"HAVE YOU COME HERE TO SEE IF MY MARRIAGE PROPOSAL STILL REMAINS OPEN?" JAMIE ASKED AS HE WALKED AROUND HER, SMILING.

She couldn't go through with it. She hated the way he scorned her with his simple words.

"I thought so," he continued. "Now let me guess. You awoke in the middle of the night with the sudden vision that you were deeply and desperately in love with me, and you could hardly bear another night without me. No? Let's try again. You woke up with the startling realization that you would never get such an offer again. That you would be a lady, a very rich lady, if you married me."

"Yes!" Jassy cried vehemently. "I never pretended to love you . . . I never pretended to like you!"

"But you are determined now that you will marry me. A man whom you hate."

"I don't always hate you." Then she emitted an impatient oath. "Why offer, then? You have no love for me."

"I, at least, want you." He grabbed her hand and pulled her over to the canopied bed and he cast her upon it. He clutched the canopy rod and stared down upon her. "This is my bed, mistress. If you go through with this, you will join me here. Nightly. Are you still willing to marry me?"

The image of the dirty attic room and the death's-head rose [illegible]ly.

He laug[illegible] "You are a whore!"

Also by Heather Graham from Dell

GOLDEN SURRENDER
DEVIL'S MISTRESS
EVERY TIME I LOVE YOU

Coming in July
A PIRATE'S PLEASURE:
North American Woman #2

SWEET SAVAGE EDEN

North American Woman #1

HEATHER GRAHAM

A DELL BOOK

To Scarlet & Joe Rios
with lots of love

Published by
Dell Publishing
a division of
Bantam Doubleday Dell
Publishing Group, Inc.
666 Fifth Avenue
New York, New York 10103

ISBN: 0-440-20235-3

Printed in the United States of America

Published simultaneously in Canada

March 1989

10 9 8 7 6 5 4 3 2 1

KRI

SWEET SAVAGE EDEN

North American Woman #1

I ❧

The Crossroads Inn
England
Winter, the Year of Our Lord 1621
The Reign of His Royal Majesty, King James I

While the cold wind whistled and raged, threatening to tear asunder the rafters of the tiny attic bedchamber, Jassy clenched her hands into fists at her sides. She didn't feel the cold as she stared down at the frail beauty on the bed cocooned in threadbare blankets. The woman drew in a rattling breath, and suddenly Jassy became aware of her surroundings, the unpainted rafters that barely held the walls together, the smut from the candles, the ancient trunk at the foot of the bed holding their few belongings, the cold that ever seeped in upon them. Jassy swallowed and her jaw locked tightly as tears pricked her eyes.

She'll not die like this! she swore to herself. *I'll not let her! I shall beg, borrow, or steal, but so help me God, I shall not let her die like this!*

But even as Jassy silently made her vows, old Tamsyn was staring at her sadly, shaking his head just slightly, in a way not meant to be seen, and certainly not understood. But Jassy understood the motion all too well; Tamsyn had already given up all hope on Linnet Dupré.

"Quinine, girl. Quinine might help to ease her misery some, but that be all I can tell you."

Tears welled anew in her eyes; she could not allow them to fall. Impatiently she brushed her small, work-roughened hands across her temple, raising her chin.

Tamsyn was wrong, she assured herself. He had to be wrong. What was Tamsyn but another beaten-down drunk to have found his livelihood with the rest of them at the Crossroads Inn? He claimed to have once been a physician who had even studied long ago at Oxford, but perhaps that was a lie. A lie like the dreams he had spun for her of a new day to come, of distant lands and faraway places, exotic voyages and emerald seas.

Her mother was dying. She had no time for dreams, and she dared not fall prey to despair.

"Quinine," Jassy said briskly.

"Quinine," Tamsyn repeated. "But ye may as well wish for the moon, Jassy, lass. The cost of a dose . . ."

His words trailed away, and Jassy gnawed bitterly into her lower lip. The cost for anything was dear when her mother's wages at the inn came to no more than one gold coin and a bolt of cloth a year.

And when she was paid nothing herself, as well. Nothing, since she apprenticed to the cook and her endeavors would not be considered worthy of coin until she had completed five years of service.

She lowered her head suddenly, whispering in desperation, "I can beg Master John—"

"Save your breath, girl," Tamsyn warned her. "Master John will give you naught."

And she knew that he was right. The customers ate great platters of meat with rich gravy, they drank tankards of ale and imported French wines. Master John was quick to buy a round of drinks, generous to all his customers.

To his servants he was mean and cheap.

And, Jassy thought was a little sigh, they had stayed,

anyway, knowing that he was stingy and even cruel at times. They had stayed, for Linnet had always been fragile, not cut out to work, and only here, where they could share this little attic hovel and Jassy could do the majority of her mother's work could they hope to survive.

A slight whimpering sound came from the bed. Jassy rushed to her mother's side, kneeling down beside her, grasping her frail hand in her own. Her tears almost spilled then. Linnet did not appear real at all, but as some fairy queen. Even now she was fine and beautiful—now, when death lay a claim upon her. Nay, not death! Jassy swore. She would be hanged before she would see her mother die here, beautiful, beautiful Linnet, never intended for such a life in such a horrid, squalid place.

Linnet's eyes opened, glazed with fever, all the more beautiful for that glaze. They were truly violet eyes, not blue, not gray, but deep, beautiful violet. A violet as lovely as the gold of her hair and the parchment-pale, but perfect, oval of her face.

A face not old in years but made to appear so by years of care and struggle.

"Mama!" Jassy gripped her hand warmly. "I am here!"

Then panic struck her, for Linnet did not recognize her. She spoke to the past, to people no longer present. "Is that you, Malden? Tell Sheffield that the curtain must be held, for I am feeling poorly, and that twit of a girl is no understudy to take on the role of Lady Macbeth!"

Again tears burned beneath Jassy's lids, and dark despair seized hold of her. Linnet, she saw, was losing her slender grip upon reality, upon life. She reverted quickly to days gone by. To a tender past, a far grander place than the present. For Linnet Dupré had not always been cast into such a lowly state in life—nay, she had most oft been cast as a princess or an heiress. She had reigned as a queen, a queen in the London theatrical community. She had traveled to Paris and Rome; she had been welcomed and applauded throughout the Christian world.

In those days she had been courted by dukes and earls, by nobility and grandeur.

Somewhere among that grandeur she had produced Jassy.

And for many, many years Jassy had lived in grandeur too. Her mother had housed a multitude of servants—and treated them kindly! There had been Remington to answer the bell and look after the house; old Mary to cook; Sally Frampton from nearby Waverly to bathe her mother in rich lotions and dress her hair in the latest styles. There had been Brother Anthony to teach Jassy French and Latin, Miss Nellie to teach her to dance, and Herr Hofinger to teach her all about the world at large, the oceans and the rivers, the Romans and the Gauls. He, too, had filled her head with fantasy; stories about the explorer, Columbus; about the New World, the Colonies, the Americas and the Indians. He had told her tales about the Spaniards and the great defeat of the Armada, and how the English still met and tangled with the Spaniards on the sea, claiming pieces of the New World. And he had told her stories about the great houses and mansions and castles within England, and in her dreams she had been swept off her feet by a golden knight and taken to a glorious castle to reign evermore as its mistress. In those dreams Linnet would never be exhausted or overburdened. She would sit at ease and elegantly pour tea from a silver server, and she would be dressed in silk and velvet and fur.

That had all been a dream, in a far distant and different life.

There had come that long dry spell when Linnet had not been able to obtain a role in the theater. And Linnet had never bothered with her own finances, so she was in complete shock and distress to learn that not only did she not have the money to take a smaller house, but also was so far in debt that the gaping jaws of Newgate Prison awaited her eagerly as her fate.

Some godsend fell upon them then; miraculously a mysterious "donor" kept them discreetly from distress.

Linnet knew what had occurred; she would not tell Jassy, as Jassy was but a nine-year-old child.

But by the age of ten, Jassy understood servants' gossip. They all whispered about the Duke of Somerfield having "done something fair" for her mother at long last.

And then they stared at her, and through little George, the cook's son, she learned that she was "illy-gitmit" and that everyone thought that the duke, who had had "illy-cit" relations with her mother, should have surely pulled them out of trouble long before.

Such rumors were lovely dreams to Jassy at first; she imagined that her father would be a great, handsome man in his prime; that one day she should appear in his great hall and that he would instantly think her beautiful and accomplished and love and adore her above all his legitimate offspring. Then he, of course, could introduce her to the handsome golden knight who would sweep her away to her own castle.

It wasn't to be. At the little kitchen breakfast table they could then afford, Linnet jumped up one morning, screamed, and fell to the floor in a dead faint.

Jassy rushed to help her, as did Mary. Mary muttered, wondering what could have caused such a thing. But Jassy then picked up the paper, being able to read as Mary could not, and quickly perused the page, learning then that the duke had been killed most ingloriously in an outlawed duel.

There was no one to pay the rent on the small house. One by one the servants went. Then the house went, and then the very last of their precious hoard of gold coins and pounds sterling. Linnet could not find work in the London theater again—the duke's vicious duchess was busy seeing that no establishment would have her.

Jassy quickly realized that they must find work. In time Linnet knew, too, that menial work would be their hope of survival, Newgate awaiting any man or woman who did not meet their obligations.

She also discovered that she was singularly talentless when it came to working for a living, and in the end she was forced to become the scullery maid at the inn, work totally unsuited to her lovely, fragile form.

Master John hired them on only because Jassy was twelve by then, in the peak of health, easily able to work the full fourteen-hour day that her mother could not.

Jassy was jerked back to the present as Linnet moved fretfully on the bed, speaking again.

"Tell them—tell them that the curtain must be held," Linnet whispered softly. The glaze left her eyes and she frowned, then soft tears fell from her eyes to her cheeks.

"Jassy . . . Jassy, Jasmine. 'Twas he who named you, for he loved the scent of Jasmine. You were beautiful, too, a babe like a flower, a blossom . . . so very sweet. And I did have such dreams! He loved us. He did love us. You were to be a lady, loved and coveted. And still . . . your hands. Oh, Jassy! What have I done to you? To leave you here in this awful place . . ."

"Nay, Mother, nay! I am fine, and I shall get you well, and we . . ." She paused, a lie coming to her from nowhere. "Mother, we shall get out of here as soon as you are well. I have heard from my half sister, one of the duke's children, and we are to travel to his estates. Her—her mother has died, and she is anxious to make reparation. We shall live in splendor, I swear it, Mother, only first you must get well." She had sworn out a lie. Would God understand such a thing? Would he forgive her? Her heart hardened, for she could not care. God had deserted her. He had left her to survive on her own, and that she must do. Linnet, though, would be horrified, for her belief in her religion was great.

But Linnet hadn't even heard the quickly spoken and desperate lie. "Ah, yes! None has ever done Juliet with such poise and innocence! That is what the critics said; that is what I shall do again."

She stared straight at Jassy, releasing her hand with a flourish. "Go now! Tell them that the curtain shall be held!"

The door to the attic loft suddenly swung open.

"Tamsyn!"

Master John stood in the doorway, seeming to bark out

his man's name. " 'Tis docked pay you'll get, me man!" he continued. "I need two kegs in the taproom, and I need them now! Jassy, if she's not up and working by morning, it's out on your arses, you are. The two of you."

Suddenly a great laugh bellowed from him, and he bowed to her. "My lady!"

He sent a curt blow reeling against Tamsyn's head. "Hurry, man, hurry! The coach has just come in from Norwood! And you—my lady attic rat," he told Jassy sternly, "had best get down to serve tonight."

"I can serve no one! I must care for her!"

Jassy quickly regretted her temper—she needed to placate Master John. She stood quickly, lowering her eyes and facing him. "In fact, Master John, I meant to come to you for help! I am desperate, sir, for coin. My mother needs quinine and—"

She broke off, for he had come before her, raising her chin with his finger so that her eyes met his. He smiled, and she saw his blackened teeth and felt overwhelmed by his foul breath.

"I've told you before, girl, if you want extra coin from me, you know how to earn it."

The room seemed to spin, and she actually feared that she would throw up her meager dinner if he came any nearer.

She knew what he meant. She thought that she knew a good deal about the private things that went on between men and women. Molly, who worked the taps, engaged in affairs quite frequently. With a cheery wink she had often told Jassy that it was a hideous business with the man grunting and panting and placing, well . . . part of his person into, well . . . parts of her person. It all sounded quite horrid, and made Jassy flinch.

"Ah, with a young and 'andsome one it ain't so bad. In fact, there's some what thinks 'tis heaven! But mark my words, lass, it's a lot of sweat and pumping. And if it were with one who was a lout, well, I think as like I'd prefer death, I do!"

Molly had her standards.

But she continued to see the " 'andsome ones"; she was very fond of the money that could be had that way.

Jassy gritted her teeth and kept her eyes lowered. Her mother was dying. Linnet was everything that she had in this world. Everything.

She stiffened her back. She would do anything to keep her mother alive.

And one day, one day! she vowed, she would kill Master John!

"John!"

The shrill cry came up from below, and Master John seemed to shrink before them. He was afraid of his goodwife, as well he should be, for she was two hundred pounds if she was a single one, and she worked quite well with a rolling pin when she was in a temper.

"Alas, girl! No coin have I this night!" he mumbled suddenly, and turned. He looked at Tamsyn and decided the man needed another blow to the head, and then he departed, wrinkling his nose at the attic odor.

Tamsyn caught his head and jumped to his feet. He was a little man, slim, graying, but strong in his wiry fashion. He caught Jassy's shoulders.

"Jassy, for the love of God! Don't ever, ever think of such a thing! Your mother will d—" He stopped. That her mother would die soon no matter what was what he meant. He had no doubt that Linnet was dying, and that there was very little if any hope at all that she could survive more than another day. But he hadn't the heart to say it so bluntly. "Jassy, your mother would rather die than have you give yourself to such a stinking oaf!"

Tears dampened her lashes and threatened to spill to her cheeks. She looked at Tamsyn, and he shuddered, for what the girl did not know was that even here, even in rags and squalor, she was twice the beauty that Linnet had ever been. She had the same fine, fragile features and more, for her beauty went deeper than anything that could be seen or touched. Hers was a fighting spirit, one that rebelliously challenged and dared from the depths of her eyes. Eyes that tilted just slightly at the corners, intriguing and exotic. Eyes that were so clear and deep and crystal a blue that they might have been violet. And they were framed by lashes so thick and dark, they might have been fashioned against the rose and cream of her young complexion by an artist with India ink.

"I must—I will do something!" she swore, shaking away his touch. She straightened her shoulders and stiffened her spine, so regally.

Tamsyn swallowed, wishing he had not, long ago, come to be such a worthless drunk that he had lost all in life except for a rather worthless instinct to survive.

"I've got to get down, girl. Bathe her face, talk to her, be with her. When she sleeps comfortable, get down to work before mean old John sets you both out in the street!"

Jassy lowered her head and nodded with understanding. Tamsyn squeezed her shoulders and left her, and she knelt back at her mother's side, trying to ease the fever that raged through her.

"Oh, Mother!" she whispered softly, not caring now that they were alone that tears slid down her cheeks and dropped upon the blanket. "Mother, we shall get out of this! I'll make you well, I swear it!"

She swallowed painfully. At the moment Linnet slept, as ethereal, as beautiful, as a hummingbird.

Jassy rose slowly. She kissed Linnet's hot cheek and then hurried out of the room.

Down below, the coach was already in. Jassy hurried to the kitchen to help the cook, but Jake, John's obnoxious doorman, bellowed out that she was to work in the taproom, serving ale.

The inn was dense with smoke, rowdy with talk. Each of the planked tables was full, some with common folk, some with gentry.

Jassy hated the taproom. It seemed always to be filled with a score of Master Johns—louts who grinned lasciviously and tried to pinch some part of her anatomy. Nor was she allowed to slap the wandering hands that touched her; Master John would have booted her out on the steps.

It seemed that she moved from the kitchen to the bar

to the tables endlessly, carrying great trays of roast beef and duckling with savory gravies, and scores of tankards. Her shoulders and sides ached from the heavy work. At one point during the night Molly passed her in the hallway from the kitchen to the taproom and gave her cheek a friendly pinch.

"Ah, luv, you look pale, you do! I know yer worryin' 'bout your ma, luv. Don't you fret, now. Cook just slipped me a bit of good wine and some soup; it's hid by the sideboard. You can get it up to her soon."

"What's this!"

Master John was suddenly behind them. "Ah, her majesty, the Lady Jasmine!" He bowed mockingly. "Missy—I see you off this floor once again and yer ma's in the street!" he warned Jassy, waggling one of his fingers before her face.

"Ah, Master John!" Molly batted her lashes at their taskmaster, pleading nicely. "Please, sir, the girl but—"

"The girl shirks work!" John roared. "If she's off this floor before midnight, she can look for her supper elsewhere!"

He physically turned Jassy about, pushing her forward. Jassy almost screamed. She thought that she might well have stabbed her mother, and then herself, before she could have abided his touch. She clenched her teeth tightly together. She was still so desperate.

Molly, with her red country cheeks and snapping dark eyes, caught up with her again.

"I'll get up there and feed her the soup and the wine, Jassy, I swear it. You just keep out of the way of mean ol' John, eh?"

Gratefully Jassy nodded. "Bless you, Molly!"

It was then that Jake told her she must bring another round of good ale to the two gents nearest the fire.

"And no uppity nose-turning from you, miss!" Jake warned in a growl. "Them two are class, they are! You serve them right!"

She knew what "serve them right" meant, and she wondered with a rush of hostility why he hadn't sent

Molly to serve the two. If they laughed and pinched Molly, she would blush and say just the right things.

Jassy walked quickly to the table. The two men, she noted, definitely were "class." More than gentry, she thought, by the quality and cut of their breeches and coats and hose.

Despite herself, she discovered that her heart fluttered just a bit as she neared them, for the gentleman on the right of the fire was handsome, very handsome indeed. He was blond and as light as dreams of heaven, with a wonderfully slim and genteel face and bright, sparkling blue eyes. He glanced up as Jassy set the first tankard down, and he bestowed upon her a smile that actually made her feel as if her senses reeled.

"Ah, and lass, where have you been all my life?" he teased.

Jassy flushed; he was kind, he was gentle. He was the type of man that once she might have dreamed of loving—in a very vague way, of course. A man to sweep her upon a mighty steed, the very knight of her dreams. He would take her back to the world she had once known, or onward to the shining castle of her imagination. It would be a new world. A world where servants moved to the slightest whim, where sheets were clean, where food was plentiful. And he would be the man she had imagined, a man to be a husband, a father, a golden, shining defender in every hour. . . .

She lowered her lashes again and stiffened her spine. What in the Lord's name was the matter with her? Men of stature did not come here to flirt with serving wenches to sweep them away to lives of dignity and grandeur. They wanted what Molly called a "dashing roll in the hay" and nothing more.

She raised her head again proudly. One day she would escape this bondage. She would escape poverty, she would travel where it was wild and free and where she would disdain all those who thought themselves above her.

"Thank you," he told her, referring to his ale. He watched her somewhat gravely, and it seemed that he flirted no more. She liked his eyes; she liked the way that he looked at her, as if he saw far more than a wench or a servant.

And she smiled slightly in return, for he was genuinely kind, and she barely noted what she was doing as she set the other tankard down. His fingers grazed against her hand, holding her there as he watched her. Still, what ensued next was not her fault.

"Robert! Quit ogling the lass and listen well, for this is not a matter that can be dealt with lightly."

The blond man smiled at her with such a touch of admiration that Jassy barely heard the other man's words and therefore could not be offended.

"Be that as it will, Jamie, we're just setting to dinner now, and you're telling me about the Injuns, as it were!"

"Robert!"

With that explosive sound he sent a hand waving with such energy that it caught Jassy unaware. She moved, startled, and the tankard she had not set down properly was caught in the movement. Ale spewed and then fell all around them.

"Damn, girl! Look to what you're doing!"

It wasn't her shining golden knight who came out with the impatient curse but the man across from him. The man that Jassy had barely even noticed as yet.

She did now, for he was on his feet, glaring at her. She had spilled ale not only over his elegant laced white shirt, but also on the documents he had been studying.

He was tall, she noted at first. Very tall, which was hard to miss, since she was slender and small. In his anger he was towering over her. Beneath the deceiving elegance of his shirt, she noted next, his shoulders were very broad, and though his hips were lean, his thighs, tightly hugged by his breeches, were as muscled and powerful as his boots were high and shiny.

His hair was as black as his boots, nearly indigo with its sheen, barely darker than his flashing eyes, cast into a rugged face that was tanned from much exposure to the sun. He was probably not much older than the handsome blond man who had been so kind; somehow he seemed the fiercer man, alive with a striking tension and a volatile energy that seemed to exude from him. He therefore appeared older, more the hardened and arrogant man than his smiling, handsome companion.

He did not stare upon her with admiration. His dark eyes smoldered with annoyance, and something that wounded her pride even worse—a total dismissal and disregard.

Without thinking about her position, she lashed out at this man who had attacked her so unfairly.

"Sir! 'Twas your arm that jolted me! The accident was not my fault."

"Jamie!" the golden man protested softly. "Take a care, please! 'Tis a tyrant runs this place; 'tis likely he'll beat the girl."

Jamie seemed to ignore him. He did not appear to care about his shirt, but he was eager to save his documents, and heedlessly he dragged Jassy to him by her skirts as he sought to use that means to dry the parchments.

"Leave me be!" Jassy cried, as indignation and rage rose within her. She pummeled against his shoulder in sudden, wild fear, for those strange, dark eyes had fallen upon her again—and lingered this time.

"Stop!"

He halted her assault simply, catching her wrists, dragging her down to the bench beside him. He might have been a devil, she thought, he was so very dark, so arrogant, so supremely confident of himself. He did not think that she would dare to fight him.

"Bastard!" she hissed in a soft, sure warning. "Let go of me!"

He laughed in amusement. She longed to move her hands, but his hold on her carried an unearthly strength, and she was suddenly quite certain that his air of total confidence had not come to him without just cause. He was a powerful man; she could feel it in the vibrant heat that passed from his thighs through her skirts; she could feel it in his very hold upon her. It meant nothing. He did not strain. But he held her fast and studied her boldly, frowning curiously as his deadly dark, satanic eyes came to her own, fell to encompass her features, her lips . . . her breasts and hips.

Something warm seemed to sizzle through her. Her heart began to thunder; she tried to jerk away from him, wanting only to do battle, thinking of nothing but his touch upon her and her desperate desire to escape him.

But then her heart sank.

Master John was bearing down upon them.

"My lords, my lords! What is the problem here? Forgive the girl—she's new. And I warrant that she will be well punished for her clumsiness!"

He was about to drag Jassy from the bench, but the beautiful golden-blond man came to her rescue. "Master John! I'd not hurt the girl."

Master John looked at Jassy as if he'd like to beat her flat down to the floor.

"Indeed, sir," the gallant blond man continued with a hauteur that could only belong to the nobility, "I should find myself in a position to see that all my friends and acquaintances were to avoid this place were I to believe that you chastised your servants too severely."

The dark-haired man finally looked at John after it seemed that the blond had kicked him beneath the table.

He sighed impatiently. "Indeed, sir, I should feel compelled to warn many from this place! Alas—and I had so enjoyed the ale and the fire!"

John appeared quite near to apoplexy. For several seconds he just stood there, his face growing redder and redder.

The dark-eyed man spoke again, this time with a deadly authority. He rose to his full height again, hands on his hips, towering over them all. "Should I hear that any harm has befallen the girl, I swear I shall return and break both your legs. Do you understand?"

"Aye!" John said quickly, barely breathing.

"Good!" The man sat again, eyeing John.

"Get back to work, girl!" John commanded Jassy.

And she did so—swiftly. She was eager not just to escape her horrid master, but also longed with all her heart to escape the dark-haired stranger.

John caught up with her quickly, whispering into her ear. "You think you're something, eh, Lady Jasmine of the Attic? Not to me, you're not!" Her heart catapulted downward as he laughed bitterly. "So I can't touch you! Well, I'll tell you this! You're docked, girl, you and her up them stairs!"

Docked! Less money when they were paid a pittance to begin with! And all over that lout of a stranger!

"Just leave me be!" she said gratingly.

"To the kitchen!" Jake ordered. "Bring out the platters of food for His Majesty's soldiers just arrived."

She headed for the kitchen. Molly crossed by her quickly there. "I reached yer ma, luv. She drank some broth."

"Bless you!" Jassy murmured, and even as the cook loaded the heavy trenchers onto her shoulders, her episode with the gentlemen faded from her mind and worry came back to it. Tamsyn's one word flooded her thoughts.

Quinine.

Linnet needed quinine to combat the fever.

She could buy some from the chemist across the lane—if she only had the coin to do so.

The cook was gossiping with one of the newly arrived coachmen even as she burdened down Jassy's great tray. The coachman, seated at the big kitchen table, tipped his hat to Jassy and offered her a friendly grin. She smiled vaguely in return, balancing her tray. Cook flashed her a quick smile, too, but gave her attention to the visiting coachman.

"Lord love us, I don't believe a word of it, Matthew!" she said, but she laughed delightedly.

"Well, 'tis true! Jassy, you should hear this one!"

"Matthew, she's a sweet young thing!" Cook protested sternly.

"But it's a great story! All about Joel Higgins, who worked in the London livery. He was such a handsome, strapping youth! He told me about this old woman, see, and she was willing to pay for his services—but he weren't that hard up! So he made her think he were willing to give when he weren't, and when the old battle-ax had her clothing a-gone, he took her purse and disappeared, saying he just had to wash up. Imagine her—a-laying there waiting while he stole away her purse!" He laughed heartily, enjoying his own story. "A good come-uppance for the old girl, eh?"

"Ah, and Joel will meet up with the hangman, that he will!" Cook prophesied dourly. "And, Matthew, you watch your mouth around my young help. Hmmph! Jassy, I be needin' you in here, I am, and he's got you out on the floor. Well, damn the man, then, if his sides of beast ain't roasted the way he'd have 'em! Sorry, girl, 'bout your ma."

"Thank you," Jassy murmured, gritting her teeth against the weight of the tray balanced on her shoulder. She paused, though, when she should have turned with her burden and hurried. "Cook, have you by any chance—"

"Lord love ye, girl! I'd gladly loan ye a coin if I had me one! I sent me last money home for me own old mother! You've my prayers, though, girl. The Lord God will provide, you just look to Him!"

The coachman sniggered. "Aye! The Lord God provides—more'n likely He helps those what help themselves!"

Jassy had already given up on the Lord, and she would fall beneath the weight of the tray soon. She gave Cook a smile and hurried out.

The night wore on. She felt that endless hours passed. At long last she was released to go back to the attic.

She ran instantly to Linnet's side, then put her forehead against the bed, crying softly as she heard her mother's great rasping attempts to draw breath.

Quinine. Tamsyn said it might ease her.

There was a soft rapping at her door. " 'Tis me—Molly, Jass."

Jassy came back to her feet and hurried to the door, throwing it open. Molly studied her ravaged face.

"Is she no better, then?"

"No better at all."

"Ah, lass!" She paused for a moment, hesitating, studying Jassy.

The girl should have had more, Molly thought. All of them had thought it. Cook, her, the upstairs maids. The girl was better than this life. Better than endless scrubbing of cold stone floors. Better than her raw, ragged hands, better than her rag of a dress. They'd all had dreams for her. She was their prize—more lovely than a human had a right to be, even if it was hard to see that loveliness, clad as she was in rags, her glorious golden hair all trussed up in an ugly net. She was fine. A rose among thorns, a blossom of spring against the dead of winter.

She was doomed. To this life; to hell on earth.

Molly sighed. "Jassy, I know your ma never much wanted you falling to our ways, but, well, that tall handsome lord was asking questions about you. He said that his lodgings were at the Towergate, across the row, and that he meant to stay up late."

Jassy inhaled sharply. An illness seemed to sweep through her stomach.

The blond man. The kind, handsome blond man had wanted her.

She stiffened. As kind as he had been, he wanted a whore for the night. She could have created an entire daydream around him; she could have envisioned him as all that life had to offer.

Her shoulders dropped. Linnet rasped away behind her. She clenched her fists together.

"Jassy!" Linnet called out.

"Mother!" She swung around and fell down by the bed. "I am here!"

Linnet's head tossed about. Jassy touched her forehead and discovered that it burned. Linnet's eyes opened for a moment, but they were glazed. She did not see her daughter. "Help me," she whispered feverishly. "Oh, help me, please . . ."

Her voice faded away; her eyes closed.

"Oh, God!" Jassy cried out. She caught her mother's

hands and held them tightly, then she stood and whirled about, almost blinded by her tears.

No! she thought, and it was a silent scream of agony. *I will not let her die here! I will beg, borrow—or steal.*

And that was when the idea caught hold of her.

Steal . . . yes.

Surely God would understand, and He was her only true judge. She had turned her back on Him, but maybe now He was helping her to help herself.

She could steal the money that she needed. And keep her daydream. If the blond man did not suspect her of a foul deed, she could suddenly cry innocence and escape him. He was so kind. He would understand.

And if he caught her in the lie . . . well, again she would depend upon his kindness.

And if that didn't work . . .

She swallowed bitterly. She could go through with the bargain. She could not let Linnet die.

"Ah—thank you, Molly. Thank you for so much."

Molly cleared her throat. "He's an exciting one, he is!" she said, trying to sound cheerful. She flushed slightly. "I—I tried to exchange myself for you; I'd have gladly given you the coin. But he wanted you, he did, were he to have any at all."

"Thank you."

"Shall I stay with her for you?"

"Oh, bless you, Molly! Will you?"

Molly nodded.

Jassy hurried to the washbowl, poured out the remaining water, and tried to scrub her face. She was shaking so badly!

Molly wandered in and sat down. "Best hurry, child," she said tonelessly.

Jassy knelt down by her mother's side once again and picked up her frail hand. It burned to the touch, and there was no response.

"Mama, I love you very much! I'll not let you die this way."

She swore it out loud, passionately. Then she was on

her feet, slipping into her worn cloak, on her way out the attic door.

One last time she paused, her beautiful features tense and dark with torment.

"Nay, I'll not let you die this way! Not if I have to beg, borrow—or steal!"

II

The savage cold struck Jassy as soon as she set out on the path from the inn to the Towergate. The two establishments were not far apart, for in this town where the road ran south from London, there was continual commerce and travel, and even a third innkeeper might have fared very well. The general consensus was that Master John set the better table, while the Towergate offered more amiable rooms—more private rooms, at that. The gentry and nobility tended to spend their nights at the Towergate even if they did sup at Master John's, while common folk enjoyed fewer amenities—and lower prices—at Master John's.

Jassy's teeth chattered. Her nearly threadbare cloak provided scant protection against the winter wind, and the ground snow—where it had not turned to muck from the countless carts and carriages passing by—had frozen to ice. She was somewhat glad of the cold, for it seemed to have frozen over her mind and her thoughts. When she stood before the door of the Towergate, she was trembling from the cold and from fear of what she was about to do.

The wind blustered behind her as she entered, drawing the door quickly closed. She leaned against it and noted that hounds and hands dozed about the dying fire alike, that there was very little commerce at this late hour, only one pair of fellows still seeming to be engaged in quiet conversation near the wall.

One of the Towergate's serving wenches came forward, and Jassy found herself furiously swallowing her pride and pulling the hood of her cloak lower about her forehead.

"What do you want, girl?" the wench demanded, and Jassy feared that she would be sick. The tavern wench was young, with well-rounded bosom and hips, and she moved with an explicit sway that brought new horror to Jassy. This . . . this was what she would become.

Quinine! She reminded herself desperately, and the thought gave her courage.

"I have been asked here," she said simply.

"Oh," the wench said, smiling slyly and eyeing her curiously. She shrugged and cast a glance toward the stairway. "Here for his lordship, eh? Well, well. Aye, he'd be expectin' you. Third door. Best room in the house."

Jassy nodded. As she moved toward the stairs the wench sauntered over to the barkeep and whispered quite loudly to him, "Why, 'tis Jassy Dupré. Imagine! Her what thinks she's better than the rest of us! Whorin' up to him that's rich and fine, same as any other lass!" She laughed delightedly.

The barkeep chuckled, and Jassy could feel his eyes boring into her back. "So 'tis her, ain't it, now? Maybe she won't be so high-flyin' in the days to come, eh?"

They both burst into crude laughter. The malicious mockery followed her all the way up the stairs and along the hallway.

Jassy reached the door and desperately threw it open, not thinking to knock. She closed the door tightly behind her and leaned against it, gasping for breath. Here she was in a man's bedchamber—as the hired entertainment for the evening.

Not any man's, she reminded herself. Robert's. The kind, golden-haired gentleman. She would not die at his touch; she would come away with coin—bartered or stolen—and with her virginity intact.

Instinct forced her first to appreciate the warmth of the room. Then she noted that it was very dark, for the fire in the hearth that provided the warmth had burned down very low, to glowing embers. The room seemed empty, and as her eyes adjusted to the dim light she stiffened, biting into her lower lip with perplexity.

Before the softly glowing embers of that fire sat a deep metal hip bath, from which steam wafted. It was definitely empty. Awaiting . . . her.

Bitterly she wondered how she would manage to scan his clothing when it appeared that she was to doff her own first. Nor could she make any attempt at playing the seductress, and then the innocent, until she had crawled into that tub, for it was understandable that such a gentleman would not want a serving girl until that girl had bathed.

Uneasily she stepped into the room, softly treading nearer the tub, wondering what had become of the man she had been summoned to . . . serve.

She gasped, her heart seeming to beat like thunder, when large hands fell upon her shoulders from behind. She did not spin around but stood like a deer, poised for flight, yet achingly aware that she dare not run.

"Your cloak, mistress," came a husky male voice from the darkness that loomed all around her. "May I?"

Panic seized her. He was behind her, it was so terribly unnerving to feel him there. The room seemed to blacken still further, and then spin, and she braced herself. Slowly the dizzy sensations faded.

She lowered her head, nodding. She tried to remind herself that this was the golden-blond, shining knight who had championed her in the public room when his towering, dark friend had so cruelly cast her into trouble.

She closed her eyes tightly, the better to remember his light, gentle eyes. So admiring.

"You are cold. As cold as ice. The bath and the fire will warm you." He spoke very quietly. His words were nearly whispers, and yet they, too, unnerved her. Soft, they were different somehow. They held a curious tension, a certain fever. He was a man, she reminded herself. A man who had hired a harlot for the evening.

He touched her. . . .

Her cloak was gone. His hands fell to her shoulders, and she tried not to shiver at the feel of those long male fingers there.

She stepped forward, eluding those fingers.

"The bath. It is for me, then?"

There seemed to be a slight, ironic pause. "Aye, mistress. For you." Then once again those fingers settled upon her shoulders, moving with expertise to the buttons on her simple woolen gown. She willed herself to remain still. She had not expected this feeling. This feeling that he should tower so behind her, seem to sear her with his hands, with the promise of his length and breadth behind her.

She narrowed her eyes, seeing the mist rise from the tub, the embers glow in the hearth. If she could just see it all like this! A red and glowing mist sheathed in darkness!

His fingers moved on down her back and skimmed the fabric from her shoulders. Once again she nearly gasped, nearly screamed out loud, for he lowered his head and pressed his lips to her nape. She felt that touch as if it were a brand of fire sweeping through her, riddling her to awful panic, yet waking her too. As if it had given her some special substance to her blood, to her veins, to her body. She felt alive, where before she had been numb. Trembling, yet aware anew that she must play this game oh so carefully to escape with her pride, her chastity—and the money she so badly needed.

His hands caressed her shoulders, and the gown fell down her arms even as she thought and planned. The wool fell over her meager petticoat, and she instinctively found herself stepping from it—and away from his grasp once again.

Her eyes lit upon the armchair just behind the tub and the fire. His frock coat lay across the top of it, neatly folded. So close to the tub. One could just reach out—and search the pockets.

If only she could escape his scrutiny long enough.

Ah, unlikely! For though she dared not look, she heard a soft sound as he whisked her dress away—and came a step closer to her once again, this time finding the hook to her petticoat, releasing it, watching it fall. In her shift she felt the cold once again. *Turn,* she warned herself. *Turn and slip into his arms. He is blond and golden and gentle, and you must woo him with a smile if you hope to leave him as a lady.*

But she could not turn. She longed to do so, but she could not. Not even to stare into those gentle eyes. Not now, not yet, for she was suddenly ashamed to be here before him in her shift and stockings alone.

Again she shivered. She felt the tension and vitality of his movement behind her, the whisper of his breath. She inhaled and felt dizzy, for she breathed in the subtle scent of him, dangerously male and potent. He clutched her shoulders, bringing her back against him, and she felt all the muscled hardness of his body.

And the growing desire within it.

She saw his hands, long-fingered and bronzed and powerfully broad as he swept his arms around her, pulling her close. She felt dizzy again, nearly overwhelmed.

And once again, ever so near to a scream, for those hands cradled around her breasts, cupping the weight, thumbs lightly flicking against her nipples through the material of her shift, so sheer that it might not have been there. She ground down hard on her jaw to keep silent, and she mentally braced herself so that she would not bolt and fly from his touch.

Then some ragged, heavy sound came to his breathing, and his fingers moved to the pins in her hair. Her hair fell from its heavy braid down her neck in a massive coil, and she inched forward again, lowering her head.

"Please . . . I cannot get it wet. I should freeze when I left here."

She heard the softest laugh and almost wished that he did not lurk in the darkness behind her, that he would step forward, smile upon her with his soft, expressive eyes.

And yet she did not really wish to see him. Not now. Not when she must forget all inhibition, all strict teachings of a lifetime. She must forget about the whispers going on downstairs, whispers about how the arrogant Miss Dupré was, after all, no untouchable thing, no ice maiden, but a whore to the highest bidder.

"I shall not touch your hair, though I long to see it free. Please, go. Take your leisure in the bath."

She bit her lip, wishing she might ask him to turn from her as she further disrobed.

She knew that she could not.

And so she was glad that he lingered in the darkness as she stepped forward, trembling, trying her best to whisk her stockings from her legs with some grace and poise, pausing uncertainly before she could step from the shift, and unwittingly performing it all in a most sensual manner.

All Jassy could think was that it was quite important to let her shift lie close to his frock coat so that she might reach the latter in pretense of seeking the first. And once that garment was gone, she was in all haste to reach the hip bath, for never in her life had she felt her own nakedness so keenly.

She sank into the water, closed her eyes, and tried to keep her teeth from chattering, though the water still steamed.

Something fell before her. Her eyes sprang open, yet she saw nothing, for once again he was behind her.

"Soap, love," he murmured, still so husky, still so low, yet there was the slightest irony there, and she wondered if he were truly as kind as she had thought him. All the better if he could be crude, she thought, for then it would be easier to deceive him, to take from him what she had no desire to earn.

A cloth followed the soap into the tub. She nervously grasped both, wishing fervently that he would not hover behind her so. He must move! He must! And she was not so sure anymore that he would gladly hand over his coin were she not to perform her services, and therefore she must reach his frock coat.

He paced behind her; she wondered if he grew impatient. She grew desperate, gnawing upon her lip as she sought a way to move him.

Mercifully it was he who moved himself, in a most obliging fashion.

"Would you like a drink?" he asked her softly.

"Aye, that I would," she whispered in reply, and he strode quickly to the door, throwing it open to call down for service.

Jassy dropped soap and towel and lunged over the edge of the tub swiftly, delving her fingers into his pocket, discovering it loaded with coins. Bitterly she realized he would surely not miss one, and it was a sorry world indeed that a man of means could purchase a woman and not even notice the cost of all that she had to give. Quickly she returned to the bath.

She heard him thanking someone curtly at the door, returning with a tray. She risked a glance at him as he set it upon the table and poured out two glasses, but she could not see him at all, for he lingered in shadow. She knew only that he had stripped down to shirt and breeches, that in bare feet he was soundless and sleek, and that he was truly a tall man, broad and trim.

Robert . . .

If she could but see his gentle eyes . . .

Ah, and good that she could not, for his coin was caught in the palm of her hand, and she dare not let him find it there!

She lowered her face into the water and started violently when she raised it, for he was hunched down behind her, one arm cast around her shoulder. He offered her a glass of amber liquid.

"Rum," he said briefly. "Caribbean rum, golden and pure. 'Twas this or weak ale."

She took the glass and drained it, gasped and coughed, and heard his laughter as he patted her damp back. "I should have taken the ale," he murmured apologetically.

"Nay, nay, 'tis fine," she responded. And indeed it was,

for it burned like a sustaining fire as she swallowed, and it eased all that seemed so rough and jagged and terrible about the night.

"You would try more?"

"I would," she murmured, her eyes downcast, and again reckoned bitterly that the cost of the rum was probably greater than that of the common whore.

It did not matter now! she assured herself, for the coin was in her palm—soon she could turn to him, then start to cry, and plead forgiveness. She would prove herself the daughter of the great actress Linnet Dupré with a convincing and magnificent performance.

Then she would leave.

And in leaving, save the dream. That in life she could come upon this golden man again, all honor intact. And by some miracle she would be rich and beautiful in silks and satins, and he would fall madly in love with her. And then . . .

He handed her the glass again. And knelt down behind her. His finger caressed her neck, from the slope of her shoulder to the lobe of her ear.

It was not so bad, it was not so bad. She had the rum.

She swallowed down that second glass and felt its hearthlike warmth and amber glow.

"You are quite rare," he said curiously. "Too slim and yet so elegant. The face of an aristocrat and, alas, the hands of a charwoman. The body of a temptress and eyes that warn of the cunning vixen, proud and sly."

She wondered at his words. That he should sound so entranced and so acidic—all in one.

And she shivered, for he suddenly did not sound at all like that gentle man with the golden head and appealing eyes.

"Mistress . . ."

The word was a whisper that was like a strange wind, quiet and yet savage, touching her flesh, filling her with a feeling of fire. Husky, it rose from the depths of him, like the deep caress of a warm summer's wind. The soap was in his hands. She could not protest him, for she held the empty glass of rum in one palm—his coin in the other. She trembled and blinked and held herself immobile. She felt the soap and cloth sweep over her, over her breasts. Slowly . . . his hands moved with an easy leisure. They moved upon her as if they had some right. As if they had known each other a long time. And she sat there and allowed the shocking intimacy. The soap and cloth coursed over her. Touching her nape, stroking against her throat, and then her shoulders, and then . . .

Her breasts once again. She shivered and trembled, shocked and staggered by sensation, feeling much as a cornered hare. The power in that touch was mesmerizing. Her eyes fell closed in confusion, and then she felt him move, move around, and touch his lips to hers.

Ah, so hot, coercive, persuasive. Consuming and expert, casting that trembling throughout her body. She felt her mouth part, the pressure of his tongue sweeping through it. And as she struggled against the overwhelming feel of it all, she was heartily sorry that she had swallowed the rum so quickly, since what had been sustaining warmth was now a rush that added to her panic and confusion. She was engulfed! Terrified suddenly at the absolute power of the man, terrified that it was all racing along in a heedless, reckless fashion and that she was quite near to losing all control.

She had never been kissed before. And this . . .

He seemed suddenly to be over her and around her, his lips upon her own, upon her throat. And his hands . . . delving into the water, sliding along her thighs, folded so crudely within the confines of the tub. Oh, now, now! She screamed inwardly. Now! She had to end it, else all would be lost.

His arms swept around her, lifting her from the tub. She let out a great startled gasp, instinctively clinging to him lest she should fall, yet somehow sure from his laughter that her weight was as nothing against his strength. His laughter . . . against the steam, against the mist, was neither light nor amused but still ironic, adding to her sense of panic.

"Please, please, sir," she murmured, and her voice, though breathless, carried the right amount of quivering pathos. Yet she discovered herself upon the vastness of the bed, the hardness of his form atop her, his dark head bowed over her breast. . . .

His hot, demanding kisses falling there.

She dug her fingers into his hair, trying to stop him. "No!" she whispered, for his mouth opened over the dusky rose of her nipple, drawing upon it, suckling it, and causing a searing to pierce into the very length of her. She could not bear it; she convulsed and trembled with the stunning sensation of it. Her flesh blazed and burned crimson as she felt that hot, liquid touch upon her, entering deep within her, shooting straight to her womb.

"No, please!" she said, fighting for coherency. "Please, gentle sir, kind sir! I thought that I could come here for you were ever so fair, yet I have discovered that I—"

She broke off in a gasp, for though her head spun with the rum and other shocking sensations and a growing panic, she had just realized her own thoughts. She stared at the hair she held, at the head of the man who so intimately used her.

Dark head. Dark . . .

"Oh! Oh, stop! By God . . ."

His face lifted to hers. No kind, light eyes with a gentleman's civility surveyed her. Dark eyes stared down at her. Dark, cynical eyes that matched the tension of his whisper. Eyes like Satan's own. Sharp and piercing, tearing into her with a scalding contempt. They were not even black or brown, as she had imagined. They were indigo and gray. Surely the devil's own. Oh, surely . . . 'twas not Robert at all, she realized in awful horror, but the rude and arrogant Jamie who held her—naked—in his grasp!

"You!"

She forgot that she had actually toyed with the idea that to gain the money she had needed, she'd have even bedded Master John. Or perhaps it seemed that this was worse—this bronzed, indigo-eyed stranger who had already treated her with such scorn. Perhaps it was his hated body upon her; his breath still scalding the dampness he had left upon her breast, his hand upon her hip.

"You!" she gasped out again in awful horror, and he smiled, a mocking curl of the lip, tight-lipped and grim, and he gazed upon her from narrowed eyes.

"Aye, yes, me. You thought to snare Robert in your little trap, eh, love? Why, you mewling little petty thief. It's a pretty game, I must say. Come like a seductress, pick a man's pocket, then cry innocence!" He made a ticking sound of disgust. "Curious. I had thought there was something special about you. I'm disappointed. You're nothing but a common whore and a thief."

"I am no thief!" she said, refuting him desperately. Dear God, she wanted to die.

"Not a thief?" His arrogant head tilted to one side.

"Get off me!" she cried. She tried to twist but found that his leg was cast over her own. She tried to strike him, but her hands were too quickly caught. She could not dislodge him from her naked body. "I'm not a thief—"

"The money, mistress, in your palm. I saw you delve your dainty little hands into my pocket. Alas! And you haven't earned it yet! Of course, I will give you that opportunity."

"No! No!"

Madly, with a strength and energy born of fury and desperation, she fought him. She struggled, swearing, to free her wrists. She arched but managed only to come closer, more surely against him. She kicked and flailed and managed to draw more than a grunt from him, but nothing else. His fingers were like steel bands, his body was immovable. It was hard as rock but hot, like the summer sun, and she could feel all his strength too keenly as she lay there naked. Vulnerable. And caught in the act of robbery. She could not win. She could only touch him more and more. Know more and more about him, as a man.

In the end she lay panting, vowing not to cry, deadly still beneath him, her wrists secured by his left hand, his right leg cast over her thigh, pinning her beside him.

She did not look at him. This was not the kind, gentle, shining, golden man of her dream. This was the other, hard and ruthless, and she would give him nothing. She would not plead. She would not tell him that she was desperate. She could not act out any charade, for he had already called her bluff. There was nothing to do but lie there and withdraw, despise him, and think herself far, far away—and pray that he did choose to call the magistrate.

He stared at her. She could not withdraw so completely that she could escape the fact that he stared at her. She was too aware of his muscular body, clad yet somehow savage to her, and her own nudity. If one could die of humiliation, she thought, she would surely perish then. Yet hatred, she had heard, was a sustaining reason to live. Perhaps she did not die because she hated him so. More determined, she stared straight into the night and waited, quivering despite herself.

He moved suddenly and she cried out, but he ignored her, securing her wrists with one of his own. He leaned over her and with his free hand opened up her palm.

And found his money within it.

She did not respond but stared straight ahead.

"Have you no excuse?"

She did not reply, and he laughed harshly.

"Ah, if I were but Robert! You would turn to me with tears in those lovely eyes and swear out your innocence. Or perhaps I should hear some story about a child needing a meal, or some other such rot! But I'm not Robert—and you did seem wise enough to know that."

"You are a despicable, ruthless bastard," she said smoothly, still addressing the ceiling. Oh, God. She had nothing, and she was in his power. If he called the hangman, she didn't think that she would give a damn. She had failed miserably.

"Ah, my love, I do protest! I tend to be fond of your fair kind, ladies and whores. 'Tis thieves alone I abhor!"

He spoke with a certain edge, and though she had just convinced herself that she did not care what came, be it death itself, she emitted a strangled gasp when she discovered him moving against her. Curtly, roughly, brusquely, rebalancing his weight—forcing her thighs apart with blunt and unyielding force.

She had thought that nothing could humiliate her any further, yet this did. She strained against him in renewed fury, swearing out her hatred, as his hand touched her, as his fingers probed her with a ruthless intimacy. She twisted her head; color and a profusion of heat filled her; mortified, she longed for death.

"I shall scream. I shall scream rape—"

"A whore who knowingly came to me?" he inquired with a certain amusement.

"Oh—God! Stop!"

The plea came from her in a ragged gasp. She could not escape him, could not escape his touch. She tried to twist, to hide, yet he surveyed her mercilessly as he examined her so insolently, ignoring her protest. Had she only had a weapon, she'd have surely slain him. He gave her no quarter, no compassion. It was not that he hurt her; it was simply that he explored where he would, his touch entering even inside her.

And then . . . his touch was gone. He still held her prisoner; still clamped her to the bed. But the terrible intimate exploration of his long bronze fingers was gone, and she was terrified to breathe.

"A virgin?" he inquired. The sound of his voice was curiously polite and distant, as if they were discussing the weather.

"Oh, for the love of God and all the saints—!"

"Mistress, do cease," he said, interrupting her. "You came to me, remember? I made my intent quite clear when I spoke to the other bar whore."

"I'm not a whore!"

"So it seems. You are a thief."

"And you are a despicable, arrogant bastard, a vile defiler of women, a—"

"Have you as yet been defiled, little thief?"

"You're touch has defiled me!"

"Ah, mistress! There is so much more that can be

shared between a man and a woman!" he assured her. "Shall we explore the possibilities?"

"No!"

"So you did come with the sole purpose to rob me blind. Ah, no. My mistake. You came to rob poor Robert blind."

"Yes, and I have failed. So let me go."

She lay there trembling in desperate fear. He was so casual, and so at ease! His hand rested very low upon her belly, his leg still blocking her escape. She might as well have been in chains beneath him. She should cry, she should act out some sweet penance. But she could not act before him. She had already discovered that. And any minute now he would take what he wanted from her. He surely would enjoy taking her brutally, for he truly seemed to hate her and he had already proven that he had no compassion.

"You think that I should let you go?" he asked quietly. His knuckles grazed her belly and she bit hard into her lip, praying that he would not delve within her again. Her flesh burned anew. She swore against him and breathed a silent prayer.

He laughed dryly, rolling from her, resting his weight upon an elbow to stare at her. For a moment she could not believe that she was really free. She returned his glare and saw fully his face. The bronzed, rugged planes, the indigo eyes—the long, arrogant nose. The lips, full and sensual, twisted into a mocking sneer. Dark hair, tumbling over his forehead. His throat, bronze against his shirt, his shirt caught tight against the corded muscles of his shoulders and chest. A medal, a golden St. George slaying the dragon, lay cast against the darkly haired section of his chest where his shirt lay open in a vee.

"Are you reconsidering, wench? Shall you stay? Ah, I see, you are enamored of me, after all. You are free, and still you remain at my side!"

Free . . . he had released her. What did she care if he stared at her so?

"Oh!"

She bolted from the bed like a hawk in flight, nearly tripping over herself to procure her clothing. She ignored her shift, petticoat, and stockings, stumbling into the harsh wool of her gown with nothing beneath, barely slipping into her shoes before she was grasping for the door. "Enamored of you! I shall hate and loathe and detest you until my dying day! Were I a man, I would slay you. Had I the chance and ability, I'd slay you, anyway, so beware, sir, lest we ever meet upon the road!" With that, she spun for the door. Hot tears were burning behind her lashes.

"Girl!" he thundered suddenly, and despite herself, she stopped, her back to him. She obeyed the raw command in his voice, and she hated herself for doing so.

Something struck the door. The coin she had taken.

"You went through quite a bit for it. Take it."

She swallowed. Oh, how she wanted to refuse that coin! How she longed to spit in his face!

She could not. Her mother was dying.

She stooped, shoulders slumping wearily, to retrieve it. She vowed in wretched silence that someday, someday she would come into affluence, and so help her, she would find and repay this man for the awful humiliation he had heaped upon her.

She jerked the door open and went stumbling out. For a moment she was totally disoriented. She stood there, desperate just to breathe, and then she rushed down the stairs mindless of the hussy Megan watching her, and of the ogling stare of the barkeep.

She rushed out of the Towergate's front door, then stopped, glad, oh so glad, of the snow that cast her into chills, of the cold breeze that seemed somehow to cleanse her.

She walked a few steps, stumbling, then stopped to stare at the money in her hand. She need only get back to the attic. Blessed Tamsyn—he would find the chemist and buy her the quinine. Any humiliation would be worth the price, for Linnet would live, and she could quickly scorn that atrocious black-hearted man!

She started to walk again.

"Mistress! Mistress Dupré!"

She stopped again, in awful pain. How had she missed the voice! Oh, how had she been such a fool? For she knew his voice now—gentle Robert's voice—beckoning her to stop.

She turned, and the red of a summer rose stained her cheeks. The gallant, handsome blond was rushing toward her, her cloak, petticoat, and stockings cast over his arm. He knew. He knew where she had been. She thought that she would die of the shame.

"Mistress! Jamie bid me catch you, as you shall need these!"

Nearly choking on the tears she tried desperately to swallow, she stared up into his sympathetic light eyes. She shook her head vehemently, unable to speak. He stuffed the things into her arms, and in horror she turned to run.

"Mistress . . . Jassy! Please, wait! If there is some problem, I would help!"

Help! Ah, too late! She could not bear to see him again. Not now, not ever.

She kept running. Running, heedless of ice and snow and wetness and cold until she reached the kitchen entrance of Master John's. Cook, by the fire, let her in, pressing a finger to her lips. Jassy gave her a grateful nod and went tearing up the servants' stairway.

She quickly went through the attic door and saw that Tamsyn was back in the room, by her mother's bed.

"I've got it, Tamsyn. Money. Please, will you get the quinine for me? I feel I must stay by her side."

"Jassy—"

Molly caught her arm. She shrugged off her friend's touch. Tamsyn stood quickly and caught her.

"Jassy, lass. Your mum's at peace now."

"Peace?"

She stared at him uncomprehendingly. Then his words began to sink in to her mind, and she shook her head in fierce denial.

"No. *No!* You must get the quinine, Tamsyn! Surely she just sleeps!"

Neither Tamsyn nor Molly could stop her. She fell to her knees at her mother's side, grasping the frail white hand. A hand as cold as the blustering wind outside. Stiff, lifeless.

"Oh, no! Oh, God, please, no!" She screamed out her anguish, then she cried, and she tried to kiss her mother, to warm her with her body. She stared down at her beautiful face and saw that indeed the Master Johns of the world could touch her mother no more. Linnet was gone.

Jassy laid her head upon the bunk and sobbed.

Molly came to her and took her in her arms. And still Jassy sobbed, on and on, until there were no more tears to cry.

" 'Tis all right, luv, 'tis all right," Molly said, soothingly.

And at last Jassy looked at her, eyes glazed but wildly determined.

"Molly! I shall not live like this, and so help me—I shall not die like this!"

"There, there," Molly said with a soft sigh of resignation.

And Jassy discovered that after all, her tears were not all spent. Because she caught her mother's cold, delicate hand once again and warmed it with a new flood of sobbing.

III

"I shall be going back," Jamie Cameron said to Robert. "And you should be coming with me."

The stableboy had saddled his horse, a bay stallion called Windwalker, but Jamie felt compelled to check the girth himself.

"I don't know," Robert said doubtfully, watching Jamie as he mounted the prancing stallion at last. They were both dressed elegantly for their travel, for by nightfall they would reach Jamie Cameron's family home, Castle Carlyle, near Somerfield. Jamie was to meet with his father on business, and he was dressed today as his noble sire would wish him to, in a fine white shirt with Flemish lace at the collar and cuffs, slashed leather doublet, soft brocade breeches, a fur-lined cloak, high black leather riding boots, and a wide-brimmed, plumed hat. He was the perfect cavalier. Robert thought with a mild trace of bitterness that his friend could deck himself in any apparel and still appear negligent of it all, masculine and rugged.

Though Jamie was not his father's heir, but rather a third son, he admired his father greatly, and they were business partners, both greatly enthusiastic about their joint venture.

"I'm starting to think that you are mad!" Robert said.

"Oh? And why is that?"

"Well, Jamie Cameron, perhaps you will not be the next Duke of Carlyle. But nevertheless, were you not the son of an extremely wealthy and powerful noble, you have used your own trust funds well. You have fought on the seas, and you have met with the savages in Virginia. Any one of them might well have skewered you through. And for what? A company that much more often fails than prospers, and a plot of land given you directly by the king. When you've so many acres here in England that I find it doubtful any of your family has ever ridden over them all!"

Jamie laughed and stared westward, almost as if he could see the New World, where it seemed his heart so often lay, even when he was home. "I don't know myself, Robert. But there is a draw. I feel it always. It is a passion that grows in my blood, in my heart. I love the land and the river and the endless forests. There are places of such beauty and quiet!"

"I've seen the sketches brought back of the Indian attacks, and of the 'starving time' in 1609, my friend. The Indians are savage barbarians. It is a savage land, so they say. Bitterly cold, then humid and hot."

"The Indians are of a different culture," Jamie mused. "But they are men and women, just as we."

Robert laughed out loud. Jamie cast him a quick glance and shrugged. He'd had the pleasure of meeting the colonizer John Rolfe and his wife, the Indian princess Pocahontas, both in Virginia, and at King James's royal court. It was said that she had saved the life of John Smith when her father would have taken his head, and the lady did not deny the story. Jamie had been saddened to hear that she had died in England. And recently, her father, the great Powhatan, the big chief of many tribes, had died too. It was as if an era were already over, when so much had just begun.

When the London Company had first sent its men sailing across the sea, and when they had first established their settlement at Jamestown on the James River in Virginia, the days had been dreary indeed. They had left England in 1606. King James had sat upon the throne then, but it was just three years after the death of Elizabeth, and three years after a tempestuous age. The age of explorers, of Sir Francis Drake, of Sir Walter Raleigh, of the Spanish Armada. Entering into Virginia, they were aware that there was a constant threat of invasion from the Spaniards, of attacks by the Indians. Many things had hindered the growth of the colony. Supplies hadn't always arrived, as planned, from England. Men had looked for profits, and they had planted too much tobacco and not enough food. They had starved, they had clashed with the Indians, the Pamunkies, the Chickahominies, the Chesapeakes.

But much had improved since then. Though Pocahontas and Powhatan were dead, the peace formed at the time of her marriage to John Rolfe seemed to have lasted. There had been few women in the colony; now married men brought their wives, and the Company had made arrangements for young ladies of good character to cross the ocean, and the colony and the various "hundreds" surrounding it were beginning to flourish and prosper. From the Old English hundred, established before the Norman Conquests. A great swath of land where a hundred families could live.

On his last trip to Virginia, Jamie had staked out his own land. He and his father were heavy investors in the London Company, but Carlyle Hundred, as he was calling his land, came to him directly from the king in recognition of the services he had rendered there.

His land was directly upon the James River, in a far more fortuitous spot than Jamestown, so he thought, for his land was higher and not so dank and infested as the Jamestown acreage. It was beautiful, high land, with a small natural harbor. The pines and grass grew richly, so profuse that the area seemed a blue-green. By the water there was a meadow, and as Jamie had stood there, alone with the sound of the sea and the very quiet of the earth, he had felt anew his passion for the land. It would be great. The country stretched forever. It was where he would dig his roots, and it was where his children would be born, where they would grow, where they would flourish. The Carlyle Hundred. "It seems to be a land of endless opportunity," he said aloud.

"I'd enjoy any of your opportunity," Robert replied with a sigh. He had gambled away much of his own inheritance and, indeed, traveled with Jamie now in the hopes of meeting a lady of fortune who would appreciate his fine lineage and ignore his lack of a purse.

"If you choose to come with me, I will deed you a thousand acres of your own."

"Acres covered with savages and pines!"

"It is an Eden, Robert. Raw and savage, yes, but with the promise of paradise." He pulled up on his bay suddenly, for they had come to the outskirts of town, and they could no longer pass easily on the road, for there was a funeral procession passing by. People stepped out of the way. An old crone looked up at the two of them and whistled softly. " 'Tis nobility! Best we give way!"

"Nay, woman!" Jamie said. "Hold your peace. All men are holden unto God, and we would not disturb those who grieve." The woman stared at him and nodded slowly. Windwalker pawed the cold earth, impatient to be on, but Jamie held him still. He watched as a bony nag dragged a cart forward. There was a gable-roofed wooden coffin upon the cart, but Jamie saw that it was constructed so that the foot of the coffin would give way. Apparently the family had not been able to afford the cost of a permanent coffin. When the final words had been spoken, the shrouded corpse would be cast into the earth, and the coffin retrieved.

The day was nearly as cold as the night had been. But behind the cart with the coffin walked a black-swathed woman. Slim but very straight, she did not cry; she made no noise and held herself with the greatest pride. Yet in the very stiffness of her spine, Jamie sensed something of her grief. Pain so great that she dared not give way to it.

"Who has died?" Robert queried softly.

The old crone snorted. "Linnet Dupré. Her Majesty, the actress. Though were ye to ask me, my fine lord, I'd say that Master John as well as killed her, for he is a mean one. She never had no strength. Were it not for that girl of hers, she'd have languished in Newgate long ago."

Listening, Jamie frowned. A gust of wind caught the black hood on the woman's head at last, causing it to fall about her shoulders. It was Jassy, the wench who had so fascinated him the night before. The thief.

His jaw hardened for a moment, then he relaxed, and he almost smiled. Well, her fascination had been for Robert. And perhaps she had been stealing for a reason. Perhaps she had longed to buy a proper coffin.

Or perhaps her mother had even lived and needed medication.

"Why, look, 'tis the beautiful tavern wench!" Robert exclaimed.

"Indeed," Jamie agreed.

"Perhaps we could help her. Perhaps we could be of service."

Jamie thought dryly of the night gone past and determined that she would not want any help from him. And yet she had taken the coin he had tossed her. He would never forget her eyes, though. They had burned like sapphires in the night, blue fire filled with hatred and a fierce, fighting spirit.

There was more about her he might not forget, he reminded himself. She was beautiful, of course. She had all her teeth, and they were straight and good. Her skin was achingly soft. Her face was fragile and fine, high-boned, exquisite. She seemed like a fragile flower, and yet there was that tremendous strength to her. No one would ever hold her down, he thought with amusement. Then he felt a flash of heat, for he had held her, and that, too, would take time to forget. She might have been created with the hottest sensual pleasure her entire purpose, for though she was overly slim, she was sweetly lush, with wonderful, firm breasts, rose-crested, beautiful. Her back was long and sleek, her legs long and shapely. Her stomach dipped and her hips flared, and she had been mercury to touch. She had left him aching in every conceivable way.

She had wanted Robert, he reminded himself. Women never seemed to realize where true strength lay, for Robert could not provide what she had needed. He hadn't the purse for it. Nor, for that matter, Jamie decided—with a certain arrogance, he was ready to admit—could his friend have provided what she needed in other ways. She was an innocent maid, but there was something about her that reminded him of his raw, untamed land. There was a promise of something wonderful and tempestuous and passionate about her. It was in her eyes; aye, even in the hatred she felt so wholeheartedly for him.

"She will not want any help from me," he said softly. He turned to Robert, reaching into his doublet for the pounds sterling he carried there. "Robert, follow her. When you are able, see that she receives these. Insist that her mother be buried in the coffin if she fights you."

"But, Jamie—"

"Please, Robert, do as I say."

Robert shrugged and smiled. "My pleasure. Perhaps it will enamor me to the lass. You should take care."

"We shall probably—neither of us—see her again, so what does it matter? Charm her into taking enough to get by on. Enough to find a new position away from such a one as Master John."

"Aye." Robert nodded. "Were that oaf to touch such beauty, it would indeed be a sacrilege."

"Aye, that it would. Go on now, the funeral party moves onward."

Robert dismounted his horse and wedged his way forward through the crowd.

She had not brought the black hood back up about her head, and from his position Jamie could see her face. No tears touched her cheeks, and her magnificent eyes were open wide upon the world. Yet she moved like some ice princess of a fantasy, forever frozen, forever made cold. No heart could beat within her breast, no warmth could thaw her. Her hair, a flow of golden silk, lifted and fluttered about her cheeks, and she seemed not to notice it. She walked straight forward, ever forward. She did not smile, and she did not crack. She was as beautiful as ice.

The wagon moved on; the crowd moved on. Jamie followed at a discreet distance, and he wondered vaguely why he took the time, and why he would bother with a maid with a temper like hers. She had tried to rob him and she had been blatantly disappointed—no, horrified!—to discover that he was Jamie, and not Robert.

It was her circumstance, he thought. Pity; had she come straight to him, he gladly would have eased her way and asked naught of her. He could be a hard man and he was aware of it, but those who knew him and those who served him knew that he was always fair and, in times of need, generous. What was his he claimed wholeheartedly, yet what was his he by rights could give, and he would have given the girl the money she needed without a thought.

He shrugged against the cold. What difference could it make?

They walked, against the winter chill, a good distance from the town. The crowd thinned. All who followed the girl now were a wizened little man and the plump, pretty barmaid who had also served them the night before.

Jamie realized that they had come to the common folks' cemetery.

No great monuments rose to the dead here. He thought of the chapel at Castle Carlyle, of the great monuments sculpted to his ancestors. Here there was earth, and the occasional poor cross, or a death's-head riding an angel. Mostly there was nothing but the barren winter earth.

A large hole awaited the cart. A mutual grave. Other shrouded corpses had been cast into it already, and more would join it before the day was done.

The priest stepped down from the cart. He waved a pot of incense, and his words rose high. God forgave all mortal sins, and Christ welcomed his own into his fold. Dust to dust. Ashes to ashes. Linnet Dupré had found a haven in the arms of the Lord Jesus.

Jamie watched Jassy, watched her standing tall and proud, the wind moving the sheaths of black gauze all about her. The priest's words fell like clods of earth, burying her mother with finality. And still she did not move, did not whisper, did not speak.

The swift service came to an end. The girl stepped forward to press a small coin into the open palm of the priest, and at last Robert stepped forward. The girl started. Her enormous blue-violet eyes opened wide, and emotion came to her at last: dismay, surprise, and a pale hint of shame.

Jamie felt his lip curl into a grim line. He hadn't known why, but he had asked Robert to return her things with a certain purpose. He hadn't known that he had such a cold streak of maliciousness, but it had seemed important that she know Robert had been aware of her activity. Perhaps she had wounded his pride. Perhaps it seemed that she believed Robert could give her more. Maybe he was just annoyed that she fawned so over his friend, believing there could be a future for her. Perhaps she dreamed of a fine house, of a title, of precious things. Perhaps he was the one who could draw the fire from her eyes and into the heart of her body.

Perhaps she even believed he was so soft of heart that he would marry her. She had misjudged her man. Robert needed wealth, and he would marry for wealth, no matter how great the beauty of a golden-blond barmaid.

As Jamie watched, Robert paid the priest for the coffin, and the toothless driver of the cart—apparently the owner of the coffin—came around, his ugly face gnarled up with interest.

The girl protested. She murmured something, and Robert turned to her and explained that she must let her mother rest in the coffin for eternity; it was a very small thing for him. The priest, who had been tipped well by now, assured her that it was important for Linnet's mortal remains to rest well in the wood.

The girl pulled the black gauze from about her and draped it lovingly over the coffin. Robert took her by the shoulders and led her away from it.

The cart was lifted and lowered.

The coffin made a thump as it landed in the ground. Only then did Jamie see the emotion that touched her face, a crippling anguish. It touched her for just a second, and then it was gone, and the ice was back about her, the crystal-cold control.

They came from the cemetery, and she saw him then, sitting high upon Windwalker. He saw her stiffen, and he saw the hatred enter into her eyes. She pulled away from Robert's hold, but Robert was talking and pretended not to notice.

The girl's eyes remained locked on Jamie's.

He dismounted from his horse. As they came closer, Molly and the wizened little man bobbed to him, murmuring, "Milord!" Jassy said nothing. She did not bow, and she offered him no title. She stood like stone against the cold and the wind. Behind them, the cart and the priest rode by, and the grave diggers hurried on with their task.

"Ah, there you are, Jamie!" Robert said. "I was telling her she must not return to Master John's, but she has said she has no intent to do so, anyway. She has a bit of money on her now, and she plans to travel southward to find her family."

"Does she?" Jamie said.

"Aye, that she does."

They were all standing out in the snow-packed road. Windwalker snorted loudly, and the breeze picked up with a vengeance.

"I've got to get back, luv," Molly told Jassy. "He'll have a strip of my skin if I don't."

"Oh, Molly!" Jassy whispered. The two women hugged each other. Jamie was treated to another glimpse of the warmth she was capable of expressing when she chose.

"And I, Jassy," the wizened little man said. "God go with you, child! Remember, we will always be here, should you need us!"

Jassy hugged him too. Fervently. He and the woman Molly bobbed to Robert and Jamie again, then swiftly departed.

"You were planning to walk to your family? Alone?" Jamie said skeptically.

"Aye," she snapped back. "And what is it to you, sir?"

"Lord Cameron, Miss Dupré," he said, correcting her with a slight bow. "Mistress, the question is of some importance to me, for my father's estates are not far, and he would be gravely distressed to hear of a young serving wench accosted and set upon and perhaps even left for dead."

"Should I be accosted and left for dead, Lord Cameron, I shall ask my Maker to see that your father does not hear of the event," she retorted. With a sweet smile she turned to Robert. "Thank you, sir, for all your kindness."

"Jassy, let us take you to the town ahead at least. We've an . . ." He paused, looking at Jamie with a shrug. "We've an extra horse. Ah, mistress! Truly the way is rough and ragged and littered with misfits and vagabonds, and I would be your escort."

Jassy smiled slightly and nodded, then looked Jamie's way. "And tell me, kind sir, is Lord Cameron accompanying you?"

"Aye, that he is," Robert said uncomfortably.

"Then I should prefer the misfits and vagabonds," Jassy said quietly.

Jamie forgot that she was a young woman, forgot that she had just lost her mother, and his infamous Cameron temper came into play. He clamped his hands down hard upon her shoulders, swirling her about. His face was darker than ever with the depth of his anger, his jaw clenched tight with the strength of it.

"Mistress, I believe you're forgetting that I might well have set the law upon you. Thievery of your type is punishable by hanging."

"Jamie!" Robert protested.

Jamie ignored him, staring into the hate-filled eyes of the woman before him. "What, madame, were you planning on stealing—a horse? Or are you so very cunning then, or is it a matter of sheer stupidity?"

"Don't touch me!"

He swore out something in absolute fury. He released

her shoulders but caught her waist. Before she could protest, he set her upon Windwalker's back. He leapt up behind her, grasping the reins with some difficulty, for she was swearing then, with the penchant of a dockhand. She tried to shift, tried to dislodge herself. Robert stood in the road, laughing.

"Well, there's one not dying to be a Cameron heir!" Robert chuckled. "Excuse me, Jassy." He bowed very low to her. "Please, do excuse me if I enjoy myself. You see, in London the ladies throw themselves all over him and he barely notices. It's nice for a change to see Lord Cameron at a loss!"

"Robert, mount up, will you?"

Jassy twisted against him. Beneath her threadbare cloak she was wearing the same garments she'd worn the night before. She tried silently to dislodge his arms from about her.

"Let me—"

"There is no extra horse, mistress. You may ride this one. Have you left anything behind?"

"I am most eager to leave you behind!" Was he mistaken, or was there a hint of desperation about her? Did the threat of tears hover in her eyes? Did her blood truly run warm, like that of other women?

"Mistress, you are a wretched witch, and in all honesty I do not know why we don't drop you here in the road!" Why in God's name was he bothering with her? She had annoyed him yesterday; he had been engrossed with his Royal Charter, his plans and his sketches, and he had sorely lost his temper when she had interrupted him. But then she had attracted his attention, and he wasn't at all sure why he should give a damn, or even if he truly did.

There's the lie, he realized. And there's the rub. He was worse than Robert, for he wanted her with an obsession. He wanted to find that thing about her which he could not see, and could not touch. He wanted the fire beneath the ice.

Her fingernails suddenly curved over his hands where they lay upon the reins, digging in. She spoke, her voice grating from her clenched teeth. "Lord Cameron, you vile heap of rodent compost—"

"Mistress, enough!" he roared. Her nails hurt. He should have been wearing his gloves. He swore, and with that, he set his heels to the bay. Windwalker took flight, sending her reeling hard against him. He heard a slight gasp. She clung desperately to the saddle pommel, and he was glad, for at least she had the instinctive sense to value her own life.

Hoofbeats sounded as Robert followed behind them. The winter wind blew about them, and though it seemed they rode the clouds, they rode hard, and it was cold.

Jassy was glad of it, for she quickly became numb. She had no adequate covering for this wild ride, nor did she know how she had found herself cast upon it. Perhaps it was all a nightmare. Within a day her life had changed so drastically. That morning she had broken all ties with the past. Linnet was gone. There was no reason for her to remain with a brute like Master John. She was young, she was very strong, she could not only read and write but also could teach geography or Latin and even history. There had to be a better place in life for her.

First, however, there was a matter of vengeance.

She was going to her father's house. She wanted nothing from anyone. All she wanted to do was to meet the duchess—and to spit upon her and let her know that she had brought about the destruction of Linnet Dupré, and that somehow, somewhere in time, she would pay for her cruelty. When that was done, Jassy could live again. She would find a better life.

She didn't want to admit that it was thanks to the gold coin that Jamie Cameron had so carelessly thrown her way that she could possibly make the long journey to Somerfield.

Jamie Cameron! she thought with scalding fury. Jassy's mother was gone, she was lost and bereft, and this dark son of Satan did not seem to care. He had no manners, no chivalry, but still insisted upon being there—ever a memory of her deepest humiliation!

She longed to throw herself from the horse! But she could not, and so she clung tight.

The wind stayed with them. They rode hard, passing frozen fields and ice-covered forests. The cold wrapped her and filled her, and at the least, it kept her from thinking of her loss. Her mind was upon him, for with each great movement of the bay's legs she was pressed against his chest. She felt his arms about her as he held the reins, and she felt the pressure of his thighs against her. How could he? she wondered bleakly. After the things that had passed between them, how could he imagine that she could bear the sight of him?

Suddenly the landscape changed, or what she could see of it, for her hair continued to lash against her face, stinging her eyes. The trees thinned, and they passed more of the barren fields of winter. There were barns and stables and cottages to the left of the road, and a frozen brook to the right. Within minutes they came upon a village.

Only then did Jassy realize that the bay had slowed, and that their wild ride had come to an end. Nor had he run the horses too wickedly, for they had come no more than twenty or twenty-five minutes from the Crossroads Inn. Suddenly they stopped. Lord Cameron leapt down from his mount and turned to reach for her. She ignored his arms at first, but though his eyes were enigmatic, they carried some curious warning or demand, and she allowed him to help her down. She hated the impact of his touch. She hated the strength of his arms and the feel of his hands upon her.

"From here, Mistress Dupré, we shall have to know where it is that you want to go."

"I want to go alone," she said quietly.

Robert came up behind them then, and two young stableboys came running out of the single tavern in the small place. Both seemed awed by the sight of Jamie and Robert, and Jassy quickly ascertained that the nobility and gentry seldom rode along this path. But the boys were quick to serve, and the horses were led away to the warmth of the stable. The tavern keeper came to the wooden steps of his establishment and stared at the lot of them with equal awe.

"Shall we dine?" Robert asked Jassy with a smile. He offered her his arm, and she gladly accepted it. Jamie followed them at a distance, then climbed up the steps and came into the establishment.

They were the only ones there, and the tavern keeper urged them into a private room with a bar and tap in the corner and a cheery fire burning in the grate. Robert brought Jassy forward while Jamie discussed the offerings with the cheery man. Robert sat Jassy down upon a bench. He knelt at her side and took her ragged hands into his own, rubbing them, warming them. She looked into his gentle eyes and saw his rueful smile, and the ever-present admiration he bestowed so kindly upon her. "You're dreadfully cold," he murmured.

"You're making me warmer," she said softly. She watched him, and she appreciated the fire's sure warmth, for she was flushing. This was what Molly meant by a handsome man. If a woman could but be his wife, maybe it would easy to lie with him. Perhaps she would not feel the humiliation and the crimson heat. Perhaps she could endure it all and return soft kisses to his gentle lips. Lips so different from those that curled with such scorn from the bronzed face of Lord Jamie Cameron. Oh, God! She would never forget that night. She prayed that he would fall off the face of the earth!

He ruined everything for her. He ruined the fact that Robert had cared, that he had come so gallantly to pay for a coffin for her mother, that he had offered her a horse that her journey might be with him, and be safe.

But he knew. He knew that she had gone to Jamie Cameron's room as a hired whore. And there was no way for her to tell him that nothing had happened, that she was still free to love where she would.

Her fantasies were taking hold of her. She could not marry him, no matter what. Men of his class did not marry women of her own.

She smiled and quickly drew her hands away. Then she realized that Jamie Cameron had long since ceased to speak with the tavern keeper, that he was staring at her with his relentless dark eyes. In silence he had watched Robert hold her hands, had watched her tender smile to his friend.

Robert stood up. "It is viciously cold, isn't it?" He warmed his hands before the fire, then turned around and warmed his backside. The tavern keeper had taken their cloaks. Jassy was still shivering.

Jamie swore softly and rudely touched her skirt. "Is that all that you have?"

She wrenched her skirt from his touch. "Aye!"

"Did your mother leave you nothing?"

"Oh, she had a dress, aye! Would you have had me set her naked in her shroud?"

Jamie took a step nearer the fire, rested his booted foot upon the stone hearth before it. He eyed her critically. "You cannot survive without warmer clothing."

"I will have warmer clothing," she said, staring at the flames.

"Perhaps this man's wife has some heavier cloak she'll no longer use," Robert said cheerfully. "I shall see."

"No, please!" Jassy swung around on the bench. "You must not spend your money on me. No more. I shall survive on my own. Honestly, I have made my way before, and I shall do so now."

"Then you'll excuse me a moment for private reasons," Robert said, and left them.

Jassy watched him go. Jamie frowned, looking down at her work-roughened hand where it lay against the wood of the bench. She wore a ring. A ruby ring with the emblem of a falcon upon it.

Jassy heard his movement, heard it like the wind, but she was not quick enough to stop his touch, nor had she the strength to battle against his sudden attack.

"You *are* a bloody thief!" he swore, catching her hand, wrenching her to her feet, and studying the ring.

"Stop it!" She tried to retrieve her hand. She could not. He sat upon the bench himself, dragging her down beside him. Then his indigo eyes found hers with seething fury, causing him to pierce into her like forks of lightning.

"Where did you get this?"

"My mother—"

"You liar! Who did you con for this ring?"

"I conned no one!"

"Who did you seduce and rob blind for this? What a fool I was! That is your act, is it not? You don't care if you are caught or not—you cry prettily—"

"I never cried before you!"

"You did not need to. I set you free. But with others you have cried! What a pity that I did not make you earn your income this time, but rather fell prey like all the others! Perhaps we should remedy the situation!"

"There were no others!" Jassy hissed furiously. "And I will never, never put myself in a position to be—to be so much as touched by you again!" Of course, he was touching her, and she hated herself for bothering with a reply. But he was on the bench beside her, and she was aware that he was no gentleman and that his touch was that of hardened steel. His hold upon her hand was brutal; the warmth of his breath touched her cheek. She could not escape him.

She gritted her teeth and went very still, but his hold did not ease. He jerked hard upon her hand again. "Who?" he demanded.

"I seduced no one!" she cried in fury. She tried to stand, and he dragged her back.

"Where did you get this ring?"

"It is none of your business!"

His eyes narrowed upon her, hard and without mercy, without a trace of compassion. "You may tell me now, Jassy, or so help me, this time I shall call the law down upon you and they will hang you by your very pretty little neck."

"You will not!"

"Test me, then, mistress."

She hesitated. She didn't know whether to believe him or not, and then, looking at his hard and implacable bronze features, she realized that he despised her and that he might do anything.

"It's my father's ring!" she snapped.

"What?"

Again she tried to wrench her hand away. "It is the crest of the Duke of Somerfield."

"Aye," she said gratingly.

"Do forgive me," he said mockingly, "but I know the children of the late Duke of Somerfield and a Crossroads serving wench is not among them."

She stared at him with the calmest loathing she could summon. "As a bastard child, she is, my lord!"

He released her hand suddenly. He was still and silent for several seconds, and then he began to laugh. "The old duke's daughter?"

"Aye, and not by choice!"

"You did not wear the ring the other night!"

"Nay, I did not, for it was on my mother's finger then. He always said that she must keep it, and she did. For this—and the taint of his 'nobility'—are my inheritance!"

He was still laughing. She hated the sound of it.

"Stop it! Oh, please, God!" Jassy groaned. "Will you not get out of my life!"

"Nay, not today, girl. I've brought you this far; I shall bring you the rest of the way."

"The rest of the way?"

"My father's lands border those of the new duke—your brother, Henry. I shall be glad to bring you to a loving reunion."

"I want no loving reunion!" She jumped up off the bench and whirled away from him. She faced him from near the fire. "I haven't come for a reunion, I have come to tell the duchess that she is guilty of murder!" She bit her lip to keep from crying out; her loss was still so close to her heart. The laughter had left him. He was watching her gravely. "She is guilty of murder! She killed my mother. I wanted nothing from him. I never saw him and I never wanted to see him. But she—his duchess! My mother was no serving wench. She was an actress, a fine one. But the duchess saw to it that she could never find work upon the stage. The duchess saw to it that she was worn into the very ground, that her health failed, that—oh, God, why am I telling you this? I hate you! I loathe you almost as much as I loathe her!"

Her words hung upon the air. The fire crackled, and he continued to survey her unblinkingly, insolent, arrogant, and ever superior. Then he smiled coldly and rose, and he towered over her, lean and hard, and suddenly she was afraid.

But he did not touch her.

"I'm afraid, my dear, that you will have to vent all that hatred upon me."

"What do you mean?" she asked quickly, backing away from him.

"The duchess is dead. She died two years ago. Well, the old duchess, I should say. There is a Duchess of Somerfield. Your brother has married."

Jassy's hand fluttered to her throat. "She . . . is dead?"

"Aye. Dead and buried."

Jassy turned away from him and studied the flames. "There is no reason for me to go there, then."

"No reason? Why, my girl! Knowing your ways, mistress, I would think that you might be most eager. Your brother is extremely rich." He paused a moment, and a curious softness touched his eyes. "And your sister is charming. Elizabeth. You should meet her."

"I will not go there."

He leaned casually against the mantel. "Then what will you do? Settle into scrubbing floors and peeling potatoes again?" He grabbed her hand again, lifting it high for her to see its work-roughened flesh. "Is this what you want for your life? To live and die in servitude?"

She snatched her hand away. "What I do or do not do with my life is none of your concern."

"I am simply trying to help. If you are so interested in scrubbing floors, I might speak with my father. He pays his servants very well, and feeds them even better."

"Thank you, no. I would not care to serve any relation of yours any more than I would ever care to serve you."

"I see. The tavern life suits you. There are always men about to seduce into parting with income for the mere promise in your eyes."

"Any man, my lord. Any five, any ten, any twenty—rather than you."

They stared at each other, and then the door swung open and Robert reentered the room. "Ah, Jassy, see what we have found!" He had an armful of garments and came to the bench, spreading them out to be surveyed by the other two. "It seems that Lady Tewesbury came through here not long ago. Do you know the story about Lady Tewesbury? I shall tell you. Her first husband died and she married a man who had pined for her for years. Well, this was a stop on their honeymoon tour, a reckless lovers' tryst in the forest. Anyway, her new husband could bear nothing of her old husband, and so he forced her to leave all her things here!" He glanced at Jamie. "The tavern keeper is willing to dispose of it all at a very modest cost." Jamie nodded slightly, and Robert went on. "I think that they shall fit you quite well!"

"Oh, but I can't—" Jassy said.

"Oh, but you must," Jamie said, interrupting smoothly. "Robert, you can't imagine what I have just discovered. Jassy is the . . ." He paused, and she wondered what he had first intended to say. "Jassy is the half- sister of the Duke of Somerfield."

"What?"

The garments fell from Robert's hands, and he stared at Jassy with renewed and keen interest.

"Alas," Jamie said, "I wonder if the duke knows of her existence."

"I wonder," Robert murmured.

"I had thought," Jamie said casually, "that we should find out. I shall hire a messenger to hurry to my father's house, and we shall take Jassy straight to Somerfield."

"Of course," Robert agreed. He was still staring at her. His breathing had gone very shallow. He smiled fully, then he let out a little cry of joy. "Somerfield, eh!" He laughed, then he reached for her hands and began to dance her around the room. Jassy thought that he had lost his mind, but he was so handsome and appealing and young and light with his laughter that she discovered herself joining in. If only Jamie Cameron weren't over by the fire, watching her with his dark, brooding gaze!

"Oh, our supper has come at last!" Robert said. He stopped dancing but still held her fingers, and the feeling was delightful. The tavern keeper entered the room with a kitchen boy at his side. He brought a feast of fish, poultry, and meat swimming in a pool of thick gravy. He brought a huge platter of bread and a dried apple tart and tankards of ale. For once, Jassy realized, she was not serving it. She was being invited to dine.

"Is it all to your liking, Jassy?" Robert asked her, and his blue eyes danced.

"It is lovely, thank you."

She managed to seat herself beside Robert, but Jamie Cameron was still there, across the table from her. And as always, he stared at her, condemning her, his dark gaze piercing into her, making her feel naked to the soul. She tried to ignore him, and she was somewhat successful, for she had never known just how hungry she was. She couldn't remember eating food that tasted this good, that was served so deliciously.

Then she looked up and found him still staring at her, and her pleasure in the meal dimmed. She did not know which of the men was paying the cost of the meal.

Jamie Cameron refilled her tankard with ale. She took it from him, sipping it, nervously meeting his eyes. Robert was talking about the fine flavor of the tart. She barely heard him, for she felt Jamie Cameron's eyes. Felt them, just as she had when they had fallen on her naked flesh, searching into her.

"Eat," Jamie said softly, "but go carefully."

"I have eaten too much," she murmured.

"Nay, it is good to see you so thoroughly enjoy that which I have taken far oft for granted. Take care, lest it be too much for your stomach."

She nodded and set down the bread upon which she had chewed. He stood up and walked to the window and watched the winter wind. "Master John should be hanged," he muttered suddenly, savagely.

Then he turned back to the two of them. "Hurry, now. Jassy, you must change. And we must be under way. I'd reach Somerfield before dark if at all possible."

"I'll see about the horses," Robert said. He squeezed Jassy's hand and strode out of the room. Jassy rose. She stared over at the clothing, and she knew that she could not go on. It wasn't right; it was making her the woman she had sworn she would not become.

"I am not going," she said.

"You are."

She shook her head. "Robert has been kind to me, but I can accept no more. I want nothing from the Somerfields, and I am certain that they will not welcome me. I wish to go on, alone."

He walked over to the bench. He plowed through the clothing there, to find a dress in dark green velvet with tiers of black lace over white lace at the bodice and sleeve. The underskirt was beige silk, daintily embroidered. There were no corsets among the things, and no petticoats. Those that she had would have to do. "Thank God you are small, and the same size. This is the one you will wear now." He came to her with the dress.

She shook her head. "You are not listening—I am not going with you."

His brow arched tauntingly. "Are you such a coward, then?"

"I am not a coward! I have no desire to be with you!"

"Ah, but I shall leave you at Somerfield."

"No!"

He thrust the dress toward her. "Do take this. I will leave you alone to dress."

"I will not—"

"I will," he said, interrupting her softly. "And I think that you know that I will, so please, change on your own. You have no secrets from me, you know. None at all."

Totally exasperated, she stamped her foot on the

ground. "I am not going with you! You may have wealth and power, Lord Cameron, but I am not a slave! You cannot make me!"

"Then what will you do? You have nothing."

"You forget. I have your coin from last night. And believe me, Lord Cameron, I have earned it!"

He smiled slowly, shaking his head. "Ah, but you *don't* have the coin I gave you last night."

"Threw at me."

"Whatever. You have it no longer."

He spoke with quiet assurance. She plunged her hand into her pocket and discovered that he was right—her one gold coin was gone.

He bowed low to her. "I'm afraid, Mistress Jassy, that you have taught me your tricks."

"Give it back to me!"

"But it is mine."

"No!"

"You performed no service. Did you intend to alter that fact?"

"Oh!" She dropped the dress and tried to strike him. He caught her arm, and she fell against him, breathing heavily. He pulled her close and their eyes met. "Now—"

"Give it back!"

"Gladly. But you earn it here and now."

"Oh! You are a toad!"

"Perhaps, but, mistress, you are no princess! Now—"

"You gave it to me!"

"Threw it, or so you say. What matters that? It is mine now. I possess it. And I will not lose it again. I try very hard to keep all that is mine."

"Possessions, all!" she cried.

"Aye—possessions, all. Now change and come along." He released her at last. She staggered for balance and he offered her his hand again, but she eschewed it scathingly.

"I do pray by the hour that the earth shall open and swallow you whole! Nay, a bear should lay claim to you!

A sea monster should seize you. Indians should roast and consume your flesh—"

"Jassy, I understand your meaning, thank you."

He strode to the door, fully assuming that she would do as he told her. And she would. She knew that he would carry out any threat, and she dared not take the chance that he would touch her again.

"Why are you doing this to me?" she called out.

He swung around and looked at her with a certain surprise. "I don't really know. Aye, maybe I do. Believe it or not, Miss Dupré, I'd just as soon not see you wind up a tavern whore or a common thief. That neck is too pretty to be broken by a noose." He smiled suddenly, and it was a surprisingly gentle smile for the man.

"You remind me of Virginia," he said softly, and then he left her, closing the door tightly behind him.

IV

Jassy was soon glad that she had dressed quickly, for it seemed that Jamie Cameron had barely gone before he returned. Smoothing the velvet down over her stomach, she stepped back as the man entered, Robert following close behind him.

"A vision!" Robert swore. He came to her and fell to his knees, then swept his hat from his head and cast it over his heart. "My lady, you are a vision, indeed!"

"And no lady, Robert, but you are very kind."

She flushed and glanced at Jamie Cameron. He didn't say a word. He studied her with his dark gaze.

"Will it do?" she demanded.

"Aye, it will do. Let's be on our way."

He stepped toward Lady Tewesbury's things once again and quickly selected a fur-trimmed cloak. He tossed it to Robert, who set it around her shoulders, then he called to the tavern keeper and asked that the rest of the things be wrapped for them. A curious silence reigned among them all the while they waited. When the clothing was wrapped, Jamie took the bundle. Apparently he had already paid the tavern keeper, and paid him well, for he was all smiles as they left. Outside in the cold again, Jassy was startled to see that a third horse was being held by the stableboy.

Jassy looked to Robert, who grinned with pleasure. "Well, she's a decent enough filly, I think."

"No bloodlines," Jamie murmured.

"She's beautiful, Robert. I thank you for letting me use her."

"She is yours," Robert said.

"No, I cannot accept her, but she is very fine, and I thank you for her use."

Robert looked sheepishly to Jamie, and Jamie firmly shook his head. "Let me help you mount."

He set his arms about her. Jamie watched as he lifted her high, setting her upon the mare's back.

"What is her name?" Jassy asked.

"I don't know." Robert looked to the stableboy. "Lad, what is her name?"

The lad blushed a furious red. " 'Tis Mary, sir." He hesitated. "Virgin Mary."

"Oh?" Robert lifted a brow in laughter.

"Ye see, me ma yelled at me pa when he bought her, she did. Said that this was a hauling place and that we needed such a filly just as a brothel might need the Virgin Mary."

"That's blasphemous!" Jassy gasped, trying hard not to laugh.

"Ah, so, 'tis an Anglican country now, thanks to good Bess." Robert chuckled and waved to the blushing boy. Jamie tossed him a coin, and the three of them started out.

For most of the journey she rode with Robert, and Jamie rode ahead in silence. They talked of the trail, and they talked about new modes of French fashion, and about the great discoveries in the world. She realized that he kept talking to keep her mind off her mother's death, and it seemed impossible that it was still so near.

Later in the day they stopped along a great forest in order to water the horses, and Robert left them alone, seeking the privacy of the trees. Jassy listened to the brook as it rippled, and the slurping sounds made by the horses as they sought water. She was sore; she was not accustomed to riding but to scouring floors and peeling potatoes.

She looked up and discovered that Jamie Cameron was staring at her as ever with his dark and enigmatic eyes. She looked over at the filly, then challenged him. "Bloodlines mean so very much to you, then, Lord Cameron?"

He shrugged. "In a horse, mistress? Often. Certain animals are bred for racing, some for stamina, and others for strength."

"Ah, yes, and in people, too, I would imagine! For certain, nobility breeds grace!"

He was still for a moment, then he shook his head slowly. "Nay, mistress. In beasts, as in people, one must be very careful. Bloodlines can be overbred and thus weakened. If you have brought in too fragile a dam for a stud, your colts will be tiny, and brittle in their bones. Sometimes it is best to go outside of the bloodlines and add new excitement to the line."

He spoke casually, yet there was that timbre to his voice, the way he looked at her, that made her feel as if hot tremors racked her inside. She turned away from him, wishing that she had never met him. There had surely been nothing wrong with *his* bloodlines. He was tall, he was powerful. He was as graceful as a big cat, as sure of his movement, as confident . . . as arrogant. He didn't have Robert's beautiful face, but surely some would consider it a handsome face, for it was well defined and cuttingly strong, the jaw so determined, the nose hard and long, his eyes so dark and sharp, and his mouth so fully mobile and finely shaped. She imagined he might fight off the women in a place like London, for perhaps those ladies were fascinated by his dark appeal, and perhaps even his very disdain enchanted them. They were welcome to him. She truly hated him.

"This is absurd," she told him. "You are going to drag me to my brother's house, and he will not have me there. Is this to further humiliate me?"

"He will have you."

"And why is that?"

"Because I will bring you there."

"But—"

"You will see," he told her, and that was all, for Robert had returned. She escaped into the trees herself, and then they mounted up again. It was growing dark, and thus it was growing colder.

Then a full moon began to rise, and in time the sky was blanketed in velvet, with the ivory cast of that moon rising high above them. Jamie urged them to hurry onward, and soon, though she sat shivering, Jassy had her first sight of Somerfield Hall.

It was magnificent, she thought. It was a palace, not a castle. It stretched across the land on the other side of a little river that glittered beneath the moon. It was built of stone, there were windows of paned glass, the front of it was built in a full arc for carriages to come and go, and there were endless steps to reach the entryway.

"It's beautiful!" she said quietly. It was her father's home. It could have been her heritage.

Her father was the man who had loved and left her mother, who had left them the legacy of poverty.

Jamie Cameron watched her curiously. Even now, even in the darkness and the cold, his scrutiny seemed always upon her.

"Come, let's reach it, shall we? The night is cold."

"Fine," she said. She dreaded reaching the manor. She was certain that he had forced her along to heap torture after torture upon her in some bizarre form of revenge. She was a fool. She didn't have to be here. She should have asked Robert for a loan. She could have sworn to have paid him back, and one day she would have done so. She meant to be a survivor.

She heard the baying of hounds, and then the circular entryway was filled with noise. A servant came to the top of the steps with a lantern and held it high, and the hounds wiggled their tails at his feet, baying again and again.

"Who comes here?" came his cry.

" 'Tis Jamie Cameron, Lydon. Tell the duke and duchess that I have come."

"Aye, milord, right away! Welcome, sir, welcome home!"

Jassy cast him a quick glance and wondered briefly where he had been. They walked their horses over the bridge that spanned the brook, and when they reached the courtyard, there was a multitude of grooms waiting to take their mounts. Jamie lifted her from her horse, not waiting for a by-your-leave, and certainly not asking for one. He set her down upon the ground and eyed her critically. He smoothed back a strand of her hair, then nodded. "You will do."

"How very kind of you!" she whispered in return. She tried to take a step, but her legs suddenly would not hold her. She could barely feel them. She nearly fell. "Robert!" she gasped. But Robert did not come quickly enough to her aid. Jamie reached her and caught her. "What is the matter with you?"

"My legs . . . the horse . . ."

"I thought you could ride," he said with impatience.

"Well, I can. Obviously I have ridden here! But I had not ridden in years and years. . . . Master John did not give us Saturday mornings for jaunts in the park, you know!"

"Hold on to me. After a few steps it will be better. You will hurt for a few days, for it cannot be helped."

He took her elbow and started up the steps with her while the man named Lydon queried him relentlessly about someplace called the Carlyle Hundred. Robert followed behind them and easily joined into the conversation, which made no sense to her at all. Then Jamie thought to introduce her. "Ah, Jassy Dupré, this is Lydon, the duke's valet and his most trusted employee. Lydon, Mistress Jasmine Dupré."

Old Lydon's eyes lit up like a freak fire, and he swallowed so fiercely that his Adam's apple jiggled. "Dupré?" he queried in a small squeak.

"Yes," Jamie said with amusement. "Miss Dupré. Have you informed the duke and duchess that we are here?"

"Aye, milord, I have, but I . . ."

"But what, Lydon?"

"Oh, nothing, milord. Do please come in. Welcome to Somerfield Hall, Miss—Dupré."

He pushed open double doors that opened upon a beautiful marble rotunda. There was a broad, sweeping staircase to the left side. To the right were double doors that Lydon hurried ahead to open, displaying a large tea room with molded ceilings, brocade drapes, upholstered chairs, and a shining wood table with an elegant silver service and crystal glasses upon it.

The family was awaiting them there.

At least she assumed they were the "family"—a group of richly dressed women and one man. He was in light silk breeches and a matching doublet with fine silk hose and buckled shoes. She gasped when she saw him, for she had always considered her coloring to be her mother's, but this man was very much like her, except for being taller and very broad about the shoulders. But his eyes were the same shade of blue; his hair, worn to his collar, was every bit as blond, and though his features were broader and heavier and very masculine, there was no mistaking the fact that they were related. And two of the women behind him were golden blondes, one the same height as she, and one taller and very slim.

The world seemed to churn and simmer. Blackness rushed upon her. She was certain that both Jamie and Robert stepped far out of the way, and that they left her alone there, like a lamb to the lions. They stared at her—the man, the blond women, and the pretty, dark-haired woman who stepped forward curiously, slipping her arm through the man's.

"Jamie! Robert! How wonderful to see you both! Henry, what is the matter with you? Lenore, Elizabeth?" She stepped forward, smiled broadly, and hugged Jamie Cameron with true, uninhibited affection, then kissed Robert on the cheek. "And who is this young lady?" she inquired sweetly.

"Jane, this is Jasmine Dupré."

"Dupré!"

The sound came out in an explosion of horror. Jane turned around and spoke sharply. "Lenore, where are your manners! Your papa would be shocked. Miss Dupré, please, you must come in and join us. Shall you have some wine? Or would you prefer ale?"

She wouldn't prefer anything. She could not talk, and she could not move, and she hated Jamie Cameron with an ever greater passion.

Suddenly the man, Henry Somerfield, stepped forward with long strides. Beneath the foyer chandelier, he grabbed and lifted Jassy's chin and stared deeply into her eyes, inspecting her. She found life at last. She stepped back and slapped his hand away."How dare you!"

He spun around on his heels and stared at Jamie. "What is the meaning of this? I demand to know."

"Careful, Henry," Jamie said softly. "I do not much care for demands. If you care to step into the study, perhaps you and I shall discuss it."

"Why bother stepping into the study?" Jane Somerfield inquired flatly. "She knows who she is, and we all know who she is. Why not discuss it openly?"

"She is a bastard!" one of the blond women hissed.

"Lenore, I will not have it!" Jane said.

"You are not my mother—"

"I am the duchess, your brother's wife, and lady of this house. You will obey me."

"Henry—"

"You will obey Jane!" he snapped. He was still watching Jamie, and Jamie was watching him. Henry smiled slowly. "Where did you discover this little gutter wench? Is this some grand joke upon me, Jamie? What is going on?"

"I stumbled upon her the other night. She is your sister, isn't she, Henry. How can I ask such a thing? I had not realized until I saw your father's ring, but now that you are together, the resemblance is uncanny. And she is no gutter wench, Henry. She is more of an abused child."

"I am no child—"

"Jassy, shut up and stay out of this. I found her in extremely unfortunate circumstances—"

"You were the unfortunate circumstance!"

"Jassy, shut up. Your father recognized her, Henry. Your father recognized her, and your mother is gone now. There is no one left to be hurt—no one but this girl."

"This . . . bastard!" the taller blond girl hissed again.

"Lenore!" Jamie snapped this time.

"Lenore, please—" Robert repeated.

"For God's sake!" Jassy exploded. "Will you please quit speaking about me as if I were not here? Lenore, your manners are the worst I have ever seen."

"I'm not about to split a copper farthing of my inheritance with you, you little fortune digger!"

"I want nothing from you!" Jassy cried.

"I will gladly share with you!" the smaller blonde claimed suddenly. She cut through everyone and came up to Jassy and reached for her hand. She blushed. "Well, actually, I'm the youngest, and I haven't much of an inheritance. Just a dowry. But I'm very happy that you're here. We knew about you, of course. Poor Mama hated the very thought of you and your mother. I think, though, that my papa loved you very much, and I'm glad that you're here."

The kindness was what Jassy could not bear. She had expected the insults; she had expected to be reviled, to be hated. She had not expected this gamine creature with her soft, radiant smile and shy touch.

Tears instantly welled behind her eyes. She blinked furiously to keep from shedding them.

"Thank you," she could barely whisper. Then she found her strength and backed away. "I did not wish to come here." She cast an acidic glance Jamie's way. "Lord Cameron insisted."

Henry stared at Jamie, and Jamie laughed. "Well, I could hardly take her home with me!"

"I think I'll have some wine," Jane said. "Let's do please quit gawking in the entryway like common folk. Oh. I am sorry. I didn't mean—oh, never mind. Lydon, wine for me, please. Girls? Henry, Robert? Jamie, a drink?"

"I'll have Scots whiskey—five fingers, please," Henry

said. He was still staring at Jassy. She had walked into the room with them. She did not sit; she longed to run, but she would not do so. She would not so entertain her brother Henry or her sister Lenore, nor so please them.

"She can have the maid's room off mine," Elizabeth said.

"She'll have to. Lord, Jamie, I can't bring a bastard into this house and try to pawn her off as legal issue! I can see that she is fed and clean—"

"Oh, she is quite clean," Jamie said, interrupting. Jassy longed to slap him. Just once. Solidly across his bronze cheek.

Jane spoke up softly. "Neither can you turn her out on the streets, Henry. She is your blood."

"And she would rather not be," Jassy said coolly.

Henry stared at her, then he laughed. "She certainly has some of Papa in her, hasn't she?"

"She has, indeed," Jassy murmured. "Her teeth are very good, you see, and her hooves are quite sound."

"We are discussing her as we might a horse," Elizabeth said.

"Lydon, the drinks, please," Jane reminded their servant.

"No dowry. I cannot afford it. She may have the room off Elizabeth's, and if she cares to help with the domestic chores, then she may stay. When there is no company, she may dine with the family."

They were still discussing her as if she were not among them. She wanted to scream and she wanted to cry, and most of all she wanted to escape. Robert Maxwell was still among them, listening to it all with amusement. He gave her a kindly smile, but her heart sank at the things he had to hear. She was coming to care so greatly for him. He was a still a dream that she coveted deep inside her breast.

"Where did you find her, Jamie? In a brothel?"

"Lenore, I do believe that I could be tempted to drag you out to the stables with a switch myself," Jamie said coolly. Lenore flushed, and opened and closed her mouth. But she didn't dispute him. "I found her at her mother's funeral, having labored for many years to keep the woman alive."

"Oh, dear!" Jane said softly. "Well, we can keep you from that fate at the very least! Isn't that true, Henry?"

"I have already said that she should stay."

"Well," Jassy spoke up, "I do not care to stay, thank you!" She turned, hoping to make a graceful exit. She did not manage it, for her legs gave out beneath her. She wavered and then fell. Her head struck the mantel and she cried out. She fell and fell and fell in a strange darkness, and still she did not reach the floor. She was caught in strong arms and lifted high. "Jassy!"

She could not answer. The darkness caught hold of her.

She woke up upon something very soft, and the light that gently glowed around her seemed to come from a single candle. She had never known such sweet comfort. She was clad in a clean white gown, and she lay upon clean white sheets, and the softest wool blanket she could imagine lay over her.

It took her a few minutes to discover these things, for they were hazy at first. Instinctively she touched her temple where it still throbbed, but there was a bandage there now.

The face of a woman wearing a bed cap hovered over her. It, too, was hazy, then it cleared. It was her sister, Elizabeth.

"Hello," Elizabeth said very softly. "Can you hear me?"

"Yes."

"That's a very good sign," Elizabeth said gravely.

"Is it?" She had to smile. "Where am I? How did I get here?"

Elizabeth sat back on the side of the bed and extended both her hands. "This is the small maid's room off my own." She frowned. "We've better rooms in the house, of course, but well, I suppose that they can't really give you the status of a legitimate child. Oh, I don't mean that cruelly. Do you understand?"

Jassy nodded. Her head was beginning to pound. "Really, I didn't want to come here. I will leave—"

"Oh, no! Please don't leave! I wondered about you for years and years. Papa and Mama had horrible rows about you. You are just wonderful. Please, stay. Jane is a darling, but then she and Henry are the duke and duchess. And Lenore, well, you've met Lenore. I have no one."

"But surely you've friends!" Jassy tried to sit up. It was very difficult to do, and her head began to pound all over again.

"Shush, and be careful! You've quite a gash upon your head. I'm afraid I haven't really friends, not as you think. Father preferred to go to London alone, I was never allowed to play with the servants, and Jane and Jamie were our nearest neighbors. Lenore is not as bad as she sounds, honestly, but still . . . please, say that you will stay awhile."

She couldn't say it. She wasn't certain that she could stay in this house very long, not when there was so much hostility directed against her.

"The room is lovely. It is by far the grandest that I have ever known," she assured Elizabeth. It was a beautiful room. It contained the wonderfully soft bed she lay upon and the fresh clean sheets and the warm wool blanket. There were drapes at the window and small, elegant tapestries on the walls. There was a trunk at the foot of the bed and a heavy oak dressing table. "How did I come here?"

"Jamie brought you up."

"Oh," she murmured, and she tried to hide her disappointment. She had hoped it had been Robert. She lowered her lashes swiftly.

Elizabeth giggled. "Take care if you've set your mind on Lord Robert Maxwell, for Lenore is taken with him. Ah, well, she is in love with Jamie, too, but he can be so very exasperating."

"That he can."

"Lenore is so demanding, and of course, no one shall ever demand things of Jamie. He barely stays within the realms of courtesy as it is. She gets so very angry with him. Then he leaves and she cries and frets for nights, and then it all happens again."

"Really." Jassy couldn't imagine caring in the least if Jamie Cameron determined to stay away forever. But Robert Maxwell was another matter. It seemed horrible to her that a woman like her sister Lenore might very well marry Robert—while she could not. Even now she would remain a poor relation. The sister from the wrong side of the sheets. It was foolish to be bitter. Molly had always told her so. It was a waste of time. But she was bitter, and she could not help it.

Elizabeth was staring at her with grave concern. They really did not look so much alike, after all, Jassy decided. Oh, the resemblance was there, but Elizabeth had a rounder face, a turned-up nose, and far more innocent eyes. She smiled, studying her sister. She had never expected to find someone like her.

"And what about you, Elizabeth? Who shall you marry?"

"Oh, no one!" she cried. "Unless, of course, Henry forces me. He shan't, I'm certain. Jane is a dear, and she will not let him force me into a marriage. I had thought for a while that I would join with the sisters of St. Francis, but I discovered that I did not have the vocation, after all."

"Then perhaps you will fall in love."

"No, I don't think so. I'm too shy. Oh, I have known Jamie all my life, and Robert is so sweet and funny. But I am no good with strangers. I love this house, but I hate it, too, for it has also been my prison. It can become a prison, you shall see! But now, tell me about your life. I am so anxious to hear."

Jassy felt a new rush of tears come to her eyes as she finished telling her story and turned her head into her pillow. *Mother,* she cried silently as she buried her face within the bedding, *I loved you. I would do anything to have you back. I still cannot believe that you are gone, that I will wake and you will not be with me.*

Elizabeth was there beside her, and it was all right that she saw Jassy's tears. They hugged each other and rocked back and forth, and Jassy tried to explain. "You buried her this morning!" Elizabeth said, shocked. "You poor, poor dear. Oh, Jassy, you must stay! They'll give you a hard time, but you must stay. The world will treat you cruelly if you do not! It will break you, as it broke your mother! The pain fades, Jassy, and in time you remember what was good and what was sweet. I promise."

The next morning Jassy was summoned by the Duke of Somerfield. When she entered his office, he was sitting behind his desk. He rose but did not invite Jassy to sit. He walked around her, observing her carefully. Then he backed away. She stared at him, not speaking, for she had not been spoken to. He was many years older than she, she determined, but was still a young man. He was elegantly dressed in wide breeches and a heavily embroidered doubtlet with wide, fashionable sleeves.

"You've no humility," he said at last. "None at all. You need some, you know."

She lowered her eyes and her head, remembering that she had decided she did want to stay at Somerfield Hall. For a time, at least—until she could fathom a way to reach her own destiny, to acquire her own wealth. A dream perhaps, but a dream that sustained her.

"You are not a legitimate member of this household!" he said sharply.

"No," she agreed softly.

"And I will not treat you like legitimate issue."

She said nothing but waited.

His voice softened. "And yet you are my sister, and very beautiful. More beautiful than Lenore, and probably more clever than us all. Your position here is a difficult one. I do not care to have a member of my bloodline living in abject poverty, so I would keep you here. We must give you a task. I imagine that you have been well educated?"

She nodded. "I had tutors until I was twelve."

"The duchess is with child. When the babe is born, you shall be the Lady Jane's nursemaid, and you must keep a stern eye on the wet nurse, for I've found only a country lass who is slow for the task. When my son is able to talk and comprehend, you will begin his lessons until he comes of such an age that I hire proper tutors. Can I trust you with such a position?"

She raised her eyes again. She had expected worse from him, much, much worse. "Thank you. I love children, and I promise that I will tend yours well."

"Then that is all. Oh, except for this: If you ever mention your birth to anyone again, I shall ask you to leave." His eyes traveled over her slowly. "Everyone will know who you are. But you are my hired governess, and that is to be that, do you understand?"

"Clearly."

"For the time you may help Jane with her correspondence."

"Thank you."

"You may go. She will call you when she wants you."

Jassy fled from the room and returned to her own, where both Elizabeth and Kathryn, the kindly ladies' maid, eagerly awaited the outcome of her interview. She told them quickly, and they both laughed happily, and the three of them decided that it was the very best that could have been expected.

Soon after that the duchess sent for Jassy. In a beautiful solar she kept an elegant secretary, and her stationery and seal. She smiled at Jassy when she arrived, and though she wasn't as effusive as Elizabeth, Jassy felt that she had another friend.

"I think that this will work out very well, don't you?" Jane asked after she had had Jassy write out a letter of condolence to a friend on the death of her husband. "What lovely penmanship! I think that we shall get along very well. Oh, and Jassy . . ." She paused, picking up Jassy's small hand. "I've some cream we must try. It will take away the redness, and in time, perhaps, heal the skin altogether. I'll have Kathryn bring it to you tonight."

"Thank you. You are very kind."

The duchess smiled and sat at the chair behind the

secretary. She sighed. "I am glad you will be tending the babe. He will be your nephew, you know, even if we aren't allowed to say."

"Yes. I promise you I will tend him or her with all my heart and soul."

"Yes, I believe that you will." She smiled but appeared tired. "Heavens! In the commotion last night I forgot to tell my brother that I am enceinte."

"Your brother?" Jassy murmured warily.

"Why, yes. Jamie is my brother. That globe-trotting pirate. Why he will not sit still in this good country . . . Castle Carlyle is big enough for a dozen families, ten times larger than Somerfield Hall. And Jamie has built his own home on land my mother left him. But then my papa, too, is obsessed with the Virginia colonies, so I suppose it is understandable that Jamie thinks it fine to sail that ocean again and again." She shivered. "You'd not get me onto one of those miserable ships for a three-month voyage. But Jamie will do as he chooses; he has always done so and he always will, and heaven help the man or woman who tries to stand in his way. I think that that is all for now. If I need you this afternoon, I will send for you."

Jassy nodded, still somewhat stunned by the news that the duchess was Jamie Cameron's sister, although why, she wasn't sure. The Camerons and the Somerfields had all grown up together. Their lands adjoined.

"Oh, Jassy!"

"Yes, Your Grace."

Jane flushed. "You need not call me that, unless my husband is present. You may call me Jane, please. When you are at leisure, I will appreciate your spending time with Elizabeth. She is terribly shy, you know, and has no real friends."

"It is a pleasure to be with Elizabeth."

"Good." Jane grinned and waved a hand in the air. "Is there anything that you need?"

"Nothing."

Jane told her what her wages would be, and Jassy

gritted her teeth not to cry out. In one month she would earn what she had slaved a year for at Master John's.

When she left Jane, she was dreaming already. She would diligently save her wages. She would buy land, or she would buy a tavern. She would become her own mistress. It would take time. So much time. But she would never be poverty-stricken again.

"Ah, my sister, the well-dressed bastard!"

Jassy was rudely jolted out of her daydream. Lenore stood before her in the hallway. Jassy said nothing but waited.

Lenore grinned suddenly. "Thank God that he has made you a servant! You would be stiff competition if you had any type of dowry whatsoever."

Jassy arched a brow, wondering just what Lenore meant.

"Oh, I'm really not so terrible. I mean, I don't wish to drown you like an unwanted litter of kittens or anything. I just want you out of my way. All right?"

"I hardly see how I could be in your way."

"Then you are blind to your own image," Lenore said flatly. "You will eat in your room tonight; Kathryn will bring you a tray. I am having company, and alas, we want you seen as little as possible."

"Fine," Jassy said, and she stepped by Lenore.

Curiously, that first day set the tone for many of the days to follow. In the morning Kathryn woke her. Elizabeth improved her wardrobe with cast-off pieces from Jane and Lenore. And strangely, Lenore did not seem to mind. "As long as you have the secondhand pieces, I do not care at all," she said airily.

Until noon she worked on correspondence with Jane, and in the afternoons she was at leisure to read or walk with Elizabeth, and even to ride. On her third day there she discovered that the horse, Mary, was in the Somerfield stables. "She is yours, of course," Jane told her, "and you must take her out whenever you choose."

"But I told Robert that I could not keep her!" Jassy protested, distressed.

Jane watched her curiously. "Jamie left her for you.

And she is your horse. Speak with Jamie if you do not want her."

"I will," Jassy said. But she could not leave the docile creature with no attention, and so she began to ride her, and each time she rode her, she remembered the conversation she'd had with Jamie about bloodlines.

Lenore was always catty, and Henry was always cold, blunt, and upon occasion, cruel, but Jane was charming and Elizabeth was sweet. As winter melted into spring she was pleased with the turn her life had taken. Things were so different here. There was so much of beauty about the Hall. There were sculptures from France and Italy, and the table was set with silver, gold, crystal, and painted Dutch plates. The Hall itself was a thing of beauty, and she discovered despite herself that she was bitter still, for she coveted the fine house and all the beautiful things within it. Her sweetest pastime was dreaming, and in that she frequently indulged.

She was so engaged late one afternoon when Elizabeth came running into her room. "Jassy! We are to have company tonight, and you are to come down to dinner as well!"

"I am? Why?" Her dreams were ever with her now. Some young squire had seen her riding about the place. He was a friend of Henry's, and he had insisted that the hidden sister be presented before him when he came for a meal. He would be fabulously wealthy, and she would fall in love with him. He would smile like Robert, sweep her away, and she would be mistress of her own castle or magnificent mansion.

"We're to discuss the May Day dance." She giggled. "Think! It's but a month away. Anyway, Jamie will be here—"

"Oh," Jassy murmured disappointedly.

"And Robert. They always come to help plan the theme. Well, it's the Duke of Carlyle who plans the event with the Duke of Somerfield, but his father has no interest in such things, and his elder brothers are in London this year, so Jamie must represent the duke. And Robert is still his guest, so they will both come. It will be fun, and very casual."

"Yes, it sounds like wonderful fun." She would see Robert again. That, in itself, was exciting.

"The May Day dance is even more fun. Lenore is in a complete tizzy."

"Oh, why?"

"Oh, well, you don't know, I guess. It's May Day. They set up a huge pole. It's really supposedly a pagan rite. The pole is actually a"—Elizabeth paused, and though they were alone, she moved very close to whisper in Jassy's ear—"a phallic symbol! But oh, the day is wonderful. And at the end of it there is a dance, a very swift and wild dance, and when the dance is over, a woman is supposed to find her mate for life, her beloved. Oh, Jassy, perhaps you will find a husband! Not that it is legal, of course, but usually lovers are able to find each other. Weddings do follow! That is why Lenore is in such a state. She doesn't know whether she will try to catch Jamie or Robert. Jassy, you look so pale. Are you listening?"

"Yes, yes, I'm listening."

"Isn't it exciting?"

"Oh, yes. Very exciting."

"Then hurry! We must dress for dinner! Kathryn will come and do our hair, and it will be very special."

Elizabeth was still talking, but a tingling sensation rippled along Jassy's spine, and she could not really hear her any longer. Lenore could not decide whether she wanted Robert or Jamie Cameron. A maid was to set out to capture her husband. . . .

Henry would probably refuse to allow her to be a part of it.

She would go, anyway, she determined. Somehow she would manage to capture Robert Maxwell. And then she would have everything; she would have him—charming, kind, tender Robert. She would be a wife and no longer a mistress, no longer a servant. She would have a house and a home of her own, and she would have realized her greatest dream.

All that she had to do was plan, very, very carefully.

V

From the start it promised to be a grand evening.

As Jamie and Robert were to be the only company, Elizabeth was pleased and in a fine mood. Jane was anxious to see her brother, and even Henry seemed to be in a rare good disposition. Lenore was highly intrigued with another chance to study both men, and to determine who she would prefer to have as a husband.

For Jassy it was her first real chance to dress up, and she felt like a princess preparing for a ball. She wore one of Elizabeth's gowns that evening, a wonderful creation of crimson velvet and soft mauve silk. The half-sleeves were ribboned and the stomacher was embroidered with gilt. Kathryn thread silver and gold ribbons through her hair, and when she was done, Jassy was ecstatic. She preened and swirled before Elizabeth and Kathryn, and laughed with nervous gaiety. For the first time she felt as if she could really play a lady. For the first time she was aware that she could appear beautiful.

"Will I do?" she asked.

Elizabeth laughed. "Lenore shall be green with envy."

Jassy didn't really want to make Lenore green with envy, but she did want to sweep Robert Maxwell off his feet. He did care something for her, she was certain that he did, and if only she could make him see that she could stand among the most refined and cultured young ladies. She knew now from Elizabeth that he was the second son of the Earl of Pelhamshire, but like Jamie, he was not his father's heir. Perhaps it was a dream, but she had halfway convinced herself that he would be willing to cast convention to the wind, if he could be made to love her deeply enough. She had to make him fall in love with her. Surely he could not love Lenore with her rapier-sharp tongue!

"Shall we go down?" Elizabeth suggested.

"Oh, yes!"

Kathryn straightened her skirts one last time, and then Elizabeth and Jassy started for the sweeping stairway. Jassy had never felt so marvelously alive and excited, her senses attuned to everything around her. She felt the rich material of her gown against her skin, and the very air as it touched her. Her blood seemed to dance within her, and her breath came short and quick.

"Oh, they've come!" Elizabeth whispered excitedly behind her. "Jamie and Robert are here, and Lenore has already gone down, and Jane and Henry are there too. You must let me go first, and then you follow and make a wonderfully grand entrance!"

Elizabeth gave Jassy no chance to protest; she raced down the stairway, greeting their guests effusively. Jassy hesitated and felt the fierce beat of her heart as she started down the stairway.

She could hear the sound of voices coming from the landing, and then they all ceased. She watched as all eyes rose to her. Her brother Henry's were startled then guarded and thoughtful. Elizabeth's were sparkling. Jane's were intrigued. Lenore's were hard and wary. Robert Maxwell's were filled with pleasure and wicked admiration. Those were the eyes that mattered. The eyes that she sought to please, and she met them gladly. But even as she smiled in return, she felt a curious draw, and she met the piercing gaze of Jamie Cameron.

He betrayed no pleasure and no surprise. Indeed, it was as if he expected her to appear no less finely attired and groomed. His dark gaze was as fathomless as ever, and he stood as still as a rock himself, striking in a white laced shirt and dark navy jerkin and trousers, white hose and buckled shoes. She thought then, though, that it would not have mattered what he wore. He had been born the aristocrat, and it was apparent in the very way he stood, in his unyielding and ever-present confidence in himself. It was in the way that he held his head, in the way he observed all things with insolence. It was in the mocking curve of his lip, and in the nonchalant way he crossed his arms over his broad chest. In rags he would appear the proud lord, the master of his world, and so his elegant attire mattered little.

She could not draw her eyes from his, and she felt her flesh grow warm. The way he looked at her was unnerving. He stripped her naked with his eyes, and easily he could, for he knew what lay beneath her clothing. She was certain that he was condemning her, laughing at her attempts to join society.

Robert Maxwell was not laughing. He did not scorn her. All the bright and wonderful admiration he felt was apparent in his eyes. He stepped forward as she reached the landing, caught her hand, and laughed. "Why, this blossom we plucked and planted here is no weed but a radiant flower for certain! Jassy, you are beautiful beyond belief. Henry, you have proven yourself a great benefactor."

"Yes, she has come along quite well," Henry said impatiently. "We are all here now. Shall we hurry along to the dining room? I admit to being famished."

There were murmurs of assent all about. Lenore, as beautiful as a snow queen in white brocade and fox fur, stepped forward swiftly, slipping her arm through Robert Maxwell's. "Robert, we are paired for the meal. Will you escort me?"

He gave Jassy a quick look of pained regret with a promise of a future meeting, then he turned with all his charm to Lenore. "It is always my greatest pleasure to be at your side."

They began to file from the entryway to the dining

room, through great double doors. Thrilled with Robert's response to her, Jassy felt as if she walked on clouds.

Then she was dragged back to earth by a vise upon her elbow.

Jamie Cameron held her.

"What do you want?" she demanded sharply.

"Merely to view this creation of mine," he replied. She did not want to make a scene, and so she stood impatiently still, feeling the heat rise in her again as his sharp eyes raked over her from head to toe.

"I am not your creation."

"Ah, but you are."

"Stop it. Stop looking at me as if you know what lies beneath my clothes."

"Ah," he murmured softly, "but I do know what lies there. I have a wonderfully clear memory of it all."

"You are hateful, and far from gallant."

"And you may wear ribbons and gold thread and all the adornment that you please, and you shall still be the gold-digging little thief I carried away from the tavern."

"Carried away! Your creation! You are an insolent son of a bitch!"

"And there comes the tongue of the tavern wench."

She jerked hard upon her elbow; he did not let go. He touched her hair instead, smoothing back a strand. Seething, she gritted her teeth and prayed that he would release her soon. She smiled. "Well, then, my Lord Cameron, what is your opinion of the adornment? Shall I suffice to grace this hallowed hall?"

His dark eyes met hers. "The adornment is wonderful. You are quite beautiful, and you know it well. But I do suggest that you take care. You are giving yourself airs, and no one here has forgotten the fact that you are the child born on the wrong side of the sheets. Don't fool yourself. It matters."

"I shall do my best to remember your warnings!"

This time when she jerked upon her elbow, he released her. With a toss of her head and a flounce of her skirts, she hurried on into the dining room.

Her place was in the middle of the table. The duchess

sat at one end of the long table, and the duke sat at the other. To Jassy's annoyance, Robert was across the table from her, while Jamie was seated to her right. He smiled apologetically as he drew out his chair. She ignored him. She concentrated instead on the beauty of the table, and of the night. Not a month ago she was a wretched servant carrying tankards of ale to lascivious louts. Now she sat here, sipping fine wine from crystal, dining with a silver fork, on a table covered in white linen and lace. She would not let Jamie Cameron ruin it all.

The meal began with a toast to the duchess, in honor of the child she would soon bear the duke. Jassy was as enthusiastic as the others as she raised her glass to Jane, for she had become very fond of the no-nonsense woman.

Then she watched as Jamie rose and kissed her, and a little knot began to form in her stomach, for then the duke rose, too, and she saw the deep affection that passed between them all. The duke's fingers fell over Jane's shoulders with tenderness, and much love was apparent in his gaze. How very sweet it seemed. In those moments Jassy envied Lady Jane with a deep and startling anguish. That was what she wanted. The knowledge that she was needed, that she was loved and cherished.

She bit her lip and stared at her plate, and then she raised her chin again. She would have Robert. She would win him and she would love him, and he would cherish her with tenderness, as she had just witnessed. And he would make her mistress of her own home.

Conversation went on to the May Day ball, with Lenore enthusiastically leading it, and Robert joining in. Lenore charmed Robert and then swept Jamie with the radiance of her warmth and smile too. She pretended to draw Jassy into her circle, for not to do so would have appeared rude. Yet Jassy occasionally felt her sister's gaze, and thought there did not seem to be hatred behind it. There was an assurance, as if she had a card to play which Jassy knew nothing about. Perhaps she did. Jassy couldn't really care.

Then Jamie no longer discussed details with them, for Henry had drawn him into a discussion on the Jamestown colony in the New World. Jassy had little interest in such a faraway and savage land. She ignored his bronze hand when it brushed hers, and she ignored the heat of his body, so close to her own. She listened while Lenore described the Maypole, and how someone was always Queen of the May, and how there was a table set for the servants, and one for the gentry and nobility. She paused and smiled, and Jassy was sure that Lenore was thinking that Jassy would definitely sit with the servants on that day. "But the meal, of course, comes after the dance of the May." She giggled and cast Robert a flirtatious glance. "It's all in costume, of course, but single maidens may seek out their true love, and if they can hold him until the music ends, then he must marry her."

"Is it legal?"

"Oh, of course not! But it is terribly romantic. Even among the poorer folk, marriage is a matter of grave concern. And when it comes to men and women of family, well, of course, there are grave details to be worked out. Dowries and contracts and the like. But I tell you, many a free maid has made her choice, and it has been honored through such play! Why, any man is honor-bound to offer the maid marriage, you see."

Honor-bound. Robert Maxwell was a most honorable young man. Jassy still could not tell if Lenore would seek out Robert or Jamie when the time came. She hoped that Lenore would seek Jamie. The two of them deserved each other, in Jassy's opinion.

"No, Henry, I think that you are wrong," Jamie said emphatically at her side, interrupting her dreams of things to come. "The first charter given to the Company in 1606 left a nebulous question of authority—the king and his council held much power, and they were across an ocean, too far away. There have been many new charters since."

"Governors have come and gone, and the Company fares no better," Henry said. His liveried servants moved about the room in practiced silence as he spoke, offering up the various platters of food prepared for the meal. A plate of fish beautifully molded to resemble a swimming flounder came Jassy's way, then a plate of parsley-sprigged lamb, and a kidney pie, and then a serving platter with a cooked pheasant, feathers surrounding the body upon the tray. It was all delicious, and Jassy gave but scant attention to the conversation as she concentrated upon the food. Sometimes it was difficult to remember that she was not starving anymore, and that she had far more than thin soup and watery gruel to fill her stomach these days.

"I beg to differ," Jamie told Henry, drawing Jassy's attention once again. "Matters have improved. The Indians and the white men are at peace. Men are learning to grow food, as well as tobacco. And there are many women in the colony now, and on the various hundreds surrounding it. And my land is an individual grant from the king. I am the authority upon it."

"I doubt not that you will grow rich on tobacco, Jamie," Henry agreed, "for what you touch turns to gold. But must you spend so much time in such a heathen land?"

"Especially when you have just built such a stunning new manor here!" Lenore said.

Jassy quickly looked over at her sister. Lenore's eyes were warm and sparkling, and they stayed upon Jamie as she smiled deeply. "It is one of the most beautiful places I have ever seen, Jamie. That you keep wandering away is a crime. It is a palace."

"It is not a palace, Lenore."

"It is grander than many a royal residence," Henry said wryly. "And still you travel on to the heathen wilderness. What is the draw?"

Jamie shrugged. "The very wilderness, I suppose. There is a pagan beauty there, raw and untamed. I am fascinated by the spirit of it. I would fight the elements, I suppose, and by God, I would win."

"And what if you lose?" Jassy asked, challenging him.

His dark indigo gaze fell to her. "I do not lose, Miss Dupré. Ever. What I set out to do is done, and what I wish to acquire is mine."

"Not every time, surely."

"Surely, yes, but it is so."

"There will come a time when it is not so."

He was no longer looking at her, but he stared across the table at Lenore, who returned his gaze. "I do not think I need to worry," he said simply. Lenore flushed, her lips parted slightly, and she seemed entranced. It seemed that Jamie had decided on her, and that in the end, no matter how she teased and pouted and tormented, Lenore would have him. It would be just as he had said—he would have what he wanted.

Robert laughed. "That is Jamie. He must win, and he will have that which he chooses."

"I should much rather talk about the dance than a heathen land," Lenore said, and shivered. "The talk of those Indians—"

"Oh, but the stories about John Smith and Pocahontas were so wonderful! She befriended our people then, and married Mr. John Rolfe, and so the colony survived. That is wondrous."

"Wondrous! Why, the pagans slice hair and flesh from men's heads!" Jane said. "The wars have been dreadful. Jamie can tell you. He fought the Indians there."

"They paint their bodies in hideous designs!" Lenore said.

"They paint their bodies in beautiful designs," Jamie said, "and the wars have been over for a long time now. When British colonists were starving in 1609, it was the Indians who fed them."

"Why, Jamie, I think that you actually admire those red devils," Lenore admonished.

"I do. Many of them. They have a sense of honor, and though many of their values differ greatly from our own, many are the same. They love their children as we love our own. They revere a man who is honest and trustworthy, and they will fight to defend what is theirs. Powhatan was a very great chief, and Pocahontas was a lady I considered myself privileged to know."

"I do suppose she was fascinating," Lenore said politely. "But not nearly so fascinating as your lovely new manor."

Elizabeth trembled suddenly at Jassy's side. "I should hate it! I should just hate the new land. It is damp, with mosquitoes and pests. And the Indians are hideous beasts, no matter what you say, Jamie. I have read about the Lost Colony, and Sir Walter Raleigh, and the poor, poor infant, Virginia Dare. The Indians carried them off and killed them, and perhaps even ate them! It is a dreadful new world."

"Elizabeth," Jamie said gently, "it is not a dreadful world, I promise. There are acres and acres for cattle to graze, acres where deer roam in plenty and where there is an endless supply of pheasant. Sometime, little one, you must come with me. You will see. But enough for now, if we distress you. Who will you come as to the ball? A Greek maiden? Helen of Troy? A fairy-tale princess, perhaps?"

Elizabeth's eyes widened. "Why, I shall not dress at all. I do not wish to capture a husband!"

They all laughed. Then Robert stared across the table at Jassy.

"And who, Miss Dupré, shall you come as?"

Caught unaware, Jassy hesitated. Henry spoke up sharply for her. "Jassy will not attend this year. She is too new to this house and needs time to adjust before indulging in such games."

Jassy felt as if an ocean of icy water had been cast over her dreams. She had to go to the ball!

Perhaps her disappointment was betrayed in her face, for Jane spoke quickly, saying that as the meal was completed, they should move into the solar, for she had hired a puppeteer to entertain them for the night.

As Jassy blindly rose, trying to swallow down her rage and disappointment, a warm breath touched her nape, and she heard Jamie Cameron's whisper. "Don't be too distressed. Occasions such as the ball are purely for show and mean little. Alas, you shall have to capture a rich husband elsewhere."

She managed to discreetly cast her elbow into him but knew little satisfaction, for he barely seemed to note the intended torment. He caught her elbow to lead her from the room. "Please don't fret. I shan't attend the ball, either. I find such charades far more savage than the practices of the North American Indians."

"A pity!" Jassy snapped in return. "You've come to plan an event in which you'll not participate?"

"It is the responsibility of the Dukes of Somerfield and Carlyle. I merely represent my father."

"I'm sure that Lenore shall be heartily disappointed. What, then, have you no interest in marriage? Why, Lenore is there, milord, quite for the taking."

"Ah, but there is Robert to consider."

"Do you really consider any man or woman in your quest for what you desire, my Lord Cameron?"

"But I don't know quite what I desire," he said. "Marriage is a most serious step. A wife must not only be winsome to the eye but a capable lass."

"Capable? Why, Lord Cameron, you need but a showpiece, or so it seems. Someone to grace your illustrious mansion, to give you illustrious children, and serve wine and comfits—illustriously, of course. Why, Lenore should charmingly fit such a bill of needs."

"You underestimate what I seek in a mate, Miss Dupré," he told her, and bowed, releasing her arm.

He moved to Lenore's side then, whispering something in her ear. Lenore laughed delightedly, turned to him, and set her elegant hand upon the frilled lace that spilled over his doublet at his chest. He seemed very tall and dark then, as striking as a prince, and Lenore, with her blond beauty, looked well with him. She sighed softly and trembled, and Jassy thought that her sister wasn't at all immune to the oft-aloof charm of Lord Cameron.

Robert was engaged in conversation with Elizabeth, and Elizabeth was laughing happily. The duke was bowed over his duchess as the puppet master prepared his show. Jassy suddenly felt very much alone—very much the bastard child, the poor, unwanted relation from the wrong side of the sheets. Her temple thundered with a sudden pain, and she hated Henry with all the venom she could muster. He could not stop her! She would go to the ball, and she would marry well. She would not know poverty again, but she would leave this hall where she was so unwelcome and become mistress of her own destiny.

None of them noticed her, and no matter how brave her imaginings, she was, at the moment, unnoticed, unneeded. She turned around and fled, leaving the solar, running on Elizabeth's soft satin slippers out through the dining room and the back of the house toward the stables beyond. Her way was well lit, for there was a full moon, and stars dotted the sky, and the house was well supplied with lanterns for the evening, as were the stables. There she raced along the length of stall until she found Mary, the poor little mare with the faulty bloodline, and slid beside her. She patted the animal's velvet nose and crooned to her softly.

"I care not that your pedigree is weak, my dear, for your heart is very valiant, and you are faithful and good and true. Wherever I go, I promise that I will see to you! They will not cast you out for not being a good worker, or a beautiful horse for the hunt, or a great breeding mare. I swear, I shall bring you with me wherever I shall go." She hesitated. "And I shall pay that bastard for you first, so that you will truly be mine."

She started then and fell silent, for she heard some sound at the door to the stables. She thought that it was late for the young grooms to be about, for they all lived in the cottages that surrounded the estate, and none of them lived in the stable. Not even old Arthur, in charge of the horses and grooms, slept here, for his pallet lay in the little room next to the tack house.

"Jassy?"

It was Robert's voice. She smiled with a rush of pleasure and came around the mare's rump. He had left the puppet show to come to her. "Robert, I am here."

"Jassy!" Wearing a charming, crooked smile, he came her way. "I was worried when I realized that you were gone."

"I felt like an intruder."

"An intruder?" he murmured. He was before her by then. He took both her hands in his own and laced her fingers with his. The light seemed to waver, the room to spin. "You could never be an intruder, Jassy."

"I do not think that my brother would agree with you," she said. She might have added that her sister Lenore would not agree with him, either, but just then, as they stood there alone in the lamplight, she didn't want to breathe Lenore's name.

"Your brother has seen this night that you have an uncanny beauty, and that your grace came inborn, and that there is a fire inside of you that fascinates and beckons."

"Has he seen this?" she whispered. Perhaps there was fire in her eyes, and she did feel beautiful, for he allowed her to feel so. Excitement crackled around her, and her dreams seemed to find full measure once again.

He pulled her closer and closer, holding their laced fingers down by his side. She stared into his light, dancing eyes, and her heart fluttered at the things she saw within them.

Then he kissed her.

His mouth was soft and persuasive. It formed over hers, and she parted her lips instinctively to his. He released her fingers, wrapped his arms around the small of her back, and pressed her hard against him. His lips moved then, wetly and sloppily over hers, and she didn't really care. She threaded her fingers into his hair and felt their hearts pounding together. He groaned against her, their lips broke, and he whispered with agony, "How I have wanted you."

"I am here!" she whispered with little thought, for her imaginings had not gone far beyond this point. But her words were a fuel to him, and his lips pressed against her throat and lowered to the rise of her breasts. Then he arched her tightly against him, feverishly kissing her. Her mind whirled, and she felt his hands upon her, here and there, and then his lips again, and his fingers, plucking at the ties to her stomacher.

No, he must not. Yet she could not find the words or the will to stop him. He loved her, she was certain. Yet she knew, too, that she could let him go no farther. Not unless he married her.

"Robert . . ." she whispered.

Her breasts were spilling from the gown, and she could neither stop nor dislodge him. He caught her lips in a kiss again. It was a sweet kiss, soft, tender. She closed her eyes and held tight to him. Then they were both interrupted by the loud sound of someone clearing his throat.

Robert abruptly straightened. He still held Jassy about the waist. He stared toward the first stall. Jassy, her eyes glazed with fascination, was slower to realize the interruption. Then she, too, stared down the length of the stables to the first stall.

Jamie was there, casually leaning against the hayrack, arms crossed over his chest, one booted foot atop a bale of hay. "Excuse me, but the Lady Lenore has been seeking you, Robert, to question you about your costume."

"Damn!" Robert muttered. "Love, forgive me." He set Jassy straight, leaving her to deal with the disarray of her gown. He thanked Jamie and strode on out of the stables.

Jamie remained. He didn't move. He watched her with dark and condemning eyes.

Trying to ignore him, Jassy lowered her eyes. She tried to adjust the gown's stomacher and retie the ribbons, but her fingers were trembling horribly.

He strode toward her, and when she looked up, there was such a dark fire to his gaze that she had to bite her lip to keep from crying out. He brushed her hands aside.

"Stop it!" she protested.

"Would you be found here as you are?" he demanded roughly. With practiced fingers he retied the ribbons. He brushed her bare flesh with his touch again and again, and she wanted to scream. He was in no way gentle. He was nearly brutal. Standing before her, he seemed ablaze with tension, so vibrant and hot that heat emanated from him and washed upon her in great waves.

"How much were you paid for that endearing scene,

Mistress Dupré? Had I realized that you were still in the market for a lover, I'd have put in a higher bid."

She shrieked in fury and tore away from him, then came for him again, lashing out for his face, his chest, whatever she could strike. She caught him, as she had longed to do, with one good cut across the jaw, but he was swift with his reprisal, capturing her wrists, twisting them harshly behind her back. She was tightly pressed to him, still alive with fury, and she tried to kick him. He easily slipped his foot behind hers, and she fell to ground, dragging him down upon her. She heard the grate of his teeth, and when she stared into his eyes, they seemed black, and the tension that gripped his features in a steel-hard rage was merciless. And still she twisted and fought against him, heedless that her hair was falling, that her beautiful gown was being torn and dirtied. "You insufferable oaf, I have had it with you—I hate you and I loathe you and I despise you—and I will never let you touch me, not for any price! I cannot bear your touch—"

"No? You are a liar, Jassy, for you are no hothouse flower but the wildest of roses, made for a tempest. You fool! You would hate Robert in a matter of months were you to have him, for indeed, you would twist him to your will. But you cannot have him. You won't see that, will you? But I will prove to you that you were not meant for him."

"No!"

He ignored her completely. He pressed his lips to hers, and they were neither soft, nor gentle, nor persuasive in the least. They were a brand, demanding, hot and searing. They forced her mouth apart beneath him, and his tongue savagely ravaged the fullness of her mouth, hot and hard. She could barely draw breath, she could not move, and she could not fight him. She could feel him only. The wild, rugged tempest that raged inside of him seemed to sweep inside of her. She did not want him, she hated his touch, she despised him . . . and still, it was as if he had drugged her. It was as if he filled her with fire and rage, and with a slow, beating tempo and hot, liquid fury. He kissed her and kissed her, and the tempo beat throughout her, and she could fight him no longer. The tempo had entered her head. She dared not move, for she could feel his body through the layers of clothing between them. She could feel the savage power in him. She shuddered, for it swept from him to her, cascaded down the length of her. His hand was upon her, upon the ribbons at her bodice, and they were untied once more. She was freed from the stomacher of her gown, and his palm swept over her nipple while he curved his hand and cupped her breast where it mounded over the lace and bone of her corset. His thumb teased the nipple through the gauze. A thread of silver sensation shot through her from that touch. She squirmed and wiggled, and merely felt his body more fully, and still she could not escape the pressure of his kiss. His heat became a part of her. She could no longer fight. She was dazed by his power, and by his touch. She lay still. The savagery of his assault slackened instantly. His hand barely touched her breast. His lips barely fell against hers, and the tip of his tongue rimmed her mouth and her inner lip, and curiously, she lay there still, allowing it all to happen.

Then, abruptly, he lifted his head. Her lips were surely bruised and damp, and they lay parted, for she was desperate to breathe. Her hair was in disarray, loosed from its ribbons. Her breast was bare, except for the sheer lace of the corset that did not cover it at all.

He smiled down at her sardonically. "A position as my mistress remains open, Jasmine, and I do assure you, my financial assets far exceed Robert's expectations."

She stared at him, longing for the words to tell him how she hated him, longing to be freed from his touch. She shrieked out something and tried to strike him again. He caught her hands and twisted them behind her back. Laughing, he lowered his head, and his tongue touched her nipple through the lace, and then he lowered his head still farther, bringing the whole of it into his mouth. She swore again, yet she shuddered as the ribbon of sensation leapt from her breast to the innermost part of her. Slowly he released her, gently easing the high peak of her breast and the lace of her corset from the graze of his teeth.

She raged against him, jerking and twisting and pelting him with her fists, but her only reward was the sound of his harsh laughter. Then he climbed from her at last and caught her hands and pulled her to her feet. She jerked from his touch, tears spilling from her eyes. She blinked them away. Her fingers still trembled when she tried to right her clothing, but when he roughly said, "Here, let me help!" she swore with ever greater menace and turned away from him.

"Leave me!" she demanded, turning her back upon him. "After all that you have done, can you not at least go!"

"Nay, I shall not go. I shall walk you back into the house when we are certain that you look none the worse for wear."

"I will never walk anywhere with you! You are untrustworthy! I cannot bear you to—"

He swung her around, staring at her with a curious passion, and the tension was ever about him. "No, don't say it again, for we both know that it is a lie. You are no Lady Lenore, and indeed, you are no lady I have ever known, for you are real, alive, and breathing, and with a heart that pounds fiercely and eyes that are full of a feminine promise." He clutched her hands and drew them between them. "Look! Look here at the unladylike calluses upon these hands! Mistress, they are admirable hands to my eyes, for they have known work and toil. Jassy, your quest is for life, you little fool! It is for life and for passion, and you cannot be made to see it, though you feel it! How long will you lie to yourself? You can bear my touch, you can bear it very well. It is what you need, it is what you require, it is what you crave! I know you. I know your strengths, and I know your weaknesses, and I know the workings of your cunning little mind and your greedy little heart! You are playing a dangerous game, you are playing it all wrong, and you are ignoring the rules—"

"Just get away from me!" she insisted, wrenching her hands from his grasp. Ah, but they were a sore spot with her! They were a reminder that she had been a cook's apprentice and a scullery maid. They were rough and reddened, and though Jane's lotion had helped, they betrayed her at every turn, no matter how she dressed in silks and fur. She cast them behind her back, lifted her chin, squared her shoulders, and cared not how disheveled her gown was as she faced and challenged him. "You play your games, Lord Cameron, and I shall play mine. And if I don't know the rules, all the better, for then I may just ignore them. Like you, I play to win, and so help me, milord, I *will* win! I will never be your mistress, and you are wrong! I crave nothing from you!"

He reached out to her. She screamed in fury, stamping a foot, and he laughed. "There is hay in your hair now, mistress. May I remove it for you?"

"No!"

"Come here, for you shall never redress yourself—"

"I don't trust you!"

"Then don't trust me. But if you ever wish to return to the house, you need my help."

"I don't need—"

"Oh, shut up!"

He dragged her close and she kicked him, but he grunted and pulled the hay from her hair. In a no-nonsense manner he spun her around, set the stomacher straight, and began lacing it into her bodice. In seconds it was properly tied, and he was no more intimate with her than a ladies' maid might have been. Once again he swirled her around, straightening her skirt, and she tried to walk away from him. "Don't!"

"Get over here."

He caught her arm, wrenched her back around, and turned her. Once again, his hands were on her hair. She gritted her teeth, amazed that fingers that could touch with such force could move so surely upon her hair.

"This is a service it seems you have performed many times!" she said gratingly.

"Enough, I suppose." She tried to move away from him.

"Stand still!" he commanded.

"Oh, I suppose that your mistresses usually do."

"And you are the unusual mistress."

"I am not your mistress at all."

"Ah, more's the pity. I thought that you had just agreed to the position."

"Never!"

"You'll dream about me," he promised.

"Only in my darkest nightmares!"

"I promise, you will yearn for my touch."

"I will yearn for your demise upon some heathen Indian spear."

"There. Now, let me see."

Without the least gentleness he pushed her from him and spun her about to face him. He critically scanned her hair and costume. "I think that the damage has been repaired."

"The damage can never be repaired!"

"How rude. After all I have done to repair your appearance."

" 'Twas your touch that destroyed it!"

"Ah, but I was not the first to touch! I merely ventured where another man had already explored."

"Oh!" She raised her hand to slap him, but he laughed and brought her back hard against his chest again.

"Shall I prove to you again that the day will come when you pine for the mere mention of my name? Alas, when we have just taken such pains to assure the demure chastity of your costume!"

"You have proven nothing, except that you are a rude and insolent rodent! Robert is your friend, yet you demean him! You laugh at his intentions, but what of your own? You must take what I would willingly give to him—"

"Fool!" he swore. She had yet to see him so darkly angry, so lacking in control. He shoved her from him and she staggered back. "So be it! Find Robert Maxwell! Give to him what you will. I cannot stop you. I can only warn you that he has nothing, and that no matter how enamored of you he is, there is nothing at all that he can give you. You dream of marriage. It will never be. Spin your dreams. You are blind, even unto yourself!"

He bowed very low to her, spun about, and left her. Jassy watched him go, her breasts heaving, her teeth grating, her mind in a tempest. "Good riddance!" she swore.

But she was shaking very badly and couldn't stand. She lowered herself down to the balls of her feet on the floor, trying to draw steady breaths. God! But how she loathed him!

Her fingers flew to her mouth, and she felt that her lips were still swollen from his touch. She still trembled but maintained some vague feeling of burning restlessness within her. She hated him with a blinding passion.

But she could not get him out of her mind, and when she slipped back into the hall at last and escaped to the haven of her own small room, it was the searing blaze of his kiss that haunted her, while the soft touch of Robert's lips faded annoyingly from her memory.

VI ❧

Jassy expected the summons that came from her brother the next day.

Henry never forgot that he was Duke of Somerfield, especially when he dealt with her. He did not speak with her casually, and when he passed her in the hall he expected a submissive curtsy from her. Like a feudal lord, he wanted those under his roof to be under his strict domination.

"Jane tells me that you serve her well."

"Then I am glad," she said, and she winced as she added, "Your Grace."

"I am not a cruel man, Jasmine."

"No, milord. Pray, tell me, have I indicated that you were?"

He shook his head, and she wondered if their father had looked like him when he had first seduced her mother, tall and very golden, and certainly splendid in his brocade and silk.

Henry walked to the window and looked out on the great curving drive before the Hall. "Let me give you a history lesson, little sister. In the late 1400s, men suspected that Richard III slew his own nephews, mere boys, in the Tower. In the next century Queen Mary had executed her legitimate cousin, Lady Jane Grey, for seizure of her throne, and for refusing to accept her Popish faith. Later, our great lady, Queen Elizabeth, had her cousin Mary Queen of Scots slain for plots against the throne. The Wars of the Roses were great, fratricidal battles. But then, you do know your history, don't you? Jane tells me that it seems your education was well taken in hand."

"Yes, I know my history," Jassy said.

"Then you will understand that blood ties mean little in this world, especially when that blood tie is tarnished by the stain of your bastardy. I have done the best that I can for you. You are not a true member of this family, and you will not participate in events of importance as if you were. Jane likes you; Elizabeth dotes upon you. But I find you a fortune-digging little temptress like your mother, and you will not step upon my back to secure your fortune. You are my wife's serving girl, and nothing more. You will not attend the ball. Lenore will find her husband then, and you will not interfere."

Jassy locked her teeth and lifted her chin. "Your Grace, how could I, a bastard, possibly interfere?"

He returned to his desk and picked up a quill and a parchment of accounts. "You know, Jasmine, exactly how you might interfere. You are like your mother, a woman men lust for. You cause trouble by your very nature. I shall do my best to see that Christian and godly ways are instilled in you. Defy me and you will be beaten. Now, I am busy. You are excused."

She didn't leave. She ran to the desk, kneeling down before him. "Your Grace! Elizabeth tells me that the lowliest milkmaid is allowed to attend—"

"But you are not. Go now! You are disturbing me."

"But your Grace—"

"If you disobey me, ever, I will strip you naked, lay welts upon your back by own hand, and send you back to the slop alley from which you came."

She rose, and she swore to herself that she would never forgive him. Blood meant nothing to him; it meant nothing to her.

She fled from the room then, terrified that she would

burst into tears. In her room she paced the floor. Robert would come to the ball and Jamie would not. Lenore would find herself in Robert's arms, and it would be right, and it would be perfect, and the honorable thing would be for them to marry.

No! It wasn't fair!

She threw herself on top of her bed and stared at the ceiling. She should be grateful for her comfort and seek no more! she told herself. But Henry's words gnawed at her. She was living by the grace of another, and it was frightening. If she offended him now, two years from now or five years now, he would send her back out into the streets. Back to abject poverty.

There had to be a way.

Kathryn came to summon her again; Jane needed her services. Jassy swallowed down her hatred for her brother and went to serve his wife. Jane dictated her letters, many of which were to stockholders in the Virginia Company. Jane, like her father and brother, had invested heavily with the Company, and with a similar venture, the Bermuda Company. When they were done with the correspondence, Jane sighed and leaned back on her bed. "I feel so weary so quickly. And so fat! Like a house."

"Milady, one can barely tell that you are with child."

"You are a diplomat, along with your other talents!" Jane laughed. "And smart," she added softly. She indicated the pile of correspondence. "Tell me, what do you think of this venture?" she asked.

"Milady?"

Jane laughed. "The Virginia Company. Jamie is so enthused. There have been many failures, but now, you see, I am determined to invest in my brother. The company travails for lack of organization. The leaders quibble with one another. Still, much has happened since 1606. Jamie tells me that there are many families in Jamestown. And in the various hundreds on the James. I think that Jamie will make us all prosper with that new land of his."

"I'm sure he shall," Jassy said politely. Her fingers tightened around her quill.

"He is an adventurer, Jamie is. He loves the wind and the sea and faraway lands. Though truly the manor he has built is amazing. Oh, well, perhaps he will settle down now with Lenore, and she will convince him to remain at home. I don't know. Perhaps it would be a bad match. He is determined to go where and when he pleases, and Lenore is no wanderer." She shrugged. "It is between the two of them. And Henry, of course, but he is quite determined that Lenore will be married this year. She must make her choice."

"And what if she chooses Robert Maxwell?" Jassy could not help but ask.

"Oh, then I can see it all very easily. They are both frivolous flirts, and they shall have to take great care that they learn some sense of responsibility!"

Jassy hesitated. "And what of you?" she queried softly. "How do you and Henry manage?"

Jane smiled slowly. "Well enough. You find him cruel, I'm certain, but you must remember that he was always taught that he would be the duke, 'His Grace,' and that he was very nobly born. Jassy, it is true, most men would not even allow you in their house."

"I am a burden to him. Perhaps, if he allowed me to go to the ball, I would no longer have to be a burden."

Jane laughed. "He wants Lenore married. When that has come about, you shall see, he will discover that you are worthy of his attention. There will always be another ball. And in time I'm certain that Henry will decide upon a proper match for you, perhaps with a prospering merchant." She smiled and winced. "Jassy, if you'll forgive me, I'm getting a terrible headache."

Jassy leapt to her feet. "If you've some mineral water, perhaps I could help. My mother used to get such headaches."

Jane arched a brow but directed Jassy to her dressing table and the mineral water. Jassy came behind Jane and dampened her fingers and set them gently upon Jane's temple. She began to move them in a lulling motion, and after several moments Jane sighed contentedly. "You are marvelous, a gift from God!" Jane proclaimed. Jassy demurred, but in a few minutes Jane was sleeping. Jassy slipped quietly from the room.

She left the house and came out to the stables and asked one of the grooms to saddle Mary for her. While she waited, Elizabeth came down and decided to ride with her. Elizabeth laughed and chatted about the ball—she loved to prepare things! And, of course, before the ball they would fast for Lent, and then celebrate Easter; there would be much for everyone to do.

Jassy brooded and listened just vaguely. She did not pay attention to their path but allowed Elizabeth to lead. Then suddenly she reined in, for they had followed an unfamiliar trail and had come to a new and gleaming residence grander than any palace Jassy had ever imagined. A high wall encircled numerous cleared acres and groves, and beyond the wall, a whitewashed palace rose against the green of the new spring grass, a tall, imposing structure in brick with symmetrical outbuildings and fascinating turrets and towers. She had once seen Hampton Court as a child; this seemed grander than that royal residence taken from Cardinal Wolsey by Henry VIII.

"What is it?" Jassy said, awed.

Elizabeth laughed. "It is Jamie's new manor. He has traveled much, you know. The symmetry is from the Italians, or so he told me. The balance is French, but we are Englishmen and Englishwomen here, and so the design is Tudor. It is wonderful, is it not?"

"Yes, it is wonderful."

"Come, we'll see it."

"Oh, we cannot! I don't wish—"

"Don't worry. Jamie is in London now. The king's council is in session, and the Duke of Carlyle is in council, and Jamie is with his father, advising him. Lymon Miller is the steward of the estate; he will take us through it."

Jassy could protest no more, for Elizabeth nudged her mount forward and they raced together to the grand wall and the massive wrought-iron entry with its emblem of the lion and the hawk. A gatekeeper recognized Elizabeth and welcomed her with respect, letting them through. Then they approached the steps to the manor itself. Grooms appeared quickly to take their horses, and even as they removed their gloves a spry bald man in handsome dark livery came hurrying down the many steps. "Lady Elizabeth!" he said with delight. "Welcome. Lord Cameron will be so sorry he missed you. He's not at Castle Carlyle, no, I'm sorry to say. They've gone on to London."

"Oh, I know that, Lymon. This is my sister, Jasmine. I wanted to show her the manor. May I?"

Lymon cast Jassy a quick and curious stare, and she knew that the entire region must have heard of her sudden appearance from a sordid past. "Miss Jasmine," Lymon said. "You must do as you wish, Lady Elizabeth. Will you have coffee? Lord Cameron has just acquired some from his ships in the Mediterranean."

"Yes, Lymon, thank you. In the blue room, I think."

Jassy followed Elizabeth up the grand stone stairway and past the concrete lions guarding the double doorway. There was a rich red runner sweeping down the length of a grand hallway, so wide and huge that it could easily accommodate a hundred guests. Portraits lined the walls, and doorways opened on either side to various other rooms. A great curving stone stairway rose from the rear of the hall, and it, too, was covered in the rich red velvet runner that came to the door. Elizabeth smiled as Jassy gaped. "It is lovely, isn't it?"

"Yes. It is exquisite."

"And imagine. He is hardly ever here. When he returns from his journeys, he spends time with his father. He keeps his belongings here, and that is it, so it seems." She laughed. "Ah, well, if Lenore has her way, they will marry, and he will have to come home more often, don't you agree?"

Jassy nodded, but she didn't want to agree. She didn't want to think of Lenore in the manor, she wanted to imagine that it belonged to her. It was fun to close her eyes and see herself in silks and furs, walking down the stairway greeting her guests. They would toast her; they would say that she was the grandest hostess in all of King James's realm, the poor little bastard serving wench who had pulled herself up and proved that a commoner could rise above her lot to grace the society of nobles and gentry.

The house belonged to Lord Cameron, she reminded herself.

"Shall we have coffee? The blue room." Elizabeth directed her to the left, where the walls were covered with light blue silk and the floor by a braided rug. Shining wooden chairs were pulled before a low-burning fire. The ceiling was molded and the mantel was made of marble. A cart that held a silver service was pulled before the fire.

"Sit. I shall pour." Elizabeth indicated a seat. Jassy bit her lower lip and smiled.

"Please, Elizabeth, may I pour?" Jassy said. She'd never had coffee before. It was an Eastern drink, and only the very wealthy were beginning to import it from places in southern Europe.

"Why, milady, do go right ahead!"

And as Jassy poured their coffee she discovered herself every bit the actress that her mother had been. She spoke about Lord so-and-so's day on the floor at Parliament, and how Lady da-de-da had been presented before the king and queen. "And where was it? Oh, they were at the Tower, I believe. And did I tell you that Lady Cauliflower stayed there recently—the queen insisted, of course—and claimed that the Tower Green was definitely haunted? Well, it is Catherine Howard who screams along the corridors of Hampton Court, but it is Anne Boleyn who carried her head about the Tower Green!"

Elizabeth convulsed with laughter. "Oh, Jassy! You would make a great lady. A very great lady, indeed!"

"Oh, indeed, she would," came a sudden, masculine voice from the doorway.

Jassy jumped up, spilling her coffee. Elizabeth dropped her cup. They both stared at Jamie Cameron.

He entered the room, stripping away his gauntlets. Lymon followed after him, ready to accept the gauntlets and take his black cloak as he cast it off. Beneath the cloak he was clad in knee-high riding boots, crimson breeches, a slashed doublet, and a fine white shirt. He handed his plumed hat to his steward, too, thanking Lymon cordially for the service.

Then he was staring at the two of them again, and though he greeted Elizabeth warmly enough, he seemed to view them with displeasure.

"Do forgive me—" Elizabeth began, but he interrupted her with a kiss on the cheek.

"Elizabeth, you are always welcome in my home."

Jassy had not said a word. She clenched her teeth and held her hands folded before her. She hated that he had come upon them. Always! Always! He destroyed her dreams. He broke into them with harsh reality, and with his ever-present mockery and scorn. Nor could she forget when they had parted. Seeing him brought back a wave of emotion, and she trembled inside. He stared at her now with polite inquiry, and without a word of welcome to her.

"I did not expect you back."

"Matters in London were solved much more quickly than I expected. Are you—er, ladies having coffee? Forgive me if I indulge in a whiskey." He went to the sideboard and poured himself an amber drink from a crystal decanter. He turned, leaned against the sideboard, and watched them both again, yet Jassy felt his acute gaze fall her way, and his lips curled into a mocking smile.

"Elizabeth, I think that we should be leaving," Jassy said.

"Yes, perhaps—" Elizabeth said, but as she spoke, she turned, catching her fragile coffee cup with her skirt, and the contents spilled upon it. "Oh, dear! Henry has so recently bought this fabric from Flanders, he will be furious with me—"

"I'm sure that Lymon can quickly catch the stain, Elizabeth, and I'm equally certain that Henry could not be distressed with you." He called for Lymon. "See, Elizabeth, it is just this bit, here, that is stained."

"If you'll come with me, Lady Elizabeth, we shall solve the problem in moments."

"Jassy, I shall be right back."

"Oh, Elizabeth, perhaps I can help—"

"I'm sure, Miss Dupré, that they can manage," Jamie Cameron said. He smiled and blocked her way when she might have followed the two of them out. She did not try to barge past him. She turned with a rustle of fabric and wandered to the rear of the room, ostensibly studying the wall cloth.

"You're good, Jassy. Very good," he said softly.

"Am I?" It seemed better to face him then. She was distinctly uneasy with her back to him. "At what?"

"At all of it. At aping your betters."

"I have no betters, Lord Cameron."

He started to laugh, and then he inclined his head slightly to her. "Perhaps you don't, 'milady.' Perhaps you don't. Your mother was an actress. You have her talent. I believe that I would dare to take you to Court upon my arm, and have little fear that your manners would be anything but perfectly correct. But you are dreaming still, Jassy."

"Do you think so?"

He approached her, and she backed away from him nervously, but then there was nowhere left to go, and so she stood her ground. He cornered her. He placed his hands on either side of her head, and he smiled, his face very close to hers. "May I tell you exactly what I read in the beautiful, cunning, and oh so betraying eyes? You love the elegance of this house, and you imagine yourself mistress here. Ah, but the house would not come with someone so loathsome as me. Oh, no! It would be Robert Maxwell's estate, and of course, he would not dishonor you with any kind of licentious proposal, but he would forget fortune and class and the society of princes and kings to make you his wife. And you and he would rule here forever and forever."

"Maybe someone will shoot you in a duel," Jassy said

sweetly. "And maybe Robert Maxwell cares more than you might think."

He turned away from her, negligently returned to the sideboard, and sat before the fire with a casual air, dangling one leg over the side of the chair. He smiled, watching her where she still stood against the wall. "Robert will never marry you. He must marry elsewhere, and quickly. He needs the income. He has gambled away a great deal of his income."

"You are a liar. You are rude and uncouth and as savage as the heathens in that godforsaken land that so excites you. You are determined to drag Robert Maxwell down at every opportunity."

He shook his head slowly. "No, Jassy. Robert is my friend. I do not seek to hurt him. I was just in London to bail him out of difficulty."

"You were there to meet your father."

"Have it as you will."

"I should be better off to come and sleep with you, right?" she said scornfully.

"Actually, yes. You could indulge in great fantasy. You could imagine that you had done away with me yourself, that the manor was entirely your own, and that you could reign here as a gracious queen forever."

"I should dearly love to do away with you," she replied.

"But then, I'm afraid that the fantasy couldn't last forever. You see, I intend to marry soon."

"The great and wondrous Lord Cameron deigns to take a wife. I hope that you shall make each other entirely miserable for a lifetime."

"No one shall make me miserable for a lifetime, mistress," he advised her. "You see, a wife has certain functions. To bear heirs, to be her lord's hostess, and his supporter in all things. And above all, of course, she is to obey him, and follow him wherever he shall choose to lead. Then again, if she should prove not so gentle and not so kind and not so pretty as she seemed before the binding words were spoken, she may be left at one estate while her lord travels on to another."

"Then the man has married himself a fool," Jassy said. "And, my Lord Cameron, you do deserve one."

His laughter followed her as she left the room at last, determining that she would wait for Elizabeth outside. A servant opened the door for her and she fled down the steps. Even as she reached the ground, the grooms were hurrying out with the horses. Elizabeth did come right along. She said good-bye to Jamie at the steps. Jassy was mounted when Elizabeth reached her. A groom quickly helped Elizabeth upon her mount.

"It's a glorious place, isn't it?" Elizabeth demanded.

"Glorious. Let's please do go!"

That night Jassy had the first of her nightmares. She saw the attic room at Master John's again, and she saw the blond figure lying there. She came toward the bed, knelt beside it, and touched the covers. Linnet turned to her, and Jassy began a long, silent scream, for her mother's flesh had rotted from her face, and she touched her upon the breast with a bony finger. Then she fell back against the pallet, and when Jassy looked again, it was not Linnet lying there at all, it was her, and she was dying just as her mother had died, in filth and poverty. For days the nightmare haunted her.

But a week later the flowers came from Robert Maxwell, and she forgot the horror, for fantasy was awakened inside of her once again.

She was at the stables when the boy arrived, a young lad with a limp and a wool cap pulled low over his forehead. He carried a handful of roses, and he came to her swiftly, nervous that someone else might be about.

"Jasmine Dupré?"

"Yes?"

He thrust the flowers to her. "Compliments of Robert Maxwell, with his greatest regard."

And that was it. The boy turned and ran away, but Jassy was left with the flowers, and they seemed the greatest gift that any woman could receive.

She brought them back to her room and laid them out on her pillow. She breathed in their sweet scent, thinking that winter was indeed gone, and spring had come.

Perhaps the cold had gone from her life forever, for Robert loved her, she was certain.

She carefully pressed the flowers into the one true gift her brother had given, a copy of the King's new Bible.

The days began to rush by; they fasted for Lent, and they atoned for their sins on Maundy Thursday and Good Friday. Easter was soberly celebrated with a long Mass, and when that day came to an end, the household began to plan for May Day with exuberance.

Even Elizabeth was excited, though she had no intention of being part of the dance. The tenants were raising a giant Maypole with brightly colored streamers to hang from it. For them it would be a grand holiday. They would all receive a measure of rum, a silver coin, and a bolt of cloth. A village girl would be proclaimed Princess of the May, while the title of Queen belonged indisputably to Lenore.

The family and the invited nobility and gentry would sup in the dining room, while a banquet for the servants and tenants would take place in the courtyard area between the hall and the stables. To attend, the duke's dependents were all to bring him a gift, and so he would hold court outside, since the gifts would most oft consist of little piglets.

"You needn't fret that you're not actually dancing," Elizabeth told Jassy. "You shall enjoy it. There's ever so much activity. Henry has hired an animal keeper with a dancing bear and ever so many musicians. There will be numerous puppeteers, and all manner and sort of entertainment!"

"Yes, I'm sure it will be wonderful," Jassy told her.

Lenore announced that she would be dressed in white, and that she would attend as a white dove. She didn't wish to leave her suitors with any doubt as to who she was.

One afternoon as the day neared, Lenore summoned Jassy to her rooms. "I have the most hateful headache," she complained. "Jane tells me that you can soothe the pain."

Jassy had little desire to soothe any of Lenore's pain. She shrugged. "I am not so talented."

"Would you try, please? I am in agony."

While she rubbed her sister's temples with mineral water, Jassy remained silent. Lenore leaned back in her chair and sighed. "Oh, Jassy, you are very good! Sometimes I wish that you were my true sister—you'd have been fun, I'm certain. Not like Elizabeth, who is too timid ever to defy Henry! Then I am glad that you are the bastard child, for you might have been some wicked competition." She laughed openly and honestly, then twisted around. "If Henry makes life too unbearable for you, you shall come and live with me when I have married. I shall keep you merely to cure headaches!"

"That's quite kind, I'm sure."

"Jassy, you shall never be meek and mild. No matter what your words say, your eyes flash."

"Who do you think you will marry?" Jassy asked.

Lenore sighed. "Well, Jamie Cameron has claimed that he isn't coming to the dance—he does not like such things. Of course, he never wanted to marry. Not before this year. I do not know what has changed him so." She hesitated. "I do adore Jamie!" she whispered, almost with awe. "When he is near, I feel that I am hot, that I cannot breathe. He is as dashing as the devil himself, so tall and dark and cynical in all things! His eyes, his whisper, make me quiver. But then, he frightens me sometimes too. He will never do as a wife asks. He will never bow down before any man or woman. He is terribly demanding. I am oft surprised that he has managed to be friends with King James." She laughed. "The king is oft so dour, and convinced that witches are after him! But that is neither here nor there—Jamie is a strong man. Too strong, perhaps. I think that Robert would be the easier match. He is quick to laugh, and to flirt, and still . . . I feel perhaps he would be the more loyal husband, for his needs are not so great. Jamie would demand both flesh and soul. Oh, but he is so handsome with his marvelous eyes. Just the way that he looks at a woman . . . but here I go, on and on. You really mustn't look so unhappy. Henry will arrange a marriage for you."

"I do not want an arranged marriage."

"No," Lenore said shrewdly. "You want to join the dance."

Jassy shrugged. Lenore suddenly leapt up. "I'll help you."

"What? Why should you?" she asked suspiciously.

"Oh, come now, I am not so awful a person as you may think! We did have the same father—even if your mother was a strumpet—"

"My mother was not—"

"Well, you are the bastard, right? Let's not quibble. We shall both go, and we shall both wear white. Henry will never know that you are there, for we are so alike that if he sees you about the room, he will think that you are me."

"He has threatened me with grave consequences, you know."

"Oh, pooh. Henry is really not such a monster, either. It will be all right. But we must plan now carefully, and in secrecy. And if we play our cards right, perhaps you will capture some handsome young knight!"

Jassy lowered her head. She could not tell Lenore that she slept with the Bible with Robert Maxwell's flowers pressed into it, nor that she had already chosen the knight that she wanted. She raised her eyes to Lenore's and could not hide the excitement in them. "Let's do it!"

When May Day came, the very air was filled with such excitement that Jassy could not be afraid of the possibly dire consequences of her deception. She heard the horses and carriages arriving, and she heard the tenants and servants playing down in the courtyard. She could hear them from her window, and when she looked down from it, she could see all manner of gaiety. Maids and youths already danced around the Maypole. The man with the bear had the animal doing circles upon his hind feet, and a marionette show was already in progress. A flutist was playing, and, in honor of King James, a group of Highlanders played the bagpipes. There was a great deal of noise and confusion. The day was bright and clear and blue and beautiful. Spring was indeed with them.

Jassy rushed along the corridors until she reached Lenore's door. She tapped, and Lenore drew her in, giggling. "Hurry!"

An hour later both girls were dressed alike. Jassy was delighted. Her hose were white silk, and her little leather slippers were white and decorated with glass stones. She wore a soft silk shift next to her flesh, and over it a binding corset, and three different petticoats. The dresses themselves were white brocade, with stomachers in a tougher velvet, low-cut bodices, and half sleeves with scores of white lace. Their face masks were covered with feathers and plumes. A little bit of a heel had been added to Jassy's slippers to make her as tall as Lenore, and they had flattened her breasts as best they could with the corset. They had both done their golden hair up in ringlets, tied through with white satin ribbons.

When they were done, they stared at each other and both burst out laughing. "We are wonderful!" Lenore insisted.

Jassy spun about and peered into her sister's mirror. She felt beautiful and as innocent as a bride. She paused, hoping that Lenore would not hate her too much if she managed to capture Robert Maxwell. No, for Lenore would be equally happy with Lord Cameron. After all, he was immensely wealthy, and Lenore had known him all her life. They would fare well enough together.

And if not, it would not be Jassy's fault. Lenore did not know what poverty was. She did not understand hunger and want. Jassy had to capture Robert.

"Come on, let's slip down together."

"Together!"

"Just to the landing. Then you must sneak outside, and I will go into the dining room. When the meal is halfway through, I will think of an excuse and change places with you. Now remember, you don't have to admit anything to anyone, or say anything at all if you don't want. This is a masked ball."

"But to come down together—"

"The excitement is in the risk!"

Certainly, Jassy thought sourly. Henry would speak firmly to Lenore if they were caught—he would whip Jassy, then cast her out.

"Let's go, then!" she hissed.

Amazingly, there was no mishap as they came down the stairway. Jassy quickly found the front entrance, came through it, and ran down the steps, encircling the massive building to come around the back. By then she was passing many people. The duke's friends, his guards, his fighting men, the farmers, and some of the merchants with their wives and daughters. The gentry mixed with the common folk. Where the pipers played a fling, a guard in half leather armor danced with a barefoot farmer's lass, and Jassy thought that many weddings were sure to follow.

She stopped before the marionette show. The puppets were beautifully crafted, and the stage scenery in the small box was excellent. Watching it, Jassy had a sense of a deep forest, and a wide ocean before it. Log buildings stood about, and houses made of wattle and daub. An Indian puppet cast herself over the body of a white man, and the white man was spared.

"There you are, minx!"

It was Robert. He caught her by the shoulders and turned her around. He was dressed in Italian Renaissance fashion, with short ballooned breeches, long hose, and pointed toe-shoes. His mask barely covered the area of his eyes. He looked briefly around, then brushed her lips with a quick, stolen kiss. "The queen of the May! You are beautiful, my love. Tell me, will you come to my arms this day?"

It did not occur to her that he might think she was Lenore. She nodded, certain that he was aware of their deception. He laced his fingers with hers. "That you insist upon this silly charade! But, love, I am besotted. I shall come where you lead me!"

Delighted, Jassy smiled. She did not speak; she did not wish to impose upon the magic. She indicated the Maypole, and with their hands laced together they came to it. Some goodwife handed them each a ribbon, and they joined the revelers singing and dancing around it. The goodwife claimed they would all be fertile, and bear many children, like the seeds of the harvest.

Looking toward the house, Jassy was alarmed to see that Lenore had made her appearance. She loosed her ribbon and ran. Lenore saw her and started in the opposite direction. Jassy raced for the house. She heard Robert as he caught up with Lenore. "Vixen! Come here!" And he laughed with the good fun of it. Lenore's laughter tinkled along with his.

It was not so amusing for Jassy. She came into the dining room and took Lenore's seat. To her great dismay she discovered that she was between Henry and Jamie Cameron. When she seated herself, Jamie poured her more wine from a silver chalice and whispered in her ear. "I had wondered when you were returning."

"I—I have returned."

Henry lowered his head to her and spoke softly. "I shall not tolerate such rudeness. Don't disappear again until this meal has come to an end."

Upon her lap and beneath the snowy tablecloth, Jamie Cameron's fingers curled around her own and squeezed. She wanted to scream. Their hands rested together upon her thigh. She felt too warm, and her heart was thundering. Jamie was staring at her. He always knew what lay beneath the coverings. He was always capable of stripping her down to the heart and soul and bare flesh.

"Lenore! Lady Renwig has just asked you about the duke's ball at Northumberland."

The duke's ball at Northumberland. She had no idea what Lady Renwig wanted. Lady Renwig wore a headpiece that resembled a giant hedgehog.

"The ball . . . was lovely," she said. Henry would note the difference in their voices. No, she was her mother's daughter, she was an actress, she could carry it off. "The weather was divine, and we danced beneath the moon. Even the king enjoyed it all tremendously."

"To James I!" someone cried. "King of England and king of the Scots! Uniting us at last!"

Then someone else said that they really didn't want to be united with the heathen Scots, and there was a whisper that such words could be treasonous. Jassy didn't care. It had taken the pressure away from her.

"Are you all right?" Henry whispered to her.

"I don't think that she is all right at all. I think that she is flushed beneath that mask," Jamie said.

"I need air, please!"

"Perhaps I should take her out, Henry," Jamie suggested. "They are crowning the princess of the May right now; Lenore shall need to be in the ceremony soon."

Henry lifted his hand with dismissive annoyance. Jassy mustered up the courage to graciously excuse herself.

Jamie's hand was on her arm. He did not lead her outside but through the door to the entryway and out to the front of the estate where there was no activity. "You've the heart of a true flirt, Lenore. The people were too much for you?" He spoke in a husky whisper. She found herself pressed against the house, and his lips touched down on hers.

"No," she protested.

"Lenore, half an hour ago you were devouring me. Now you are playing the coy maid. What shall it be?"

Her heart was thundering. "I must get out back." She hesitated, then stood on her toes and kissed him quickly. She mustn't forget that she was Lenore. "I promise to devour you again, my Lord Cameron!" she whispered. Then she fled. Her knees were weak and her flesh was aflame, and she could still taste his lips upon her. She tried to wipe away the touch as she fled around to the gaiety in the back.

She came around the house just in time to see Lenore mounting a dais. Jassy, catching her breath, tore into the open doorway of the tack house. Desperately gasping for breath, she watched as Lenore was made queen of the May by her brother, the duke. Jane, now noticeably with child, stood at his side. They all laughed and kissed one another. It was a pretty scene. Pretty pageantry for the poor people, Jassy thought. But then, she promised herself, from this day onward she would never be poor again. She would love Robert and support him in all things. She would check his gambling—if he really had such a habit!—and make him eternally happy and proud.

Henry stood before his people, and they cheered him. He raised his hands—the magnanimous landlord!—and the crowd fell silent. With a flourish he announced the dance of the May.

The musicians began to play. The beat was slow. Men and women moved into one another's arms.

Lenore disappeared into the crowd.

Jassy saw Robert Maxwell. He was far across the crowd, on the other side of the dais. She had to reach him. She slipped from the doorway of the barn and began threading her way through the costumed dancers.

She walked into Henry and Jane and froze. "Choose carefully!" Henry told her affectionately. She nodded, breathed again, and started through the crowd once again. The tempo of the music picked up. Laughter rose, and the slow, staid dance became wilder. She saw Robert. He was just ahead of her.

A hand clamped down upon her shoulder. She was whisked into strong arms and swirled about with startling force. Stunned, she looked up into Jamie Cameron's eyes. They began to circle and circle. Jassy tried to jerk free. "No!" she said in panic.

She felt faint. She twisted and saw that the real Lenore was now in Robert Maxwell's arms. They were swirling to the furious beat with its pagan thunder of drums. They were laughing in each other's arms.

She looked into Jamie Cameron's eyes. She saw their hated dark indigo depths, tearing into her soul. She felt the force of his arms around her, felt her dreams plummeting to the bottom of the deepest ocean.

"Now!" the duke commanded, and the music ceased.

She tried to pull away, to free herself. Jamie Cameron ripped her mask from her face. "Jasmine," he said.

She turned around, dazed. She still could not free herself from his hold. She saw Lenore, and Lenore was with Robert, and he was kissing her tenderly, and they were both laughing.

Then she saw her brother, Henry, and she saw the raw fury in his face as he came toward her.

"Please, God, have some pity! Let me go!" she told Jamie Cameron, and she wrenched away from him at last and ran.

VII

Jassy fled around to the front of the house, running like a cornered fox. When she reached the entryway, she didn't know what to do or where to go. She had to flee. Henry would carry out his threat, she knew. She would be best off if she left by herself.

Her fear was little greater than her disappointment. She was still stunned that Lenore and Robert could be together, and so very happy in each other's arms.

Jassy heard voices, and men running behind her. She ducked into the house—and ran straight into her brother's arms. He was still red with rage. As if he might have an attack of apoplexy at any moment.

"I'll leave!" she cried.

"When I'm ready for it, mistress! You disobeyed the one edict that I gave you!"

"Henry!" Jane came hurrying up behind him. "Henry, please, have some mercy—"

"The girl disobeyed a direct order! Haven't I been kind, haven't I been decent? I have done more for her than our father did, and still she defies me."

"Henry—"

"No, my God, woman, leave me be!"

He had Jassy by the wrists, and he dragged her along

with him up the stairway. "You have made a fool of me before my guests, girl, and this you will pay for!"

"Please, I have told you I will leave!"

He ignored her, and in minutes they reached his study. He threw her into the room, then closed the door behind them, but he did not bother to lock it. Jassy prayed that Jane would try to intervene again. No one came. Henry stared at her for a minute then came after her and caught her wrists again. She struggled against him. He was far too powerful. He threw his desk chair into the center of room and forced her down upon her knees before it. He tied her hands to the back of it, having wrenched the satin ribbon from her hair for his bond. He grasped a quill-sharpening blade from his desk, and Jassy, so tightly bound to the chair, cast back her head and screamed in terror, certain that he meant to slay her. He did not. He came around and slashed the fabric of her gown and wrenched it down her back, leaving it bare. From a hook upon the wall he snatched a riding crop, and he flourished it before her, slapping it against his palm. "You want all things due the legal heirs of our father, Jasmine? This he called judgment, and we were all privy to it! Perhaps it is just that if you would come here, you would feel the mark of his anger."

She did not know if she was more afraid of the bite of the whip, or more mortified by her position, for her torn garments hung from her and she was nearly naked from the waist up, and forced upon her knees, and desperate with her hands so brutally tied. She wanted to speak to him, to reason with him, but she dared not open her mouth, for she was so afraid that she would cry. "You see, my dear, the bastard children do find certain benefits!" He stroked her bare back with the crop of the whip.

"Your Grace—" she began, and then she screamed, for he brought the whip down upon her naked back with a violent force that was shattering. She had never known such agony. Tears stung her eyes, and she didn't know how many more she could bear.

The door opened, but she was barely aware of it through her haze of pain. She wanted to brace herself, to prepare for the next, but Henry knew how to punish, and how to extend the pain.

"How many lashes, Jasmine? How many do you think before you would obey me? You see, I fear that I could tear your flesh to ribbons, and still it would help little. Still, I must try."

"Henry, no!" came a commanding male voice.

The lash fell again, and she could not help herself; she cried out with the agony of it.

"Henry, stop!" came the command again. There were footsteps before her. A man approached her brother and wrenched the crop from his hands.

"Damn you, Cameron, what right have you to stop me! You brought me this chit to harbor, and she has defied me! It is my right to punish her as I see fit. She deserves what I give her."

Jassy tried to blink back her tears. She wanted to die. Now Jamie Cameron was witness to this humiliation too.

Her gown was completely awry, her breasts were bare, tears stung her eyes, and she prayed only that the tall, towering, dark man who had brought her a respite would disappear into thin air. She would rather bear the whip than the damning glare of his indigo eyes.

"By God and all that is holy, Jamie, we are friends, but this is my business now. Do not interfere!"

"I have the right!" Jamie declared. He knelt down before Jasmine. She wished he would go away. He untied the ribbon that held her. She had no strength left. She fell from her knees to the floor. He came around to her side, lifting her. She cried out, for the cuts on her back stung painfully, and she cried out in protest, for she was so exposed and vulnerable and didn't want him witnessing her in this state. He stripped off his doublet and wrapped it around her gently, taking care when she flinched as the fabric hit her back.

"Damn you, Jamie Cameron!" Henry swore.

"It is my right, for I will marry her."

"What?" Henry said, astounded.

There were others in the room then, Jassy realized, for they all repeated Henry's exclamation.

"But that's foolish, man! Think of your position. You will have to have a special dispensation. You cannot marry this common—"

"Take care!" Jamie warned. "It is my betrothed you speak of now!"

"Jamie, you have lost your mind!" It was Jane speaking. She was kind, but she had a strong sense of propriety. "Think of who and what you are, and think of your life and your life-style—"

"That is exactly what I am thinking of," Jamie said curtly. He scooped Jassy into his arms. Instinctively she clung to him. He whirled around to face Henry. "Where is her room? Where shall I take her?"

"I'll show you!" Elizabeth said. Jassy saw her sister's pretty face dance before her. "Come, Jamie, I will show you."

"This is madness, Jamie!" Henry called after him.

"I held her when the dance ended, did I not?"

"I would never hold you to a marriage with a bastard!"

"I hold myself to the bargain," Jamie replied, and he followed Elizabeth out into the hallway.

"Jamie Cameron, you'll not interfere with me this way! You cannot mean this! You don't want the girl punished, though God knows why. I do not maim her!"

"I play no game," Jamie said softly. "I have decided. I will marry her."

They walked along the hallway. Dazed with pain, Jassy stared up at him. His neck seemed very bronze and powerful, and his jaw was hardened with determination. He glanced down at her, and his eyes were dark and menacing.

"I won't marry you," she said.

"No? Not even for all that money I've got?"

She shook her head. "I hate you. I'll never marry you. You should have let Henry whip me."

"Perhaps I should have," he said.

"Here, this way," Elizabeth said before them.

He entered into her room, and he laid her down upon her bed. He set her upon her side, then rolled her to her stomach, freeing his doublet from her and baring the strokes of the whip.

"Please, go away!" Jassy said breathlessly.

"Some salve will heal them. Henry does care something for you; I saw him lash a groom for thievery once, and there was little flesh left," Jamie said flatly. "Elizabeth, my sister has a lotion that will be soothing. Other than that, the marks should fade in a few weeks."

"Please, go away," Jassy implored him again, her face in her pillow. He didn't go away. He sat at her side and continued to study her back.

She didn't turn around and she didn't look his way; she felt him pick up her hand. He slid a ring onto her small finger. "This will be the mark of my betrothal. It will keep you safe from . . ." He paused. Jassy thought that he meant to say she would be safe from her brother, but he did not. "You will be safe from all harm," he finished.

"I will never marry you,' she said dully. "And you do not mean this. You needn't continue the charade."

"But I do mean it," he said very quietly, and she felt the whisper of his voice against the bare flesh at her nape. "I do mean it, with all of my heart." Something hot and frightening filled her as the fever of his words touched her again. She turned suddenly, seeking his eyes. Her torn bodice and shift fell, and flushing, she retrieved them, staring at him in amazement. "Why? Why would you want to do this thing? Henry is right. No one will hold you to it! I am a bastard, and you are the son of a duke. Why?"

He shrugged. His eyes were dark and dusky, and his face was hard set. He crossed his arms over the breadth of his chest and rose, and she trembled, watching him. She remembered Lenore's words. He would bow to no man. He would do what he chose with his life: he had asked her to be his mistress and now he was willing her to be is wife.

"Why? Well, because I do desire you, I suppose. I want you, and marriage seems to be one kind of a price to pay. You do demand your price, don't you?"

She couldn't speak. She burned beneath his gaze and felt as if they had barely scratched the surface of things, as a tempest brewed between them both. She was afraid but swore that she would not be afraid. Lenore knew him, and the strength of his will. Jassy swore then that she would fight it.

"Excuse me, love, till we meet again," he said. He kissed her forehead and bowed to Elizabeth, and Jassy still hadn't spoken when she realized that he had left the room.

"I will not do it!" she said in panic. "Elizabeth, I will not do it! He saved me from Henry's wrath, yes, but if he were in a temper or if he had been defied, I would fear him far more than I would Henry! He can't mean it, it will never happen—oh, why did he have to step out in front of me! He meant to catch Lenore, and Lenore meant to have him—"

"Oh, don't worry about Lenore!" Elizabeth said happily. "Lenore has Robert!"

"Oh!" Jassy said, and suddenly she burst into tears. Elizabeth, distressed, tried to comfort her. "You're in pain. I shall get the lotion. Kathryn will come. We'll clean you up and get you a hot drink laced with rum. Then you'll sleep, and it will all look so much better in the morning."

In the morning it looked even worse. Jassy woke to find Lenore beside her. Lenore kissed her cheek effusively. "Oh, Jassy, but you do carry incredible luck with you! I had thought that we were all doomed, and what happens? Of all men, Jamie Cameron determines to marry you! You! A commoner and a bastard! Henry would have whipped you and ordered me to my room until my marriage, but he is so bemused, he doesn't know what to do! Jassy, I had thought at first that I begrudged you so very much. But I am happy. Honestly, I am so very happy! And we must be friends. Oh, you needn't worry about the London snobs, either. I shall handle them. And the king will accept you for Jamie's sake, so you've really nothing to fear at all. It will be wonderful! We'll all be very close. You, me, and Elizabeth!"

"I cannot marry him," Jassy said.

"Don't be absurd. Oh! I had thought that you might trap yourself a young soldier or a merchant, and now . . . now you shall be Lady Cameron!"

"I cannot marry him."

"Oh, you're jittery, that's all. I suppose I might be a little afraid myself if I were to wed Jamie. He does have the devil of a temper and the will to match. But he is so handsome, and so very rich. Robert isn't nearly so rich, you know. Thankfully there is my trust fund, which is my dowry. We shall do very well, for we love each other dearly. Well, I'll admit, I had decided on Jamie at the beginning of the day. He kissed me and I could scarce stand. Or perhaps I kissed him. I don't remember. But it is quite all right that you marry him. It is fate, I think."

"No. I cannot marry him."

Lenore did not believe her; neither did Jane, who came to see her later in the afternoon. "He wishes the wedding to take place by the first of June, for he will have to leave shortly afterward for his holdings in Virginia. Naturally he wants some time with his new bride. I have spoken with him at length, all to no avail. I have wondered myself if you are not completely a scheming and fortune-hunting little strumpet, but none of it means a thing to Jamie. You do not know my brother; when he sets his mind on something, there is simply no stopping him."

"I will stop him. I will not marry him."

"What are you, a complete fool? One might take you for many things, my dear, but never a fool. He brought you out of a gutter; now he is willing to marry you. He is one of the richest men in the country. And you say that you will not marry him. Fine, then, return to your gutter! Wallow in it."

Still, for the rest of that day she lay in bed, and she shivered and swore to herself and to anyone else who came near that she would not marry him. Then, that night, Kathryn came to her room and told her that she must get up and dress, Lord Cameron was waiting to see her in her brother's office.

When she entered Henry's office and saw Jamie, her heart began to beat too fast, and trembling sensations seized her. She could not cast herself to his mercy. He knew that she hated him. This was some great and final mocking joke on his part. It had to be.

Nor did he act much like the loving husband-to-be. He eyed her critically when she entered, and in silence. Then he spoke at last. "I have made arrangements for a dressmaker to come here. You will be available to her at all times. You must have a completely new wardrobe, for my wife must not wear hand-me-downs, no matter how fine. You will need much in wool, and I suggest that you have her fashion you warm woolen stockings and pantalets, for winters can be harsh. Also, see to it that you are supplied with ball gowns, for one never knows. Henry has seen that the church has cried the banns, and we will be married on the first of June."

Her throat was dry, and she could barely move her parched lips. "No. I have said that I will not marry you."

He arched a brow, and his mouth curled into a smile. "You mean it?"

"Yes."

"Well, then, the offer has been made."

He stepped by her. She stared up at the powerful breadth of his back and his dark head, and she shivered.

The door closed behind him. She opened it and ran, returning to her room. She asked Kathryn to pick her a few warm things, things given to her by Elizabeth, her one true friend. Henry would have her leave in the morning, she was certain.

"Relax, love, it will work out!" Kathryn assured her. "I'll give you warm milk and you'll sleep, and it will look better by morning."

The morning did look better, for by night she had slept, and in sleeping, she had dreamed. She was back in the awful attic, and the wind was raging. It was dark and dreary and cold and filthy, and she was approaching the bed, for Linnet was dying. She had to reach her, she had to touch her, warm her. She reached out for the threadbare blanket covering her mother, and it was awful, for even before the figure turned, Jassy knew what she would see.

She would see death.

And still she had to touch the figure. And the figure turned, and indeed she saw the death's-mask, awful, pitiable, horrible. It was the face of starvation and misery and age come by wear, not by years. It was the ravaged, torn face of disease and hunger and desperation.

She started to scream. It was not her mother's face. It was her own.

"Jassy! Wake up!" Elizabeth was there, shaking her. The dream had been so horrible, it was hard to come from it. Elizabeth shook her again. "Jassy! It is a nightmare, nothing more."

Jassy looked around her. She saw by the windows that it was nearly dawn. She threw off her covers and ran to her wardrobe.

"Jassy! Where are you going, what are you doing?"

"Is he still there, do you know?"

"Who? Where?"

"Jamie Cameron. Is—is he staying at his house?"

"Yes, I believe so. He is not due to sail until the middle of June."

Jassy dressed quickly. She was barely aware of what clothing she wore. She started for the door, then she came back and kissed Elizabeth's cheek. "I love you," she whispered. Then she ran out the door and down the steps.

The servants were barely awake. She had to call for a groom to come and saddle Mary for her. Impatiently she mounted with no help, and she kicked the little horse with much more vigor than was needed, then she apologized to the faithful mare as she raced along. The sun still had not risen completely when she came to the gates of Jamie Cameron's magnificent estate. She had to wait for a gatekeeper to come, and as she waited, she stared at the house. It would not be so bad. Nothing would be so bad, for this would be her home; she would be mistress of this magnificent mansion. If she married him, she would never want again for anything.

She would have to lie with Jamie Cameron, she reminded herself. Night after night, into eternity. That would be her payment for security and riches. She started to tremble, and she almost turned around to ride back. She could remember his bronze fingers on her flesh all too clearly. She could remember his kiss, and the hot way it made her feel. She could not do it.

She nearly turned the mare about, but then the gate opened, and she rode through. Lymon was waiting to greet her on the steps. A groom took the mare, and she started up the steps. "Is—is Lord Cameron awake as yet?" she asked him.

"He is, mistress, and is aware that you have come. I'll take you to him."

She hadn't been up the grand staircase yet. As she mounted it, her heart hammered and she breathed with great difficulty. She tried to look at the finely carved wood, and on the second floor she looked over the fine portrait gallery, the silver sconces on the wall, and the superb deacons' benches that lined the alcoves of the hallway. Lymon came to great double doors, and he pushed them open for her. "Lord Cameron awaits you, mistress."

He ushered her into the room. The doors closed behind her.

She was in his bedchamber. It was a huge room with a canopied four-poster bed to the right of a large stone mantel. Huge Elizabethan chairs faced the fire around a circular, inlaid table. By the windows was a large desk, angled so as to make the most of the sunlight. There were brocade drapes tied away from the window. There was another door, which stood ajar and led to a dressing room and privy. It was fine; it was a palace. She could be mistress of it all! she told herself.

Then her eyes wandered to the bed, for there would lie the crux of it all. To marry him gave him the right to have her. To touch her whenever he chose. A shiver ran down her spine.

He was seated casually upon the thick carved window-sill, staring out at the day. He wore only a white shirt, plain brown breeches, and his high boots. He stared at the sun, and his arms were crossed over his chest. He did not turn to face her.

"Mistress Dupré, to what do I owe this honor?"

She tried very hard to speak, but no sound came. "I—"

He turned to her, and his eyes fell upon her sharply. "Come, come, speak up! You can do much better than that. I cannot believe that the cat could have gotten the better of your very adroit tongue!"

Anger smoldered within her.

"You could make things easier!"

"What things? I have no idea what you're talking about."

"You do!"

He arched a brow. He leapt from the windowsill and walked around her, smiling. "You want me to help you, mistress? Well, then, I shall try. Have you come, perhaps, to see if my marriage proposal still remains open?"

She couldn't go through with it. She hated the way he scorned her with his simple words.

She had to go through with it. She would not live as her mother had, nor would she die that way. She lowered her head and nodded.

"I thought so. Now, let me guess." He strode around her again, slowly, rubbing his jaw. "You awoke in the middle of the night with the sudden and amazing vision that you were deeply and desperately in love with me, and you could hardly bear another night without me. No? Ah, alas, I did not think so. Let's try again. You woke up in the middle of the night with the sudden and startling realization that you would never get such an offer again. That you would be a lady—not that I think titles matter to you much. Ah, but you would be a rich lady. A very rich lady. Money. That is it, isn't it?"

She kept her head lowered. She locked her jaw and remained silent.

"Isn't it!" he snapped, and he came before her and jerked her chin up.

"Yes! Yes, that is it exactly!" she cried, wrenching from his hold. "I never pretended to love you—I never pretended to like you! This has been a bizarre accident and nothing more!"

"But you are determined now that you will marry me. A man whom you hate."

The passion left her. She lowered her head. "Yes."

He was silent. She lifted her eyes at last, and she could read nothing from his harsh, dark gaze. "I don't always hate you," she said. Then she emitted an impatient oath. "Why offer, then? You have no love for me. Why do you make this proposal?"

"I, at least, want you," he said softly. He grabbed her hand suddenly and pulled her over to the canopied bed, and he cast her upon it. He clutched the canopy rod and stared down upon her. "This is my bed, mistress. If you go through with this, you will have no room of your own, you will join me here. Nightly. You will not have headaches, nor will you suffer distress. And you are still willing to marry me?"

She furrowed her brow. The image of the dirty attic room and the death's-head rose before her.

"Yes," she said coldly.

He laughed then, and pulled her up. "You are a whore," he told her.

She lunged at him furiously, and he caught her wrist. He did not pull her close but just held her. "If you would engage in battle, my love, be assured that I will ever be ready to enjoin it. Take care, lest the injury you would inflict upon me fall home upon you. I saved you from Henry's wrath only because I had made up my mind that I would wed you. I think a few more lashes would have stood you well, but should they ever be administered, I think I would prefer to raise the rod myself."

"Let go of me!" she raged, jerking her wrist.

He quirked his brow. "Come, love! Are those the words

of a tender fiancée?" He held her a moment longer, then released her. He returned to his window seat, and she saw then that he had a number of documents there and had been studying them before her arrival. He had dismissed her, she thought. And she was all too glad. She was ready to turn and flee.

"The wedding will be on the first of June, as I have said. I shall send the dressmaker today, for there is very little time. Tell her that she is free to hire as many seamstresses as she deems necessary to finish your wardrobe by June. Jane and Lenore have excellent taste if you wish advice, though I wonder if you are not as talented with style as you are with accent and manner. I shall send a purse to Henry for anything else you might require before the wedding."

"There is nothing that I will require."

"What? You are marrying me for money, and you are shy about taking it?"

She did not know how to tell him that she was marrying him not so much for money as she was for the mere security of steady meals, a soft bed, and a sturdy roof over her head. For heat against the chill of winter and bread against the bite of hunger.

"There is nothing that I require," she said simply.

He was silent for a moment. She wondered what he thought as he watched her. "That will be to your discretion," he said at last, and he turned his attention back to his documents.

Jassy didn't move. Now that the arrangement had been made and she had refused his purse, she thought of a few things she might have done with it. She cleared her throat, and then was annoyed with herself for her manner. When he looked up at her again, clearly irritated by the interruption this time, she spoke sharply. "There are a few things that I would—that I would like done."

"You will be mistress of the house. You may do as you please."

She lowered her head. "Molly . . . the girl at the tavern. She was very good to me. Always. May I bring her here?"

"You may. I'll have her sent for. She can be here for the wedding."

"And . . . and Tamsyn too?"

"Tamsyn?"

"He was a doctor once, I believe. He works at the tavern."

"That old drunk—"

"He is not an old drunk. He is a man down upon his luck. I can make him work well. He will be sober, I swear it!"

Jamie shrugged. "The servants are your domain. I have vast holdings, and we shall need many of them. Hire whom you will. If this Tamsyn can be found with Molly at Master John's tavern, then I will see to it that he comes here with Molly. Is there anything else?"

She shook her head. He waited. She moistened her lips.

"Thank you," she managed to say to him, and then she fled.

The dressmaker came that afternoon, and the afternoon after, and the afternoon after that. Her small room became filled with velvets, taffetas, silks, laces, linens, and brocades. She was fitted for day dresses and evening dresses, warm dresses and summer wear. She was to have several warm muffs, jewelry, caps, elegant hats, and fashionable purses. Jane and Lenore were very much into the spirit of things. Jane produced numerous fashion dolls from Paris. "One must be careful, though, for the king was raised by strict Presbyterians. Alas, fashion hasn't changed much! At least the ruffs are gone. I remember as a little child that we had to wear them. So uncomfortable!"

"The queen is very fashionable," Lenore protested.

"Anne of Denmark adds jewels to old styles!" Jane complained.

Jassy barely heard them. She watched her wardrobe grow around her. Sometimes she would touch the soft fur that rimmed a collar or a sleeve, and she would marvel that such beautiful, costly things could be hers.

Then she would realize that the cost of a single muff might have saved her mother's life and she would be morose again. The days were rushing forward. May passed in a blaze of glory.

On the twentieth of the month, Jamie came to dinner. He and Henry were cordial friends again. Henry, in fact, considered himself the extreme benefactor. Thanks to his good graces, Jassy had been given the opportunity to rise above her station in life.

The meal was good, duckling and early vegetables, but Jassy could barely eat. She could hardly lift her glass to her lips. Robert was with Jamie, and he and Lenore were planning their own wedding. It would take place two weeks after Jassy's.

Jassy was seated next to Jamie. She could not speak to him, nor could she join into the other conversations. Lenore laughed and said that it was nerves. Jamie commented that it certainly was.

When the meal was over, Jassy fled outside. She went to the stables, and to her mare. Robert found her there again. Bitterly she remembered the first time he had met her there.

He kissed her soundly on the cheeks. "Ah, Jassy, it has come well for you, hasn't it? Had I but had Jamie's resources, it might have been different. You are so beautiful."

"And you are a man betrothed to my sister," she said to him.

"The sister with the dowry," he murmured.

"Be good to her," Jassy warned.

He laughed. "Oh, I will be. Lenore is a beauty too. There's something about you, though, Jassy. Alas, it is my best friend to wed you. You've come so very far. Who would have imagined this of the wench in the tavern?"

"The wench in the tavern makes her own way, Robert," Jamie said, entering the barn. Jassy did not like the sizzle in his eyes. It was harder than usual.

"Robert was congratulating me," she said.

"So he was."

"I'm happy for both of you," Robert said, and grinned.

"Ah, a haystack! I shall leave you two young lovers alone."

Jamie remained at one end of the stables. Jassy nervously stroked the mare at the other.

"Strange, how it comes to mind the way that I found you two together the last time I was here."

"There was no contract between us then," she said.

"Ah, but there is a contract now. I've even the king's blessing upon my endeavor."

Jassy held quiet for a moment. He was still; he had not raised his voice. Yet she sensed the leashed fury of him down the length of the stalls, and she spoke defensively. "There was nothing between us."

"Did I say that there was? I accused you of nothing."

"Because there is nothing to accuse me of."

"I came quickly."

"You are absurd."

"You claimed to be in love with him once. I am merely hoping that you have curbed the emotion."

"Don't threaten me."

"My love, this is no threat. This is a deep and grave promise. If I ever find you so close with any man again, you will find the lashing you received from your brother to have been a tap on the hand, and nothing more, compared with what you shall receive from me."

Jassy urged Mary back into her stall with all the control that she could summon, then she started walking down the length of the stable. He was between her and the doorway. She tried to walk around him. He blocked her.

She tried again. This time he caught her shoulders. She cast her head back and stared at him coldly.

"Please, milord, take your hands from me."

"You are something!" he murmured. "Airs and graces lie all about you."

"You are about to marry me. I thought that you wished me to play the part of a lady."

He shook his head. "Not in front of me, mistress. Not in front of me. For I swear, I will strip those airs and graces from you."

"Never, milord. Now, may I step by you?"

His hand moved. It traveled from her shoulder to her throat. He cupped her chin and she held still. She willed herself not to shiver, not to betray the rampant tempest that played throughout her like a storm, hot and windswept. His fingers moved down her throat. He spoke to her harshly.

"Aye, mistress, you are beautiful." He lowered his face to hers. His lips touched hers. They were gentle enough at first, then they moved with force. She was in his arms, her mouth was parted, and he played within it easily and with leisure, with the wet blade of his tongue. She clung to him, for she could not stand. The weakness seized her, and the shivering came violently.

She tore away from him, afraid of the volatile emotions and sensations inside her.

"Please! Let me by. We—"

"We what?"

"We are not married yet."

He smiled with humor, with the patient grace of a stalking tiger.

"Alas. We are not married—yet. But that is soon to be rectified, isn't it?"

She started to run by him. He caught her arm once again. "No cold feet, milady?"

She looked from his hand upon her to his eyes and back down to his hands again. "No cold feet, my Lord Cameron."

"You haven't forgotten that I shall expect everything from you. And that I am not a patient man."

"I have forgotten nothing."

"It is all an unfortunate price that must be paid."

"Yes, yes! What difference does it make?"

For the briefest of moments she thought that he appeared disappointed in her. Then he seemed nothing more than hard and cold and ruthless again.

"There is no difference to any of it, Jassy. No difference. We both know what we want, and we are going for it. You are the adventurer, as much as I. The savage heart, my love." He released her. "Go. Run. You've only a matter of days left now. Oh, my father will be coming by in the next few days. Be cordial to him."

"Why? Shall he command you not to marry me? Shall he stop your allowance?"

He touched her again, his fingers digging into her arm cruelly. "I do as I choose, mistress, in all things. You had best remember that. And my fortune is my own, I receive an allowance from no man. You will be decent to him, at your most courteous best, because he is a fine old man, and I would have him think that I chose a beauty for her spirit, rather than that I made a deal with a harlot, my money for her person."

She jerked away from him, blinking furiously at the tears that stung her eyes. "May I go now, my Lord Cameron?"

"You may. Oh, I have your friends. They are already situated at the manor."

"Molly? And Tamsyn?"

"Yes. Both of them are with me."

She hesitated and lowered her head. "Thank you. Thank you very much," she told him. Then she ran back to the house.

Three days later his father, the Duke of Carlyle, arrived in a magnificent coach. Jane and Henry sat with her in the receiving room while she greeted him.

He was a wonderful man. She had trembled before meeting him, wondering if he would despise her as a strumpet who had ensnared his son. He greeted her as if Jamie had chosen a grand duchess for his bride. As tall as his son, with the same dark, flashing eyes, he reached out his arms to her and stood on no ceremony. "Welcome, Daughter," he told her, and he took her into his arms.

She nearly burst into tears but managed to avoid them. He did not speak of her past, he spoke of the future. Jane teased him and they all laughed, and when the duke had departed, Jassy tried to run out of the room. Jane called her back. "Jassy, whatever is wrong? Papa was not so bad, was he?"

She shook her head. She was going to burst into tears.

"Your father is wonderful," she said. And then she ran, and Jane did not try to stop her.

The wedding came too soon. The morning dawned ominously dark, with rumbles of thunder and lightning. Kathryn, Elizabeth, Jane, and Lenore ignored the weather. They all met in Jassy's room early, decking her out in her wedding gown. It was in ivory satin, with pearls and glass beads sewn throughout it. The bodice was low, and lined with white fox. She wore a tiara of diamonds that held her veil in place, and the veil, too, was embroidered and studded with pearls and little sapphires.

Jassy stood still the entire time they dressed her. She could eat nothing, she could drink nothing. She clenched her hands nervously, and released them again and again.

At one o'clock it was time to go down. Henry called for the carriage, and she was handed into it. They arrived at the old Norman church in the village within minutes, and she was handed out of the carriage. Thunder cracked and rolled. "Get in, get in!" Henry urged her impatiently.

He would give her away. Robert was to stand as Jamie's witness, and Jane as her own. Jane and Elizabeth walked down the aisle before her, and then Henry tugged on her arm. "Jasmine!" he urged her. "Now!"

She started to walk. Jamie was at the end of the aisle, resplendent in black breeches and doublet and a red silk shirt and silk hose, his hair just curling over the lace at his collar. He watched her as she came down the aisle, and he betrayed neither impatience nor pleasure. As usual, she did not know at all what he was thinking.

Suddenly she was there, beside him, and she was handed over to him. She felt his touch, his hand hot, his fingers a vise upon her own. She felt the startling heat of him, as he was close. She saw his clean-shaven cheeks and breathed in the scent of him. She was trembling again before the service ended. She could not speak her vows, and the priest had to prompt her twice. Jamie stared at her curiously, a smile curving his mouth. She managed to answer.

He spoke his own firmly, with no hesitation.

Then it was over. He kissed her, and kissed her freely, and the young men in the pew called to him with laughter. Robert cleared his throat, and told Jamie that they must depart; the wedding feast awaited them.

She left the church in her husband's carriage, suddenly very aware of the band of gold on her middle finger. She moved it nervously, aware that he stared at her while they rode, that he assessed and studied her with curiosity. He moved the curtain on the carriage. "Your prize, milady. Your manor looms before us."

The carriage moved through the gates. When he lifted her down from it, she stared at the beautiful mansion, and a thrill rippled through her. He had called her "milady," and it was her rightful title now; he had made it so. And this was her home.

If she could just keep from thinking that the night must come!

"Come, love," he whispered to her. The other carriages were arriving. He lifted her off her feet and into his arms, and he carried her over the threshold of the house for luck. Applause followed them, and then the manor came alive. Liveried servants were everywhere, supplying guests with plates and crystal glasses of wine and ale in the hallway. Her father-in-law kissed her, and Jane kissed her, and Elizabeth gushed, and even Henry kissed her. She was introduced to nobility and gentry, for she was a lady now, the wife of Lord Jamie Cameron.

It was a fairy tale. She was the bountiful mistress of this. She had become a princess, and this was her palace.

"You should have taken your bride to Paris," Lenore told him good-naturedly. "I should have demanded it."

"Ah, but my bride could have demanded and demanded, and it couldn't have been, for I sail in two weeks. No . . ." He paused, and his gaze lingered as it fell over Jassy. "In the time we have as newlyweds, I shall seek the comfort of my bed, the service of my trusted friends here."

Jassy turned away. Her head was pounding. Musicians began to play, and she was happy to dance. She even laughed when she danced with Robert, for he was always funny, and he was able to lift her mood. Until she discovered Jamie watching her again. Still, she wanted the music to go on and on. But, of course, it couldn't.

And finally the last carriage rolled away. Lymon announced that he would seek her council about the household in the morning.

Lymon left them at opposite ends of the hallway. Jamie lifted his wineglass to her.

"I shall give you thirty minutes, Jassy. No more."

She could not breathe. The time of her reckoning had come. She could not set down her own glass and turn to the stairs.

"Thirty minutes. No more," he told her again.

She gripped her glass more tightly and turned to the stairs. She fled up them. She knew the way to his room. She ran into it and closed the door. Leaning against it, she closed her eyes. She swallowed down the last of her wine, and in a sudden pique, she sent the glass flying across the room and into the fire.

"Jassy!"

She looked up, and there stood Molly, all beautifully dressed, her eyes bright and her cheeks rosy. "Molly!" Jassy hurtled herself across the room and into her friend's arms.

"Lord luv you, girl, but you've married a lord! Oh, bless you, lass, and you remembered me and old Tam. Oh, Jassy! We're together again. I cannot believe me own eyes! This fine place is yours!"

She swallowed. Yes, this fine place was hers. The crystal and the silver and the silk and the marble. Fine things, and they were all hers.

Molly mattered more than any of them. "Oh, Molly! How are you? Tell me, how have you been? You look wonderful. I've missed you so. Tell me—"

"Lord luv you, lass! But 'tis your wedding night, and I've no mind to be here when your handsome groom appears. Come, let's undress you. I've laid out your nightgown; now let's get all this off!"

She was tempted to cling to her clothing. Panic was setting in on her again.

Molly set to work. She carefully removed Jassy's veil and gown. Then she made her sit, and she removed Jassy's shoes and stockings and untied the constraining corset. Jassy was down to her shift, and suddenly she turned and clung to Molly.

"I can't do it. I can't go through with it."

"Why, Jassy! It will be nothing. He's a fine, striking man. Many a lass would trade years off her life for the opportunity of one night with such a one! And you're so very beautiful. He will love you with all his heart."

No, he hates me, she thought, but she could not bring herself to say that to Molly.

Molly reached for her shift, and she was suddenly naked and shivering. Then the soft silk nightdress was falling over her shoulders. It was high about her neck, and long to the floor, and the sleeves were long, too, but there was nothing modest about the gown, for it was almost entirely sheer.

There was a knock upon the door. "Oh!" Jassy cried. She tumbled into the big bed beneath the canopy, crawling beneath the sheets and blankets and pulling them tight to her chin. Molly hurried, stuffing her shift into the trunk at the foot of the bed. She raced to the door then, and threw it open, grinning in her broad, country, good-natured way. "Evening, milord!" she said. And then she hurried by him and Jassy was alone.

He entered the room and closed the door. He moved into the room, casting off his doublet and casually allowing it to fall on the trunk at the foot of the bed. Heat coursed to Jassy's face and she watched him with a growing panic. He went on over to his desk, where he poured himself a large measure of some liquor, then sank negligently into the chair before it. His eyes sliced like indigo steel into her soul as he stared pointedly upon her and sipped his drink.

He lifted the glass to her and spoke softly. "So. Here we are, my love, together, alone, at last." He smiled, and his brow arced. "And we are married now, aren't we, milady?" He set his drink down upon the table, and he stood, and there was nothing negligent or casual about him anymore. He strode toward her with purpose and wrenched the covers from her fingers. "Let's see if this bargain is worth its measure, shall we?"

VIII

Jassy cried out at his touch. She had not meant to, but he startled her so when he wrenched upon the sheets that the sound escaped her. She tried to retrieve her covers, but they remained tight in his hands while his eyes condemned her. A dark cast of annoyance tightened his features, and she tried very hard not to gasp out again. She was no coward, and she didn't fear his anger, she assured herself. She was indebted to him; he had made her his wife. He had made her mistress of this glorious house, and he had given her crystal and silver and silks and gems. But those things meant nothing to him. They were not given out of love or regard, but as a matter of course. As his horses were well shod, so would be his wife.

He smiled slowly, cynically, as if he read her mind again. She would have run, had there been a place to go. But there was nowhere to go. Nowhere but the streets or the gutter. She was his wife, and she had married him willingly.

"What? Second thoughts, love?"

If only he didn't smile so hatefully, knowing her every thought, reading her mind! Locking her jaw, she released the covers and fell back against her pillow. She crossed her arms over her chest, and her eyes snapped with the glow of the fire as she stared at him.

"I have no second thoughts."

"I see. You have been breathlessly anticipating this moment for many a lonely night?"

"I have no second thoughts."

"Good." His smile faded. He wrenched the covers from the bed, dropping them upon the floor. Then he moved away from her, sitting at the foot of the bed. He cast off his fine buckled shoes, pulled his shirt from his breeches, and cast it over his head.

Before he had come, the room had been cast in the shadows of the night. Now it seemed that there were candles everywhere, burning from the desk, from the trunk at the foot of the bed, from the mantel. The fire that had seemed to burn low in the grate had cast out only a pale glow, but now the logs snapped and crackled and hissed, sending out a fierce light. The draperies were pulled against the night sky, and the massive room seemed very small, for they were encapsulated within it, just the two of them. Light played and flickered over his bare back and chest, over muscle and sinew. His shoulders were very broad, and his back and breast were as bronze as his features, from constant exposure to the sun. She wondered briefly how he had come to such dark color upon his chest. She bit softly into her lower lip to keep from shivering as she watched him. The muscles in his arms were very large; they tightened and flexed naturally with his every movement, like those across his chest. They were the arms of a blacksmith, she thought, and not of a lord. All together, he seemed like some heathen then, so paganly bronzed and built, like one of the strange red men he so frequently defended from the new land across the Atlantic.

His shirt fell on top of the covers on the floor. He stood in his breeches and hose. A profusion of short, dark hair grew upon his chest, narrowing to a thin line as it tapered to his waistband, forcing her to wonder what lay beneath the band. She wound her fingers together tightly, praying for some miraculous salvation. She burned one moment and lay cold the next. She willed herself not to bolt, for she was certain he would merely drag her down. She had only to imagine herself somewhere else and she could endure this. She had to endure it, for she had married him.

Paying her scant attention, he walked to his desk, moving silently, with a curious grace and ease, like a great cat in the night. With his thumb he smothered the candle there. He repeated the action with the candle upon the trunk.

And still, Jassy thought, the light blazed too brightly, and Jamie knew too well how to draw out torture. With each second that passed, she trembled more fiercely. She grew more aware of his strength and his manhood, and of one irrefutable fact—that she had married him. She had done so for a life of fine things, and in doing so she had given him the right to her.

He walked to the mantel, his footsteps silent, and smothered out the flame there.

And still, light poured from the hearth. From the dying fire lit against the chill rain of the day, sparks flamed and glowed, casting their glaze upon him. He rubbed the back of his neck, and for a moment Jassy actually thought that he had forgotten all about her.

He had not.

Standing there before the fire, he stripped away his breeches, and then his hose, and they lay where he had dropped them. He turned then to Jassy and came around to where she lay, again his stride so silent, as if she were being stalked, and indeed, she believed that she was. She longed to run. She had to keep reminding herself that she had nowhere to go. She wondered if there was anything that she could say or do to put the moment off, if she could not plea or beg or seek some gentle spot within his heart. She wanted to keep her eyes level with his, but she could not. They fell against the length of him, and her cheeks burned. His stomach was flat and hard, with the delineation of tight muscles. His thighs were long and as hard as his arms, his calves shapely. The trail of dark hair that tapered to his waist tapered below it, too, then flared again to a thick nest, and from that nest his male shaft protruded like a blade—strong, bold, and sure. He approached her with no hesitance and no modesty, but with firm and unfaltering purpose.

He did not smile. There was no mockery to him then, and neither was there humor. He planted his hands upon his hips and stared down upon her coldly. "Off with the gown."

She backed herself against the bed as best she could. She willed her fingers to cease trembling, but they would not. She hated his proprietary tone of voice, and she was suddenly determined that she would fight him.

"If you had the least bit of care, milord, you would not force the issue this evening."

"What?"

"Perhaps in time—"

"Get the gown off, milady. Now."

"Robert Maxwell would never have behaved so crudely! He'd have given his bride the time to know him."

"Madame, you know me, and you do know me well! So your dreams are of Robert Maxwell still. Then know this, Jassy. I am not Robert Maxwell, and if naught else at the end of this evening, you will know that for a certainty." His words were clipped; a pulse ticked in his throat. She thought that she had seen him angry before, and yet this sudden wrath he unleashed seemed more terrible than any ire she had provoked in him before. In fear, she lashed out.

"You have the manners and finesse of a wild boar," she told him scathingly.

There was no challenging him. "And you, my dear," he said, leaning over her, his palms upon the headboard on either side of her head, "have the scruples, manners, and morés of a London slut."

Jassy cried out, lifting her hand against him in fury. She caught his cheek, and the mark of her fingers burned brightly against it. His lip tightened, and in a split second he wrenched her to her feet. She was barely standing before the bodice of her sheer white gown was caught between the power of his strong bronze hands and ripped asunder. She swore as the soft material fell to her feet and they were left naked together. She slammed her hands against his chest, as he lifted her into his arms, and the ruthless darkness of his eyes blazed into her own as he walked the few steps back to the canopied bed.

"You bastard!" she cried out to him. "So this is nobility! This is the behavior of a lord!"

"You play the grande dame well, Jassy, very well. But in our particular circumstance I find your modesty a jest, and though your airs are very pretty and will certainly have their place, I promise that you'll not bring them into this bed with you." So saying, he tossed her upon it. There was nothing to grab to shield her from his relentless gaze, for the covers were gone. There was nothing, nothing at all. No barrier against his slow, critical scrutiny of every inch of her body. She lay still and miserable beneath his gaze.

"Have you no mercy whatsoever?" she demanded, "Are you forgetting that I—that I—"

"That you are innocent, my love? Oh, it is a strange form of innocence, but I do not forget it."

"We could wait—"

"Preferably until I leave? Alas, no, love. I get little enough from this contract as it is. No wealth, no riches, no titles. Your dowry lies in the verdant field before me, and as it is all, I would avail myself now. So come. You are the consummate actress! Welcome your lord and husband, lady."

"Oaf!"

Tears stung her eyes. She swore that she would not shed them. Then he came down upon her, once again moving as silently, as powerfully, as sleekly as a great cat. He stretched out his naked length upon her, taking her into his arms. She struggled against him in silence, her fingers upon the hot, muscled feel of his arms, her legs trapped beneath the casual curve of his own. She could not move him; she could only feel him more fully, his chest against her breasts, his limbs entangled with hers; his sex, hard and prominent, seemed ablaze against the apex of her thighs. She went very still. He was all steel. He did, for a moment, let his indigo eyes blaze above her, then his fingers threaded into the hair at her nape, and his lips fell upon hers.

He did not hurt her. His mouth molded slowly over her own, and when his lips had possessed hers, he pried them open and filled her mouth with his tongue. A curious warmth filled her. The heat that he always brought about was like a fire that rippled and cascaded along her spine, but it entered into her, and it came from within her too. It swept from the liquid warmth of his tongue to her lips, and it came from the encompassing and volatile heat of his body, pressed hard to hers. It came from the pulsing masculine blade of him, as insinuative as the stroke of his tongue within her mouth. In and out and sweeping, and deep within her again, until she was breathless. He freed his hand from her hair. He cupped her breast as he kissed her, his fingers winding around the firm weight of it. His thumb grazed over the rose crest of it, and he rubbed that peak between his thumb and forefinger. She shuddered at the streak of sensation that bolted through her, from that touch, to the very core of her. A streak like a sizzle of lightning, so very hot.

She was terrified of that heat, frightened that it might seize her completely, and if it did, then she would have no defense against him ever again. He did not love her, he scorned her, he called her whore. She could not give anything to him. Nothing.

She twisted her lips from his and drew in a ragged breath. His face was over hers again, hard and taut and relentless, "Please!" she hissed. "Do what you will, but must . . . must you kiss me?"

He went dead still, then she felt the furious shudder that rippled through his hard body, and she saw the dark contortion of his features. She had wounded him, and for a moment she was glad, for she often hated his smugness.

Then she cried out, for as his eyes locked with hers, he

caught her knee, and with swift and brutal determination he parted her legs, and his weight fell between them. "We shall have it your way . . . milady," he told her. "But have you this evening, I shall."

His hand moved down the length of her, along her thigh. He lifted her legs high against him, and she swallowed sharply when she felt the touch of his hand intimately upon her. His eyes remained hard upon hers. She knew then that she could have cried out, that she could have whispered a single word, just one plea, and he would have taken her differently, more gently, tenderly, even. Perhaps. But she could not whisper that single word; she could not plead, and she could admit to nothing, give nothing. She would not ask for mercy. She clenched her teeth, her lashes fell over her eyes, and she shivered against the raw honesty of their bodies together, terribly aware of all of him, of the naked sexuality that lay between them. Still, she would beg no quarter, would seek no mercy.

And she would receive none. She felt the hard, pulsing shaft of his sex against her, then thrusting, plunging, deep, deep, within her. Blatant and bold and with no hesitation, he claimed her. Then she choked and screamed, and stretched and struggled to free herself, like a trapped and panicked animal, for she had never imagined such a searing pain. The size and breadth of him were too much; he would tear her apart.

Instantly he went still. She trembled, choking on her tears, wishing that she could free herself from him. He swore, and she did not know if it was at her, or at himself.

"Easy," he told her softly.

"You are—killing me!" she told him brokenly. The intimacy was unbearable. He was a part of her. He lay atop her and within her. All that was personal and vulnerable lay naked and open to him. His breath mingled with her own, and their heartbeats were one upon the other.

"You will not die, I assure you. Women have been accommodating men since the beginning of time," he said wryly. She met his eyes again. He held himself very still, staring at her, and still he was there. She could barely meet his gaze, and neither could she look away. "Part your lips," he told her.

"I—"

"Part your lips to mine. Part your lips, and lay still to my touch. Cease to fight me."

He dipped his head, and the tip of his tongue flicked over her mouth and delved into it. Then the blaze of his kiss ran a path down the length of her throat. His tongue laved over the valley between her breasts, then circled the nipples, and then the full weight of each of her breasts. And all the while she felt him within her, still but pulsing with life, so alien, so ferociously alight with fire and promise. The pain was keen, and she lay still herself, with each new intimate assault upon her senses, with the practiced play of his mouth and hands upon her.

The pain began to fade. The warmth filled her. She parted her lips to his command, and she did not protest his hands upon her body. He stroked her breasts until she cried out, and still she was aware of the hardness of him inside her, achingly aware of the sexual intimacy. And acutely aware of the combustile warmth. She could not give in to it. She must never give in to it. . . .

Suddenly he withdrew from her. The burning was still all about her. She wondered with rising hope if he meant to leave her be now, if that was all . . .

It was not. It was to be worse. His eyes upon her, he stroked the length of her torso with his hands. He covered her breasts, came down to her waist, and lifted her buttocks. He raised her high. She gasped and cried out, burning crimson that he should look at her so, then she realized his design, and she cried out in protest. "Nay, oh, please—"

"Lie still, madame. I will ease your pain."

"No! No—"

But the complete, intimate invasion had begun. Her fingers wound into the bed sheet, and she tossed her head, continuing to protest. It stood her no stead, for he took his leisure. She tried not to think, but she had never felt anything more keenly in her life, not the pangs of hunger, not the fear of death, not the promise of heaven. With a touch of sizzling, wet fire he stroked her and laved her, and she burned with a terrible ache, felt a crimson tide threaten to seize her. She twisted and writhed and begged him to cease. He touched and probed and laved her again. She wanted to die and felt that she could.

Then he released her. He crawled over her and thrust deep inside of her once again, and when he was there, the feel of him was absurdly right. He filled her still, a massive blade that cut inside her, but her body gave to his. Where her heart could not give, her form surrendered, and she yielded to his command.

When he began to move, she gasped. Her fingers dug into his hair and into his back. He moved slowly at first. His whisper touched, brushed her cheek. "Do I hurt you?"

She shook her head. She could never look at him again. She would never be able to face him. She burned still from that very first thrust, but he caused her no new pain. She buried her face against his shoulder. The scent of him was not unpleasant. It was clean and masculine, and somehow it was better than to be against him.

She shuddered suddenly, fiercely, as a surge of power seized him. It was a storm, a tempest, come upon him. Nothing was slow and nothing was easy, and she clung to him tightly, lest she be lost to the storm. On and on it raged, a tempest of power, of driving thrusts and strokes, of tension, terrible and sweet. She lay there, aware of the rising fire all around her, vaguely aware that something sweet lay within her reach, something that made this wild storm the tempest that it had become for him. She could give in to it, she thought, as he moved against her again and again, indomitable. She could give in to it, to the strength of the arms that held her, to the curious promise of glory.

No, no! She must never . . .

He rose above her high, and he came into her again,

shuddering and rigid. He fell against her. Something honeyed entered into her, a warm liquid seeping from his body into hers.

His arm lay over her breasts; his fingers touched her nipple with absolute possession. Jassy felt the burning between her legs, and his casual and negligent touch with his complete assumption of right. It was over. He had taken what he wanted, and now she had no secrets from him. She had been, she was certain, as well used as a woman could be.

She swore savagely. She tossed his arm from her, and she turned and crawled to the far corner of the bed, her back to him. To her dismay, tears spilled down her cheeks.

He never let her be! He touched her shoulder and pulled her back.

"Stop, please, leave me be now, for God's sake!" she demanded.

But he ignored her. His indigo eyes pierced her as thoroughly as his body had done. "I did not seek to hurt you."

"I am not hurt!" she lied.

"I told you that if you married me, you would lie here. You were in agreement."

Her lashes fell over her eyes. She felt his fingers again, light, idly stroking her breasts. "Please!"

"It is never easy the first time, so they say. Damn you! I did not seek to hurt you! 'Tis your tongue; it is a vicious thing, a weapon few men could withstand."

"Does it matter?" She looked up. She did not protest his touch. She gritted her teeth against it, and his hand stopped its movement.

"Nay, madame, perhaps it does not."

He turned away from her. Jassy rolled again to the far side of the bed and curled into a ball. She shivered, but she dared not reach over him to the covers on the floor. She tightened into herself as much as she could. She closed her eyes and tried to imagine being mistress of the house. She thought of the graceful pillars and the beautiful lines, of the crystal and the silver and the gold.

It did not work. All that she could see was the passion in his dark eyes as he moved over her. It still seemed that he was with her. It seemed as if he would always be a part of her from now, until forever. She would never free herself of the feel of him. She had sold her soul and would never find peace.

But she did find it. In time she heard his even breathing. She lay awake, aware of him there. She thought that she would move, that she would find the remnants of her gown, that she would sleep in a chair. But she did not move; exhaustion claimed her and she found the peace she so desperately sought.

The instant Jamie awoke, he longed to touch her. He did not, no more so than he did already, for the cold of the night had sent her against him. She lay, beautiful and naked and sleek, against his side. She was at a half curve, her back to him, her arm cast out, her knee curled high. Her breast peeked out from a tangle of hair and the crook of her elbow, and it was such a temptingly ripe fruit, he barely restrained himself.

Yet he did. He stared at her, and he bitterly mocked himself. He had been certain that when he had her in his arms, he could make her come alive! That he could touch a fire and ignite the spirit within her.

He was a fool who had been taken in by a fortune-hunting piece of baggage. He had seen a sensuality in her that did not exist; he had sought a promise that had never been given.

He sighed softly to himself. Well, it was done. He had married her, despite the protest of friend and foe alike, and even the king. She had never pretended not to hate him.

Yet, he thought gravely, it might have been better. Had she not turned from his kiss, and by God, had she not brought Robert's name into their bed, he would have taken a far greater care before touching her in violence. He wondered if it could ever be rectified now, and then he thought of the years and years before them, and it was a chilling thought.

No, he promised himself, he had not made a mistake. She was what he wanted. She was strong and willful, and if she despised him, perhaps that was well, for she would need the power of her emotions to endure the hardships ahead. And all the better for him. He wanted a wife, he needed a wife to complete his life in the New World, and he was determined to have children, many of them. She was young and strong. She could detest every single minute of her duty, but she would accustom herself to it, and she would give him sons.

He wondered what had driven him with such determination to marry her. She was beautiful, but it was not her beauty. Lenore had much of her look—in fact, he had decided that he would marry Lenore, as he desired a wife. But from the beginning Jassy had bewitched him. It was something that he could not touch, not even now, now that he had married her, that he had bedded her at last. It was elusive; he still could not touch it. It was her will, it was her determination, it was the very strength of her hatred and determination. It was the spark in her eyes, the fire . . . fire that he could not tap. . . .

She sighed. Her lips parted, and they were soft and beguiling. By God, he would find it. He would reach for the fire, until it blazed to an inferno, for him.

He touched the tangle of her golden hair, and he drew his finger down the length of her spine and over her buttock. Still sleeping, she stretched, sleek and lovely and sensual. Her breasts jutted out then, and she sighed softly again.

He came behind her. He wrapped his arms around her, pressed his lips against her nape, and filled his hands with the full, round firmness of her breasts. He had never seen a woman more beautiful naked. Her skin was silken, her waist was tiny, and her hips held a fascinating, sensual flare. Her legs were long and very shapely, and her nipples were large and an exquisite deep rose color. It was there! he was certain. It was there, a deep and sultry passion! He tightened his jaw, and he swore savagely to himself that he would find it—and if he did not, he would tame her still. She could vent her rage all she chose—she would learn that it would do her no good.

She sighed softly again in her sleep. He cupped her breast, curved his body to hers from behind, and flicked her nipple with his thumb. She moved against him, awakening. He pressed his lips against her shoulders and ran his hand down her flanks. She arched, then awoke, stiffening.

"Lie still," he commanded her.

"It's morning—"

"Lie still."

"It's light—"

"I like the light."

She swore softly. He ignored it and ran his hands over her buttocks again, lifting her thigh slightly and urging it forward. She turned her head away from him again, some sound escaping her, and he stroked her inner thigh, again and again, roaming every higher. He kissed her nape, bit lightly into her shoulder, and moved his tongue over her upper vertebrae. She lay very still, as he had commanded, and he wondered at her eyes, if they would be filled with fire and hatred, if she would fight him at the end, or if she had determined to honor her bargain. He slipped his thumb into her and felt her stiffen and shudder, but she did not protest, and to his surprise she was even sweetly wet and ready. He entered her from behind, pulled her close, and felt the blind, driving passion seize him. He swept into her stronger and deeper, and then with a raging abandon.

When it was over, she did not cry, scream, or protest. She lay on the bed and stared up at the ceiling, her beautiful sky-blue eyes blank. Entirely irritated, Jamie pulled the bell cord. Jassy came alive then, leaping from the bed. Curiously, after the evening and morning was spent, she still tried to hide herself from him. She sought her gown, and when it came up in shreds, she swore. He did not help her. He sought his wardrobe and donned a robe, and while she was still searching in her trunk for something, there came a knock on the door.

She cast him a scathing glance. He smiled. "Get back

into bed. I'll give you the covers. Come in, please, Lymon."

She hurried back into bed. As he had promised, he threw her the covers and she hid herself beneath them. The door opened and Lymon entered. Jamie bid him good morning cheerfully, then asked for milk, coffee, and rolls to be served in the room. "And the hip bath, too, Lymon. With lots of hot water."

Lymon cast a quick glance at the figure beneath the rumpled covers, then promised that it would be done right away. Jamie thanked him. When Lymon was gone, he walked back over to the bed and wrenched the covers from her hold again. "Madame, you are supposed to be found in my bed by morning, you know. You are my wife."

She grabbed for the covers again, coming to her knees, leaping up and seizing the sheets. He watched her movement. He watched the spill of her golden hair over her back, curling to her rump, and he watched the tendrils that fell over her breasts and curled around them. He watched the spark in her eyes, and the angry purse of her lips, and he watched the graceful sway of her hips and the movement of her legs. His eyes wandered to the juncture of her thighs, and he felt his loins tighten and harden.

He wanted her again. He took her and exploded with the force of it, and then he wanted her all over again. He didn't know quite what it was, but he vowed to himself that he would discover it.

"May I have the first bath?" she asked him, tossing back her head of golden curls.

"Certainly. But you cannot wash away this marriage, you know."

"It is not the marriage that I wish to wash away."

"Ah, that's right. Marriage is the manor and the servants and the estate. 'Tis only me you wish to wash away."

"Those are your words."

"Well, think of it. In two weeks I shall be gone."

"Across the ocean," she agreed.

"A perilous trip. Storms plague ships at sea. One never knows when one will meet up with a Spanish pirate."

"I shall pray for you."

He cast back his head and laughed. "I daresay that you shall be praying. But take heed, milady. Unless you bear me an heir, my estates will revert to my father. So perhaps you should pray that I do live for a while."

"Have I no widow's compensation?" she asked him sweetly.

"You do."

"Well, then, that, I imagine, should be sufficient."

He curved his lip into a smile and inclined his head toward her. "Alas, the emotion within you wrings my heart."

"You know I have no feelings for you," she said suddenly, passionately. Her eyes were very wide, somehow frightened, and very blue. "You chose to marry me. Would you have me pretend now?"

"No, love," he said wearily, "we will have no pretense. If nothing else lies between us, let it be honesty."

"You do not care for me!"

"But I do want you. More noble than mere marriage for money, I think."

"I see. Lust is preferable," she said grandly.

"You are an adventuress, Jassy. Perhaps we shall make out very well."

He hesitated, for there was a knock on the door. He raised his voice and said that the caller must enter, and the door opened. Lymon entered with a half score of serving boys. He carried food, while the servants brought the carved wood hip bath and buckets of hot water. The household was very efficient, for while Lymon set out the milk, coffee and rolls, the boys brought more water. They all bowed to Jassy in her nest of covers. She colored and nodded an acknowledgment.

Then they were gone. Jamie poured two cups of coffee and brought her one. She accepted it with a soft "Thank you."

"Breakfast is usually in the dining room," he told her,

"and usually much more substantial. In good weather we eat in the back, on the terrace."

She sipped her coffee, then she set down her cup. Jamie watched her broodingly as she suddenly streaked from the bed and into the tub. She howled at the heat of the water, and, he was certain, had he not been standing there, she'd have jumped back out of the water. She sat, though, winding her hair above her head to keep it dry. She realized then that she hadn't the soap or a cloth.

Jamie brought her both, still sipping his coffee. He dropped the cloth and the soap upon her and moved to the mantel, where he had a wonderful view of her. She lifted a long leg and scrubbed it, and then she remembered that he was there. With a scowl she slipped back into the tub.

"Please, don't let me disturb you."

"You do disturb me."

"Do I?"

He set his cup upon the mantel. Her breasts were level with the height of the water, her nipples even with it. She saw the intent in his eyes as he approached her, and she let out a little sound of protest. He barely heard her. A rush of desire raged in his head, and he heard nothing but the driving wind of it. He knelt by the tub and took the soap and cloth in his hands. He laved her breasts with the suds and the piece of linen. "Don't!" she whispered, leaning back, swallowing. He stretched his hand downward and between her legs, and she cried out, but he ignored her. She brought her hands against him, but then they went limp, and she lay back in the tub. Her lips were slightly parted, her eyes closed. Her head rolled back and forth. "Don't . . . please, don't."

He lifted her out of the tub. He laid her down upon the sheets, and when she tried to twist away, they both saw the stains on the sheets where her virginity had been lost. She twisted again and met his eyes. "No . . ."

He unbelted his robe and let it fall to the floor. She closed her eyes again and started to roll away. He straddled her, stopping her, whirling her around to face him.

"I just washed *you* away!" she cried.

He arched a brow. "No, madame. You washed for my pleasure and convenience."

"*Oh!*" She tried to sit. He caught her shoulders and led her back. Her eyes were wild and somewhat panicked as she stared at him then. "Lie still!" he commanded her impatiently. "It should not be loathsome, and you should not feel pain. You should lie there, seeking me, as I seek you."

"No!"

"But you will in time, I swear it."

"You are an insolent pest!"

"Lie still, madame. I will prove it." He took his hands off her. She bit into her lip and tried to squirm from beneath him. "Uh-uh, milady. Still. Unless, of course, you wish to scream and weep and writhe with passion."

She swore again. He laughed, caught her wrists, and pressed her back to the bed. "I will kiss you whenever and wherever I choose, Jasmine," he whispered, and then he set out to prove it.

She did not protest, twist, or fight. Her lips parted easily beneath his, and he kissed her deeply, feeling the rise of passion, of haunting, desperate desire. At last he raised his lips from hers. They remained parted, moist, and her breath came from her in little gasps. Her eyes, glazed and wide, met his. He smiled. Thunder and lightning raged through him, demanding he take her there and then, but he did not. He met her gaze, and his smile was wicked. He held her eyes while touching and playing with her breasts, and moved his hands ever lower and more intimately upon her. She tried to close her eyes. "Look at me!" he told her, and for a moment she did. But then he moved from her and parted her thighs. She closed her eyes again. "No!" she protested in a weak whisper. "No, no . . ."

He caught her foot, kissed the sole of it, and ran his tongue over her toes. He parted her thighs wider. When she tried to bring them back together, he spread them with his shoulders, allowing her no retreat. He stroked her thighs, and then he gave deliberate and piercing attention to the golden triangle of her sex. He took his leisure, touching, exploring, savoring the honey taste of woman and soap, and leaving her drenched. And still she gave nothing to him. She remained as still as he had commanded her to be.

He crawled over her. Her eyes were open and glazed over, and her fingers were knotted into the sheets. She tried too hard to deny him! He swore in silence and caught her knees, then brought them high over his shoulders. He swept into her with a single stroke, and she encapsulated him easily with the sleek, sweet feel of honey. He placed his hands on her shoulders and thrust farther, and she tossed her head to the side. He drove harder into her. She cried out once, and then she was silent. He gritted his teeth, and the storm of his passion swept over him. The explosion of it was violent, and he fell against her, gasping for breath. She curled quickly away from him.

Furious, he caught her shoulder and swirled her back around. "Why? Why, damn you, must you fight me?"

"I did not fight you!" she cried.

"Nay, lady," he said scornfully, "you did not claw or beat me, or try to run, but you fight what you feel yourself. You do not give yourself to me; you deny me every step of the way."

She was trembling. She wanted to escape him. He was so achingly familiar with the beautiful naked length of her now that he could not bear it. He held her hard and fast. "Why?"

"Because I feel nothing!"

"You are a liar!"

"You take what you want; that is all there is!"

He let out a furious oath and moved away from her, stepped into the now-cold bath, and loved it. He washed with a vengeance, aware that she lay immobile on the bed, afraid to move. When he finished, he grabbed a towel and dried himself harshly.

He ignored her while he dressed. His tastes were simple that day, dark breeches and a white shirt and a leather jerkin and his high black riding boots. While he tugged them on, he spoke to her coldly, not glancing her way.

"I am sorry to leave you so, my dear, on the first day of our wedded bliss, but I'm certain that you'll find it in your heart to forgive me. I have to see a man about the supplies for the ship."

He stood. She was on the bed, in a cocoon of covers. She was, he thought, a whore who had married him with no pretense for his money. Well, it was a bargain well met. A bargain crafted in hell. He had married her for her youth and her health and her strength.

And her beauty. Even now, even in his raw anger, he saw that beauty. Her golden hair was completely tangled, and a tempest about her. She was swathed in the covers, but her shoulders were sloping and bare, and the rise of the sheets barely covered the full slopes of her breasts. She looked very young then, and lost and alone and vulnerable. He almost wanted to offer her some assurance.

Vulnerable! he thought with a snort. She was as vulnerable as one of the sharp-toothed barracuda that lurked in the warm southern waters off the American coast. She was hard, as hard as stone. She didn't even play at gratitude.

He did come by her, and run his fingers over the top of her hair. "Take heart, madame. Two weeks is not such a terribly long time. Then you shall not see me for a minimum of four months." He walked on by her, heading for the door.

"Four months!" she said in surprise. "But I thought it took three months to cross the ocean? And three months to come back again. And surely you intend to spend time there—"

"More time than I had thought at first," he told her. He watched her, curious to her reaction. "Much more time. That is why I have decided that you must sail, too, as soon as possible."

"What?" She gasped. She must have been truly stunned, taken completely by surprise, for she forgot her nudity and leapt from the bed, running after him. She seemed small as she grabbed his hand. But then, he was booted and clad, and she was like a golden Eve, naked, with her hair tumbling down about her.

He smiled wickedly; he could not help himself. "Aye, lady. My pinnace, *Sweet Eden*, will leave the London dock on the twentieth of July. You will be upon it with whatever supplies and servants you shall require. My love, you will follow me to the New World."

"No!" She cried with horror.

He tapped her chin closed for her. "Yes, my love."

She shook her head violently. "No! I will not leave England! I will not come to that savage land full of Indians and insects! You have said yourself that it is dangerous. That Spanish pirates roam the seas! That there may be tempests at sea—"

"You will come, madame. And you will come when I command, for you are my wife."

"No—"

"And you will come when I command, milady, because if you don't, then I shall come back for you. And if you force me to do such a thing, then I swear, heaven will need to help you, for you cannot imagine what violent paths my wrath may take, and what tempest it is that you should truly fear."

His smile deepened; he shook himself free of her touch and exited the room, slamming the door sharply behind him.

IX

Ten days later, at her first chance to entertain in grand style, Jassy still turned pale at the very mention of the word *Virginia.*

Robert and Lenore and Henry and Jane and the Duke of Carlyle and, of course, Elizabeth came for their first visit. Jassy should have found it her greatest triumph, for she, an illegitimate child of the streets, had come to reign in grandeur on an estate far grander than her brother's. She was dressed in the finest fabric, in the newest style, and she entertained with the Venetian crystal, the Dutch plates, and the English sterling flatware, in the room where the walls were covered in silk. She had everything that she had coveted within her hands.

And the man she had married was telling her that she should leave it all behind and follow him to the savage wilds of a new country inhabited by wild men.

The day had not been without its triumphs. Her father-in-law the duke had greeted her with warmth and pleasure, telling her that she graced his son's fine house. Jane had laughed; Henry had muttered that there was, after all, much of their father within her. Elizabeth had whisked her into a corner where she had giggled delightedly. "Oh, Jassy! Remember the day when we came here and it was all pretense? And now it is real. Oh, truly, you are the grand lady!"

Not for long, she thought, but she refrained from speaking, for if this was to be her one shining moment, she wanted to cling to it. "Come, Elizabeth. What will you have? some wine?"

"Oh, yes, please! Wine will be grand."

Conversation was casual as they gathered in the blue room, much of it regarding Lenore's coming nuptials. Jassy often felt Robert Maxwell looking her way. Once she caught him doing so, and he raised his glass to her. She flushed and quickly looked away, but then, when he found her alone for a moment, she felt a bitter pleasure in his company. He caught her hands and kissed them both, and his admiration was unmistakable. "I have never seen you so beautiful. Marriage becomes you. Or *something* becomes you. You are radiant. I should have swept you away when I had the chance."

Yes! she wanted to cry. You should have done so!

She remained silent, but she felt her heart pound. A new excitement filled her, and the day was fun once again. She could forget that she had married a dark, demanding man who gave no quarter, ever, and even now watched her from his stance at the mantel. He rested an elbow upon the mantel, but lifted his brandy snifter to her sarcastically as he caught her eye. Her smile and enthusiasm faded, and she quickly turned away. Still, she felt his eyes upon her.

Their days of newlywed "bliss" had been fraught with tension. Most of the day Jamie was gone, and at night Jassy went up to the room alone. She dressed in the plainest gowns, and feigned sleep the moment she heard his footsteps near their door. And every night he laughed at her attempts to avoid him, and it mattered little what she had chosen to wear, for she did not wear it for long.

She did not fight him, ever. She willed herself to lie still, and she realized that it was herself she had come to fight. He was not cruel to her, nor was he brutal, though she knew that he would have brooked no resistance from her. Every night and each time he touched her, she grew more sensitive to him. Sometimes she ached for his hand before it came to her flesh, and she despised herself for the weakness. She bit into her lip when she would cry out at some sudden sensation, and she forced herself to remain still and impassive. She knew that he watched her, and she knew that he was vastly disappointed in her. She had to resist him. There was so little that was hers, and hers alone, to give.

So it had been . . . she thought pensively, until the last two nights had passed them by. On the first she had pretended sleep, and he had allowed her the deception, lying on his side of the bed, staring up at the canopy. To her surprise, she had lain awake very late, stunned that he had not touched her.

Then last night he had said wearily that she should snuff out the candles when she crawled into bed. And again he had ignored her, and again she had lain awake a long, long time.

To add fuel to the fires of discord, Jamie's mind was on his coming voyage. Jassy was determined not to join him, and she argued with him at every opportunity. And at every opportunity he argued back, and informed her that she would do as she was told. If she wasn't careful, he would demand that she come with him on the *Hawk* when he left on the fifteenth.

"Truly, Jassy, you look marvelous today. The lady born and bred. More noble than any of us!" Robert said, laughing ruefully and drawing her from her introspection.

"Thank you, Robert," she said.

"And you, Jamie. How do you find marriage, now that you have succumbed to the state at long last?"

Jassy felt Jamie's eyes upon her. "I find it deeply rewarding," he said. "Infinitely . . . rewarding. And intriguing."

They were spared further conversation on the subject, for Lymon came to the door, announcing that Captain Hornby was there.

"He begs not to disturb a private party," Lymon said, addressing Jamie.

Jassy was somewhat startled when Jamie deferred to her. "My love, what an unexpected guest, a man of esteemed character." He watched her still, and she wondered if he tested her. She wondered if he ever spoke with Robert and told him what a disappointment he really considered her to be. She did not believe so, but neither could she be grateful for the fact that if his marriage was less than he hoped, he gave no hint of such a thing in public. He was a proud man and would never admit to defeat.

"Good old Hornby?" Robert said. "Is he really here?"

"You must invite him in, Lymon," Jassy said. Lymon bowed to her and left them.

"A wonderful old soul," Robert said cheerfully to Jassy.

"Robert, really! What a way to refer to the poor man!" Lenore protested, but she smiled, taking the sting from her words. Maybe she really was in love with him, Jassy thought. She had grown far more gentle as of late.

"Well, love, he is old. He was old when Jamie first sailed with him in '08. He must be ancient now."

"And the finest mariner I have ever met," Jamie said. Then Lymon was back with the man in question.

He *was* old, Jassy thought. His hair was snow white, as were the whiskers at his chin, and his face was heavily lined. He had bright green eyes, though, and he walked with the agility of a man half his age.

Captain Hornby apologized for the interruption, and assured Jamie that they could speak later. Jassy insisted he sit and have a drink, and he chose whiskey. She was glad that Lymon served the drink, for with Jamie's next words, her fingers trembled in sudden spasms.

"Captain Hornby sails the *Sweet Eden,* my love. He will bring you to me in the Virginia colony."

"Oh!" Lenore cried suddenly, looking at Jamie. "So Jassy is to come?"

"Aye, Jassy is to come."

Lenore turned to her. "Oh, I'm ever so glad."

"Why?" Jassy asked.

"Oh, well, you see, Robert has determined that we

must sail too. He wishes to take his chances with Jamie, and seek his fortune in Virginia."

Jassy shook her head, forgetting her husband. "But, Robert, you are a fool! The land is full of warring heathens—"

"Oh, lady, nay, not so much as before!" the good captain said, interrupting her.

"No, it is not so bad as it once was," the Duke of Carlyle told her, gazing affectionately at his son. He took Jassy's hand in his own. "There were bad times, of course. When Captain Smith and the others arrived in 1607, the Indians were hostile. Some of the party believed that Powhatan's people might have been responsible for the annihilation of the Roanoke colony at the end of last century. There have been reports of curiously light boys among their number, so perhaps the survivors were taken in by the confederation tribes."

"The Indians had some good reason for hostility," Jamie said from his stance at the mantel. "They had seen French and Spanish and English ships in the Chesapeake by the time the Jamestown settlers arrived. In 1524 Giovanni da Verrazano, Gomez the year after, and in 1560, Pedro Menendez de Aviles, who captured and enslaved the son of a werowance."

"A heathen spiritual leader," Captain Hornby informed Jassy.

"They all came with their guns blazing ceremonially, and few came in peace."

"Ah, Lord Cameron!" Captain Hornby said. "You should know that the heathens are not so peaceful themselves!" He looked at Jassy. "He knows, milady, your husband does! On his first voyage he went with Captain John Smith up the peninsula to find Powhatan. It was the starving time, and the men were desperate to secure food. Powhatan tricked Captain Smith. Pocahontas warned them of the trick, and they survived. And the heathens are savage to their captives. Why, they mutilate their prisoners. They dismember them and throw the body parts into the fire to burn while they still live and breathe, and then they disembowel them."

"Captain Hornby!" Jamie said sharply.

"I believe I'm going to faint!" Lenore gasped.

"Elizabeth *has* fainted!" Jassy cried. She was quickly on her feet, and she managed to catch her sister before she could fall. Then Jamie was beside her, lifting Elizabeth, carrying her to the massive chair before the fire. Her eyes flickered and opened. Someone had brought water for her. She looked about.

"Oh, I am sorry! So very sorry."

"Nay, milady!" Captain Hornby apologized. "It is I who am sorry. I am not accustomed to the company of ladies. Forgive me."

"You are forgiven, and gladly," Elizabeth said. She looked up at Jassy and smiled wanly. "Well, don't you see? If you go, and Lenore goes, then I must go too."

"Don't be mad!" Jassy said harshly. "You have a beautiful home here. You needn't risk any of it. You won't be alone. Jane and Henry will be here. And—and we will be back as soon as possible."

No one said anything. Jassy realized that the silence was for her sake. Jamie was demanding that she come, because he knew that he would be gone for a very long time.

"I want to come with you," Elizabeth said, and she squeezed Jassy's hand.

"You are a wonderful, brave girl," Jamie told her, "and we will be delighted to have you."

Elizabeth smiled radiantly.

Jassy glanced quickly at her husband. She had always struggled too desperately through life to pay much heed to the news of distant lands, but men in the tavern had often spoken of the Jamestown colony. She had heard of the "starving time." Over nine hundred settlers had traveled to Jamestown by that time. After Indian raids, disease, and starvation, only sixty or so had survived. She couldn't imagine that a man of Jamie Cameron's means could have risked his life on such a foolish quest.

She still hated him for even contemplating such a thing now.

"Other than the Indians, it was still a bad time, the

starving time," Captain Hornby said. "Why, white men, good English men, feasted upon the dead of their own kind."

"Captain!" Robert warned, "the ladies!"

"If the ladies are to travel to Virginia, perhaps they had best hear it all," Jane said softly. "Are you all right now, Elizabeth?"

"Oh, yes, I—I am fine."

"They ate Indians that year too," Captain Hornby said cheerfully. "One fellow went mad and murdered his wife. Then he salted and ate her."

"Captain, enough!" Jamie warned.

"And we call the Indians the savages," Henry commented with disgust. "I am glad that you are the lot that has chosen to go." He affectionately touched his wife's protruding belly. "My son will be born on this land, as a good Englishman should be born."

"A good Englishman? Henry, we've all heard of an instrument called the Earl of Exeter's daughter, a good English torture device named for the charming man who invented it." Jamie smiled at Jassy. "The rack, my love. The good, civilized, English rack. We disjoint and cripple and maim more slowly than the savages, perhaps."

"Powhatan was a crafty old warrior," Captain Hornby warned.

"Powhatan is dead."

"That is true, and when his brothers, Opitchapan and Opechancanough, shared the rule of the Powhatan Confederation, it seemed that peace might be assured. But I am not so sure. Now Opechancanough rules alone. He is a crafty one, I'll wager. Much like his brother."

"Thank God I'm not having my child there!" Jane said, and shuddered.

Jassy's stomach churned. She couldn't imagine bearing a child in the wretched wilderness in which her husband was determined she would live. The child would die, she would die, they would all die.

"It sounds like a horrible place," Jassy said aloud.

"Oh, no, milady, that it is not!" Captain Hornby protested. "I'll grant you, milady, that there was confusion at the first. A profusion of leaders. There was Edward Wingfield, who was unpopular for his Catholicism, Captain Newport, and John Smith himself. Lord de la Warr made it just in time to save the colony when the survivors were leaving in '09. He was a harsh man, but he saved the colony, he did. There have been a number of charters." He hesitated, looking at Jamie. "The Company did not always make the right decisions, and the king did not always judge the situation well, being here while the colony was there. With the lottery disbanded, one of the principal means of income has been lost, but now the tobacco crop flourishes, and the colony is making money of its own. Not that any of it will matter to you, milady," he told Jassy. "The hundred is not Jamestown."

Jassy stared reproachfully at Jamie.

He shrugged. "The hundred is my own land, and we are not subject to the rule of Jamestown. We will abide by the laws of England there. At the Carlyle Hundred we will be self-sustaining. We've already many families living there. Five carpenters, three gentlemen of means, fifteen farmers, ten laborers, two bricklayers, two tailors, two blacksmiths, and three masons, and all their diverse servants and so on. I interviewed them all myself before they sailed, and I am certain that we shall prosper."

Why did he care? She wanted to scream it, to demand it. She wanted to cry and rail that he was a fool, but she could not do so, not here, not now. She had company, and her company, all but Elizabeth, still watched her for some flaw in the porcelain mask of her manner. She would not let them find a flaw. She stood. "I'm sure that our dinner is served. Shall we adjourn to the dining hall?"

With murmurs they all rose and left the room for the hall. Jassy realized that Jamie hung behind, that he watched her until the room had emptied. She paused. "Well, have I passed inspection? Do I manage well enough?"

"You manage well enough. You know it."

"Not that it will matter. An actress's bastard child can

surely greet a heathen tribe of Indians as well as a grand lady."

"I'm sure that you will do well, my pet, whichever and whomever you choose to be." Calmly he strode by her. She hesitated, breathing hard, hating him.

He waited for her before the doors to the dining room. He took her hand. "You do sparkle today."

"Do I?"

"Is it because Robert Maxwell is here?"

"You must think what you will, milord."

"And you may think what you will, but I have determined that I will find the woman with the sparkling eyes tonight. When the company has gone, when we are alone."

"She is the same woman you're standing beside."

"She is not. But so help me, lady, I will meet her, in my bed, this very night."

"This is a crude conversation. We've guests."

"I will crush those airs, lady, mind you." He did not lead her into the dining room but propelled her there with a hard shove upon the back. No one noticed them, though, for Lenore was busy chuckling, demanding to know what clothing was worn in the wilds.

"Oh, it's all very civilized," Captain Hornby assured her. "Men wear what is proper, as prescribed by Parliament in the days of good Queen Bess. For laborers, homespun linen or canvas jerkins, breeches, and hose. On Sundays they wear their best, with their flat caps, while the gentry, and nobility, milady, deck themselves out in their finest, in their taffetas and satins, decorated with embroidery and slashes and pinking. You needn't fear. None has forgotten that it is a God-fearing, English community! There are some concessions, of course, to the wilderness. But I believe you will be heartily pleased with the goodness of the colonial manners and ways."

"Well, that is encouraging, isn't it, Jassy?" Lenore said. Jassy offered her a halfhearted smile and wondered how Lenore could be so cheerful about the prospects of their lives. Lenore had never known anything but comfort. She knew very little about the lives of the common man in England, much less across the distance of an ocean. She didn't know that people starved. She didn't know that there were game laws, that men could be hanged for stealing a loaf of bread because they starved. She had no true conception of dirt, let alone a life of hardship and travail. No matter what Captain Hornby said, Jassy was certain that Virginia must be a grim place indeed.

Jassy took her place at the head of the table, her husband seating her. And when the lord himself was seated, the meal was served: soft, flaky founder; baby eels; roasted pheasants; new potatoes; and fresh summer vegetables. It was a wonderful and elegant feast.

Tears pricked her eyes. There was so very much! The cost of this meal alone might have saved her mother's life. It could have spared her two months of scrubbing floors.

She realized that Josh, one of the kitchen lads, all decked out in Cameron livery, was standing beside her with the steaming platter of fish. She smiled, took a helping, and thanked him softly. She could not eat the fish. She looked down the table, her beautiful table, with its chandeliers and cloth and crystal and silver. The Duke of Carlyle was engaged in heavy conversation with Captain Hornby. Elizabeth laughed at something Henry said, and Jane, smiling bemusedly, paid them both heed. Robert whispered to Lenore, and Lenore smiled radiantly.

She felt Jamie's eyes upon her long before she met his gaze. He had noted the way that she watched Lenore and Robert.

He lifted his glass to her. She lowered her eyes.

Later that afternoon they danced. The grand hallway was cleared, and musicians sat up in the minstrel's gallery and played. Even Jane, so very pregnant, joined in the fun, for though she had protested that it was entirely improper, Jamie insisted that they were all related by blood or marriage, except for Captain Hornby, of course, and the good captain promised not to notice. The Duke of Carlyle brought his daughter out on the floor. Henry danced with his sister, Lenore. Elizabeth turned to Jamie, and he escorted her to the floor, leaving Jassy alone for Robert. And while they whirled around the floor, Robert, who knew her misgivings, made her laugh about the trials and tribulations of a long sea voyage. He told her cheerfully that they would chew upon plenty of lemon peel and thus avoid scurvy. "And we shall hang a ring of sachets about our necks, and thus avoid the odor of those who have not chewed upon their lemon peel!"

He spun her about, and she was laughing again, but her laughter faded and the light fled her eyes, for he spun her into her husband's arms, and the dark brooding she discovered in Jamie's eyes was grim, foreboding worse to come.

"May I take my wife, Robert?"

"Aye, but of course!"

And so she was swept away into rigid arms of steel, and his eyes pierced into her. "Where is it, milady? Where is the laughter? Where is the smile that animates, the glow that comes to you so seldom?"

"I don't know what you mean," she said sullenly.

"You know exactly what I mean."

"We are being rude. Captain Hornby is standing alone."

"Don't play the grande dame with me. I want to know. Where is the girl with the laughter, with the sparkling eyes?"

"She does not exist for you!" Jassy snapped, and thankfully the Duke of Carlyle chose that moment to claim her, and Jamie cordially acquiesced to his father.

But he watched her still.

Jassy avoided her husband for the rest of the afternoon, but when night fell, their company left them. Thankfully Captain Hornby was the last to leave. He required a few moments business with Lord Cameron, and Jassy was given a certain respite. She was certain that he had not forgotten his irritating determination to plague her.

She stood in the hallway while the men entered Jamie's study to the left of the hall, behind the dining room. She could hear their voices droning on and on, as Jamie gave the captain requisitions for supplies. Four more cannon, twenty-five muskets, a thousand feet of match, barrels of black powder, ramrods, balls, twenty-five suits of half-armor, breast- and backplates, and helmets. Captain Hornby should also bring five more ewes, five good Hereford cows, twenty chickens, and a rooster.

"The weapons are necessary," Captain Hornby said. "But bear in mind, the muskets will stand you well in hunting, milord, but they are not much good against the Pamunkee. You will need swords and knives. Not even pikes are much good against a Pamunkee lying in wait in the grass."

"Yes, you're right," Jamie said. There was a rustling sound; she heard the clink of glass and she knew that the men were pouring drinks.

"You know them better than most men," Captain Hornby said.

"Yes, I know them, and we should be at peace. Powhatan's brothers are not as powerful as he was; the confederacy has loosened. Many of the Indians are interested in trade with the white men. And still . . ."

"Still?"

"They can be a savage lot. I traveled with Captain Smith often when I was a lad, when Father decided that a third son must see the world and seek his place. I have been to their camps. I have seen them prepare for their torture rites. They are renowned cooks among the Indians. The women prepare great feasts. They cover themselves with tattoos, and they eagerly await their entertainment. When a man is not dismembered and disemboweled, he is beaten to death. So was the case, Smith told me, when Pocahontas saved his life. She was just a child, but the great Powhatan's favorite, though the lord alone knows how many children he sired, for he had many, many wives. The girl laid her head over Smith's so that none would beat him."

"But you seem to like them, Lord Cameron."

"Call me Jamie, we are alone. I like the Indians, yes.

They have a sense of honor, and many of them are peaceful. I simply never forget that our cultures differ. That they worship first Okeus, a dark demon, and that they sacrifice their own children to this god."

"Well, the Carlyle Hundred will be well prepared to meet with any threat," Hornby promised. "Now tell me, Jamie, is there anything else you would have brought aboard the *Sweet Eden*?"

Jamie seemed to hesitate. "Aye, Captain. Buy me a fine bed, with a good down mattress, in London."

"And shall I see to the silks and draperies for it?"

"In the colony?" Jamie said, and laughed. Then he hesitated again. "Aye. See to it. Women like that sort of thing, don't they?"

"Her ladyship will surely appreciate it, aye."

"Will she?" Jamie mused, and Jassy sensed the bitterness in his words.

"You married wisely, milord. She is a beautiful lady, and sure to do you proud in the New World. She has the spirit for it."

"So I had thought," Jamie said.

"She does not wish to come?"

"She does not, but she will do so."

"Ah, milord, can you be sure?"

"If she does not willingly step aboard the pinnace, then you will have your orders to see that she comes aboard it trussed in a canvas bag. I care not how you bring her. Perhaps I shall send her back in time." He suddenly sounded weary, very weary. "Perhaps life will prove more palatable without her. Time alone will tell."

Jassy stood in the hallway, her face burning. She had frozen when they spoke of the Indians. She had frozen, and then felt ill. Then they had spoken of her, and the burning glow had slowly come to her cheeks. She still could not move.

The men spoke for a few more minutes, then the captain took his departure. Jasmine, aware then that she had been eavesdropping, shrank against the wall. The captain did not notice her. He walked on out the entrance. Lymon closed the door, bidding the captain good night.

She heard Jamie's glass clink down upon his desk, and she realized that he would soon be up to the bedroom—to join her. To finish what he had begun during the day.

She turned in a sudden panic and fled up the steps. She dared not be in the room, and yet she still clung to the belief that she might one day convince him that she slept, and slept too deeply to disturb, when he arrived.

She had difficulty with the fasteners upon her dress. She kicked off her shoes and thought of calling for Molly, then decided that it would take too much time, and she had so little left. She tried to calm herself and find the hooks, but she could not. She was trembling fiercely. She grasped the bedpost and tried to breathe slowly, but she could not, for all that she could see was a horde of Indians before her, naked and tattooed and leaping before a fire and dismembering some poor captive. . . .

The door opened. She whirled in dismay and stared across the room to it. Jamie was there. He arched a brow to her, and his slow, mocking smile as he looked from her to the bed indicated his surprise that she was not already in it.

"You are still up?"

"My hooks have caught—"

"You should have sent for Molly."

"Yes, perhaps. I shall do so now."

"Never mind." He strode across the room. She tried to turn away from him.

"I can manage."

"No, you cannot. Stand still."

Quickly he unhooked her dress. Then he walked over to his desk and poured himself a snifter of amber liquid, propping his feet up on the desk and watching her. Jassy stared at him awkwardly.

"Please," he told her, "do go on."

"If you were in the least the cavalier, you would exit the room until I—"

"I am not the least bit cavalier, and you are my wife.

If you need more assistance, I am eager and willing to oblige."

She wondered what it was about him that could make her temper flare so quickly. She swore softly and turned her back on him, and still she felt his eyes, and still she felt awkward, and her fingers trembled. At last she drew her fine dress over her shoulders and tossed it carelessly on the floor. She stepped from her petticoat and saw that Molly had laid out one of her nightgowns, but one of Molly's choosing, of course, in peach silk with satin ribands at the sleeves and at the low-cut bodice and hem. She grabbed the gown, aware that there was no other she could find easily, and then tried to hold it as she struggled with the ties of the corset she wore. It was then that Jamie moved. He came behind her and deftly worked the strings, and the garment fell free. She muttered a curt "Thank you," and he returned to his desk and his drink, and she felt his burning gaze again as he continued to watch her. She halfway dropped her shift and slipped into the nightgown, then let the shift fall. She forgot her garters and hose and got into the bed, drawing to her own side of it, her heart pounding in a fury. She was there for several seconds before she heard him rise. His fine doublet and shoes hit the floor, and she tried not to listen; she tried to close her eyes and feign sleep.

She heard nothing more. Cautiously she opened her eyes. He was standing above her, staring down at her, waiting for her to do so. He smiled, and his hand fell upon the valley of her breast, and they both felt the frantic beat of her heart. "Sleeping?" he inquired pleasantly enough. He carried his drink in his hand. He was barefoot and bare-chested, and clad only in his breeches.

She didn't answer him. She didn't like his mood at all that evening. It was cynical, and he had been consuming a great deal of liquor.

He touched her chin. He moved it backward and forward, studying her eyes. "Where is she?" he whispered.

"I think that you are drunk," she said haughtily.

"The brandy? My love, it helps to make life palatable. You must have some."

"I don't want any."

"You are refusing to drink with me?"

If he poured her a brandy, he would go away, she decided. "I will drink with you."

"Good." He walked back to the desk and poured her drink. Warily she kept her eyes upon him. She leapt out of bed then, thinking that it was a dangerous place to be. But her movement might have been more dangerous, she realized too late, for her gown was far more revealing than concealing, and as soon as Jamie turned to her and his eyes moved over her, she saw her mistake.

But he did not touch her. He handed her the snifter. Still, he studied her eyes. She turned away from him and walked to the window seat. The windows were open to the warm summer breeze. It wafted in upon her, touching her hair, lifting it.

She didn't hear or feel him coming up behind her. She cried out, startled, when he touched her. He lifted her from the waist and set her upon the window seat. She clenched her teeth, for his hands moved upon her calf to her thigh, discovering her garter and loosening it and her stocking. He peeled the silk stocking from her leg, the rough pads of his fingers brushing over the soft tender skin of her inner thigh, and she was shocked by the strength of the sensation it evoked. Her eyes met his, and the indigo depths within them burned.

"Where is she?" he murmured tensely. "Can I reach her?"

Frightened, she tensed. He ignored her, his hands slipped up the length of her other leg, and his fingers tarried upon the flesh of her inner thigh again. She bit into her lip and swallowed fiercely, but his eyes were keenly upon her, and his touch did not cease when he reached the height of the garter upon her leg. His fingers moved higher and higher, teasing her. She swallowed down the brandy in a single instant. It burned down her throat and into her belly, and then lower, where the sensation met with his fingers and seemed to explode in aching heat.

"Stop," she whispered, but he paid her no heed.

He studied her eyes. "Where is the spirit, the passion, the life? The fire . . . I saw it today again but only briefly."

"Perhaps you haven't the fuel to ignite it!" she cried out.

He shook his head slowly. "No, no, I do not believe that, and so help me, lady, this evening we will discover it, no matter what it takes."

"No . . ."

He plucked the brandy glass from her hand and pressed her back against the enclosure. His lips met hers, and they were fierce and hungry and demanding. His one hand rounded the curve of her breast while he held the other beneath the silk of her gown, between her thighs, teasing, probing.

His tongue entered her mouth again and again. She wanted to twist away. She could not. The pressure of his naked arms and chest were too much.

Suddenly he pulled her down, and she lay across the window seat. She stared up at him, at the dark, demanding passion in his eyes. She gasped when he tore open the soft peach gown, and she lifted a hand to draw the gaping sides together.

"No," he told her firmly.

"It was one of my favorites," she complained.

"You may buy another." Their eyes met, and she remained silent. He caught her hands and drew them high above her, and he kissed her lips again. He drew his lips and the tip of his tongue down the valley of her breasts, and then he circled each nipple. Then he touched her with that wet fire again, down to her navel and below. The June breeze came in the window and brushed over her naked flesh where the dampness of his lips and tongue remained, and she quivered. The heat of the brandy seemed to touch her everywhere, and the feel of the air upon her was curiously fascinating . . . delicious. His lips traveled to her belly, below her navel. His breath was warm. His dark head moved upward again. His lips seared her, and his tongue laved her flesh. He came to her breasts, and he played with one while he sucked lightly, then passionately, upon the other. She caught her breath, swallowed, and held rigid, and then his mouth wandered upon her again, and his tongue plundered into her navel, and then below. He caught her thighs, spread them apart, then bit lightly upon their inner flesh, rising higher and higher to the tender, intimate flesh at her apex.

And it was then that the fire bit fiercely into her, seeming to explode throughout her. Her body trembled, she gasped, and she thought to stop him while the myriad sensations cascaded down upon her. The feeling was so good and so sweet that it was unbearable. She arched and she twisted, and the steaming, sweet ache and hunger remained with her, and to her astonishment she did not seek to escape him but to avail herself more fully to him. Starlight and the black velvet of the night and the June breeze all played over her, and she burned, sizzled, and craved from the inside out. She was barely aware of the intimacy between them; she desired the wet, encompassing hunger of him, and the rugged feel of his hands upon her body. She cried out, twisted, and yearned. She trembled and arched to him mindlessly.

Sensations exploded and burst inside of her again, and she reached a curious peak of ecstasy and splendor, and she felt her body shudder and convulse and give. In awe, she gasped out, and felt the honeyed liquid inside of her flow like a river, and she was washed again in little spasms of ecstasy and delight.

And then she met his eyes, triumphant, over hers.

"Oh!" she gasped in horror, and she yearned desperately to escape him, to escape his eyes, but she could not, for he wouldn't free her. He caught her lips, and she heard him tugging upon his breeches, and then he stepped away to free himself from the restriction of them. In the starlight he was extraordinary, like an Adonis, bronzed and created of nothing but muscle and sinew and the long, hard staff of his desire. He lifted her high in his arms, she flushed with the embarrassment of her actions, and he was still triumphant with his throaty laughter. "Please . . ." she said to him, and she hadn't the faintest idea of what she meant by it. He laid her down upon the bed and crawled atop her, driving into her as he took her breast deep into his mouth again. She gasped, for it was all with her again so easily, the sweet need, the ache deep inside of her, the desperate, undulating desire to have more and more of him.

And that he was willing to give. He held himself above her, and his face was strained with the harsh fever of desire, dark and striking. She did not look at him long; she could not meet his eyes. Her breath came in quick, desperate pants, and she moved with him rhythmically, accepting his every thrust with fervor, feeling the sensations rise in splendor and beauty, knowing what she reached for, and the cascading climax of it all. She was as wet and sleek as he, and achingly aware. Then she felt the explosion burst upon her again, the glorious, sweet answer to her need. She felt the sudden, shuddering ferocity with which he thrust within her, again and again. He cast his head back, a guttural groan escaped him, and he fell down beside her.

She lay in silence. Even as the breeze cooled her, her face flamed, and she wondered if a lady was supposed to behave so wantonly. She wanted to burrow into the pillows, she wanted to hide herself away somewhere, curl into a little ball in a hole deep in the darkness of the earth.

It wasn't to be. Just seconds passed when she felt his hands upon her again. They were light and idle, his fingers just brushing over her naked flesh.

Then he pounced over her and caught her chin, and she hated the victory and the laughter she saw in his eyes.

"So she does exist!" he said. "The woman of passion, the creature of fire."

"No . . ."

She closed her eyes and tried to deny him. She heard his husky laughter again, and felt his lips upon her throat, and then upon her breast, and she was so sensitive to his lightest touch by then that she cried out and shuddered and instinctively reached out, digging her fingers into his shoulder.

"No more!" she whispered. "Oh, no more!"

His dark eyes swam before her own. "I must have more while I have this woman of fire," he told her, "lest I lose her when I shall seek her again."

And he would have more. Nor could she deny him, or the miraculous new sensations she had discovered. There was little difference in her surrender to him when he made love to her again and again that night. . . .

Except that instinct took over completely, and she was not aware herself that she made love in return, that her fingers moved sensually up and down his back, that she bit into his shoulders and laved each little hurt with the tip of her tongue. . . .

She was not aware of it, but Jamie was, and for the splendor of that evening he gloried in her every abandoned breath and movement. He bitterly rued the fact that he was due to leave her soon.

And so he used the evening well, determined that she would not forget him, nor their marriage, when the time came that he must sail away. The dawn had long broken when he let her sleep at last, and even then he brooded upon her. He stroked the long, golden strands of hair that lay across his pillow like a sunburst, and he followed the elegant lines of her features to the slender and beautiful curves of her body.

Was he a fool, he wondered, to whisk her away, across a treacherous ocean?

She sighed, and smiled in her sleep, and he wondered of whom she dreamt. He had touched her passions. At long last he had reached inside of her, and he had found the deep sensuality he had been certain must lie beneath her sizzling eyes. But he was truly a fool, bewitched and besotted, if he didn't realize that it meant little between them. When morning came, she would despise him anew, and perhaps ever more so, for he had proven himself the victor on this curious battleground.

No . . . he was right. His dream of the hundred had

always been his true passion. He had married her, aye, because he had wanted her, and because he was his own master, and he had chosen to do so. But he had done it, too, because there was about her an innate strength. Her passion was for life. He would not live without her. Happy or not, she would come, and she would be his wife in all things.

Already he missed her. Already he longed for her again. There was so little time left. . . .

He rolled her over. Her sleepy gaze widened to his, and she whispered in protest.

"Nay, Jasmine, no words and no pretense, for I want you, and I will have you!"

She gasped, and the world spun into splendor again. When it was ended that time, he rose, quickly washed and dressed, then exited the room. A new day had dawned.

And she was left alone, small and spent, naked and tangled in the covers of their huge bed, and suddenly aware that she had given in to him. She had submitted, surrendered, and given away all.

She cursed, she cried, and she threw a pillow across the room with a vengeance, and then she lay back and cried violently into her pillow.

X

Jamie had barely left the room when Jassy heard the sound of horses' hooves and the clatter of carriage wheels on the cobblestones below the open window to their room.

Shouts and commotion assured her that someone of import had arrived. Drawing the sheets about her, she rushed to the window, crawled upon the seat, and stared down to the ground.

There was, indeed, a carriage below, drawn by four perfect bays and bearing the crest of King James I. Jassy gasped and shivered slightly, and her eyes widened. She suddenly realized the importance of the man she had married, that a royal messenger would come to him from the king.

A portly man with a set of lush, dark curls stepped down as the footman ran down the velvet-clad ladder. By the time he stood upon solid ground, Jamie himself had appeared below to greet him. The visitor was dressed in green taffeta with red stockings and ribbons upon his doublet, and he wore a richly plumed hat. Jamie was in simple black breeches that morning, and a loose linen shirt, and his high black boots. He stood tall, whipcord-hard and lean beside the stranger. No elegance worn by another could ever diminish the nobility of his bearing, Jassy thought, and she startled herself. She bit into her lip and realized that he was an extraordinary man. From the proud carriage of his head to the sharp intelligence of his eyes, he was striking. There was much about him that was extremely fine. He had the grace of a cat, and its sleek power. He was always vital, even in stillness, even in silence. Like the sun, he radiated heat; like a forest blaze, he swept in an indomitable fury against any opposition. His passions were hungry ones; his demands he saw as law. And yet he was strikingly sensual, and that morning she at last saw the raw magnetism of him as a man, and understood that London might well be filled with women who had coveted her husband's touch. He could stir and elicit the wild winds of the heart with a touch, with a breath, with the pressure of his lips upon naked flesh. . . .

He greeted the newcomer like an old friend, and received a rolled parchment from him. Then, as if he sensed some scrutiny, he looked up and saw her there, her hair tumbled all about her face, her fingers clutching the covers to her throat. He stared at her long and hard, with a curious cast to his eyes. Then he smiled slowly, and it was a smile that acknowledged not his own demanding sexuality, but hers. It was his smile of triumph, and it was a sensual invitation all its own. Then his smile faded as he heard something that the portly man said. He paid Jassy no more heed, but a dark, annoyed frown fell over his features, and he was hard and unapproachable.

Jassy gritted her teeth, flushed, and drew back inside. She found the pitcher and bowl and hurriedly washed. She quickly dug into her chest for a clean linen shift, slipped it over her head, and found her petticoats upon the floor, where she had discarded them the night before. She paused, picking up her gown, running her hands over the silk. She pressed it to her face. She was seldom so careless with things of value. She had traded the value of her life for the value of a fine bed and a strong roof, and silk against her flesh.

Her fingers started to shake, color rushed to her face,

and she felt nearly faint and very warm. The previous night had been no part of a contract, no deception. Thoughts of it still made her long to bury her face from the world, and yet they made her feel as if her bones melted inside of her, and she wondered now if the shattering ecstasy could have been real. She was shamed to realize that deep inside herself she yearned to discover it all anew.

No! She would not think about it; she could not admit to the exquisite pleasure, nor allow herself such abandonment again. She was certain that a true lady would not do so, and that when he'd looked up at her from the cobblestones below, with her hair awry and tumbling down, he'd determined that he had indeed married a whore.

She bit her lip and straightened, realizing that Molly would come and cheerfully straighten the room. She was the lady of the manor, and as such, she must hurry down and greet the royal messenger. But standing there in her petticoats and shift, she was startled when the door to their room burst inward. With her eyes very wide, she watched Jamie as he purposefully strode back into the room, a fierce scowl tightening his features.

"What—what has happened?" she said.

He cast her an irritated glare, striding toward his desk and jerking open the drawer. "God rot his Royal Majesty!" he swore in what was surely a treasonous statement.

"What—"

"The King is inconstant. The man was four hundred thousand pounds in debt when he inherited the crown from Elizabeth; five years later he is seven hundred thousand pounds in debt! He and Anne provide masque after masque for their own entertainment, when what income he has could so better be used to support his colony. One day he supports his bishops and swears that he will prosper in the New World, that he will see the Virginia colony grow and expand and fight the Catholic cloak of the Spaniards. Then he is apologizing for his colonists to the Spaniards, eager for the alliances of his children to the nobles of Europe. He is inconstant, I tell you, and seldom knows his own mind. He creates havoc by mere whim."

"I thought that he was your friend."

"He is the king, madame, and as such, I serve him. Yet he is part of the very reason I hunger for the new land, for though it is the king's dominion, it is far away, and a man is judged far more for his measure than he is for his title."

"But what is wrong?"

He cast her a sharp gaze. "You will be delighted, madame, I am sure. I have been summoned by the king to receive and deliver some of his correspondence to the Jamestown colony. I leave earlier than expected. I leave now."

He found what documents he sought and slammed the drawer shut. He strode across the room to the door. "Lymon!" he called.

Jassy, standing there in her shift and petticoat, gasped in protest. "Don't you dare call Lymon, and don't think to vent your wretched temper upon me. I'm not decently clad, and I tell you, I will not have it—"

"You!" he seemed to growl, coming to her quickly and setting his finger upon her chin to lift it. "You, my grand lady, will not tell me anything. You will sit still and await my convenience." He lifted her up by the waist and cast her in a flurry of her petticoats upon the bed. Tears stung her eyes, and she swore at him, and she wondered how, after the previous night, he could still be so carelessly rude to her. By then Lymon had reached the room, and she backed against the headboard, pulling the covers to her. She sat in brooding silence as Lymon assisted Jamie with the final touches to his packing, for he had been nearly prepared for the voyage. More servants arrived to carry down the heavy trunks, and when they were gone, Jamie at last turned to her. He leaned upon his desk and crossed one booted foot over the other, and his arms across his chest. "I had thought to have more time to express the vehemence of my determination. Lymon will see to it that a coach is prepared to bring you to London with your immediate household in time for the *Sweet Eden* to sail. You are free to bring your horse, Mary, if you desire, for you will definitely need a mount in Virginia, and as you seem attached to the creature, you may bring her. I know that you are still totally against the voyage, but I stress to you, my love, should you not arrive upon the *Sweet Eden*, you had best pray that your remains rest at the bottom of the sea, for I swear it will be a better end than what I shall have in mind."

She did not know if it was his words, or the insolent way in which he said them, but her temper seemed to burst and shatter, and she'd have gladly torn every last hair from his dark, arrogant head. She leapt from the bed in a blur of motion and flurry and catapulted herself against him, her fists flying, her words incomprehensible, her nails bared. She came in such distraught passion that he was unprepared, and her palm and nails caught his chin and drew blood. She was scarcely aware of it, though, or of the leashed rage that grimly tautened his flesh over his features. He caught her hands and dragged them behind her back, and she swore on in a vengeance, suddenly very lost and confused, and hating him fiercely. "How dare you, how dare you speak to me this way, how dare you continue to abraid and abuse me—"

"Abuse you, madame? You know nothing of the word! Alas, perhaps I do abuse you! I drag you away from the china and the crystal, and the elegance of the manor. And you do covet fine things, do you not, milady?" He pressed her ever backward as he spoke. She stared up into the smoldering blue fire in his eyes, and the battle was still with her.

"Yes! Yes!" she cried. "You thought that if you married a tavern wench, she would not care that you brought her to a barbaric mud pit! Well, you are a fool, for I shall hate it with every breath in my body, just as I hate you—"

"Despise it, Jasmine, but find yourself there. And you may despise me, madame, but so help me, you will not forget me, or that I command your life, ever."

"No? I have forgotten you already!" she swore violently.

He had reached the foot of the bed, and she was startled when he suddenly cast her free, shoving her upon it. He loomed over her, and she had been a fool not to realize the tempest of anger, or that the blaze in his eyes had come from anger to something more. Stunned and dazed, she struggled up to her elbows.

"Lady, we shall see that you do not forget me!"

"No!"

She struggled fiercely, slamming him hard in the chin with her elbow. He grunted in acknowledgment of the pain, and it was then that she saw the blood she had drawn upon him. She cried out, in a fury to avoid him, to twist away from him. His mouth ground down hard upon hers, and his body pinned her to the bed. There was nothing tender about his kiss, it was brutal and punishing, and still, it was searing in its heady passion. She felt a warm rush about her, the male scent of him, the unyielding strength of his arm. The pressure of his knee increased. She freed her lips from his, breathing in ragged gasps. He caught tendrils of her hair, golden in the sunlight, and wound his fingers into them, then found her lips again. She twisted from him, tears stinging her eyes. "No, you will not! You cannot order me about and have me at your whim. You will not—"

"But I will, madame," he said grimly, "and when I am done, you will never dare jest that you have forgotten me, not for a single moment."

"Bastard!"

"Nay, I married the bastard, you will recall. The scheming, grasping little wench who yearned for my money. How ironic! But, madame, think of it! None in the New World will know you as anything but a very grand lady, indeed. You may reign over the savages supreme!"

"Get off me!" Jassy raged. "I have paid for this bargain, and dearly. I hate you, and I hate you—I hate you atop me, and—"

"Do you? Last night I was convinced otherwise."

"You, sir, are the one who called me a magnificent actress! Get off me!"

"Never, madame, for you will give me my due—"

"I owe you nothing—"

"At my leisure, my dear wife. The bastard, the actress, the whore—you have come to perform very well. Let's see if we can draw such a performance again!"

"No!" She clawed at him anew, but he was in command, and she was pushed back, back—into the softness of the down mattress. It was quick, it was violent, and it was shattering. He secured her wrists as she swore and struggled, pushed up her petticoats and the linen of her shifts, and fumbled with the draw of his breeches. She didn't think that she had ever despised him so fiercely. . . .

And yet when he took her, the fire had never been so brightly lit within her. Her struggles ceased, her hands were free, and she was sinking endlessly into the soft clouds of the bed. She cried out at the fierce impact of his thrust, and she shuddered. He paused, and then his lips lowered and took hers, and his tongue came warm into her body, as did his sex. She came alive, wild and desperate, and dug her fingers into his shoulders. She wanted him, more than she had ever learned to want him the night before. She arched for the feel of his hand upon her breast through the linen of her shift, and her hips shifted and moved and undulated in a fever. So much came so quickly. The soaring rise of sweet need, the thunderous beat of his deep strokes. She wound her limbs around him and held tight, straining against his body. His dark eyes loomed above her, and with a sob she pulled his face to hers, and her lips, curiously wet with the salt of tears, demanded something of his. He kissed her deeply, raggedly, and then tore from her, an anguished, shuddering groan escaping him. Fulfillment raged through her, cascading like a warm blanket of liquid sunshine, seeping through her limbs and into her womb. Little tremors seized her again and again, and then she fell down to earth once again, down to the tangle of sheets and linen and petticoats, and the man who still lay heavy upon her.

Wordlessly he pushed himself from her and rose. He straightened his breeches. She lay still, dead still, spent and dazed.

Jamie stared at her for one minute. She did not meet his eyes but stared at the canopy above her. He swore softly, vehemently, then turned from her. She heard him sweep up his hat and his doublet from his desk, and then his long strides bore him swiftly across the room. The door slammed in his wake.

She lay there a long, long time. She heard the coach departing below, and she heard the grooms and the milkmaids and the servants as they set about the business of the day.

She realized that she lay in dishevelment and shame, her shift and petticoats pushed up high to her waits, the sheets beneath her twisted and dislodged. Her limbs were so sore, she scarcely could move them. She drew them together, and she rolled over, and despite the June day, she began to shiver. He was gone, she thought dully. He was gone, and it would be many months before she saw him again.

She could run away, she thought, but she did not want to. She liked being Lady Cameron; she *needed* to be Lady Cameron.

No matter what it entailed.

She would not be on the ship, the *Sweet Eden*, she decided. He could rage and protest and swear and thunder all he liked, but he would be three months away on another continent. She would not go; that was all there was to it. She would not go.

She shivered, remembering his conversation with Hornby. She would be dragged aboard the ship if she did not walk upon it. Not if they couldn't find her, not if she disappeared . . .

She lay there miserably with her arms curled about her chest, cold, her teeth chattering, despite the June sunlight streaming in. As time passed, she realized that she would be on the ship. Even across the vast distance of time and an ocean, she hadn't quite the nerve to defy him. He would hunt her down, she was certain, and he would find her.

Three days later, Robert and Lenore were duly married. Jassy sat in misery through the ceremony, then smiled brightly for them both.

That night she lay awake a long, long time, tossing and turning. As dawn came, she realized with horror that she missed her husband beside her. She missed the startling rapture he had taught her to feel. She missed the strength of his arms.

The next morning, she was summoned to her brother's house. Jane was in labor. After fourteen hours, a beautiful little girl was born. Jassy came home exhausted, but happy.

A week later her happiness faded when morning sickness began to plague her. She lay in bed in terror, looking about her beautiful room. It would be one thing to bear a babe here. . . .

But hers would be born in the wilderness, with savages.

She hated Jamie fiercely.

But still, she was missing him. Every bit as passionately.

XI

Their crossing was one of the fiercest Jamie had ever endured. Storms beset them across the Atlantic and continued to plague them as they neared the American coastline. Heavy crosscurrents pressed the flagship of his four-pinnace fleet, the *Hawk*, ever northward. Jamie stood with Captain Raskin at the bow, his glass in his hand as he observed the distant shore beneath a gray day and a dripping rain.

" 'Tis what happened to the Separatists, the 'Pilgrims' who left London late last summer," Captain Raskin said morosely. "They meant to settle somewhere southward, in the land chartered as North Virginia. But the currents swept them northward to the point that John Smith had drawn as Plymouth on his map, and there they stayed."

Jamie cast Raskin a quick stare. He wouldn't have minded a side trip to the Puritan community under normal circumstances. He would liked to have seen how the men and women of the Plymouth colony were faring now that their first brutal winter was over and they had learned something of survival. In London he had heard that the death toll had been tremendous. He hoped that they were surviving well.

The death toll in the Jamestown colony and its surrounding hundreds had often been tremendous, he reminded himself. And yet Jamestown had survived thus far, and with the plantations and hundreds arising along the peninsula on the James, the area seemed destined to endure.

The Pilgrims were escaping religious persecution, while the Jamestown settlers had come for more commercial reasons.

He had come for the adventure himself—and because his father had deemed it appropriate for a young man of his situation to see the world and seek his place. When he had first seen the land before the starving time of 1609, he had felt its draw. Within the Chesapeake Bay lay hundreds of fine natural harbors. The bay was fertile, and the Indians had proven that the fields were rich. The forests were verdant, and he had thought he had never seen a more natural state of the earth, nor a more beautiful one. The very loneliness, the very wildness of the land had excited him.

By 1613, he had turned twenty-one and taken over the trust his mother had left him. Wise investments, backing hardworking London merchants, had tripled his income. He had invested in the ships then, and his little fleet had carefully traveled the Caribbean, avoiding the Spaniards, who liked to claim the whole of the New World, and moving onward to the Bermuda colony and then back to England again.

He needed no more commerical gain. He was well set for life, and he had built his beautiful home in England. He didn't know why he felt the obsession to build here in Virginia. It was as if the land was a comely mistress, a tart who flirted and laughed and seduced, and in the end, would have her way. Like a woman, the land was unpredictable. To reach it, one challenged dangerous shoals. And once upon it, a man faced starvation and the hazards of hurricanes and Indians' arrows and knives. But to Jamie Cameron the rewards were endless. To touch the land, to build upon it, to create a new world. He could not deny the fascination. It was like something that stirred in his blood, ever driving him. It was like the passion and obsession that had seized him when he had first seen Jasmine. . . .

"Let's move inward and anchor for the evening," Jamie said. He handed the glass to Captain Raskin. "I don't want to lose a month's time by being forced northward. My wife will be arriving by the start of fall, and there are things that I would have prepared."

"Aye, aye, milord!" Captain Raskin said, and he called out orders to his men.

Jamie stood on deck while the sails were furled against the treacherous power of the wind of the dreary gray day. Though his cloth was finer, his clothing that day was much like that which the sailors wore: loose breeches and a simple jerkin of tough leather. He was known to take the wheel of his own ships, and to pitch in with the men when a heavy wind threatened, or when any decisive, demanding change of course was commanded. He liked to sail. He liked the wind and the tempest of the sea. One of his mistresses had told him once that he was hot-blooded, that he loved anything that demanded challenge or fever or high passion. He wondered idly if it was true.

He watched as the mainsail came down, then he turned away and headed toward the aft, and his cabin, which rode high above the waterline and was graced starboard and port with paned windows and heavy damask drapes. It was an elegant cabin with a velvet interior. There was a cherrywood desk and a big bunk and a wardrobe, and all were well nailed into the floorboards against the whims of the waves.

The difficulty with it now was that he sailed alone.

Inside the cabin, he drew open a desk drawer and pulled out a bottle of whiskey. He swallowed some, plopped down upon his bunk, and closed his eyes.

He should have made her come with him, he thought, and wondered why he had not commanded her to do so.

He had married her under false circumstances, he mused. He had known from the beginning that he was determined to come here, and that was why he had determined to take a wife. For the first time he had been seized with the concept of destiny, of future years and future generations. This was where he wanted to build, and this was where he wanted to raise a family. He wanted to see his sons cutting down the forest, and he wanted to see the day when a fine brick government house might rise in the wilds. In a hundred years when Virginia flourished, he wanted his grandsons to be a part of it, a part of the founding of the New World.

He swallowed again on the whiskey, and he winced against the burning sensation that trailed down his throat. He should have made her come with him. He wanted her, now, beside him. Perhaps she would not have been so dismayed by the savage rawness of the new community if she had accustomed herself to life with him upon the ship. Perhaps she would have believed that they could one day create a home as elegant as the cabin. Perhaps he could have inflamed her with his own enthusiasm and passion for the land.

He swallowed again upon the whiskey, and the fire of it all seized him, and he gritted his teeth and shuddered. He had believed in the promise in her eyes, and at last he had discovered that there was, indeed, a steaming sensuality that lay beneath the genteel airs with which she had cloaked herself. He had married her because he had wanted her—and more. He had married her because of the fire and spirit with which she had challenged him that very first night at the Crossroads; he had married her for the very sizzle of her hatred. He had married her because he had longed to take her between his two hands and force her to turn around and see him, to tame her, to live a life in a raw Eden with a savage passion and a never-ending flame of life and desire. . . .

He had married her, he admitted bitterly to himself at last, because he had fallen in love with her.

He swallowed down more of the whiskey, and he wondered if he hadn't been wrong to force so much upon her. Perhaps he could have won her heart in a more gentle fashion. He remembered that last time between them with a surge of shame, for she had so seared his temper that his violence had surpassed all tenderness and care. He could remember her now . . . the sight of her sprawling in the tangle of covers upon the bed was forever etched in his mind. She had never seemed more vulnerable to him, more soft and fragile and feminine, her hair splayed in soft, golden tendrils and tangles across the pillow, her eyes so wide open and glazed. . . .

He had touched her at long last. He had grown weary of seeking a response from her. He had believed that he had been wrong, that he had indeed been a fool. That he had married a cunning little wench with no warmth, no heart, no soul whatsoever. That he had doomed them both to a life of bitterness and hatred.

And then had come their last night together, when she had come alive, like kindling set to a sudden flame, like a fierce blaze raging through a forest. He had found the passion within her; he had discovered that the warmth, indeed, existed. And in the aftermath of his violence and fury, she had met him again in a rage of desire, and remembering her, even now, locked him in an anguish of longing once again. She detested him still. But he had at least discovered that her blood ran as hot as his. He twisted and hardened his jaw, and he thought of the eager young ladies, the daughters of dukes and earls, who had batted their lashes his way, and he thought of the eager mamas who had longed to wed their girls to the Duke of Carlyle's third son. Women had teased his senses before, and he'd known many of them. But none of them had so swept into his heart as the one he had married, the bastard waif who had despised and defied him at every turn. It was ironic and painful to love her. He, the proud Lord Cameron, brought low by the waif.

He laughed aloud, and the sound was dry. They were cast to their fate now. Perhaps he never could make her love him, but he would be damned if she would continue to crave another. She could rue the day that she had met him every moment of her life, but she would be his wife in all ways, at all times. That was the bargain, the covenant they had made. Perhaps he could be a bit more like Robert Maxwell and offer her the laughter and the courtesy she so craved. After all, she would spend two to three months upon the *Savage Eden* with Robert. Robert Maxwell was his friend, but he knew his friend's faults. Jamie once had saved him from Newgate for indebtedness. He was a charmer, but one with little sense of responsibility. The New World was his last chance at respectability, and Jamie had promised Robert land when his father had sworn that he had washed his hands of his son and his careless ways.

He tensed, remembering the time he had come upon the two locked in an embrace. She would not deceive him now. Surely even she would not go so far. Still, the thought plagued him, as it had a number of times. The pinnace was not so large. Robert would be aboard ship with his own wife, and certainly Jassy would be in Elizabeth's company.

He rolled over, clenching his teeth. He had seen passion in her; he had never known her laughter. An ugly vision reared its head, of his wife riding upon his best friend, her breasts firm and beautiful and dancing above him as her eyes shimmered and her mouth curved with laughter. Rage came so sharply to his mind that he nearly blacked out with it, and then it subsided. Robert was his friend, and in his debt, and though he might covet Jassy, he would not touch her. Jamie knew it. And still, the vision haunted him. He had found her passion; he had never seen her laughter. Not for him.

Maybe he could try to woo her. Maybe he could attempt a more tender approach. If he could just dispel the haunting image and the anger, he could give the laughter a chance.

There was a fierce pounding upon his cabin door. "What is it?" he said.

Captain Raskin, with a broad smile splitting his bewhiskered mouth, entered. "The wind, milord! The wind turns in our favor!"

Jamie leapt up, corking the whiskey bottle and slamming it down upon his desk. He followed Captain Raskin out. Indeed, the wind was in their favor. It had picked up from the northeast, and it would drive them homeward.

Homeward. Aye, the Carlyle Hundred was his home.

Three weeks later they came upon the natural harbor of the hundred. From the deck of the ship Jamie stared toward land, and his heart swelled with pride and pleasure. When he had left last fall, his plans had been drawn and his instructions clearly set out, but little had stood then, except for the wall and the palisade and the few small houses where the farmers and laborers had lived, the kiln, the chapel, and the storehouse.

Now, as he looked, the homes had already spilled beyond the palisade. The cannons he had sent in the spring were mounted upon the wooden palisade in four places, three facing inland and one facing the sea. Though he doubted that the Spaniards would invade this late in the game, it seemed only wise to be prepared. The fields to the right and left of the hundred center had been cleared. Cattle and sheep and goats grazed close to the coast, while farther inland, he could see the summer growth of tobacco and corn and grain. Dead center of the palisade, he could see his own home.

Once it had been a hastily constructed creation of logs and wattle and daub. Now, though the materials remained much the same, the house had grown. Though there were no glass panes for them, Jamie could see that the windows he had drawn had been cut and completed, and that a second story had been added to the structure, and two long els on either side.

"She's grown, eh, milord?" Captain Raskin said.

"Aye, and finely so!" Jamie replied. "Captain, let's get her berthed, then see to the unloading of the vessel. Give the sailors double rations. We've come home again, and I'm eager to touch foot upon the soil!"

Twenty minutes later the pinnace had been drawn to her deepwater dock. Before the slips were tied, Jamie leapt onto the wooden dock and strode toward its end. It was a hot day, with the sun fiercely shining down, and it was late summer and glorious. At the end of the dock he met with Sir William Tybalt, sergeant at arms of the ten trained fighting men he had in his employ, and governor of the community in Jamie's absence. They were old friends, having fought Indians together as lads, and an occasional Spaniard upon the sea. William rode a bay gelding and led a mount for Jamie. William dismounted and greeted Jamie with a firm handshake, then the two men mounted together and rode toward the palisade.

"How fare things here?" Jamie asked.

"Well!" William assured him with a broad grin. He was a man of thirty years with dark brown eyes and sandy hair and a quick grin. Like Jamie, he had found a fascination with the land. He had not cared for the Jamestown community life itself, with its ever-changing authority, but he had well liked Jamie's determination to build a new hundred.

William grinned. "We are working diligently here, and I think that we will have plenty of grain for the winter ahead. And young Tom Lane has become an expert marksman, and brings down wild turkeys with little effort. We've carefully planted food and gardens as well as tobacco, and still the tobacco does well. Come, let's hurry onward, for the men have arranged a display of arms, Father Steven is eager to greet you, and when the good father is gone, I've arranged a surprise for you myself."

They came before the palisade. The gates were open, for no danger threatened, and the people came and went. The wives of the laborers, hurrying along footpaths with their water buckets or laundry or produce, stopped to greet him, bowing low, and hailing him with true enthusiasm. He responded to all of them with nods and a deep smile as he rode into the palisade and saw that the soldiers were lined up before his house, dressed in their steel helmets and half-armor, front- and backplates, and prepared for an exercise with their pikes. William rode to the end of the line of men and began to shout out his commands. The men assembled impenetrable formations with their sharp, long shafts, went at ease, and grouped formation again. Jamie applauded their efforts, and William excused them from their ranks. Jamie informed them all that there would be a feast that night; they would slay one of the huge hogs that had come with him on the ship and roast the pork over a spit throughout the afternoon. Cheers went up, and he was glad of it.

"There's some business to attend to," William cautioned him. "A few cases on which we've awaited your judgment."

"It will wait until I've seen the house," Jamie told him. Dismounting from his horse, he cast the reins down and hurried the few steps to the heavy wooden door and pushed it open.

There had been vast changes in the dwelling. The floor was laid with boards, and the carpenters had fashioned a sweeping staircase that led up to a gallery. The entryway stretched into a long hallway like his house in England; at the end was a large, beautifully oiled, polished dining table, with a bowl of flowers atop it. To either side lay the els, and up the stairs, he knew, were the family bedrooms.

He took the stairs two at a time and found that the right side of the upper floor, behind the gallery, was intended for his use. An arched opening broke the long room into two, one a bedroom—where the bed he had ordered in London would lie but now held a lumpy pallet on a boxed wood frame—and one where his desk was set, and where the walls were lined with shelving for his books. A stone hearth lay to the side, which he had specifically requested. He did not care for the colonial habit of building open fires beneath flues.

Jamie left the bedroom and looked across the hall and found two more bedrooms, then he came back down the stairs. To the right he found a row of small rooms, sleeping quarters for household servants. To the left of the hallway was a large room that held a dais to the rear and had numerous chairs. It could be a ballroom or a courtroom, and certainly would be used as both.

The house in no way compared to the magnificent manor in England, but Jamie was pleased with it. It had been hewn from a raw wilderness, and it was a beginning. Each ship that came would bring more comforts, and eventually it *would* be a grand manor.

When he came to the entryway, William was there. "Well?"

"It looks fine."

William exhaled with pleasure, then grinned. "Well, the hog is about to sizzle. The sailors have come ashore and are causing havoc with the unmarried servant girls and the daughters of the laborers. But, as I said, Lord Cameron, there is business."

After Jamie settled a few disputes among people living in the hundred and William introduced him to the new house servants they came out to the hallway and sat around the dining table. Jamie stretched out his legs upon the table and cast his plumed hat over his head.

"An order of rum sounds in good standing," Jamie declared, and William laughed, approving heartily. Jamie called for Mrs. Lawton, the housekeeper, and the woman brought them a bottle and small glasses, and then discreetly departed again. The men filled their glasses, and William talked more about the events of the time passed—four infants had been born, but two of them had died soon after birth and were buried in a plot of hallowed earth outside the compound. A group of men from Jamestown and the surrounding hundreds had visited with Opechancanough, and they believed that the Indians were as pleased with the peace that lay between them all, as the white men were.

Jamie frowned. "I don't know. He is a warlike man. Clever, like Powhatan." He shrugged. "But I am for peace. It is productive. And my wife will be here soon. She has glorious golden hair, and I'd not like to see it worn upon a warrior's mantle."

"A wife!" William said. "Ah, so one of the fawning London beauties caught you at last!" He chuckled.

"She is not from London," Jamie said. The day lay upon him hard; the prospect of a hanging was not a pleasant one. He wondered what William would think if he told him that he had married a bastard scullery wench who had once come to him as a whore and a thief. He said nothing but swallowed more rum. "She is from the outskirts and travels with at least one of her sisters, Robert Maxwell, and a few serving maids, no doubt."

William arched a brow with a bit of a smirk. "You'd bring a lady here, milord? From your fine marble-and-brick manor to a house of wood and daub?"

"I have done so," Jamie said simply. He stood. The room was growing dark with the shadows of the late afternoon. "Come, William, I can smell the roasted pork, and I am famished."

In the center of the compound, the pork was indeed nearing completion. The people were gathering around the fire with contributions of their own: fresh Indian corn, bread, summer peas swimming in rich butter. The laborers, artisans, and gentry gathered together, and though Jamie and Sir William were given respect accordingly, there was a camaraderie here that could not exist in England. The men who served him welcomed him. Daughters were shyly introduced to him; wives came to offer him bounty from their kitchens. He sat cross-legged upon woven mats on the ground with them. Rum flowed along with the good food. Instruments appeared in the compound, fiddles and trumpets and drums and even a spinet, and soon there was dancing on the grass and dirt. Jamie was soon pulled to his feet by a group of giggling girls, and he gallantly bowed to each and, one by one, danced with each girl beneath the moonlight. When the night lay full upon them at last, he excused himself to the remaining revelers, found his own door, and stumbled up the stairs. Exhausted, he stripped, then cast himself down upon his pallet, and was startled to hear a soft giggling sound. He moved his hand across the bedding and encountered bare flesh.

"What's this?" he said. Groping for a candle, he carried it to the low-burning hearth and lit it.

A girl lay within his bed, as naked as he, propped up on an elbow and staring at him with huge green eyes. He had danced with her that evening, he realized. Her name was Hope, but it had once been something else, though she did not remember what. She was a Pamunkee Indian who had been taken in at Jamestown, since her green eyes had convinced him that she was a descendant of some white settler from the lost Roanoke colony. She was a bewitching child, no more than seventeen, with glowing copper skin, fascinating eyes, and full breasts with huge brown nipples. He did not resist the temptation to look at the length of her, for from the tip of her coal-dark hair to her dusty feet she was sensual and fascinating.

"What are you doing here?" he asked her.

"I have come to serve you."

Jamie paused for a moment. Now his eyes had adjusted to the darkness and the candlelight, and a soft glow played over both of them. He had missed the heady passion he had discovered so briefly with his wife, and he was a man with heavy appetites. He had never refrained from such an invitation before, and his body ached to accept the girl now. It was a novelty to be wanted so. It would be interesting to lay with a woman he needn't fight. Especially this exotic creature from two worlds.

He knelt down beside her, and he took her hands between his palms. He smiled ruefully, because something inside of him revolted at the idea. She wasn't Jassy. She had sultry, beautiful eyes, but not eyes that burned with crystal-blue spirit. She had wide, sensual lips, but not Jassy's defined mouth with the lovely color and pouting lower lip. Her breasts were tempting, but they did not cause the breath to leave his body, his fingers to itch with anticipation, his mouth to water for the sweet taste of their crests.

"I am married," he told her.

She frowned, and Jamie smiled, because she was apparently accustomed to men who gave the matter little thought. Perhaps he was a fool to do so. If he had any sense, he would lay with the little white Indian again and again and cleanse his ever-grasping, calculating, but exquisite wife from his system.

"Married?"

"I have a wife. A woman of my own."

"Where is she?"

"She is coming. She sails across the sea."

"But she is not here now."

"No. And still, she is my woman."

Hope smiled. "Sir Tybalt said that I was to be a surprise for you."

So that was what William had been planning. He had probably sent the girl still, leaving the matter to his own discretion.

"You are a beautiful surprise."

Her eyes lit straight upon his loins, caressing a certain part of his anatomy. She stared at him with pleasure and triumph. "You are pleased with me. I will stay." She snuggled down into the pallet.

Jamie laughed and lifted her up, and set her on her feet. "Hope, you are a sweet surprise, but I must wait for my wife."

"You are ready for Hope."

Her hands came upon him, encompassing his shaft. He caught her wrists. "Hope, no. You will meet her soon."

"She is so beautiful?"

"Yes, she is beautiful."

"And you—you love her so very much?" Her green eyes were wide, questioning. She was a precocious girl, and she had lived several years with the settlers in Jamestown, but she still seemed something of the pagan with her long, thick dark hair and demanding, uninhibited gaze.

"I—she is my wife," he insisted. "Now come, dress. I have had a very long day and I must sleep."

He paused then. "Hope, you speak the Powhatan language well, don't you?"

She nodded.

The language the tribes of the Powhatan Confederacy spoke was a derivative of the Algonquin family, the Indians many of the explorers had met in the northern regions while searching for a northwest passage. Jamie knew many words himself, but he preferred having an interpreter when he traveled into the Powhatan lands.

"If you want to help me, Hope, you may come with me

on a trip. I wish to find Opechancanough and offer him some things. You will come with me?"

"When?"

"Oh, maybe a week. I have a few things to settle here, and then we will go. I must bring letters and documents from the king to Jamestown on the ship, and from there we will travel inland."

"Oh, yes!" she said. "I will love the ship. I will take great care of you."

"I don't need great care," he said. "But I would be glad if you will sail on the ship."

He found her simple homespun dress upon the floor. He handed it to her. Unabashedly she slipped it over her head. "I will still serve you, anyway."

"Thank you. But I am married."

"You can handle more than one woman."

He laughed. "In some ways, maybe, but then, I'm not so terribly sure. I will have you work for me, very soon."

Hope left him at last. He lay down on his pallet, and her image haunted him. He should have kept her with him and snuffed out all the light.

It would have done no good. In pitch blackness he would know his wife; he would know her scent. He would know the softness of her hair. He would know the shape of her, and the sound of her, and he would know the feel of her breast and the undulation of her hips beneath him. He would know her forever. He had sworn that she would not forget him. He would not forget her.

At long last he closed his eyes and slept.

A week later, with the pinnace loaded for the journey home, the supplies settled, Jamie boarded the ship again with Captain Raskin and the crew. He left Sir William at the palisade with five of the men-at-arms, and he took Father Steven, the chapel's young Anglican priest, and two of the laborers with him—along with Hope—in the ship on a sail up the peninsula.

The wind was with them, and the afternoon brought them to Jamestown Island. It, too, had grown, with houses spilling in row after row around the wooden palisades of the town. His ship had been seen coming in, and the royal governor was there to greet him, quick to ask about the most recent affairs in London, and determined that Lord Cameron join him for supper. Jamie stayed, and while he listened to the governor, he thought of the years gone by, of the many mistakes of the London Company of Virginia, of the confusion and mismanagement—and still the colony was thriving. There had been very few white women before 1619, and now there were many wives and sisters and daughters. He assumed the white population—including the various hundreds, bought by subsidiary companies or parceled out by King James—had to have reached three thousand. And in the governor's house he ate off fine plates with silver, and he saw that the governor's mantel had been decorated with delft tiles. He would try to remember to order similar pieces, thinking that Jassy would like them.

Jassy . . . he could never push the haunting image of her dazed blue eyes and her spread of golden hair far from his mind.

That afternoon, though he was encouraged to stay, he determined to set out. Opechancanough was at Rasawrack, he had been told, one of the Indian capitals. In Jamestown, he bought several horses accustomed to the overgrown trails and started out.

That night they slept in the wilderness. Jamie heard the owls and the night creatures and looked through the spidery branches of the trees to the sky. He felt the cool air of late summer, and was curiously at peace. He heard new sounds in the night, but the others slept, and he refrained from bolting up to call out an alarm. Though the footsteps in the night were furtive, he didn't believe that he was under attack. Nor was it Hope, determined to find him. She knew Father Steven, it seemed, and had already discovered the young priest's penchant for long sermons on the proper behavior for young women.

In the morning he discovered footprints, and he knew that the Indians were watching him and allowing him to come forward. He wondered if the chief had sent out the scouting party. The Pamunkees, the Paspaheghs, the Kecoughtans, the Nansemonds, and the Chesapeakes were all under the rulership of the Powhatan Confederacy, and in neighboring areas lived the Chickahominies and the Potomacs and the Monacans. Jamie did not know who followed them, but he sensed they would not be harmed. Still, as he packed up their gear, he was careful to see that his sword was belted at his waist, and that his knife was sheathed at his ankle. Muskets and pikes were little good in forest fighting. To be aimed, the muskets had to set upon rests. One had to carry several feet of burning match to assure that the black powder could be lit when the time was right. Loading a musket was a slow process—load the powder, ram in patch and ball. Though skilled men could fire off four rounds in a minute, it was still a tricky business at best, and near impossible when a lithe Indian leapt down upon a man from the shadow of the trees. Swords and knives were far more useful weapons here.

It took them three days to reach Rasawrack. Before they came upon the Powhatan capital, warriors came rushing out to greet them. Barely clad and heavily tattooed, they danced and let out curious cries but offered the party no harm. John Smith had once warned Jamie never to give up his weapons to the Indians. They asked him to, but he refused, and they let it be.

Jamie was taken to the chief's house, a long, arborlike structure created by implanting double rows of saplings and bending the tops to make the arched roof. The roof was thatched, with a smoke hole in the center. The other houses in the community were much like it, but Opechancanough's house was larger. They were brought into the large center room, and the chief came out to greet Jamie.

He seemed pleased, and reminded Jamie that he had been a very small lad when they had first met. What words Jamie did not understand, Hope filled in for him. Jamie was glad to see him, and to hear of his power. Opechancanough smiled slyly, and Jamie again worried that trouble was in the offing. The chief was a very tall man, ten years Jamie's senior at least, and strongly built, with very handsome features. His eyes were dark, his nose long and flat, his cheekbones very high and proud.

He invited them to a feast, and Jamie said that he would be glad to attend—as long as it was not a torture feast. The chief laughed and assured them it was not. It was a feast of creation.

Outside the chief's house, cooking fires raged, and men in breechclouts danced around long poles. Father Steven appeared frightened and appalled, and Jamie mischievously whispered that it reminded him of May Day.

"This is creation," Opechancanough told them. "The Powhatan were created by a giant hare, and he kept us prisoners for many years, while old women battled him for his prisoners. Finally he determined to let us be earth dwellers, and he gave us down to the soil and the forest."

Women moved about with bowls of food. Father Steven seemed leery; Jamie knew that the Powhatan were good cooks. For their celebration they had made a tasty stew of rabbit meat. It was eaten with the fingers, with flat bread to sop up the juices.

The men danced, then naked women in blue paint with leaves about their loins joined the men. They sang and moved with erotic abandon. The men-at-arms enjoyed it thoroughly, Father Steven looked as if he would have apoplexy, and Hope moved back and forth to the music, her lips parted.

They stayed with the Powhatan that night, and for the two nights following. Father Steven tried to tell the Indians about Christ, and they were quick to tell him about their gods, Okeus and Ahone. The chief and Jamie spoke affectionately about Pocahontas, and Jamie reminded him that John Rolfe was back living in Virginia, and that he was assuring a future for the princess's son. Jamie tried to explain the king, and Opechancanough told him about Powhatan's funeral, about the temples of feathered mantles and war paint and copper and jars that had been prepared for his death.

When their stay came to an end, Jamie saw that Opechancanough was given a large supply of glass beads in radiant colors, two ivory-handled knives, and a blue linen shirt with inserts of cloth of gold. The chief seemed very pleased, and insisted that Jamie return with numerous bags laden with dried fruits and grains.

It had gone well, Jamie thought. He and Opechancanough had made a vow of friendship, and he was certain that the Powhatan chief remembered and respected him. But something about the chief was crafty, and made Jamie wary.

They were longer coming back to the hundred, for they could not make the distance between Jamestown and the Carlyle Hundred by ship. When they came through the trail in the woods to the clearing of the fields and the palisades at last, Jamie was stunned to see that a ship lay out at harbor.

It was the *Sweet Eden.*

Jamie calculated swiftly. It was only the fifth of October. He had not expected the ship for at least another two weeks, but there she lay, in the harbor.

A thunder came to his head, and to his great irritation his palms went damp, and his fingers trembled where they locked around the bore of his musket.

He urged his mount forward, galloping hard over the fields to reach the dock. His heart thundered, his loins ached, and his mouth grew dry. He was about to see her again.

He was properly clad in a silk shirt, leather doublet, fawn breeches, and his high boots, for the Indians understood such things as the proprieties of English dress. He was even clean-shaven, for Hope had performed that barber's function for him not with a razor but with the Powhatans' method of a sharp, honed shell. He was clean, for the Powhatan bathed daily in the rivers, and he found it a very palatable custom. Still, he had not planned to meet her this way. He had wanted to see the house, to assure himself that it was ready. He had wanted to have time to think . . .

And to dream. But then, he had dreamed of her often, and always it had been the same. He had seen her lying as he had left her, disheveled and spent and curiously beautiful and also . . .

Hurt.

"Milord, the ship is in!" someone called as he raced by the palisade. But that was evident. The *Sweet Eden* had already pulled to the deepwater dock. Sir William had come down in his absence, to greet his wife.

Racing pell-mell upon his mount, he felt his body heat and churn, and he gritted his teeth, swearing that he would behave the noble lord and husband and not wrench her into his arms to soothe his loneliness. He would not take her brusquely, or in anger.

But neither could he forget in those moments that her passions could be reached, that though she denied him in her heart, she could not do so with her body, and his appetites that day were sorely whetted and keen. He had missed her and she was his wife.

And perhaps she had missed *him*. Perhaps she would come down the dock and stare at him, and at long last there would be a radiant smile upon her face, and the spark in her eyes would blaze for him.

The horse's hooves thundered beneath him, but already the passengers were beginning to disembark. He saw her; he could not miss the golden glow of her hair. She was dressed in soft blue, with a darker velvet cloak thrown over her shoulders and encompassing the length of her. She had seen Sir William, but she had not yet seen the rider racing toward the dock.

She looked over the hundred. He could see her pale, beautiful face, her sapphire eyes . . . her soft red lips.

Aye, he could see her face.

She stared upon the wooden palisade and the wood-and-thatch-and-daub houses with horror. Sir William spoke, and she tried to smile, but it was a lame effort.

"Jamie!"

It was Elizabeth, walking behind her, who called out with such joy. He reined in upon his horse and dismounted quickly. William saw him at last, and grinned.

Then all the others seemed to drift away, or perhaps in that moment, they simply didn't matter at all. His wife stood before him after the long months apart, and they stared at one another.

She did not smile, and her eyes did not come alive. She was so pale that it worried him, and she was thin. Her flesh seemed nearly translucent, and she was even the more beautiful for it, ever more a crystal goddess. He ached to touch her. He ached to shake her and grab her down from the pedestal of her aloofness. He longed to strike her down to her knees and demand that she cease to hate him so.

He locked his jaw tightly, for what he wanted truly was to take her into his arms and hear her cry with joy, and that was not going to happen, either. He had not realized that a hum had filled his whole being, that words and other sounds had escaped him, that he had been aware of nothing but her, until he heard her voice again. He walked down the dock, his strides long. He reached her, and the sweet scent of her washed over him as she cast back her head to stare up into his eyes.

"Welcome to Carlyle Hundred, milady," he said. He bent and would have kissed her, but she moved her face so that his lips brushed her cheek.

"Jamie!" Elizabeth cried. His eyes remained coldly on Jassy as Elizabeth stepped forward, hugging and kissing him warmly. "Elizabeth . . ." he kissed her back, and then he ignored his wife. Robert came up, shaking his head industriously, and then Lenore met him, cheerfully railing against him for having missed her wedding.

William spoke up, and Jamie introduced him around. By then Captain Hornby was on the dock, and Jamie applauded the time he made across the Atlantic.

"Fortuitous winds," the captain said, pleased.

Then Jassy spoke softly but with an undercore of bitterness that startled him.

"It was a very long and horrible trip."

Some agony touched her beautiful eyes, but then it was gone.

"Come to the palisade and the house," Jamie said. He reached for her hand, and she cringed. His temper snapped. "Come, Jassy, you will ride with me quickly to open your own door to your guests," he said. "They will follow in the wagon."

"No—" she began, but he did not allow that rebuttal. His good intention fell from him with the chill river of her disdain, and he caught her hand firmly and dragged her along. She struggled, but his grip was so firm that none could see. Halfway down the dock he paused, spinning her about and lifting her into his arms. Holding her so, in a grim silence, he hurried toward his horse. He set her firmly upon it and leapt up behind her.

She was trying to dismount from the creature already.

"Don't!" He jerked her so that she sat still, and then his whisper fell against her neck. "I have done everything that I can think to do for you, madame. I have hired on your friends, I have given you clothing and jewels, and even here, in the wilderness, you will have servants aplenty. And still, madame, at every turn you attempt to humiliate me. May I warn you, madame, don't ever, ever do it again!"

"If you would do anything for me," she cried, "free me!"

"Free you?"

Her head lowered. "I—I hate this place. I cannot be your wife here. I cannot."

He nudged the horse, swallowing down a bitter, bitter disappointment. His arms around her, he lifted the reins and guided the horse toward the palisade that meant so much to him.

"Jasmine, you will be my wife here. Tonight. I promise you."

His heels touched the bay, and the lathered horse broke into another gallop, bringing them quickly onto the palisade, and their new home in the wilderness.

XII ❧

The wind rushed over her face, the horse pounded its mighty legs beneath her, and Jassy could hear cheers all around her. But most of all she was aware of Jamie behind her—the hard, vibrant wall of his chest; the entrapment of his arms, warm and unyielding as they came around her to hold the reins. She felt absurdly giddy, as if she might pass out at any moment. She felt a rush of warmth within her, because he touched her. She didn't want this . . . this gruesome place, and she didn't want to sail again, not when infants died and were cast, tiny and pitiless, into the sea. Not when even sailors sickened and died, and weevils chewed into the food. Not when storms raged and buffeted a vessel until not even the screams of the passengers could challenge the moaning of the wind.

From the moment they had boarded the *Sweet Eden*, things had gone badly. A scream had brought Jassy down to the hold where she discovered Joan Tannen, the wife of one of Jamie's men, in the midst of a cruel labor. A day later, Joan had borne a dead, blue-faced baby, swearing her loyalty to her husband and Jamie even then.

The wind howled; the rain slashed. Jassy divided her time among the sick children and Joan, trying not to leave her side for long. It did no good.

Two weeks after the baby had been cast into the sea, Joan had followed. She had bled to death, begging Jassy to give her husband the very last of her love.

She didn't want to be a part of this place. . . .

There was nothing here, just the log palisade and the looming cannons that warned of further death, and the little houses made of wood and wattle and daub. Beyond that, beyond the fields, there seemed to be nothing but the endless forests. By night it would black, as dark as any true pit of hell.

She didn't want to be with child. She didn't want to bear a child, not here in the wilderness.

But even as she longed to escape the voyage and the land, she again felt her husband's touch, the sweet dizziness; the rush of warmth encompassed her, and she lowered her head, feeling her body grow warm, for she was stunned to realize how she had missed him, how she had wanted to feel him beside her again. . . .

And how she had longed for the expertise of his intimate touch. Even if that touch had cast her into her present, frightening predicament, she longed for it. She had even lain awake at night aboard the wretched ship and thought that perhaps, had he been there, had she been able to turn to him and cry out her loss and her fear and her anguish, it might have been better. If he had been there to hold her and soothe her, to take her into his arms.

He had never taken her into his arms, not to be tender, or to gently soothe her, she reminded herself. And he probably never would, for she had seen the stark disappointment in his face when she had spoken on the dock, and even now she felt the harsh power of his anger.

They rode through the palisade and followed a trail through thatched-roof houses and structures that brought them to the largest of the buildings. Jamie reined in, leapt down to his feet, and reached for her. His eyes were dark and cold and fathomless. His face was more bronzed than ever, and he loomed taller than she had remembered, and when she placed her hands upon his shoulders while his hands wrapped around her waist, she thought that he seemed more tightly muscled, more savagely and perfectly honed, than ever before.

He set her down before him. "Milady?" He indicated the house. She held tight to her cloak and preceded him up a stone path. The door opened before she reached it. A plump, middle-aged lady bowed to her quickly, then offered her a cheerful smile, then nearly fell back upon herself with another courtly bow.

"Amy Lawton, my dear," Jamie said behind her, and she didn't know if the wry tone of his voice was for her, or for their very respectful servant. "She will be in charge of the household, and, I'm sure, eagerly awaits whatever commands you might have."

"Oh, yes, milady."

Jassy took her hand. "Amy, I am glad to have you, and as I know nothing about living here at all, I will be grateful for your guidance."

Amy flushed with pleasure. Someone giggled behind her, and Jassy was introduced to the two young maids, Charity and Patience. A youth, bobbing and nervously twirling his flat cap in his hands, stepped forward next. He was Simm Tyler, the groom. Jassy gave him a smile and asked him if he would be especially good to her little horse Mary, for the mare had not liked the crossing one bit. The young man, with freckles and ears too big for his slender face, promised that he would see to the poor creature.

The last of the servants was Jonathan Hayes. Jamie introduced him as their cook, and she looked at him with special interest, for she never forgot that she had been apprenticed to Master John for just such a position. He was a very skinny man for one who spent his time in the kitchen, but he had nice, warm eyes, sunk into the near cadaverous hollows of his face, and Jassy decided that she liked him very much. There were others about. Men arrived, bearing supplies from the ship.

They smiled to her: they bobbed to her with respect. She liked them all very much.

It was Virginia that she did not like. It was the wilderness, the savage threat of the forest beyond them.

"My dear, you had best release Jonathan and the girls to their duties," Jamie said, his hands upon her shoulders. "We've guests coming along shortly, as weary as you are yourself from the voyage, no doubt."

"Of course," Jassy murmured.

Jamie started to take her cloak. She pulled it back around her, wrapping it tight. She heard his teeth grate, and she whirled from him defensively. "Milord, I am still chilled."

"Then we shall stoke the fire," Jamie said. He left her, walking down the hallway to the huge brick hearth that burned halfway down the length of the room.

"Ah, milady, I shall pour you some warm mead with a good shot of cinnamon in it. 'Tis warming, it is!" Amy Lawton assured her. She urged Jassy into a chair by the hearth while she sent Charity Hume to the kitchen for the mead. Seconds later a crude mug was in her hand, and Amy was telling her with pride that it had been crafted there, in the hundred, in their own kiln.

She sipped the mead and gasped, for it was potent, but it was good, and after the trip she felt that she could drink many, many cups of Mrs. Lawton's mead. She looked up and saw Jamie where he stood by the mantel, one elbow resting upon it, his eyes pensive but giving away nothing in his thoughts. Even as he looked at her they heard a commotion in the front and knew that the others had arrived in the wagon. Amy Lawton smoothed her skirts and hurried to the door. In seconds they were all filing into the house, Robert and Lenore and Elizabeth, and behind them, Tamsyn and Molly and Kathryn, and then Captain Hornby and Sir William Tybalt. "Oh, how quaint, how crude!" Lenore proclaimed.

Jamie smiled indulgently at her, and Jassy wondered what his response would have been had she uttered the statement.

"We're very proud of this house," Jamie told her.

"Oh, dear, you mean it goes downhill from here?"

"I'm afraid we have a one-room hovel," Robert said ruefully, "and for that, my love, we must be grateful."

"You've no hovel, Robert. I'm afraid that the two of

you are guests in this house for now. I was not sure that I could convince you to come, and so your house is not yet built. But we shall get our carpenters working upon it immediately, and it will not take long. Now, drinks all about, I think. Amy, Patience, if you will. Whiskey for the gentlemen, I think, and more mead for the ladies."

"Me, too, milord, I'm hoping!" Molly piped in, and Jamie laughed, in good humor again. "You, too, Molly. And Kathryn. And Tamsyn. Be assured, today you've no duties but to acquaint yourselves with your new home."

Jassy watched him covertly. He was good with servants, she thought, with men—and with women. With servants he was gentle, with his peers he was knowledgeable and determined, and with women he was not gentle, but there was something about his dark good looks and very indifference that seemed to seduce them all. Molly was taken with him, as was Kathryn. Lenore had once admitted her fascination with him. And Jassy, herself, had learned the heady lesson that he had promised—she never forgot him, not ever. He entered into her dreams, he touched her by the coolness of dawn, and by the darkness of the night, ever in her imagination.

"Jamie, I do love it!" Elizabeth cried with sudden enthusiasm. They all stared at her. She flushed, then came to sit beside Jassy. "Oh, did you see the colors in the trees! Fall is coming, and the forest is lush now in yellow and green, and I can imagine that in a number of weeks it will be radiant with red and orange . . . it is so raw, a beginning. Like a Garden of Eden!"

"Serpents stalked the Garden of Eden," Jassy reminded her.

Captain Hornby laughed gruffly, then once again there was a certain amount of commotion, for their traveling trunks and the new four-poster bed that had been specially purchased in London had arrived, though in a number of pieces. Again Jassy was struck by not only the respect but also the affection with which these people viewed her husband, and how eagerly and cheerfully they served. The men who had come to lift and carry bobbed to her with real pleasure, and if they cast her a sly glance here and there and grinned to one another, they still did so with such good humor that it was difficult to be offended. She wondered if Jamie had seen the glances, and turning to look at him, she found his eyes upon her. He had. But the way that he stared at her disturbed her, for it was not with the lust she had expected but with some deeper emotion, and she realized that once again she had disappointed him heartily.

She tossed her head. To the devil with him! She despised this place, and longed to go home. She did not want to have her child in this savage wilderness. Still, tears stung her eyes, and she wondered why, and then she knew that she wanted him to look at her with pride, and with respect, and with . . . tenderness.

"When things are set, milady, we will see that our guests are comfortably settled, then we shall gather once again for supper," Jamie said.

Time passed with them all together, but for Jassy, things were set too quickly. Captain Hornby said he would return to his ship, and Sir William had business to attend to as well. The workers finished with the upstairs, and departed. Amy quickly showed Kathryn, Mary, and Tamsyn to their rooms in the servants' wing, and Charity led Lenore and Robert and Elizabeth up the beautifully carved and polished stairway to their rooms at the left of the second floor, while Patience brought Jassy to the suite of rooms she would share with her husband.

Alone, at last, she stared down at the desk and then at the bookcases, and she saw that her husband had brought many of his fine leather-bound books to his new home. There were candles in copper holders upon the mantel, brick in these rooms too. There was a screen, and behind it she discovered a washstand and pitcher and bowl and the chamber pot. A huge armoire was in the corner of the room, and her traveling trunks were aligned at the foot of the bed, by the window, and near the door. There was also a beautiful dressing table beside the bed, and then there was the bed itself.

It seemed very large, and was grander even than the

one in Jamie's room at the manor in England. Four simple, straight posts held up heavy draperies, secured by loops at every post. It was piled high with pillows and covered in a tapestry-woven blanket. She walked over to it, gingerly placed her hand upon the down mattress, and discovered that it was very soft. She knew Jamie had ordered it in England, that men had worked quickly to assemble it for her comfort.

"It is much like the one that King James once sent to Powhatan, the gift of a king to a king. I hope you like it."

Jassy spun around. Jamie had silently entered the room and stood with his back to the door, leaning against it. His dark eyes fell broodingly upon her, and still she had little clue to his thoughts.

"It's—fine."

"Is it?" He walked on into the room, his arms crossed over his chest, circling her but not touching her. She felt him with every breath of her, and she wondered that he did not touch her, for they had been so long apart that they were nearly strangers, and yet it was as if the flesh and blood of her had lived in wait to know his touch again.

"It is the finest of all the colony, madame. As is this house. I believe it is even grander than the house in which the Jamestown governor resides. Alas—it still is not grand enough for the scullery maid from the Cross-roads."

She stiffened as if he had slapped her. "If you are disappointed in me, then it is your own fault, milord. I did not wish to wed you, and I made it amply clear that I had no desire to come here."

"Then why did you come?"

Suddenly he was closer. His hands were on her shoulders, and his fingers bit into her arms ruthlessly. She cried out softly and tried to free herself, and he shook her so that her head fell back and her eyes met his.

"Why?"

"Because you commanded that I must!"

"You are a talented woman, in many ways. You could

have eluded my men, if not me, and I was traveling an ocean."

"You said that you would come for me and that I—"

"Ah, but it would have taken me months to realize that you did not come, and months to retrieve you. And perhaps by that time I would have decided that you were not worth the bother. So why did you come?"

His eyes were fire and his touch was steel, and she was desperate to escape him. She twisted to bite his hand, and he hissed out in surprise. then suddenly he lifted her and sent her flying onto the mattress of the beautiful new bed. He joined her there, catching her shoulders again.

"Let me go! I shall scream!"

"Enjoy yourself."

"We've guests in the house."

"Then let them wonder if you are screaming from pleasure or pain; this is my room in my house, and you are my wife." For a moment she thought that he meant to lean over her, to kiss her with the same savage passion that glittered in his eyes. She felt the heat of his body, cast beside hers, and breathed in the subtle, seductive male scent of him. She was dizzy again, filled with a aching rush that left her trembling. It was wrong, and it had to be shameful, for they were such bitter enemies, but she wanted him desperately. She wanted even the anger, so long as it came with the explosion of passion. She wanted his hands against her bare flesh, his lips burning into her, and the flame of his body warming hers.

His fingers bit tightly into her shoulders again. "Why are you here?" he demanded.

"Let me go!" she shrieked, for she had to fight him, and fight this place, this wilderness. He held her so tightly, his breath came in raw and ragged anger, and everything about his hard body seemed vital and alive, streaked with lightning. The very room seemed alive with it, with combustible sparks, with tension that ripped the air between them. He would touch her, he would take her, and she could fight no more, for she could not . . .

"Answer me!" He shook her again.

"No! No! I have answered you! I mean that I want you to let me go!" Her eyes, wide and sapphire blue and sparkling with the hint of tears behind them, met the savage indigo of his. "Let me go home."

"Your true home is in the gutter, milady."

"An *English* gutter, milord, and I believe that I should prefer it!"

"Bitch!" he swore suddenly. And then, to her astonishment, he was gone.

He left her, and she was cold and alone in the beautiful new bed that might have been made for a king, encompassed in her royal-blue cloak. Bereft, she moved her fingers over the bed and cried softly. She hadn't even told him about the baby. She hadn't told anyone, because she did not want the baby to exist. She did not want her baby to be born in the primitive wilds.

She did not want to be so alone. So terribly alone. She had her sisters . . . she had Molly and Kathryn and Tamsyn. But she did not have Jamie, and she was alone, hurt, and frightened. If even the passion had left them, then there was nothing remaining at all, except for a bleak life of bitter hatred.

She curled her fingers into a fist, for she still longed to touch him. She wanted to run her fingers over the strong lines of his face and down to the slope of his shoulder. She wanted to see him prowling naked and supremely confident and graceful again, and she wanted his arms around her, safe and secure. She wondered if he would come back. He did not. She closed her eyes in misery, and she still felt as if she experienced the rocking of the ship. She closed her eyes and slept.

In the end he did return. She felt him shaking her shoulders and calling to her, as if from some great distance. She was so exhausted, and so very weary. She tried to awaken and she tried to smile, to show him that she was glad to see him.

But he tossed her over curtly and spoke with blunt,

commanding words. "Get up. Dinner is being served, and you have many guests. Wear something very grand—we would show our friends and family and the people that we can have elegance here in the wilderness." He pulled open her various trunks and began pulling clothing out and tossing it upon the bed "Get up!"

She didn't move; she was exhausted. He grasped both her hands and dragged her to her feet and tugged upon the tie to her blue cloak. It fell to the floor, and she instinctively touched her stomach. No one could tell, as yet. She could feel the hard swelling in her stomach and the fullness of her breasts, but no one else had fathomed her secret, except for Molly, perhaps, and Molly wasn't telling. But Jassy didn't want Jamie touching her this way. If he had come to her gently, or even with passion, she could have coped. But she would not have him discover it so.

"Leave me alone!" She turned away.

"I said—"

"Oh, yes, milord! And I will obey! Yes, milord, no, milord, whatever your whim, milord. You did take me from a gutter to a primitive forest, and I must be forever grateful and at your command!"

She didn't like the set of his jaw when he took a firm step toward her, and she moved away again. "I will dress in whatever you have chosen!"

"I will send Molly—"

"No. You said that they have no duties today. I will manage if you will just please let me!"

She watched the pulse tick at his throat, and she wanted to burst into tears. Apparently he had changed while she slept, and she had never seen him appear more masculine and exciting. His shirt was white against the bronze of his throat, his breeches were royal-blue satin, and his doublet was black. His hose hugged the muscles of his calves, and he wore buckled black shoes. His hair was long, curling far over his collar, and though he was clean-shaven, he had some of the rugged look of the place about him, and it was very appealing.

"Five minutes, milady."

He turned and left her.

She didn't manage to make it downstairs in five minutes, but in ten. Elizabeth had come before her and was sitting with Jamie before the hearth, listening with enchantment to some tale he was telling her. Elizabeth looked up when she arrived. Jamie stood and greeted her with a proper murmur.

"Jamie has been telling me about a delightful stream, not far from here." She flushed, bringing her hand to her mouth. "The Indian maidens swim naked, and so do many of the white women now, because the water is so wonderfully clear and cool."

"The Indian maidens seek to catch husbands," Jamie said.

Elizabeth laughed. "Do they? So things are not so different among peoples, after all."

"No, they are not," Jamie said, watching Elizabeth with tender admiration.

Robert and Lenore arrived then, breathlessly. Jamie said that he would call Mrs. Lawton to prepare their drinks, and then they might sit to dinner. Amy brought French wine that had arrived with them upon the *Sweet Eden*, and when they were all served a glass, they gathered around the table. Lenore giggled and apologized for being late, and she looked at Robert and said sweetly, "Oh, but it was nice to . . ." She paused, realizing what she had said, and blushed prettily. "It was nice to be upon solid ground again."

Everyone burst into laughter except for Jassy. Lenore stared at her with innocent eyes. "Wasn't it nice, Jassy?"

She gazed down at her plate, because the innuendo was there, and of course everyone was assuming that she and Jamie couldn't wait to make love once they were alone. She could not bear to say that her husband had not wanted her, nor could she look across the table to where he sat. She felt his eyes upon her.

"The ship was tiresome," she said.

"Milady?"

Jonathan—dressed now in Cameron livery—stood beside her, offering her a huge silver trencher. He lifted the cover, and the sweet aroma of the food made her mouth water. "Venison, milady." She nodded. "Jonathan, it looks wonderful. Thank you so much. If you will serve Lady Maxwell first, please."

Jonathan served the meat, Amy Lawton served buttered squash and beans, and the girls came after them with breads and puddings and slabs of wild turkey. The meal was delicious, and there was plenty, and it was difficult to believe that there had been a starving time here. Sir William Tybalt arrived when they were halfway finished; and apologized for being late, explaining to Jamie that one of the little children had wandered into the woods.

Jamie frowned. "Why didn't you call me?"

"It is your first day back—with your wife."

"I know the woods well," Jamie said. "In the future you must summon me immediately."

"She is back, alive and well," William said.

Robert looked at Jamie. "Your responsibility here seems heavy, Jamie. You are the lord of the manor, do you not rest?"

Jamie shook his head. "No, Robert. Here we all toil with the earth, you will see. No man rests easily. There is always forest to clear, homes to be made, land to be plowed. Our ships come sporadically, and we must become as independent as possible if we are to survive. I can buy many things, but if the ship they are due upon is caught by a storm and swept astray, then my money is as worthless as the goods I have imported. We are not so savage as you might imagine, and still we pull together. Candles must be made, and soap, and the animals must be attended. I hunt food with the men when I am here, and I saw logs, and I think, Robert, that you might come to enjoy it."

"Well, we shall see," Robert agreed pleasantly. He smiled at Jassy. "You should fare well enough, milady. You were a regular angel aboard the ship."

"Down below, administering to the common folk,"

Lenore said. " 'Tis a wonder she caught no diseases or creatures from them!"

"Lenore, really—"

"Jassy, you must be more careful. You could infect us all."

"The woman who died bled to death from childbirth, Lenore," Jassy said softly. She looked up. Jamie's eyes were on her again. He was silent, and yet she felt that he did not stare at her so condemningly as he had before.

Jonathan cleared his throat at the head of the table, and Jamie turned to him. The man whispered discreetly to Jamie, and Jamie rose. "Bring her in."

"Excuse me," he said to his company. "I will return as quickly as possible."

Elizabeth asked Sir William about his customary day; and Sir William politely answered her, promising that he would teach them all the proper use of the matchlock musket. Jassy listened vaguely, but her curiosity got the better of her, and she excused herself, too, hurrying down the length of the hallway to the front where Jamie spoke with a soldier in half-armor and a woman.

The woman was unlike anyone Jassy had ever seen before. Her hair was incredibly long and sleek and black, her skin the color of honey, and her eyes bright green. She wore a simple homespun dress with no petticoats or corset, and the pendulous size of her breasts seemed indecently evident.

"You must see that the chief is thanked, and is assured that my bride will value the gift greatly—" Jamie was saying. He broke off, realizing that Jassy stood behind him. He brought her forward. "Jasmine, Lyle Talbot of our patrol, and Hope. Lyle, Hope, this is my wife, the Lady Jasmine."

Lyle knelt before her and handsomely offered her his service.

Hope did not stir at all. She studied Jassy with her eyes, then bobbed a bit. "Lady," she said. She looked over Jassy's head to Jamie with a glitter in her eyes. "I will convey your message."

"Thank you."

Hope smiled. "I shave you well, yes?"

"What?" Instinctively Jamie lifted his hand to his cheek. He had forgotten Hope's administrations with her honed oyster shell. "Yes, you did well. Thank you."

Before him, Jassy stiffened. Lyle Talbot hurried Hope out the door, and Jamie closed it tightly. Jassy stared at him until he turned about, and it was her opportunity to stare at him with condemning eyes.

"Jassy—"

"The meal grows cold," she said, and swung about with great dignity.

She prayed that he didn't see that she was trembling and seething as she walked. It had not occurred to her that he might do to other women what—what he had done to her. She was dismayed at the rage that swept through her, and the pain. He could not! He could not desire that curious heathen over her! He would never, never touch her again; she would not allow it.

Her teeth were grating when she returned to the table. Then she did not know what struck her, but it was wanton and wicked, and she set out with sudden cheer to charm both the other men at the table. She grew animated and bright, and she asked endless questions of Sir William, and when the voyage across the sea was mentioned again, she took Robert's hand. "Robert has ever been the most gentle man and the best of friends. Why, I should not have borne the voyage at all, were not for his every assistance. The loneliness would have been unbearable—except that he was there."

Lenore, who had known that her husband had been at her own side during the voyage, thought nothing of her sister's sweet words of praise.

On the other hand, Jamie, who knew full well that his friend had once deeply desired his wife, knew nothing of the kind. Jassy saw the wrath that tightened the muscles in his throat, sending a blue fire to his eyes. She delighted in it. How dare he touch the heathen girl and bring her into their house!

They moved downward to the hearth when the meal was finished for whiskey and pipes and mulled wine, but

Elizabeth wearily declined any substance at all, and Lenore quickly yawned and excused herself too. Sir William was explaining the musket to Jassy, and she listened avidly to his every word, widened her eyes, and said that he must teach her. He stumbled over his promise to do so.

"Jassy, hadn't you best go up too?" Jamie said, irritated.

"Oh, no! I am not tired at all. I am desperately eager to meet the challenge of this new world!" she claimed innocently.

His gaze then frightened her, and she dared only flirt with Sir William a moment longer. Then she fled up the stairs.

She would undress like mercury, she determined, don her nightgown, and plummet into the bed. And if he thought to waylay her this evening, she would send him to his Indian harlot. He would not dare touch her, she swore it.

The plan went awry from the beginning, for he entered the room, closing and bolting the door, while she was struggling to bring her dress over her forehead. She felt his presence as he remained by the door, watching her, then he stepped forward and pulled the gown from over her head.

Pins loosened from her hair and fell to the floor, and she met his eyes. He tossed her dress to the side and stared at her as she stood there, her shoulders bare, the soft, white mounds of her breasts rising high over her corset, her eyes liquid blue pools, and her petticoats streaming from her waist. Soft tendrils of golden hair curled over her shoulders and around the fullness of her laced breasts, and blue veins pulsed against the slender column of her throat. He had never seen her more desirable. Longing seared through him with the vigor of a shot. He shuddered with the stark heat of it. "Come here," he told her, his voice caught in a rasp.

"You have lost your mind!" she said gratingly. "You will never touch me again, you savage."

"The hell I will not—milady!" he told her, and he wrenched her into his arms.

Her fists pelted against his chest, but he held her tight and lowered his mouth upon hers, forcing it open, taking her lips with a bruising passion. His fingers threaded into her hair, and he dragged back her head as his lips traveled downward to the pulse at her throat, and onward to her shoulders.

"Don't you dare!" she gasped, shoving hard against him.

He ceased his motion and held her still, his eyes blazing into hers with fury. "What, milady? You played the whore tonight for Sir William, and now, in this room, you would be the nun?"

"I was polite and nothing more to Sir Tybalt."

"The grande dame! Your performances are so fine, milady. Tell me, what of Robert Maxwell?"

"For him, milord, I play the dedicated friend! What he has given me, I seek to give to him."

"In this room, milady," Jamie insisted, sweeping her from the floor, "you will play my wife!"

She fought him with a fury she had not known she possessed that evening, for imbedded in that fury was anguish. She could not bear that he had turned to another. Especially when he had forced her here and she was terrified that she would die with the birth of his child.

She was flung upon the bed, and he was quickly atop her. She lashed out for his face, but he secured her wrists. She kicked at him savagely, and he cast his weight over her.

"I will scream."

"Scream loudly, then. I'll not have you taking half measures."

"Go to your Indian whore!"

"What?"

"Take your stupid, panting lust to your Indian whore!"

"Are you jealous, love?" He paused, arching a dark brow, comfortably situated as he held both her wrists in his one hand and held her down with one leg cast over her thighs.

"Never, milord. I am humiliated."

He moved his free hand over her cheek. She wrenched away from his touch. His fingers wandered down her throat and fell upon the laces to her stays. He deftly untied them. His gaze and his fingers roamed freely, lightly, over her shoulders and her breasts, teasing her. His thumb and forefinger paused over an achingly sensitive nipple, rubbing it to a long, darkened peak. Jassy tossed her head, twisted, and looked away, and she wondered if he had held the Indian girl so, and if he took more pleasure from the honey-colored flesh than from her own.

He lowered his mouth against her. "I hate you!" she choked out. His hand cupped her breast, his lips and teeth encompassed her nipple, and she cried out at last, shuddering at the searing rage of deep, molten desire that swept through her. "Stop it, I hate you, I hate you, I hate you—"

He had stopped. He held her wrists in a fierce, merciless grasp and tore at her petticoats and shift with a sudden, startling violence. Frightened, Jassy writhed to be free of him, wondering at his intent. She swore, she twisted, but in seconds she lay entirely naked, with her petticoats and shift a pile of debris beneath her, only her garters and stockings covering her legs.

His hand fell heavily over her abdomen, large, his fingers nearly covering the entire area of it. He inhaled sharply, and his eyes found hers once again.

He knew. He knew about the child.

"You're pregnant," he said crudely.

"It is scarcely my fault!"

He stiffened like steel. His fingers bit into her wrist, and his hand tensed upon her abdomen. "Whose is it?" he asked in a deceptively pleasant voice.

It took her several seconds to realize the accusation of his question, and when she did, she exploded with fury and broke his grip upon her. The tears she had held back, and all the desperate fear of the ocean voyage, surged into her, and she became a wild thing, crying, screaming, tearing at him, striking out with her fists and her feet and barely coherent words.

"Jassy!"

She didn't hear him. She managed to rise to her knees, and he rose to meet her, but she slammed her fists against his breast with such a vengeance that he grunted in pain. She leapt from the bed and started to run in her stockings and little blue satin shoes, but he caught her hair and spun her back. She slammed back against the bed again, and he was on top of her.

"Jassy!"

"No, no, no!" She tossed her head in furious distress while he straddled her. "You will not speak to me so, treat me so, and think that we can do . . . this!"

"Jassy, shush!"

"Go to her, go to your Indian mistress!"

"She is not my mistress, I have never touched her."

"But she serves you so well!"

"She shaved me this morning, that is all. While you—"

"You hateful, loathsome snake! It is your baby, but that doesn't matter to me. I don't care whose baby it is, I don't want it! I want to go home! I do not want to die here—"

"Jassy, you're not going to die!"

Silent tears streamed down her face. "Why not? The baby died upon the ship. It was born blue. They wrapped it up and they threw it overboard, and the fish have surely eaten it. And then Joan died too. She bled to death. She lay there and she bled to death, and there was nothing—nothing!—that could be done for her."

She hadn't realized that he had freed her hands until she saw that she was pounding them with little strength against his chest. He was dead still, tense, watching her, and ignoring her blows. Finally he caught her hands. He held them between his own. "Jassy, you are not going to die. You are a very healthy young woman."

"I don't want this child!"

"I do."

She opened her eyes wide and stared at him. "Why did you marry me?"

"What?" he said wearily.

She started to laugh. "You did not want me. You wanted a vessel who you could force here. You wanted someone who could survive childbirth in this place. You—"

"Stop it, Jassy."

"No!"

"Stop it!"

"No!"

She opened her mouth to speak again, but this time he found a more direct route to stop her. He closed her mouth with a kiss.

It was a deep, searing . . . and tender kiss.

His tongue delved into her mouth again and again. It filled her mouth insinuatively, and then withdrew, and each time her lips parted more fully in anticipation, and then she met his tongue with her own, and their mouths met again and again. He began to stroke her body, and she had never known such care from his hands, such a tenderness. He touched her so lightly that she arched, aching to feel more his palm against her breast. He breathed and nibbled against her earlobes, and his tongue drew a fiery trail down her throat and over her collarbones and into the deep, shadowed valley between her breasts. And again she writhed and arched to meet him when his mouth fell full and wide over her breasts and sucked upon her slowly and completely. His hands wandered and roamed and found the moist center of her, and she cried out and pressed him there too. Trembling from head to toe, she closed her eyes and writhed, awaiting him. Suddenly he was gone.

And she had what she had wanted, what she had longed for.

He stripped impatiently.

She watched him through half-closed eyes. He moved toward her, bronzed and sleek and powerfully muscular. She admitted as she lay there with the air caressing her body that she loved the proud, leonine quality of his head, the indigo of his eyes, the rich, dark hair upon his head, his chest, and nesting the protruding manhood of him. She wanted him. . . .

He crawled atop her and caught her palm and brought it to his lips. He kissed it and brought her hand downward.

"Touch me," he whispered.

"No . . ."

"Touch me."

"No . . ."

"Touch me."

"Yes . . ."

He cast back his head and let out a male groan of pleasure and triumph that might have shattered the house. Jassy did not care. She was fascinated by the powerful shaft of him, by the seething pulse, the massive life. His lips found hers, and he kissed her, and he touched her, too, and in the end she was nearly delirious. He groaned out again and twisted her and turned her, and there was nowhere upon her that his lips did not brush her flesh. His teeth nipped against her buttocks and his tongue ran hot and wild over her spine, and she was seeking access to him, too, all the while. She indulged herself in her whims, and in her dream, and she stroked the fine muscles of his chest, she played the touch of her fingers over his tightly muscled rear, and she teased his earlobes with her teeth and bathed his shoulders with her kisses. She was half sobbing when he rose above her at last, and she screamed with incredible pleasure when he plunged deep, deep within her, burying himself.

She screamed again when it was over, the sensation was so strong and so volatile. Embarrassed, she buried herself against the slick dampness of his chest and tried not to think of all the very wanton things she had done.

His arms wrapped tightly around her. His chin rested on her forehead, and he stroked her hair. He was as silent as she.

The fire in the hearth burned low. Jassy thought that perhaps he slept. She turned slightly, but he held her still, his hand beneath her breast, his fingers very lightly splayed upon it. She felt the length and warmth and strength of his body, curled flush to hers.

"Jassy . . ." he whispered. His fingers moved from her breast to her belly. "Don't be afraid. You are not going to die. I want my son. I will be with you."

"I—"

"What?"

"I want to go home," she said.

He stiffened, and his arm went still. She trembled and caught his hand when he turned away from her. She was suddenly terrified that he would spurn her.

"Jassy," he said, and he held her again. "This is your home."

"You will not let me go?" she whispered.

"No."

Another tremor ripped through her, and she was not sure if his answer distressed her, or made her sweetly pleased. Her fingers tightened around his, and he paused and laced his slowly and carefully with hers. "You are my wife, for better or worse, and I will never allow you to leave me."

"You accused me of lying with Robert!" she said.

"I do not think that you would."

"And why not?"

"Because you know that I would be forced to slay Robert."

She shivered, suddenly, violently, because it was certainly true. She wished that he had told her that he knew that she would not because she would not dishonor him, her sister, or herself.

But then, Jamie certainly did not think the best of her, or of her motives.

He had gone silent. He held her still, warm and secure against him, and for that she was glad. But she could not bear her life here if he were to turn from her.

"What of the Indian girl?" she persisted.

"She is an interpreter. Nothing more."

"Would you swear it to me?"

He released her suddenly, rising above her to study her eyes in the darkness. "What?"

She swallowed, meeting his eyes with a mixture of determination and innocence in her own. "Please, I want you to swear it to me."

He smiled slowly. "This once, milady, but I am not a man accustomed to having his word doubted, so do not think to challenge me so again. I swear—Hope is an interpreter, and nothing more. We think that she is a descendant of a white hostage from Roanoke, the lost colony. I have never touched her, I promise. Is that all?"

"Yes," Jassy said complacently. She hesitated and added a prim "Thank you."

"You're welcome."

He lay down beside her. His arm did not come around her until she nudged her buttocks against him and sighed softly. Then he turned, holding her against him once again, his hips to her derriere, his hand resting upon and below her breast.

It was a very comfortable way to rest, Jassy determined.

"One more thing, milady."

"Yes?"

"I shall teach you how to fire a musket; you need ask no other man."

"No, milord," Jassy said sweetly. "I will need to ask no other man."

"For anything."

"For anything."

Her fears had receded remarkably, and to her amazement she quickly closed her eyes and very quickly drifted into a sound and dreamless sleep.

XIII

Jassy awoke when a firm hand made sound contact with her derriere. She jerked up in indignation and discovered that Jamie was already dressed, and staring down upon her like a tyrant. The fire had burned very low and the room was cold. Adding insult to injury, he pulled her covers away. " 'Tis morning, love. And we've things to do. Up."

It wasn't morning, not at all. There was only the palest flicker of soft pink light finding its way into the room. Jassy stared at him with sure hostility, reprocured her covers, and burrowed back within them. She had not risen so early in a very long time. Not since she had scrubbed floors before dawn to save her mother the labor at Master John's.

"Come, milady—up!"

The covers were swept away again. Jassy cried out in protest, coming to her knees to retrieve them. She came flush against Jamie, who was laughing at her, a wicked gleam to his dark gaze. Men, she decided, were impossible. She had submitted and surrendered to him, answered his every demand in life, and he was behaving like the devil's own autocrat.

"I'm freezing!" she said.

"Then dress quickly and you will not be so cold. Wear

something warm, for it seems we have an early cold snap."

"Fine!" she promised him. He started to turn, and she snatched back her covers and sank back into the down of the bed. She was startled to hear the sound of his laughter, and then feel the weight of his body as he leapt down beside her. Her eyes opened wide upon his, and the mischievous glare within them.

"If I cannot get you up, then I suppose that I must come down."

She gasped softly and rolled quickly from the bed, just evading the grasp of his fingers. Shivering, she landed upon the floor but quickly leapt up and snatched the covers around her nakedness. She frowned, seeing the good humor in his face as he propped upon an elbow to watch her. He was completely dressed, down to high boots and greatcoat and plumed hat.

"You've been out already?" she said.

"Aye, madame, I have. The hunting is best in the very early morning, when the creatures of the forest awake to break their own fasts of the eve."

"You might have let me sleep—"

"Nay, love, though I'd a mind to, in appreciation for the wondrous quality of the night."

She flushed and bit into her lower lip. He was amused; she wished that she did not so easily betray her ardor, for she was certain that it gave him good cause to reflect upon her background. "If there is a certain time—"

"There is, and it is now. The day begins early, at dawn. We hunt, and the farmers take in the first hours of the day to work the fields, for with winter almost upon us, darkness comes early. And now is the time when we dine, and since the days are so busy, it is best if we all dine at one time."

"I will dress."

He sighed with drama, and his eyes fell fleetingly over the length of her. "Be damned with a meal!" he declared, pushing off from the bed and striding toward her. She let out a little gasp, but he was upon her, taking her hard into his arms. "Be damned with a meal, and with time, and with schedules. I cannot bear it. I fear that I must sweep you into my arms. . . ."

He kissed her, sweetly and deeply and tenderly, and though she knew that he was teasing her and being entirely dramatic, the kiss was sweet and enflaming and entirely decadent, and quickly sent a surging stream of molten flame streaking through her. His lips left hers to land against the pulse at her throat, and she whispered to him in sudden panic. "No, Jamie, it is morning! People will expect us downstairs, we must go down. I'll dress quickly, Jamie, they will be waiting for us—" She choked off, catching her breath, for he pulled the sheet away from her in an instant, baring her body to the cool air of the morning.

"Let them wait," he said, and he was teasing her no longer. His eyes were hungry, and they ravaged her with no uncertainty. She was indeed freezing now, for the room was chilly, and she had no sheet about her, nor did he touch her to warm her. Her teeth chattered, goose pimples broke out on her flesh, and her hair streamed out over her breasts where the peaks of them teased through golden strands, hardened by the chill, and fascinatingly enlarged by her pregnancy.

"Jamie . . ."

He came back to her, laughing. He took her into his arms and kissed her again, then his laughter faded and his lips found her shoulder blades and collarbone, and he very slowly lowered his length against her. Her fingers fell upon his well-clad shoulders and she could have pushed him away, but she did not. "I am cold—"

"Nay, lady you are hot as fire."

And soon she was. The light of day was upon them, and it seemed dangerous and sinful and very exciting. She shivered still against the cold of the room, but where his lips touched her and where his hands fell upon her, she was aflame. He traveled the length of her, and she gasped and bit back a scream when he touched her searingly and intimately, and she cast back her head to the abandon of it, her fingers moving over his shoulders and then into his hair, her body alive with trembling.

She could not think, but only feel the sheer, sweet assault upon her senses.

She was not cold. . . .

No, not cold at all. The molten fire raged the whole of her, like sunlight streaking from the center of her being, wherever he touched and ravaged and laved. She gasped and cried out, incoherently mouthing his name, pleading that he stop. But he did not, and the sunfire did burst and explode and cascade throughout her, and then she heard his pleased, husky laughter, and flamed crimson as the nectar of her ecstasy escaped from her body.

She thought that she would fall, but he quickly swept her into his arms. He laid her upon the end of the bed, adjusted no more than his breeches, knelt down, and swept into her with the driving velocity of a sudden summer storm. He held tight to her shoulders and met her eyes, until she cried and twisted so that he could not stare at her eyes and see the betraying and forbidden things that were surely alive within them.

The storm spent, he lay against her, his dark head just below her breasts. She was tempted to run her fingers through his hair, but she bit into her lower lip and held back, suddenly afraid of the very depths of the thing that raged between them. She must not give *so* much, *so* freely. She could hold nothing back, nothing at all, and it was frightening, when he still held so very much of himself away from her.

He shifted slightly, and his hand moved over her abdomen. She stiffened; she could not resist, for no matter what his words, the thoughts of the child brought new horrors to her.

"What is the matter?"

"Nothing," she lied quickly.

He swore slightly, turning away from her. "I wish I knew what it was that could unlock your mind!"

"Unlock my mind!" she cried. "You have everything! You have even that which I would hold away from you—"

"That's it, my love. Exactly. You try to hold back."

"But I am the daughter of a whore and unable to do so?" she whispered bitterly.

He caught her shoulders, pulling her up. "Jassy, you are my wife, and a beautiful and passionate woman, and nothing else beyond that matters."

"Because we are in this wilderness."

"Because I have said that it is so."

She flushed and lowered her eyes, for she thought that he was in earnest, and that he did not mock her. He rose and adjusted and tied his breeches, and before she could curl away from him, he was beside her again, his hand lightly upon the swell of her abdomen. His fingers rose and encircled her breasts, and she bit her inner lip, staring toward the door.

"You frighten me," he said softly.

She stared at him, amazed for one that anything could frighten Jamie Cameron. "Why?"

"Because you do not want the child and you are capable of impetuous and dangerous measures. Tell me, is it because it is my child?"

She didn't understand his question at first, and therefore she hesitated, then hoped she had not hesitated too long. "No," she said quickly. "I—"

"Never mind. I don't want to hear it. But you will hear me out, and hear me out well. If you think to avoid this pregnancy, you could very seriously be risking your own life."

She stared at him for a minute blankly before she realized what he meant. Then she tried to twist away from him, only to be dragged firmly back. "Jassy?"

"Had I thought to do something, milord, I would have done so long ere now!"

He stared down at her, apparently satisfied. "Joan Tannen might have died in her own bed," Jamie said, "in England."

"But she didn't. She died on the ship, trying to reach this pagan land." Her eyes came to his once again. "I must see the laborer John Tannen. I—"

"He has been told about his wife and child."

She shook her head, and she was afraid that she was

going to cry. She had to see the man herself. No one else knew as she did how Joan had loved him, and he deserved to be told. "I must see him!"

"Jassy—"

"Please!"

Startled, he hesitated, watching her curiously. Then he shrugged. "After breakfast I intend to give you your first lesson with the musket. Supper is at four; you may find John Tannen between the two, if you are so determined."

"I am. Please."

He nodded, and still he watched her, holding her still. She felt a flush rising to her face again, and she lowered her lashes over her eyes. "What is it? We will be very late if you do not let me rise and dress. You are ready rather easily," she said with a certain resentment edging her tone.

He laughed again, and she liked the sound of it; she even liked the look of him when she dared meet his eyes again. His hat had fallen, and rich tendrils of dark hair fell in disarray over his forehead, and his eyes blazed their deep, rich blue from the bronze hues of his well-structured face. He was startlingly appealing then, ever more so with his laughter.

"You used my Christian name," he said.

"What?"

He leaned down very close to her and whispered above her lips. "When we made love, my dear. You called out to me and used my name. You have never done so before." He kissed her lips lightly, her forehead, her left breast, and her belly, then rose quickly. "Come on! We are frightfully late."

"Late!"

"Aye!"

He pulled her to her feet. She ran, freezing and naked once more, behind the screen to the washstand. There was a discreet knock upon the door, Jassy heard footsteps behind the screen, and then Jamie cast the door open. She heard his deep, well-modulated words to the caller who had come for them. "Good morning, Molly, did you sleep well enough in your new bed?"

"Aye, my Lord Cameron, that I did!"

"Are we so late, then?"

"Well, milord, Amy is fretting—"

"There is no need. I shall talk to her right now. And, Molly, your timing is wonderful, for your mistress is just this moment in need of your services."

The door shut, and Jassy heard a rustle of skirts as she doused her face and hands with water from the pitcher on the washstand. "Jassy!" Molly called.

"Aye!"

"What'll you be needing?"

"Everything!" Jassy said, and in a moment a shift appeared over the screen and she slipped it on and came around. Molly, her eyes bright and her cheeks flushed, awaited her in high good humor. "Late night, love?"

"Molly!" Jassy said, stepping into her petticoats.

Molly laughed delightedly, then hugged her. "I'm just so very happy for you, love. I always did think that he was the one for you. There's a grain of strength in him, not like the blond—"

"Robert Maxwell?"

"Aye, that one." Molly came around with her corset and tied up the ribbons as Jassy adjusted the stays.

"Robert is a wonderful man."

"And you, no doubt, were in love with him when you snared this one, eh? Well, mark my words, love, and I know men, that I do. You acquired the better of the two."

Jassy's head popped out of the plain blue wool she had chosen from her trunk. "You're mad, Molly. Robert is very gentle and caring, a fine man."

Molly narrowed her eyes. "So that's the way it is!"

"It is no special way," Jassy retorted. And it was true, she thought. She liked Robert more and more, like a brother. She was not in love with him. She could not be in love with him, for she could never forget her husband's hands upon her, nor the power of his being, the possession in his eyes. Whether she hated him or nay, he had encompassed something of her, and she no longer envied her sister Lenore her husband. She was too busy grappling with her own, in her dreams and in her flesh.

"Take care, love—"

"I am late, Molly. Thank you for your concern."

Jassy was angry, and so she quickly departed the room, leaving Molly and the mess within it behind.

Everyone else was already downstairs at the table: Lenore and Elizabeth and Robert and Jamie. The men rose when she approached the table, and Lenore offered her a wistful smile. Jassy apologized for being late. Robert Maxwell looked at her with knowing eyes, and she flushed. Jamie noted her reaction to his friend. She saw his jaw harden and his eyes grow dark. She tossed back her head. She was innocent of any wrongdoing, and she would be damned before she spent her life tiptoeing about his suspicions.

She sat and complimented Amy Lawton on the good breakfast of fish and bread and fresh milk and cheese. When the meal was finished, Jamie was the first to rise, pulling back his wife's chair. "I shall start with Jassy on musketry. Tomorrow, if you are so inclined, Elizabeth, I will bring you too."

"I—I don't think that I could fire a gun," Elizabeth said.

"It is your choice."

Jassy added to her sister's sentiment. "Jamie, I don't know if I will be at all capable myself—"

"Jassy, come on. Now." He had picked up his musket, resting on the wall by the hearth. He procured a length of match from a roll beside it and lit it from the fire at the hearth. Then he came back for her. He led her out by the hand, and they left the others sitting at the table. At the front door Amy met them, handing Jamie a leather bag of powder, a small satchel of balls, and a long stick with a forked end, a "rest," as Jamie murmured to Jassy. He thanked Amy. Jassy forced out a smile and told the housekeeper good morning, that she would be back soon.

As they walked through the buildings in the palisade, the housewives about their business and the occasional workman they encountered all greeted Jamie with respect and pleasure, and bobbed prettily to Jamie's wife.

"The lord and master, eh?" Jassy breathed sweetly.

"Aye, my love. Remember that."

"Did you think I might forget?"

"I think that I like not the sparkle in your eyes—that I see for other men."

"You are imagining things."

"I am not."

"But you know that I would not tarry with Robert Maxwell, for you would slay him, and then me, too, surely. I have not forgotten."

"Oh, I would not slay you, love. I would allow my son to be born, then I should lay your tender flesh black and blue and lock you away in a high tower where you could repent at leisure."

He mocked her, she thought, casting him a covert cast. Or did he? She knew him so intimately, and she didn't know the deep corners of his heart or mind at all.

They walked through the gates of the palisade, and he kept her hand held tightly in his own. They kept walking. The morning, Jassy decided, was beautiful. The sun was rising full and bright against the coolness of autumn, and already more of the leaves on the trees in the forests were changing colors. A few crimsons splashed against the golds and yellows and greens, and even the river seemed exceptionally blue and calm. In the distance Jassy could see the fields where the men were working, harvesting their spring crops. "Tobacco, our cash crop," Jamie told her, seeing the direction of her gaze.

She smiled, ignoring his words. "You would not dare beat me," she told him.

He laughed pleasantly. "Don't try me, love," he warned her.

"I cannot help that you see what is not there."

He stopped suddenly, and the humor was not about him, but something serious and tense. "What do I see? And what *is* really there, milady?"

"I—I don't know what you mean," she murmured, moving back, and wishing she had not spoken so cockily.

He advanced on her, not touching her, but towering dark and powerful over her. "Yes, you do, madame. You do not love me. That is established. Am I to believe that you have fallen *out* of love with our dashing and illustrious friend?"

Her heart leapt and careened, and she stared with a dangerous fascination at the pulse that leapt with a furious beat at the base of his throat. "*You* do not love me," she reminded him. "So what may I take that to mean?"

"Ah, madame, but I desire no other woman as I desire you. Answer me."

She lowered her head, suddenly very afraid of him, afraid also of the powerful range of his temper. "I—I love no man," she said, and lifted her eyes to his again. "It is money I cherish, remember, milord?"

His jaw tightened, but he said nothing more. He caught her hand and jerked her along again until they came to a cleared place with a single line of wooden fencing.

He took the long stick. "This is the rest," he said matter-of-factly. "The musket is heavy and difficult to aim. The rest will hold the weight and help to keep your hand steady. Do you understand?"

Icily she repeated his words. He slammed the rest into the ground. "That," she said, indicating the firearm, "is the musket. Black powder and balls. And you've an incredible amount of match." The match hung from the musket, one end burning.

"Milady, if the match is not long enough, a hunter finds his prey and discovers he has no firepower, or worse. A scout meets up with a feisty Indian and discovers that he is weaponless. Never leave without a good length of match. You do not know when you will need your weapon."

"Never leave without a good length of match," she repeated between clenched teeth. "Even though you have repeatedly assured me that the Indians are peaceful these days."

"I have never assured you so."

"You like the Indians."

"I respect their right to their own way of life," he said, drawing up the gun. "I have never suggested that a man need not take grave care around them. There are many tribes and many rulers, and a man may never know whose temper has been sparked when. Now take heed. This compartment is for the powder." He sprinkled from the bag into the powder dish, showing her how much. "Take care that the burning end of your match is away, lest you blow your fingers to ribbons," he warned her. "Close the compartment. Drop your ball and your packing, and then ram both down the barrel. Now you are ready to aim."

"And by now your feisty Indian has surely slit my throat."

"You will gain speed when you become adept. Aim low. The musket will kick back."

He fired off a shot, hitting a target upon a distant tree dead center. He reloaded, showing her how quickly all of the separate acts could be performed. Then he set the musket upon the rest for her. She aimed, low as he had suggested. The match ignited the powder, which shot off the ball. There was a tremendous roar and a mighty recoil. It sent her flying backward, and she would have fallen had he not caught her.

"You will get used to it," he said, setting her firmly upon her feet. "Now, let's do it again. You do all the steps this time."

She was exhausted when he at last determined that she should have a rest. The musket was monstrously heavy and difficult to manage. He yelled at her when she forgot to close the powder dish, and he yelled at her again when the long match dangled too close to her skirts. She yelled back and tried again, sweat beading upon her brow and trickling between her breasts. She determined that she would come to fire the damned thing better than he could. On her last effort she did very well. She loaded, aimed, and fired in a matter of a minute or two, and she did not fall back with the kick of the firepower. Triumphantly she handed him the heavy musket.

"Have I passed for the day, milord?"

"You have," he said calmly. "But then, I expected you to do very well indeed."

"Oh, yes. That is why you married me."

He stared at her hard. "You know why I married you. Let's go. You wish to see John Tannen. Now is the time to do so."

Silently they walked back to the palisade. Jamie knew his way about. He wound through the rows of houses and buildings until he came to one of the small wattle-and-daub thatched-roof homes with a smoke hole in the center. He started to knock upon the door, but the door opened and a young bearded blond man stood there, his thin face ravaged and weary but a surprised smile coming quickly to his features. "Lord Cameron, 'tis a pleasure."

"John Tannen, this is my wife, Lady Cameron. She has something she wishes to tell you."

The man looked very awkward. He pulled his flat cap from his head and squeezed it between his hands, then indicated that they should come in. "I'm so sorry, milady, milord. I'm in a bit of upheaval. I was awaiting me Joan, ye know, and, well, I'm not much of a housekeeper. And I've the older boy with me, and Joan's little sister, and we don't seem to be able to keep up much."

The small house was something of a sty, Jassy thought, for there was clothing everywhere, and the pots and pans and trenchers and jugs from many a meal were strewn about a rough wood table. A dirty little girl with huge, brown, red-rimmed eyes stared at her dolefully from the center of the room, and a boy of about ten watched her from the table where he tried to mend a pair of hose with a needle and thread and brass thimble.

Jassy looked from the boy to John Tannen. "I—I wanted to say that I was with your wife at the . . . at the end, Mr. Tannen. She spoke of you with a great deal of love, and I wished to convey that to you. I thought it important."

He suddenly took her hand in both of his great, rough worker's hands and knelt down upon the rough floor of his dwelling. He bowed humbly over her hand.

"Milady, I have heard of your tender care of my wife, and as God is my witness, you've my eternal gratitude."

Jassy stepped back, reddening. She hadn't thought much of a man who had allowed his wife to travel to meet him, especially in Joan's condition, but John Tannen seemed a sincere individual, bereft, and doing his best to stumble through the trying time. She tugged upon his hand. "Mr. Tannen, please get up. I did nothing, really."

He nodded, not really hearing her words, and he did not rise. "Mr. Tannen." She looked helplessly to Jamie. He was watching her with curious eyes, and he shrugged, leaving the situation to her.

"Mr. Tannen, get up! Now, I know that you are in pain, but indeed, this place is a hovel, and Joan would have been sorely disappointed in it." She pulled her hand away from him and looked to Jamie again, but Jamie intended to give her no help. She felt a slight quivering in her chin, wondering if the action she was contemplating would assure him that he had married beneath his class, but then she didn't care. He had cast her out to sink or swim, and so she would do as she chose.

She walked over to the table. "What's your name, boy?"

"Edmund, milady." He jumped up quickly. He was growing fast, Jassy saw. Too fast for his clothing, so it seemed.

"Edmund, fetch a good bucketful of water and heat it for me over the fire. Have you had your meal yet? Jamie will send some venison from the house, and he will send Molly over, too, and we will shortly have this place to rights."

"But you must not, milady!" John Tannen had stumbled to his feet at last. Aghast, he looked from Jassy to Jamie, back to Jassy, and then to Jamie once more. "Lord Cameron, you must explain to her that I am a common laborer and that she is your wife, and that it—that I am grateful, but . . ." He paused, talking to Jassy. "I am ever so grateful, but . . . Lord Cameron, please help me."

Jassy looked to Jamie too. If he denied her, she knew that she would defy him. This man needed help. Jamie was his master, and John Tannen had lost his wife in Jamie's service.

And she wanted to help. She *needed* to help. She held her breath and lifted her chin high.

Jamie watched her with his dark, fathomless gaze, then replied slowly to John Tannen. "I am afraid that she is determined, John, and there is little that I can say to her. You cannot deny that you need the help, and I promise you, my wife will see to it that you are quickly in some state of repair. I will send her maid, as she has suggested, along with a side of venison. Edmund, see that you escort her home after dinner."

His eyes fell upon Jassy one last time. She watched him in return, and she could not tell for sure, but he did not seem to be judging her or condemning her. If she sensed anything at all in his gaze, it was pride, and it was a good feeling. It warmed her deeply.

"Edmund! Come along now, these things must be done. What is your sister's name?"

"She is Ma's sister, not mine," Edmund said. "Her name is Margaret."

"Margaret." Jassy lifted the girl off the floor and set her upon the table. She found a mop cloth on the table and a bowl of water, and began dabbing at the little girl's face. "Ah! There is a child beneath the dirt! And truly a girl. A very pretty little girl. Come now, let's move along. There's much to do."

Molly soon arrived with the venison. She reviled poor John Tannen for the state of his house, and when he tried to explain that it was the harvest season, she found fault with something else. Jassy ignored them both and set about making a good and palatable meal. With Margret's help she found vegetables for a stew and a bit of salt for seasoning, and cooked it all in a pot above the hearth. With Molly in charge, the place quickly became more habitable. She had everyone moving about, including John Tannen. She had the poor man so befuddled that when he at last sat down to eat, he did so with a sigh of great impatience. "Woman!" he muttered to Molly, "you do make a body long for solitude!"

Molly rapped him on the hand with her serving spoon. "John Tannen, get your filthy fingers off that bread. You will wash for this meal, or you will not consume it!"

With a quick oath he threw the bread down and rose. Then he looked at Jassy and apologized profusely. "Milady, she could make the good Lord rise and shudder himself, she could!"

"I've no doubt," Jassy said, laughing at Molly's quick look of frustration. "Now run along and wash. She is right about your hands at least."

He went along and did as he was told. When the meal was over, he went back to work, his son coming along at his heels. Jassy determined to bathe Margaret and dress her in a clean gown. She only had one other, but it was better than the first. With her face and body scrubbed, Margaret was a very pretty little girl, and she very much resembled her sister Joan. "I am going to make you another dress," Jassy promised her. "From one of my own. Would you like that?"

"Oh, yes, milady!" Margaret said. Jassy looked at Molly and found that her friend and servant was studying her solemnly.

Promising a gown to this little waif . . . it was another of those things that she was able to do because she had been swept from the gutter by Lord Cameron.

She stood and kissed Margaret's little cheek. "I hear John and Edmund coming back. Edmund will walk Molly and me home, but we shall come see you tomorrow. All right?"

Shyly Margaret nodded. John and Edmund were inside the door. John Tannen tried to speak, but Molly interrupted him. "We shall finish tomorrow. Until then, Mr. Tannen, you keep from destroying all that has been set right, eh?"

Jassy grinned and shrugged. It was the most fun she had had in a very long time. She had done something for someone that day, and it seemed that it had even worked out right.

Jamie was awaiting her in the hall when she returned. He sat at the table sipping wine, and he offered both her and Molly something to eat and drink while they spoke about the day. Molly was more verbal, tsking and telling him about John's slovenly ways.

"But he's a very good worker," Jamie said. He poured Jassy a glass of wine and held the earthenware jug above a third glass.

"Milord, I don't mind if I do at all," Molly said, and Jamie laughed and poured out the glass. The fire was still burning in the hearth, and Molly sat right beside them at the table.

"John will have his own acres soon enough," Jamie told Molly. "He labors in the township, and he works in the field. He is a man who will prosper, and I am heartily sorry that he lost his wife and child."

"Well, in another day or two he shall be set!" Molly said firmly. She drained her wine, then seemed to realize that she sat between the lord and lady of the house. She stood quickly. "Good night, Lord Cameron, Jass—er, I mean, Lady Cameron."

"Good night, Molly," Jamie said.

Jassy echoed his words, then nervously finished the wine that her husband had poured her. She wanted to show her gratitude in some measure, not so much for any material thing that he had given her but because he had bestowed his faith upon her.

She stood up, then yawned unintentionally. It had been a very long day, and she had worked very hard. "Excuse me!" she murmured self-consciously.

"You're excused," he said gravely.

"I . . . I wish to thank you."

"For what?"

"I suppose my behavior today was not the best. Perhaps I should not have insisted I stay in the house and work. I realize that I did not appear the lady at all—"

He stood, taking her glass from her hand, cutting her

off. "On the contrary, love. I think that you appeared a very grand lady today. A very grand lady, indeed. Now, come to bed. It is late, and the morning will come early."

She meant to respond to him that night. She meant, with all her heart, to respond to him fully and willingly.

But he had some business to attend to at his desk, and as soon as her head hit the pillow, she fell asleep, soundly exhausted and very comfortable. In the night she felt an even greater comfort, for his arms came around her. And in the morning she was awakened by the soft pressure of his hands caressing her breasts, moving over her buttocks. She started to speak, to turn to him. His whisper touched her earlobe. "Sh . . ."

Then she gasped, startled with the pleasure as he slipped into her erotically from behind. She had been barely awake, and it all had the magical quality of a dream, yet he was real enough, very real, and the sensations that erupted over her were the same.

Then he rose quickly, kissed her cheek, and reminded her that breakfast was early.

Her first weeks in the township went much the same. Molly quickly had the Tannen home in good order, but she and Jassy continued to spend time there, for Jassy had become very attached to little Margaret. And when she finished helping out at the Tannen home, she discovered that there was much to do in her own home. They could not depend upon supplies from England. Nor could any lady be idle, for there was not just the management of the household to be kept in order, but also there was always some food to be dried and stored for winter, meat to be smoked or salted, candles and soap to be made, bread to be baked, and so forth. Having servants was one thing, Jassy quickly discovered, but here, it meant having someone to share the work, not having someone to do it all. Monday through Saturday were workdays, and Sunday was a day of worship, and everyone from Lord and Lady Cameron and their noble guests to the lowliest laborer or serving wench attended services at the church. They wore their best clothes, and they celebrated the day with grace and good humor.

Jassy had been in the hundred for nearly a month when Jamie left her for a week, traveling into the interior at the request of Opechancanough. She was startled at the distress his departure caused her, and she tried to talk him out of going. So far, the only Indian she had met was Hope, and she wasn't sure that Hope would count as a representative of the Powhatan Confederation. She had seen some of the Indians, walking along or riding by the palisade. She had even seen Jamie pause to speak with the wildly tattooed men and children, but Jamie had been high atop his horse with his knife at his calf, his musket upon his saddle.

She did not like the idea of his going into the interior.

"Do you care so much, then, my love?" he asked that night, teasing her. She brushed her hair, and he lay in bed watching her.

"I think that you are being foolish."

"I have been invited. For the sake of the settlement, I must go."

"Someone else should go. I have heard what these Indians can do to white men."

"If I am slain, milady, think of the benefits that will come your way. You carry my heir, and so all of my property will rest in your hands. You can return to England, if you so wish. You can do whatever you will."

"Stop it!" she hissed to him. "They *do* kill white men, you know. *Savagely*. They mutilate and burn them and skin them alive, or so I have heard."

"*Do* you care, then?" Jamie said softly.

Jassy kept her eyes from him and concentrated upon the length of her hair. "I should hate to think of you overly bloodied."

"I shall ask them to kill me quick."

She threw the brush at him. He laughed and leapt out of bed, naked and sleek and graceful, and swept her up into his arms. He dropped her down upon the bed, and he stared at her a long time, holding her tight, feeling their hearts thud together and smiling at the sizzle of anger in her eyes. "I think that you do care, my love. Just a little bit. So kiss me. Let me bring the feel of you, the scent of you, the taste of you, into the heart of the fray."

"There is no fray—" she began, but his lips had found hers, and in a matter of moments she was caught up in a tempest again. He kissed her everywhere and swore that he would remember her taste, just as he would recall, in the cold and lonely nights to come, the fullness of her breasts and the curve of her hip, the musky perfume of her soap mingled with what was all woman about her. His words, his kisses, inflamed her again and again. She was amazed that he could leave her so sated one moment and be back to touch her again even as she sighed and closed her eyes. It was a long and tempestuous night, and in the morning she could barely awaken. Jamie rose, left her, and came back again. He kissed her lips. "I leave in an hour. You must come down."

To her own surprise she clung to him, her arms about his neck, her bare breasts crushed to his chest. She buried her face against his neck until he slowly released her. "You must come down," he repeated huskily, and then he was gone.

She awoke fully at last, stretching her hand across the bed and finding that it was cold where Jamie had been.

She crawled out of bed, shivering. The November morning was brisk and cold. She thought about calling for Molly or Kathryn. The fire had died out in the hearth, and she would have dearly loved a long, hot bath. But she was very cold, so she quickly washed, pouring water from the pitcher to the bowl, and scrubbing with the cloth neatly folded on the stand. She dressed in one of the warm wool gowns she had made, and came out on the landing.

She ran into Robert Maxwell, who was just coming from his bedroom. He offered her a wry smile, rubbing his freshly shaven chin. "Good morning, Jassy. You're up and about."

"Yes. Jamie is leaving soon."

"Lenore is still sleeping. I should awaken her."

"Let her sleep, then."

"Ah, but this is the New World, and a new way, and I believe that we all must get accustomed to it."

He was still very handsome, Jassy thought. He had always had his quick smile ready, and he was ever courteous. Sometimes he could still make her heart flutter, and he could make her laugh when she was low. But something about the way she felt about him was changing, and it had been doing so for a long time now. She wondered it it was because Jamie more and more filled her thoughts. Whether she was hating him or longing for him, he was always on her mind, a strong, definitive presence, and one that she could not shake.

"I suppose we must," she said softly. "But then, you can go home if you choose, Robert. I cannot."

"I cannot go home," he assured her, "for I have no home." He laughed suddenly and touched her cheek with gentle affection. "Ah, Jassy, you are the best of the lot of us, do you know that? They would label you a bastard, but you've inherited the best of the nobility, and the very finest of the common lass. You will survive, and survive well, and put the rest of us to shame. We shall flounder, as we did on the ship, and you shall lead the way."

"I did nothing—"

"You did. You were brave and determined, and we admired you very much, with all of our hearts."

His tone was earnest and his voice was soft, and it was a calming salve against the fears that had lived with her so long. She stretched up on her toes to kiss him. It was not with passion of any kind, but with nothing more than the deep, sisterly affection she was coming to know for him.

"Good morning, Jassy, Robert."

The startling sound of her husband's voice drew Jassy back to her solid feet, and she spun upon the landing. Jamie stood at the foot of the carved stairway, a curious smile twisting his lips, his dark eyes hard upon them.

"Good morning, Jamie," Robert said heartily. "And you are off, so I hear. I wonder what I shall do without your leadership."

Robert offered Jassy his hand, and she took it. She was innocent, and she was not going to let Jamie's hot eyes condemn her. At the base of the stairway Robert handed her over to Jamie very properly, and Jamie accepted her hand from his friend. She felt the simmering ire within him. She lifted her chin, ignoring it.

"Robert, I imagine that you shall do fine in my absence," Jamie said dryly. "See to your house, man, for it is almost completed, and I find that the workmen have done very well. Let's sit to breakfast, shall we, for then I must take my leave."

He led them down the vast hallway to the table at the rear of it. Here the fire in the hearth burned healthily, and a cauldron of something simmered above it. Amy was there, stirring the stuff inside. She smiled happily at Jassy. Jassy smiled back, aware of Jamie's fingers, a burning vise upon her.

"A Scottish porridge," Amy advised her. "Good against the cold and damp here, milady."

"It smells wonderful."

"Of course, we've game too. His Lordship is a fine hunter, and we never lack for fowl or venison. There's cold meat atop the table already, and bread and milk.

Jassy freed herself from her husband's touch and found her place at the table. Robert and Jamie joined her, and she gave her attention to the meal, complimenting Amy, who admitted that she had prepared the porridge as Jonathan was busy plucking the wild turkeys that Lord Cameron had brought in that morning.

Jassy cast her husband a quick glance and found that his eyes were upon her speculatively. He smiled. "The day always starts early here, my love."

"You've been hunting already?" Robert demanded. "*Today?*"

"Aye, that I have."

"On a day that you will leave? And imagine, you could sleep late and be damned with labor back home in England."

"Perhaps."

"Well," Robert said, "it is the life that I would choose."

"And you, Jassy?" Jamie inquired, his tone light, "I believe that you would have preferred such a life."

Things had gone so well between them for so long. Had it all been illusion? That morning he was angry and mocking, and it infuriated her and cut deeply. She did not wish to fight that morning, but he had seen her kissing Robert, and his temper had flamed, no matter how he attempted to conceal it. He did not trust her. What had they between them, then?

She replied to him bitterly. "I did not come from such a life, milord," she reminded him, aware that Amy Lawton heard her every word. "But I was not given a choice, if I recall. Besides, my home, sir, is the gutter, as you deem important to remind me at times."

Amy, about to set down a bowl of porridge, stiffened. Jamie's eyes glittered, his temper rising. He idly drew his finger upon the back of Jassy's hand. She did not dare draw away.

He smiled above her head to Amy, his dark eyes alight, his mouth curved into a sardonic, wickedly appealing grin. "She married me for my money, you see. It has been a grave disappointment for my lady to discover that she had married not for silver and crystal, but for a raw log home in the wilderness."

Amy flushed crimson. Jassy longed to kick Jamie beneath the table. Robert laughed uneasily.

Jassy stood. "How dare you, Jamie Cameron—"

"I only ended what you chose to begin, my love," Jamie said, his eyes narrowing. He used his foot to pull in her chair, causing her to fall back into it. "Sit, my lady. You have not dined as yet. And you must. Mustn't she, Mrs. Lawton? It is cold and hard here, and she must keep up her strength."

"Milord, I am sure—" Amy Lawton began.

"That it is none of your affair. Quite right, Mrs. Lawton. You are the very soul of discretion, and we are well pleased with you." He stood suddenly, impatiently. "Lady Cameron is with child, Amy. Our babe will be born in February, though she conceals her state well in those voluminous skirts. You will, I trust, see to her welfare while I am gone?"

Amy gasped softly, staring at Jassy. "Milady, I did not realize—"

"So you are with child," Robert breathed, startled.

Jassy kept her furious eyes pinned upon her husband. "Yes."

"You said nothing on the ship," Robert said. "None of us knew. Even now you did not tell us—"

"There was little reason to do so."

"We should have been taking greater care of you."

Jassy stood again and smiled down at Robert ruefully. "Why? Joan Tannen received no special care. They sent her down to the common quarters. Her baby died and she died. And no one thought a thing of it. She was a commoner, as I am myself." She turned to leave.

Jamie caught her arm. "You are my wife," he reminded her softly, "and for that reason alone, madame, you will take care."

She pulled away from him, wondering just what his words meant, if he thought that she should take care for her health's sake, or for their child's sake . . . or if she should take very special care that he not discover her again as close to Robert Maxwell as he had that morning.

Tears suddenly stung her eyes as she lowered her head and rued the argument that had sprung up between them. He was entering the Indians' territory, and they were at tragic odds.

They had always been at tragic odds, she told herself. The change had been an illusion.

"Jassy—" Jamie said, catching her arm again.

"I do intend to take the greatest care, milord!" she said, raising her lashes at last, and meeting his eyes with her own, glazed with tears. "And may I suggest, milord, that you do the same yourself?"

He smiled suddenly, tensely. He pulled her against him, there at the table. "Kiss me good-bye," he whispered to her.

She did not need to kiss him. He kissed her. Passionately, forcefully, violently . . . then tenderly. Her heart thundered, she could scarcely breathe, and she could taste him and all the salt of her tears. When he released her at last, she was dizzy, and she could barely see, for she was blinded with her tears.

"Good-bye, milord, take heed!" she said, and she pushed away from him, ran for the stairs, and fled up the length of them.

XIV

Jassy saw her first Indian brave on the tenth of December, when Jamie had already been gone for almost two weeks.

She was beyond the palisade with Sir William Tybalt as her escort, and she was covered with soot and smudge, industriously studying the art of musketry. Elizabeth was at her side, shivering with each recoil of the weapon, and warning Jassy that she could bring harm to her child.

"Elizabeth, this is very important—" Jassy was saying when she saw the curious red-skinned man upon the pinto pony.

He was perhaps fifty yards away from them, observing them. There were a half dozen men behind him, but none of them was noticeable, not when the startlingly proud figure sat before them on his horse.

"It is Powan," Sir William said, standing between the women and the warrior. Jassy peeked around Sir William, fascinated.

Even atop the pony it was evident that Powan was a tall man. His buckskin-clad legs were very long, and dangled far below the horse's belly. He was not so much red as he was a deep, deep bronze, and his eyes were the darkest mahogany color Jassy had ever seen. He carried his head with the air of a king, and his features were somehow noble, too, high-boned and broad, long-nosed and square-jawed. He looked at them with a penetrating gaze, an autocrat who wore a cloak of blue-and-white plumes over broad, heavily muscled shoulders. Despite the growing December chill, he wore no shirt beneath the cloak, and Jassy could see tattoos of primitive hunting scenes upon his arms.

"Powan?" she murmured.

He carried a feathered and sharpened shaft, some kind of a spear, but he held it more like a scepter than a weapon. He nudged his pony and advanced upon them. Despite the fact that they were basically alone with Sir William by the fencing, Jassy was more curious than frightened. Perhaps it was a dangerous fascination, brought on by the endless stories she had heard of the Algonquin family savages. But surely there could be no real danger. The men were busy collecting the last of the winter harvest from the fields, and carpenters and laborers worked on various dwellings within and without the palisade. Nearer the river, a number of the women were busy with candlemaking, dipping and stringing their tallow. Powan had come with only a handful of braves. Jassy was aware that her knowledge of the Indians was limited, but instinct told her that this was a peaceful venture.

"Powan!" Sir William said, and he lifted his hand in a gesture of friendship. The Indian dismounted and came forward. He was very tall, as Jassy had suspected. As tall as Jamie at least. And there were other curious resemblances between the men, she thought. They were built much the same, lean but tightly muscled, graceful, and supremely confident in their silent movement.

"Good day, William Tybalt," the Indian said, and Jassy started at his use of the king's good English. His eyes fell upon her and, in a leisurely and insolent fashion, traveled up and down the length of her. Jassy flamed beneath the pagan regard and wondered at the red man's thoughts, for in a month the pregnancy she had concealed for so long in the pure volume of her petticoats and skirts had become quite evident. Still, he seemed to find her as fascinating as she found him.

"Powan, it is always good to wish you good day," Sir Tybalt said. "This is the Lady Cameron, Jamie's woman, his wife."

A curious flicker of emotions passed over the Indian's strong features. "Jamie's wife?"

"Yes."

"Good day, Jamie's wife," Powan said.

"Good day, Powan," Jassy said. Impulsively she stepped forward. She took his hand and shook it. He watched her with a mixture of amusement and pleasure, then laughed and looked at Sir William. "She is a fine woman for my friend, Jamie. She grows heavy with his seed. It is good."

Elizabeth still cringed behind Jassy. Jassy dragged her sister around. "This is Elizabeth. Lady Elizabeth. She is my sister."

Elizabeth could not speak. Powan looked her up and down with a certain contempt and spat on the ground. He muttered something in his native tongue, then lifted his hand, and one of his men came forward, carrying a broken musket. The firing mechanism had disjoined from the wooden barrel.

Powan moved on to matters of business. "Where is Jamie? I would like this fixed."

"Jamie has gone to see Opechancanough," Sir William informed Powan, "at the chief's request. In his stead I will give you this musket . . ." He paused. Jassy was leaning upon the weapon. She smiled quickly and lifted up the heavy weapon to give to Powan. He took it from her and laughed. "She is a strong woman. Good for Jamie. She will work hard in his fields and give him many children."

Then Powan had nothing else to say. He shouldered the musket and lifted his feathered shaft in a gesture of farewell. He leapt upon his saddleless pony, lifted the gun and the shaft again, then whirled the horse around and headed for the forest, his men jogging along after him.

Elizabeth let out a gasp of relief, then started to fall in a swoon. "Oh, catch her!" Jassy cried, and Sir William did so, lifting Elizabeth into his arms. Elizabeth's blue eyes opened, wide and dazed. "Oh, he could have killed us!"

"Nay, nay, lady!" Sir William said assuringly. "We are at peace with the Indians."

"Let's go back to the house and have some warmed mead, shall we?" Jassy suggested. She didn't want Elizabeth to see it, but she was still shaking herself, and she didn't know if it was with fear or excitement.

Sir William carried Elizabeth, but near the palisade she determined that she could walk; she did not want someone making a fuss over her. At the house Jassy quickly searched the wooden shelves behind the big table for a ceramic jug of mead and, finding it, poured out a glass for Elizabeth. Elizabeth choked it down, then smiled dazedly at Jassy. "Oooh, he was so frightening!"

"Nonsense, Elizabeth, he did nothing frightening at all!" Jassy protested.

"Powan is a friend," Sir William assured her. "Jamie is his *good* friend. In the winter of 1608 to 1609, Jamie was here with Captain John Smith. The whites were nearly betrayed by Powhatan, and a ruthless killing started up between the two sides. Powan and Jamie were just lads, but Powan stumbled upon a group of bitter Jamestown settlers on the river. They meant to string up Powan, but Jamie let him go, telling the men that the king's good Englishmen did not murder children. They have never forgotten each other. Powan is a chief of his people now. Opechancanough is still the final law upon the Confederation, but Powan does have a certain authority."

"He is a savage!" Elizabeth insisted, shivering. She swallowed more mead.

"Savage, yes, but a part of this land," Sir William said. He smiled ruefully to Jassy. "You handled yourself very well, Lady Cameron. Jamie would have been proud."

Sir William bowed low to her and Elizabeth, then took his departure. Jassy watched his retreating back and wondered just what her husband would think about his Indian friend's approval. She made a good wife—she would work hard in Jamie's fields and give him many children. Well, it was what Jamie had wanted.

That night when she lay in bed, she thought about her husband, as she had every night since he had left. She ran her fingers over the bed where he usually lay, and she was swept through with a curious shivering and anguish. She missed him sorely. Even hating the way that they had parted, she missed him. She did not care if they fought, if they came together in tempest or in anger. She wanted him beside her, touching her. She liked the security of lying with him, and she was anxious for the deep sound of his voice. And now she missed the laughter, too, and the tenderness that they had shared so many times. No matter what she tried to hold from him, she gave all of herself too easily. She lay down upon the bed, and he swept her to new heights. He touched her if she feigned sleep, and he awoke her with the dawn. Sometimes he was fierce and impatient, and sometimes he was achingly slow and gentle, and yet she could never lie still, never pretend that he did not unlock the deepest secrets and passion within her, for he would always persist, and in the end she would submit to the overwhelming sensation. Now, with him gone, she had only her dreams, and they were usually sweet. She dreamt of him, of his indigo eyes, naked in their intent and purpose. She awaited him in a bed of white down, and he strode toward her, bronzed and savage and beautiful, and she lifted her arms out to him.

That night the dream changed. It began the same way, but then it changed. Jamie was coming to her. Tall and towering and muscled and sleek and bronzed and blatantly sexual in his sure, silent approach. She awaited him, aching for him. But then he was no longer purely naked; he wore a cloak of white feathers, and his look had been altered, until he was coming upon her like one of the pagan Indians. It was Jamie still, but then it was not, and she was afraid. He caught her ankles within his hands and wrenched her down toward him, brutally parting her legs. She started to scream, but no sound would come, and she was drowning in a sea of white feathers. . . .

The feathers were lifted into mist. She was walking now, approaching a bed. She didn't want to lift the covers, but she had to do so. She started to scream again. There were corpses there, a line of them. Her mother's emaciated body was riddled with worm holes. Jamie, in the white feather cloak, lay beside Linnet, and an ax protruded from his heart. Beside him she lay herself, white and wide-eyed, the head of her scalped infant child cradled in her arms.

She bolted up and discovered that she was not alone. Elizabeth and Lenore were in her doorway. Robert was at her side.

"It—it was a dream," Jassy said. She was trembling still. Robert took her into his arms, and she started to sob. He soothed her, smoothing back her hair.

"It is all right. It is all right," Robert said.

"It was the Indian," Elizabeth said bluntly. She looked at Lenore. "She had ceased the nightmares, and now she has them again. It was the Indian, I know it."

"We shall all be slain in our beds!" Lenore said, distressed.

Listening to them, Jassy realized her own weakness. She pushed away from Robert, quickly and ruefully wiping the tears from her cheeks with her knuckles. "I'm sorry. I'm such a fool, really. I do have dreams now and then. It's all right. I'm all right. Lenore, we will not be slain. Powan is Jamie's friend. We have a good guard about the hundred. I am so sorry that I disturbed you. Please go back to sleep, and don't be alarmed."

By then Amy Lawton had come up the stairs, and she stared at Robert and Jassy together. "What is it?"

"A dream, Mrs. Lawton, nothing more. I am so very sorry," Jassy said.

Robert kissed her forehead. She rose quickly, hugged both her sisters, and offered Mrs. Lawton another apology. "Please, forgive me. Go to sleep."

When she was alone again, she did not think. She lay

awake, not dreaming, but imagining her husband. She saw his dark eyes, his tall, proud build, powerful, exciting, arresting. She respected him, she knew. The dream had reminded her that he was his own man, and that he made his own rules. He had defied propriety and class and had married her. He had swept her from poverty and starvation, and the cruel grip of a life of labor. He had quickly demanded her respect. But there was more to it now. She might be angry, but she did not detest him. She wanted him, she desired him, with a fever that was surely indecent. She was afraid to fathom what she felt, but she promised herself that night that when he came home, she was going to be a good wife to him in all ways.

The next day, another of her husband's ships appeared on the river. It was the *Lady Destiny,* and her captain, Roger Stewart, quickly sought out Jassy. The *Lady Destiny* had brought many gifts from England. Jamie had ordered Jassy a wool-and-ermine cloak for the winter, and a whole assortment of fur muffs. Crate after crate of soft silks and laces and taffetas and brocades was delivered to the house. There was also a set of gold-plated chalices, and a multitude of ceramic jars and vases from Italy and Spain. The finest of the gifts was a delicate filigree necklace from which suspended a fine blue sapphire surrounded by diamond chips. With her sisters about her to help her, she laughed joyously as they opened box after box. Jamie, she thought, was very good to her. She would quit complaining about this place, she thought, and she would strive to like it. Perhaps it would not be so hard. More and more, the hundred became a complete community. There were now two kilns, and two talented potters at work. Another weaver and a metalsmith had arrived from England.

Mr. and Mrs. Donegal had opened a trading center where the artisans sold their crafts. Even John Tannen was doing well, with Molly more frequently with him than with Jassy and the household.

Tamsyn was no longer an old drunk. He was clean-shaven and neat in appearance and never imbibed too much liquor these days. He was not even so old, Jassy realized, and she enjoyed his company often in the afternoons. She would come out to the large stable built off the back of the house, and while he worked upon the horses, he would spin tales for her about things he had learned during his days at Oxford. He opened the world to her, and once, when he realized that she was brooding, he reminded her that he had been a good physician once, and that he would readily die himself before letting anything happen to her in childbirth.

Aye . . . the days were growing good, and far less grim than Jassy had imagined. Tamsyn had regained his soul and his strength, and Molly might well become the wife of a free man with a fine future. Little Margaret looked happier and prettier by the day, and it was all a magic *she* had created . . . by her husband's largesse, she admitted. A husband who now haunted her dreams and inflamed her senses.

For the first time Jassy realized she might do more than survive. She might also have a chance to be happy.

With her palm upon the bed where Jamie should be, she smiled, and at last she slept, in peace.

Jamie and his party, Father Steven among them, arrived home in the early-dawn hours of December seventeenth. The first soft snow of the winter season came floating down to the ground, and though the day was cold, it promised to be beautiful too.

Jamie was weary and confused as he rode. Opechancanough had been behaving very strangely, he thought. He had invited—summoned—Jamie to his home; he had assured Jamie that he liked him well, and then he had suggested that he go home. Not to the hundred, but home, to England.

Jamie—alone with his ten men in the midst of hundreds of Pamunkees—had promised the chief that he would think about it, but he had expressed his confusion. Sharing a pipe with the chief, he had told him, "But if I leave this place, what benefit will it be to our people?

The Englishman has come here to stay, Opechancanough."

"The land belongs to the Powhatan. My brother fought to bring the tribes here to order. Order will remain."

Jamie had left laden down with gifts once again, with dried meat and bags of grain and maize corn, and he had left Opechancanough with several scores of old buttons with the Tudor rose emblemed upon them. The chief had seemed pleased. And still, the entire visit had disturbed Jamie. He intended to take care in the months that followed.

He had not realized the extent of his worry until he left the forests and came upon the clearing for the fields of the hundred. He looked toward home, and the palisade still stood, with the cannons rising westward in the shadows. He let out a pleased cry that brought laughter to his men, then he nudged his horse and shot like a bolt ahead of them. The palisade gate opened as he approached it, and he was glad and relieved again, for it meant that an armed man was on duty, keeping careful watch.

Few people were about as he hurried his way to his house. The man Tamsyn was up, and he sleepily took Jamie's horse. "How fares my wife?" Jamie asked him.

The man smiled and answered him with an articulate tongue. "The lady fares very well, Lord Cameron. She blossoms daily."

Jamie laughed and hurried for the house, pulling off his gauntlets. At the door to the hallway he paused.

He had not thought of their parting argument since the early days of his departure, when the words they had exchanged had haunted him nightly. He was wrong, he knew, and he had no right to taunt and bait her about Robert Maxwell. Robert had his faults, but he was a trusted friend. And Jassy . . .

She had never lied to him. She had married him with the truth of her feelings upon her lips, and yet she had never really given him reason to believe that she would betray him.

It was his temper, he thought, his damnable temper,

and the jealousy that soared from his heart—and his loins—when he saw the sparkle in her eyes when she spoke to another. Aye, it was bitter medicine, but he loved her, and he must hide the emotion from her. Anger was easier than betraying his heart. If often seemed that she had none, and therefore a wise man would build a careful shield around his own. He was, perhaps, a man possessed, but proud nevertheless, and he'd not let his heart or his loins rule his mind. He would be master of his own house despite the minx, and if she never learned to *love* him, she would come to *obey* him.

He wondered bleakly if she would ever cast aside the barriers that she had set before him. If she would ever come to him with husky laughter on her lips and the bright fire of passion in her sapphire eyes. That was what she kept from him, he realized. That was what she held away, like some sacred prize.

It was a prize, he thought, for he longed to obtain not her submission but her partnership.

He inhaled and exhaled, and a hot shudder swept his body, piercing his loins. For the time being, he thought, he could live with submission. He had thought of nothing but her soft, creamy, naked flesh during all the nights of his journey. He had thought of her sky-colored eyes, of her hair tumbling about the fragile structure of her face, and he had thought of the evocative swell of her breasts and the darkened shade of her nipples, and he had imagined the curves of her body as she lay awaiting him. He had seen her lips, parted, damp, and he had awakened many times in a cold sweat, wanting her. She would be further along now . . . but not too far along.

He had to see her.

He pushed open the door impatiently. Amy Lawton, in her nightcap with her long gray braid streaming down her back, hurried out with a candle to meet him.

"My Lord Cameron! Welcome home." She looked at him a bit askance—he was dressed in soft, warm buckskins given him by the chief, and his head was bare. He might well have resembled a savage himself.

"Thank you, Mrs. Lawton, I am glad to be home." He

spoke softly, for it seemed that it was still night in the house. He had ridden through the darkness, anxious to be here. The days of Christmas were almost upon them, and he wanted to be among his own people for the Christian celebration. No . . . he wanted to be back with his wife. He wanted to know if she was still angry for the way they had parted, or if she had forgiven him. He had just wanted to touch her again. If she did not give in to him, he wanted the passionate, frenzied response that he could draw from her, he wanted to see her lips parted and damp, and slightly swollen by his kiss, her eyes open and blue and heavy-lidded with desire. . . .

And he had wanted to assure himself that their child grew well in her womb. "Is all well?"

Amy Lawton seemed distressed, and so he moved to the fire with a frown, warming his hands. "Is all well?"

"Well enough, milord. But . . ."

"But? Speak up."

"Lady Cameron had some horrid dreams, I think, while you were gone. One night I awoke and came to her, but she did not need me, for her brother-in-law was already with her. The poor lady! I was heartily sorry, for she seemed so distressed."

"Really?" He did not want to feel it, but the dark anger cascaded over him again. Robert! Always she was reaching to Robert!

He gritted his teeth. He reminded himself of the anguish he had endured, wanting her through the long nights. He tried to remind himself that his jealousy was invalid, for though she might still feel some draw to Robert, she would not act upon it. Surely she would not.

But no logic worked upon him. Robert Maxwell had soothed Jassy in the bed she shared with him, and the thought of it infuriated him. What else had happened there?

"Milord, shall I get you something?" Amy said.

"No, I think that I will see to my wife."

"Oh, she slept peacefully and well last night, milord, I do believe. She bathed late in the outhouse and drank warm milk before bed, and I am certain that she did not awake distressed. Oh, and, milord, the *Lady Destiny* arrived with your gifts, and your lady was quite pleased."

"Was she?" Aye, Jassy would be pleased. She was like a child with a present. She had married him for his wealth and position, he reminded himself. The lady could be bought.

"Thank you, Amy," he told his servant, and headed for the stairs. "See that Sir William is informed that I will speak with him later. And tell Captain Stewart that I will see him too. I am sure that he is anxious to sail southward before winter comes upon us any more viciously."

"Yes, milord," Amy told him, but he barely heard her, for his attention was already upon the door at the top of the stairs. Still, when he reached it, he paused again. He stood there, his palms growing damp, his heart beating too quickly and too hard. She was a harlot, he reminded himself. She had sold herself into marriage, but it had been a payment, nonetheless. She was his wife and was honor-bound to obey him. He did not need to tremble like a lad in the schoolroom.

He pushed open the door and stepped into his room.

She slept, and she slept as sweetly and as innocently as a child. He could smell the soft rose scent of French perfumed soap upon her body even as he stood over her. She was clad from head to toe in a soft white gown, laced and beribboned on the bodice, entirely chaste. The covers were swept over her to her waist, but her gown dipped precariously from her shoulder, exposing a fascinating expanse of clear ivory flesh. Her hair was a profusion of sunshine splayed upon the pillow, and her lips were as he had so often dreamed of them, softly parted as she breathed evenly with her sleep. He ached to touch her; he burned to touch her. His loins ached, and only the tightness of his buckskin breeches kept his naked desire from showing as clearly as the king's flag upon a pinnace.

He reached to touch her naked shoulder, and then he drew away. He ground down hard on his teeth and walked around to his desk. He sat and plopped his feet upon it. He stared at her, then searched for the jug of rum in the bottom drawer of his desk. It was early morning, and he did not need his mind fogged. He drew deeply on the rum, anyway.

In a matter of moments she began to stir. Like a cherished child, she stretched, and a soft, smug smile touched her lips. And well she should be pleased, Jamie decided sardonically, for she thought him still gone, while his gifts lined her trunks. Robert slept across the hall and could come at her first call of distress. Robert, who she had planned to trap in her matrimonial web. . . .

Robert would sleep across the hall no longer, Jamie determined. The Maxwell house would be hurried along. He did not wish to fight the urge to smash his friend's pleasant features every time they chanced to meet.

Her eyes opened suddenly, falling full upon him. Then they widened and she sat up, and to his chagrin he thought that she was about to scream.

"Is my appearance so distressing, then?" he said harshly.

"Jamie!"

"Yes, my love, returned alive and well," he said.

"Oh!" She placed her hand over her heart. Her gown spilled farther down, and her breasts rose and fell in tempting agitation. Her hair, tousled by sleep, was a wild glory about her. He fought to remain still at his desk. "Who were you expecting?"

She pointed to him, indicating his clothing. She smiled ruefully and beautifully, and it did seem that her face was alive with welcome. "I—I—your outfit. It frightened me."

"Oh?" He stared down blankly at the buckskins. "Forgive me, love. Were you about to scream for Robert?"

The welcoming smile quickly faded from her features. "I don't know what you're talking about."

He wished that he hadn't spoken, but he couldn't take the words back now. He leaned deep into his chair, watching her through a bare slit in his eyes. "I have heard, madame, that your distress in the night is eased by Robert Maxwell."

She stiffened and did not reply. She sat there like a queen, entirely regal and disdainful in her silence. His throat grew dry, and again he longed to take back his words, but they had already been spoken and could not be taken back. More than ever, he ached to touch her, to slide his trembling fingers over the naked expanse of her shoulder so displayed to him. He wanted to move but could not. At last she did so. With her head proudly carried and her hair tumbling about her, she slipped her legs over the side of the bed, discreetly adjusting her gown to stand. But when she stood, he saw the startling change in her, and a hoarse sound of surprise escaped him. She whirled to him in alarm.

His boots landed on the floor and he was upon his feet. She was back toward the wall, her eyes wide with sudden alarm, her hands splayed protectively over the swell in her abdomen.

"Come here!" he whispered. She ignored him, and he swore vehemently. "Do you think that I would harm you, madame?" Impatiently he strode to her, and she backed away again.

"You *have* threatened grave harm!" she reminded him.

"Only under damning circumstances, madame, and you've done nothing damning, have you?" His strides brought him to her. She choked back a gasp and seemed to brace herself, but he offered her no force or violence. He came down upon one knee before her and cast his hands upon the swell of her belly. Fascinated, he felt the hardness of the child growing within her. He swept his palms slowly over the swell again and again. He reached higher and encompassed her breasts with tenderness, then he rose, pulling the gown up and over her head.

"No!" she protested in distress.

"I have ached for the sight of you," he said.

She tried to elude his arms. "I am large and awkward of a sudden, and not much to see," she murmured.

He could not see her eyes or her face, for she had lowered her lashes and her head against him, and since she could not escape his hold, she had pressed against him. He caught her chin, and when he lifted it, there was the slightest glaze of tears touching the exquisite sapphire of her eyes. He felt suddenly as if they had never parted. Tension filled him, and he wondered what was truth about her, and what was pretense and lies.

"Give me the gown!" she implored him.

"No."

"Please. I am so . . . fat!"

He had expected anger or denial, and not this. A smile touched his lips, and he whispered, "To me, madame, you are more exquisitely beautiful than ever."

He threaded his fingers through her hair and tilted her face to his. He kissed her deeply, the fire in his loins exploding again with the searing hot contact of their lips. He lay hold upon the ache that plagued him, for he had determined that he would be gentle now, and so he would. He knelt before her and explored again the hard curve of her belly where his child found life. Her fingers curled into his hair. Distressed, she tugged upon him, but he ignored that pain and pressed his cheek against her flesh.

"Jamie . . ." she said, tugging upon him. But then she ceased the effort, and her knees began to tremble, and when he looked up at her, she had her head cast back, her lips were slightly parted, and her breath came in ragged pants. He rose and swept her into his arms and then onto the bed. He tugged off his boots and hose and buckskin breeches and jerked his leather doublet over his head. He shook with the fever to have her, but even as hunger swamped him he took a tender care with her, greater than any he had exercised before. And still, when it was over, he knew a satisfaction like nothing he had ever known before. She reached for the sheet, and he stopped her, lethargically propping himself up on an elbow and running his fingers with idle abandon over her belly. He paused, his heart slamming against his chest, for he felt a sudden movement. He looked to her. She was flushed with embarrassment, and he laughed with sudden joy. "The babe?"

She nodded.

Holding his weight upon his knees, he straggled over her. He cupped her abdomen again with his hands and smiled as he felt the sudden power of a kick against his hand. "He is strong."

"*She* is not so fond of you this morning either."

"Alas, did you not miss me?" he said tauntingly.

Her lashes fell quickly over her eyss. "Milord, I had Robert Maxwell, don't you recall?"

His jaw tightened, and the movement of his hands ceased. "This is a wound into which you rub salt, my love. Take care."

Her lashes flew open, and her eyes met his again. She was so achingly beautiful that he wanted to shake her. He wanted her to swear that she was loyal, that she had been a fool . . . that she loved him.

She did not do so, but she swallowed and answered softly with an admirable dignity. "I have done nothing but suffer your slings and arrows, milord, for what is a friendship with the man who is my sister's husband—and your dear companion, or so the past has claimed. If you would taunt me, milord, than you must expect my ridicule on the subject."

He lowered his face, taut with emotion, until it hovered over hers. "*Did* you miss me, madame?"

She hesitated a long time, then her dignity was lost in an angry cry, and she tried to wrest him from her person. "Aye! My Lord Cameron, I have missed you. I have felt the snow of winter and the chill of frost coming upon us, and I have ached for the searing fire that you can bring against the cold."

His breath caught; he had not expected such an admission from her. Slowly, slowly, he lowered himself beside her, his eyes locked upon hers. She swallowed again, nervously lowering her lashes. "Have *you* missed *me,* milord?"

"More than I have ever yearned for water to drink, or air to breathe. With every fiber and drop of blood within me, milady, I ached to hold you in my arms again."

A smile touched her lips. He pulled her close, and he

pulled the covers over them both. It was good to be home.

In seconds he was sleeping.

When he awoke that afternoon, Molly was in the room straightening up, and his wife was nowhere to be seen. He frowned to Molly, who was painfully cheerful. He had a splitting headache from the rum he had drunk with the dawn.

"Where is Jassy?"

"Why, milord!" Molly said innocently, "Jassy is about business. One cannot sleep late and tarry here, sir. This *is* the New World. Nay, milord, not even nobility and gentry can while away precious time here."

"Molly, where is my wife?"

"Why, she is seeing that the meat in the smoke shed is coming along properly. The game has been slim of late, as you can imagine, I am certain. But Powan and his men were by recently. Jassy made him a satin shirt from some of the fabric that arrived upon the *Lady Destiny*, and he was quite pleased with it. He has brought up many rabbits, and a great deal of pumpkin bread in turn."

Jamie shot up, then remembered that he was naked, and jerked the covers up. "Powan?" he demanded.

"Oh, yes, the chief has been around often, as have many of the Indians. Lord Newbury was in from Jamestown, and everyone seems to be getting along very well. The Indians are often helping the settlers these days. Isn't it wonderful?"

"Wonderful," Jamie murmured. Powan was an old friend, but he had not expected to see him this far south upon the peninsula at this time of the year.

And he had certainly never expected Jassy to make the Indian a shirt. Wryly he realized that he had not expected Jassy ever to speak to an Indian, much less form the facsimile of a friendship. He would be curious to hear more about the affair.

A man could never fathom what might happen in his absence, he determined.

"Has anything else happened which I should know about?" he asked Molly, crossing his arms over his chest.

"No, milord."

"Did you know that Jassy has distressing nightmares?"

Molly's eyes lowered quickly. "We are all plagued by dreams now and then."

Molly wasn't going to say any more. Jamie grunted. He noted the warm, luxurious fox fur that stretched out at the foot of the bed. "So the *Lady Destiny* arrived with her cargo."

"Oh, yes!" Molly was all animation again. "Jassy—Lady Cameron—was so pleased with the things!"

So pleased . . . oh, yes, his wife could be purchased.

"Milord, is there anything else?"

Jamie scowled. "Yes, Mistress Molly, I would like you out of my room so that I might dress. Now!"

Molly jumped and fled. Jamie rose and folded his buckskins and sought out his good Englishwear. In satin breeches, silk shirt, and a woolen doublet he set out for the day, anxious for the business at hand.

He met with Sir William, and William told him about the day when Powan had come and first met Jassy. William grinned. "He told her that he thought she was a good choice for you—she would work hard in your fields and bear you many children."

"That must have gone over well," Jamie murmured.

Sir William was amused.

"She handled herself most admirably."

"I am sure that she did," Jamie said. Then he told William about his visit to Opechancanough, warning Sir William that he was worried, though he could not pinpoint the danger. "We must keep up a careful eye," Jamie warned, and Sir William agreed.

Later that day he met with Captain Stewart and gave him his sailing orders. The captain's cargo of tobacco for England was loaded. He chewed on his pipe, enjoying the Virginia tobacco himself while he watched the loading with Jamie on the dock. He would return in the spring with the supplies ordered from the mother country.

Late in the afternoon Elizabeth found him, and she proudly showed him that she had not only learned to carry one of the heavy muskets but to load and fire it, and actually to hit a tree as well. "Jassy taught me," she told him proudly.

Jamie wasn't sure why, but he was further irritated.

Then Jassy did not appear at the dinner table—she was still engaged in some task or another, Lenore told him. Jamie liked Lenore well enough, and he was very fond of Elizabeth, and Robert was his friend. But they needed to be in their own home, and he would see that they moved quickly, he vowed to himself.

Still weary from his all-night ride to reach home, he climbed the stairs to his room, his temper seething as he wondered about the whereabouts of his wife.

He was not to wonder long.

She was seated upon the foot of the bed, her legs curled beneath her. She was dressed in a diaphanous gown that clearly delineated every full, sensual, and sexual curve of her body. She brushed her hair into silky strands. Her movements were slow and sensual, and the mere sight of her sent him floundering into a stream of desire. He took care, though, walking to his desk, sitting behind it and folding his hands and watching her thoughtfully.

He wondered at her motive.

He did not see the hurt in her eyes as he ignored her; he only saw that she was playing at seduction, the actress again. He did not want an act, and he did not want a game.

"Why weren't you at dinner?" he asked her.

She stretched, graceful, entirely feline, feminine, and exciting. The deep rouge crests of her swelling breasts strained against the silk gauze of her gown, and she smiled lazily. "I looked after the meat we are still preparing for the winter today. I seemed to be filled with the scent of smoke, and so I bathed and washed my hair, and then I needed to dry before the fire.

The fire . . . the firelight played all over her. It enhanced the curves that teased him beneath the evocative gown. It made her hair gleam like goldleaf, and her skin, too, seemed to gleam golden. He gritted his teeth and watched her from narrowed, suspicious eyes.

She yawned deliciously, and stretched again. Graceful, unbearably sensual. He rose and walked over to her. He took the brush from her fingers and leaned over her with twisted tension that forced her back upon the bed. He planted his palms on either side of her head. "What is this display, madame?"

Her eyelashes flickered uncertainly. "I did not get to thank you this morning for the many gifts you sent aboard the *Lady Destiny*—"

She did not finish speaking; he swore with a startling violence and pushed away from her. "You really are a whore, milady, aren't you? Determined to pay your debts."

Shock registered on her features, a look of naked pain that passed by so quickly that he might have imagined it, and then a look of raw fury and hatred. She lashed out in rage, railing against him, trying to strike him. He caught her wrists, and to his astonishment she fought on, kneeing him curtly in the groin. Stunned and in agony, he fell from her.

She leapt up and swept her new furred cloak around her and stared down at him scathingly. "You needn't worry, milord, you haven't the price to pay any more, ever!"

"Jasmine . . ." he began in a growl. He meant to catch her. He was in pain and his temper was seething, and he meant to have it out then and there. She was too quick for him. She was gone. In her sheer gown and her furred cloak, she was gone.

Of all the people that Jassy did not want to see at the moment, the half-breed girl, Hope, might surely have topped her list.

No one else was about when she reached the downstairs hall, but the beautiful, honey-colored girl sat at the table eating stew with her fingers. She saw Jassy and smiled at her agitation.

"What are you doing here?" Jassy asked her.

Hope licked her fingers very slowly and completely. "I am eating my dinner. I traveled with Lord Jamie, and so now I am here, in his hall." She stared pointedly at Jassy, then looked up the stairway and rolled her eyes. "What are you doing here, lady?"

Jassy fought back the temptation to slap the girl's face. "It is my house, Hope. I belong here."

"You belong up there, with him. It is *his* house."

She stiffened, because the girl was right. And she had to sit, suddenly feeling very ill because she should have been with him, but she should have never, never made such a fool of herself. She was incapable of being a temptress, and now she hated her husband all over again because . . .

He had spurned her advance; he had called her a whore. And here was this half-pagan strumpet instructing her about duty!

Hope began to chuckle. "So you do not please him so much anymore. You should try harder. He is a man to be cherished." She seemed to purr the last words, and the sound scraped along Jassy's back. She gritted her teeth together hard.

"Hope, you are an insolent creature. *I* am none of *your* business, and neither is Lord Cameron."

"Lord Cameron might well be my business." Smiling, Hope sat back. Then she leaned toward Jassy, and it was evident that she wore no stays beneath her simple gown; her large breasts swayed with her every movement. To Jassy's amazement, Hope spread out her hands, making an imaginary measurement. "If you do not care for Lord Jamie, I will, lady. He is the finest man I have ever seen."

Jassy realized that Hope was measuring the most masculine part of her husband's anatomy. Anger flared within her so hotly that she seemed to see red. Dizziness swept her.

She stood. "How dare you!" she grated out. Without much thought she set her hands firmly upon the girl's shoulders, wrenching her like a little child from the table. She set her down upon her feet and turned her toward the door. "Out! And do not come back!"

By that time, Jassy heard footsteps hurrying down the stairs. Jamie—she had forgotten him in the depths of her rage.

His hair was mussed, and he was barefoot and clad only in a pair of breeches. As soon as he appeared, Hope set up a wail. She raced for him, throwing herself against his chest when he reached the landing. She set up a horrible wailing.

"What in the Lord's name—" Jamie looked from Hope to Jassy. Jassy stood silent in rage, and Hope began to cry. "She beats me, she sets her hands upon me and beats and throws me out into the snow—"

"Jassy, is this—"

Jassy didn't let him finish speaking. She came up to the two of them, slapped him across the face with a stunning blow, and headed for the door. "No, I did not beat her. And I will not throw her out into the snow. *I* am going!"

She didn't realize until she stepped outside and bitter cold knifed into her that she wasn't wearing shoes. She had walked at least twenty feet before it registered in her mind that she had nowhere to go, and *had* she had somewhere to go, she could not make it there barefoot.

It didn't matter. By then, Jamie was behind her. He ran like light, sweeping her into his arms, catapulting her into the snow. She gasped and sputtered the white flakes from her mouth and looked up to see that he was bare-chested and shivering and furious.

"Madame, once we are both back in that house and thawed, I intend to wring your neck."

"My neck! You bloody, lying knave!"

"What? Never mind!"

He rose, wincing, swearing once again that if they both lived with all their limbs and extremities intact, she would pay dearly. He pulled her up, lifted her into his arms, and, looking straight ahead, carried her back to the house.

Hope was gone and the hall was empty, but were it not, she was certain that her husband would have behaved in the same heedless manner. He thundered up the steps, tearing into her verbally, swearing that she was a fool, and a fool risking the life and health of an innocent child as well as her own.

She fought his hold. Once they had reached the harbor of their room, he freely let her go, setting her before the fire while he came close to singeing his hand and feet, trying to warm them. "I should beat you—" he began, his teeth chattering, but Jassy was already on her feet.

"Beat me? Nay, milord, you snake! You cast doubt upon an innocent friendship while you lie in my face!"

"What are you talking about?" he said, exploding.

Her cloak was tangled about her and falling. Jassy impatiently tossed it down and leaned forward as Hope had done, displaying the fullness of her breasts temptingly before him. "What am I talking about?" she repeated, mimicking Hope. "I am talking about you—and the piece of your anatomy that rules your heart and stupid mind!" She put her hands out as Hope had done, showing him an extremely accurate measurement of size.

"What?" he repeated.

She swung, intending to strike him again. He wouldn't allow it. He caught her arm, she spun into his arms, and he held her tight. "Let me go!" she demanded, wild with fury.

Suddenly he was laughing. "You're jealous."

"You will never touch me again, I do not care about marriage vows or—"

"Jassy, I never touched her!"

"She has seen you—bare. I know it!"

He whirled her around and looked into the wild tempest of her eyes, and it made the pulse of desire within him shoot and sear like gunfire. He carried her over to the bed and set her down, and when she tried to rise, he cast the weight of his leg over hers, taking care of the babe but pinning her down. He started to untie his breeches, and she went wild, tossing like a wild pony beneath him. "You will not—"

His breeches were free. He leaned over her, pinning her wrists with his hand, finding her body unbearably evocative beneath the gauzy gown. He caressed the full, firm weight of her breast while she squirmed and swore, and when she tired, he spoke again. "She saw me, yes. But I never lay with her, Jassy, never, and I will swear it upon the Bible before Father Steven. She appeared here one night, determined on seduction, but I did not touch her."

She went still, watching him suspiciously. He bent his head and sucked her breast over the gauze of the gown. He felt her grow taut beneath him. "Why not?" she whispered.

"You were on my mind," he murmured, lightly closing his teeth over her nipple. Her head twisted and her body suddenly surged against his, and he slipped his hand between her thighs, and then rolled suddenly, dragging her around. His eyes heavy-lidded and sultry, he smiled at her vulnerability. "I swear!" he repeated, tugging her gown high. "Love me, wife. I've no need for any woman—nay, any life or sustenance!—but you."

He tugged up her gown, caught her hips, and brought her slowly down upon him. When he began to fill her, she suddenly resisted.

"I tried!" she choked out. "You—"

"You tied my heart and mind and loins all in a knot together, and I humbly beg your forgiveness!" he claimed. He caught her hips and brought her fully down, and he watched the beauty of her face as the passion caught hold of her. Moments later he found the hem of her gown, tossed it over her head, and he was swamped with the heady passion that possessed him as she moved, fluid as a river, graceful and sweet, her back arching, her breasts full and bouncing before him. In the end he caught her to him, and she was soaked and exhausted and completely sated. She didn't speak. She fell silent beside him.

He waited, and smiled. Then he kissed her forehead.

"Jassy, it is the truth. I never touched her. I will be glad to swear it."

She was quiet for a moment. Her eyes remained closed, and he thought that she slept, but then she answered him. "And I, milord, swear that what I feel for Robert Maxwell is a deep friendship; he is my brother, my sister's husband, and nothing more."

Her eyes opened and met his.

"It will be a long, cold winter, my love. Truce?" he said.

Her eyes fell closed again.

"Truce," she agreed.

XV

As Christmas neared, winter came upon them in full, cold and hard and brutal. Jamie left very early each morning in search of game and came back later every afternoon. Jassy quickly realized that there could be little class distinction here, for the settlers were forced to band together to survive. Jamie had managed to bring many supplies from England, but they must be shared, and being a "lady" here—especially Lord Cameron's wife—was a matter of responsibility and not leisure.

She did have help, for their household servants had come to the New World for a new life, and were willing to work hard to survive the rigors of the winter. It wasn't, however, England. There were no major social obligations for nobility or gentry, and though Jassy did spend time writing a letter to Jane and Henry to be taken back on the next ship to arrive, it was her only correspondence. The settlement did not yet provide the customary activities for ladies of means. Jamie assured her that in the spring they would entertain the governor of the Jamestown colony, and that they would ride to the other settlements. But on the whole, she certainly had no demanding social schedule; she didn't need to prepare to travel to Court, nor was she expecting any royal visitors. She did have a busy household, with constant tasks, and if she occasionally mourned for the grand manor in which she had reigned so briefly in England, she was also quick to forget the elegance when engaged in some necessary chore. The days were short, and the nights were long and cold. Men of all classes cut trees and stacked wood; women sewed, salted and smoked and preserved meat and foodstuff, made candles and soap, and engaged in the endless task of laundry.

The Indians began appearing more frequently. They came to the palisade to trade; they came in friendship. In winter they wore buckskin, the men *and* the women. Jassy did not see Powan again. She was fascinated by the Indians but also wary, and she tended to keep a careful distance from them. A few of the settlers who had been with the hundred since Jamie had first chosen the site knew some of the Indians' language and managed to communicate with them effectively. Jamie knew enough of it to get by very well, and she saw him greeting various of the Indians many times. He knew them by name, welcomed them, and encouraged Jassy to get to know them. But even then he warned her that she must take care around them too.

"Why?" she asked him one night. She was bundled into a long blue nightgown, and he was at his desk, setting the last of some entry for the day into his calendar. He looked up at her, startled.

"Why?" he repeated.

"*You* seem to like them very much, but you warn *me* away."

"I do not warn you away. As my wife, I expect you to greet them always with courtesy."

"I am courteous," she told him, her temper simmering at his indication that she had not.

He shrugged, then set down his pen. "I have seen you near them, madame, upon occasion. You are stiff, and careful not to come too close. That is not exactly courtesy."

"I met Powan and—"

"You did well, yes. It seems that you are deeply fascinated, but I think, too, that you forget that they are men and women just as we are. They are made of flesh and blood, and they are born with hopes and fears and emotions."

"I am aware of that," Jassy said coolly. "I did not think that you had complaints about my demeanor as your wife."

"The little actress," he said softly. "I do always wonder what you are *really* thinking or feeling."

"I would assume, milord, that you expect me to do better here, with savages and farmers, than with your friends of the nobility and gentry back home."

"I assume, milady, that you will do just fine, no matter with whom you are cast."

"So, have I done well here?" she demanded, her chin high. She knew that he watched her often; she never knew what he *thought*.

"You know that you have done very well. You need not seek a compliment. In fact, you have done exceptionally well, considering your hatred for the voyage, and for leaving England. I think you hated it all enough to regret the marriage, no matter what it brought to you." He watched her pensively. "Tell me, milady, have you regretted it?"

She kept her eyes upon his, and her throat went strangely dry. Her eyes lowered. "I—I have regretted nothing," she murmured. "You forget, I could still be a servant in my brother's house."

"You are an ingenious woman, milady. I'm rather sure that you'd not have stayed there long."

She ignored his words and pleated the sheets beneath her fingers. "Tell me, milord, have *you* regretted your marriage?"

He took a long time to answer, sitting back in the chair. He stared at her so long that she flushed, and very deeply regretted the question.

"My passion for you has not died, milady," he said at last.

"That does not mean you do not regret the marriage," she murmured, her cheeks aflame.

"I do not regret the marriage," he said. He looked back

to his paper but continued speaking to her, returning to the subject of the Indians. "Remember, Jassy, that you are to take care with the Powhatans. In their beliefs they are very different. They did not spring from Adam and Eve but from the pouch of a giant hare. They fear their evil god more than they love their benevolent one, and they have sacrificed their own infants and children to that god. They have little mercy for their enemies."

"Are we their enemies?"

He set his pen down and walked over to the hearth, stopping to watch the fire burn. "If Opechancanough's brother still lived, I would have felt more secure. He was a man of peace, while Powhatan earned his great power by violence, and Opechancanough is a man who is quick to violence too. They have at times befriended us; they have never really accepted us."

Despite herself, she was shivering. "Why are we here, then?"

Annoyed, he stared at her. "Madame, we are here because I choose it so." He walked over to the bed, and she flushed, realizing the intent in his eyes. He tilted her chin so that their eyes met. "And *you* will take grave care, milady, because I have commanded that you do so, will you not?"

She was not sure what he meant, but she nodded to the dark demand in his eyes, and she trembled then, for his arms came around her with every bit as much demand as stoked his eyes. This she could not regret, this magical flame that leapt between them.

But later, when she lay by his side and heard the even whisper of his breath as he slept, she wondered uneasily of the future. Her fascination for him grew daily. But would the time come when the passion he felt for her died, when the flame ran its course? If so, she would be lost, and she would not even have the strength of her hatred to sustain her.

She was his wife, she reminded herself. She was about to bear his child. But was that enough?

For the first time she realized that she wanted his love.

On the twentieth of December, Robert and Lenore

moved into their new home. The entire settlement had worked upon the finishing of the house, including Robert and Jamie. They were all very excited, as the house was nearly as grand as Jamie's, and put together very quickly but very well. Jassy was somewhat startled by Lenore's enthusiasm, for her sister was often very conscious of class, and the house did not compare to the home she had known growing up.

"That was always our brother's home, Jassy," Lenore explained. "This is the very first home I shall have of my own."

The three sisters worked hard upon a set of tapestries to keep the cold out. "Ladies' work, and very proper!" Lenore assured Jassy. She had never approved of Jassy's involvement with John Tannen and his pathetic little family, but Jassy had shrugged aside her objections. It was surprising, though, to realize as they worked together on the last day that she would miss Lenore. And when night fell and the men came back to tell them that it was time to move, she embraced Lenore warmly, and Lenore hugged her fiercely in return. Then Robert kissed her and smiled at her. "Good-bye, little sister. Take care."

"We will not be so far," she said.

"Merely a stone's throw," he agreed.

"It is a very small community," Jamie said dryly. "I daresay that we will see as much of one another as we always have. We shall merely . . . sleep in different places." He drew Jassy away from Robert and back to his side. He seemed tense and somewhat irritable. He did not seem to mind, however, kissing Lenore very warmly before it was time for them to depart.

Jamie was to see them to their new home. Jassy assumed that she would accompany them, too, but when she asked Molly to fetch her cape, Jamie whirled her around, shaking his head. There was a curious fever about his eyes. "Madame, it is late and bitterly cold for you to come out in your condition. Your good-byes have been said, and you can take a walk to the new house in the morning with Elizabeth."

She wanted to argue with him. She longed to see the new house, with the last of it completed. And she didn't like being left alone when surely they all would have a welcome toast and Jamie would probably stay very late while she sat upstairs alone.

"Jamie, there is no reason—"

His jaw twisted and set. "There is every reason."

She lowered her head, then tossed her hair back, ready to challenge him. "Jamie—"

His hands fell upon her shoulders, his eyes burning. "It is not a good night. The snow has iced over, and you might trip or stumble, and fall. Would you risk my child so readily?"

"We shall all get together in the morning," Robert said cheerfully. "Well, maybe not." He grimaced. Robert was learning the way of the settlement. He was accompanying Jamie on his morning hunting trips outside the palisade. "I shall be out with Lord Cameron, but then you ladies shall probably enjoy each other's companionship well enough."

"To bed," Jamie told Jassy firmly.

She set her jaw, kissed Lenore, and then Robert once again, and hurried for the stairs. Jamie nodded to Molly, and Molly nodded gravely in return, and followed Jassy.

Jassy fumed to Molly about her ill treatment, and Molly, setting out one of her bed gowns and folding the lace ruff Jassy had worn fashionably about her neck, cheerfully ignored her. "Women do get temperamental in your state, so they say, pet! Oh, I do hope that I shall find out soon enough! Crawl into bed now."

Curious, Jassy obediently crawled beneath the covers. "Now what does that mean, Molly?"

"John Tannen has suggested that we should marry." Molly was trying very hard to subdue her excitement. "He is asking Father Steven if we might marry before Christmas Day."

"So quickly!" Jassy gasped.

"And more proper than not," Molly murmured. "Jassy, I spend so much time there with the children and . . . all. Oh, Jassy, I am so excited! I am getting on, you know.

And once I felt so old and worn and I thought that no man would ever have me . . . I have been honest with John, he knows all about my past, and he cares nothing of it. He says that all that matters is what lies between the two of us. He said that I was a whirlwind of giving energy, and that he cannot help but love me, for he has watched me with his son and his little sister-in-law, and thinks that they could have no finer a stepmother, nor could he choose a more tender bride."

"Oh, how beautiful!" Jassy cried. "I am so very pleased for you, Molly."

"It is all thanks to you, Jassy."

"Molly! I did not make you kind and good and loving!"

"You gave me a new life. You and Lord Cameron."

And Lord Cameron, Jassy silently acknowledged. She lowered her eyes and bit into her lower lip. He had made life good. He had made it a tempest, and he was still a horrible autocrat, but she could no longer imagine a life without him. He infuriated her, he stimulated and excited her to sheer abandon, and he was the force of her life.

She kissed Molly warmly. "I wish you the very, very best."

"Oh, thank you, Jassy. I will need your blessing, and Lord Cameron's."

"He will give it freely." That much she thought, she could say with confidence. Jamie would be pleased for Molly and John. In many aspects these were his people, far more so than their loyalty or lives belonged to any king. He was the governor here, the law, the only king that any of them knew, or could touch, reach, or recognize.

Both women started suddenly, for they heard Jamie's footsteps upon the stairs. He was coming to the room, long-strided, swift and, sure. "Good night!" Molly told Jassy, and slipped away quickly. Jassy listened, curious, as Molly and Jamie greeted each other, and then Molly scurried down the stairs. The door to the room opened, and he was there, his heavy cloak covered in snowflakes. He cast it carelessly aside, his eyes still hot, curiously excited, and fevered as they fell upon her. He stumbled out of his boots, watching her all the while. She kept a wary eye upon him in return. Was he angry over Robert again? He had snatched her quickly enough from his friend, and he had ordered her upstairs. . . .

He wrenched off his doublet, and practically tore off his shirt in his haste to get it over his head. Approaching the bed, he pulled away his hose and garters but went no further. With some kind of a barbaric cry he leapt upon the bed, seized her to his side, and kissed her with a dizzying passion. She struggled against him at first, then gave way to the honeyed sensations that swept warmly and deliciously through her. His hands gently ravaged her, and when he broke away at last, a blazing and devilish smile touched his eyes and curved his lips.

Jassy moistened her lips. "What is it?"

"It? It is passion, and an obsessive desire, and I can bear it no longer, and, madame, we are so much more *alone* in our house!"

"Jamie, how can you be so crude—"

"Not crude, madame," he said, shimmying from his trousers. "Delighted."

"Robert is your friend."

"Um. And your friend, too, milady. Tell me, do you ever think of him?"

"What?" she demanded, startled.

He cupped and cradled her breast and brought his body, naked and hard, flush to hers. "Do you still think of him? Wishing that you had not been so rudely caught within my arms on May Day?"

She went very pale, wondering at the tension within him. "What do you want from me?" she asked harshly. "I am huge with your child, and still you would taunt me so! What do you want?"

He gazed at her a long time, his eyes indigo fire, so dark and enigmatic that they seemed black. "Your very soul, perhaps, milady. That which I do not hold."

"No man should hold everything of a woman!" she cried. For then the woman, she thought silently, would be so sadly at his mercy.

"And what of the woman, milady? Should she hold everything of a man?"

"You are talking in riddles, and I do not understand you. You have whatever you choose you take."

"What I choose to take . . ." he repeated savagely. His head lowered to hers, his lips seizing upon her mouth, and he filled her with the potent surge of his desire. He made love to her with tenderness, and with a searing and shattering sensuality. She rode the wild wind of the reckless emotion that haunted him, and she was cast higher into a realm of abandon and ecstasy than she had ever gone before. She had once thought that this thing between them could know no higher bounds, yet he taught her again and again that she could soar farther into distant heavens. When he had finished with her, she felt entirely sated and spent, somewhat awed, and thoroughly dazed. Exhausted, she curled against him and felt his hand sweep around what had once been her waist. She expected some arrogant comment from him, some taunting assurance that she was *his* possession and she would learn not to think of another.

He was silent for a very long time, then she heard him sigh, and he touched her gently. "Alas, my love, my fiendish pleasure comes too late. I should not have had you this night, fiercely or otherwise. Feel? The babe kicks. He protests his father's rudeness. Did I hurt you, Jassy?"

She was glad of the darkness, for she flushed crimson. "No, you did me no harm."

He kissed her forehead. "Well, milady, my wife, you will be free of me now, for some months to come." Again he was silent. He teased her breasts with the idle play of his fingers, just touching the tip with his tongue. He hovered over her in the night. "Tell me, Jassy, will you be glad? Or will you not miss this . . . just a bit?"

"Jamie, please . . ."

He rolled away from her and got up from the bed. "Go to sleep, Jassy," he said harshly.

"Jamie—"

"Go to sleep."

She watched him miserably as he moved across the room, his naked back and buttocks tightly muscled and sinewed, and beautiful in a curious manner. He did not gaze back to her but stood before the fire.

She wanted to cry out to him, but she could not. The words would have tumbled from her lips fast and desperately, and she would have given away more than her soul; she would have cast her naked heart before him, and that she dared not do. She closed her eyes, and exhaustion overwhelmed her.

The house was very different in the morning. Lenore and Robert had taken Kathryn with them, and Charity had left to serve in their house, too, if only for a week or so, or until some girl was found to help with the household tasks. Elizabeth had opted to stay with Jamie and Jassy, if Jamie didn't mind. Jamie didn't mind Elizabeth at all—it was only Robert he had wanted gone. With Elizabeth, Jassy set out to see her sister's new home, and Lenore was glad to greet them both, showing them about as if she had acquired a palace.

"This," she said, showing them a little loft, "will be for the baby."

"Oh, Lenore, you too!" Elizabeth cried with pleasure. "How far along are you?"

Lenore giggled. "Well, I am not yet. Except that I think that maybe last night . . . well, Robert was quite determined." She gave Jassy a smug, conspiratorial smile. "Men . . . Mostly he is so courteous, and not at all demanding. Last night he said that we must have children too. He has pointed out how very well you manage in your condition. He also pointed out how quickly you arrived in your condition." She idly curled a lock of hair around her finger, studying Jassy. "But then you married Jamie Cameron, and he must be the devil himself in—in private."

"Lenore!" Elizabeth gasped.

"Oh, don't be such a little church mouse!" Lenore laughed. "Honestly. I was the one Jamie intended to marry. Sometimes I do wonder."

Jassy was pink by then, but Lenore didn't intend to let the matter drop. "It isn't a 'duty,' is it? It is exciting and decadent and—"

"Lenore!" Elizabeth said entreatingly. "You're making Jassy very uncomfortable."

Jassy smiled suddenly. "Lenore, I am quite content."

Lenore laughed good-naturedly. "Jassy, *I* am quite content. *You* are something more, I think."

Perhaps she was, but in the next few days it seemed that a breach widened between her and Jamie. He was gone long in the morning, and had much to do in the afternoons, and he started working at his desk until very late at night.

As Jamie had expected, Lenore and Robert were still with them almost as much as they were not. It was an evening only three nights after they had left the house when they returned for dinner. Jassy learned from Molly that Father Steven had approved her immediate marriage to John Tannen. With all of them present, Jassy broached the subject to Jamie.

Jamie was thoughtful at first, arching a brow to the very suggestion. In England, such a marriage would have been a breach of morality, for poor Joan was barely dead and cast to the sea for six months. In the hundred, it was a matter of good sense, for John Tannen needed Molly, and it seemed that Molly's temper had been a matter of her mixed emotions.

"Father Steven has approved this?" Jamie asked Jassy.

"He has . . ." She hesitated. "I would like to have a reception for them here, following the ceremony."

Silence greeted her suggestion.

Then Lenore spoke up, quickly and certainly. Such an event would have been an outrageous breach of society had they been home in England, she was quick to point out. But they weren't in England, Jassy was just as quick to counter. And, standing by the mantel, her hands lightly resting upon her rounded abdomen, Jassy quietly reminded her sister that at home, in England, Jassy could barely muster into the ranks of society herself. "And you are forgetting one thing," she reminded her sister, her head held high. "Molly is not just my servant; she is my friend. Her circumstances are much the same as my own. She was always at my side when I needed her, and I wish to do for her now what I can."

Lenore stared at her sister, shaking her head, then turned to Jamie. "Can't you stop this? Life is certainly different here, but . . ."

Jamie, paying little heed as he scoured his musket barrel, looked up at last, shrugging to Lenore. "Jassy must do as she chooses. It is her home."

The matter was settled, and Molly was duly married, and amid the white snow of winter and with everyone in attendance, from the maids and carpenters and laborers to Sir William and Lenore and Robert and Father Steven, Jassy held her first party for her friend. It was fun, and it was a relief from the rigors of the weather and the dampness that could so easily chill the bones. Jassy danced happily with Sir William, the groom, and Robert. It was then that her husband cut in upon her. His eyes were grave, and she stiffened, wary lest he have some comment about Robert. He did not. He swept her around himself, saying merely, "I think it is time that you rested. In England, my lady, a damsel so far enceinte would not be so gaily upon a dance floor." He hesitated. "You could harm the babe, love. Or yourself."

Flushing, she dutifully left the floor and set herself the task of handing out warmed mead and ale. And when the party came to an end, she was filled with pleasure as Molly kissed and hugged her, promising her that she would forever serve her, and do so with love.

She was grateful to Jamie that night, but she was hesitant about making any overtures to him, for she still could not forget that she had attempted either to please or seduce him once, and had failed miserably in the attempt. He had said that he would not touch her again, but she did miss him. Still, she might harm the babe, and she grew more awkward daily. She was very heavy with the child, and she wondered sometimes with dismay how she could have grown so large so quickly. And so she did not attempt to seduce him; she crawled into bed and watched him as he disrobed. Even in the shocking cold he slept naked, and—in the days before his determination not to touch her—she had usually wound up so herself. After her first protests he had laughed and assured her that the warmth they generated together was the greatest form of heat they could achieve. She could not tell him, but she did not mind. She liked the feel of his hard body flush to hers while they slept. She liked the possessive splay of his hands upon her, and the tickle of the hairs upon his chest against her back. It was exciting—all of it, just as Lenore had suggested—it was comfortable, and there was also a soft and pleasant intimacy about it that caused her to yearn for more, for something she could not quite see, and for which she was afraid to reach.

With the covers about her, she watched Jamie as he finished some notation at his desk, stretched with his hands upon his lower back, and stood pensively before the fire, his elbow resting upon the mantel, idly stroking his cheek. He looked at her at last, and her cheeks burned, for he caught her scrutiny of him, and he smiled slowly, his brow arching.

"Did you mind the party so much?" she asked him.

"I did not mind it at all. And you enjoyed it."

"Ah, but *you* did not come from the gutter," she said, and as a scowl darkened his features she quickly repented her words. She looked down quickly at her hands, wanting to apologize, but not at all sure how to do so.

"This is a new world, indeed, milady. And I'm not at all sure that it matters where one was born to excel here."

He turned away from the mantel and started across the room for his cloak. Jassy was startled, realizing that he intended to go out. Once she would have been inordinately pleased to have him leave her alone in their bed. Now her heart quickened, and she wondered if she hadn't finally become so misshapen that she could no longer hold his interest, and she couldn't help but wonder where he was going.

"Jamie?"

He paused, then came back by the bed. He lifted her chin and studied her eyes. "Go to sleep," he told her softly. "I won't be long. I feel a certain restlessness and want to see that the gates are locked, and that the guard is awake."

Once he was gone, she lay awake, foolishly fighting a wave of tears. She didn't know what she was feeling, except that she was in a tempest. She would never sleep. But as seemed usual of late, she was exhausted, and she fell into a restless sleep.

Somewhere in the night, he crawled in beside her. She sensed his presence, and her rest became more peaceful.

On Christmas Eve, Father Steven held church services, and the settlement crowded into the small chapel. They sang English carols, and despite the cold and the hardships, the night was one of revelry. Even Elizabeth was in good spirits, and she spent much time with Sir William Tybalt, which intrigued Jassy and gave her hope for her sister's future. She would love to see Elizabeth happy and wed.

The family exchanged small gifts in the hall when the services were over. Jassy had muffs for her sisters, and for Robert and Jamie she had sewn soft leather jerkins. She was anxious to see Jamie with his gift, and when he had lifted the doublet, she showed him the shirt beneath. It was made from the best of the silk that had come to them on the *Lady Destiny*. He sat across from the fire, and Jassy was pleased that they were a certain distance from the others. She was anxious to see his reaction to the gift.

He looked at her quickly and curiously, fingering the cloth. "It is probably the best piece brought over. And you've certainly used the best of the lace upon the sleeves and collar. I had thought that you would have wanted a dress made from this."

She shrugged, fingering the pendant that lay against her breast, his gift to her. It was a gold medallion, engraved with the Cameron crest and studded with precious jewels. "Do you not like the shirt?"

He studied her carefully. "I like it very much. Who made it?"

"I did."

"I never saw you work upon it."

"I meant for it to be a surprise. I worked when you were out of the house. Are you surprised?"

"Very. The cloth is rich, madame. You did not take it for yourself. If you do not take care, I will begin to imagine that you did not marry me entirely for my money. I thought that you craved the best of everything, my love."

Jassy flushed, still fingering the precious golden medallion. He taunted her, but it was Christmas, and she did not care.

"I never craved the best of anything . . . material, milord. I did seek not to starve, I admit. And I did seek . . ."

"What?"

"Never mind," she said, swiftly turning aside. He would not let her go. He stood, catching her arm, pulling her back to him. "You did seek what, milady? Tell me."

"Jamie, it is Christmas. We have guests—"

"And may God bless them. Answer me. You did seek what?"

She lifted her head and met his demanding stare gravely. "I sought not to die, nor to live, like my mother. Please, could you be so good as to release me now?"

His hand fell away from her arm. She lowered her eyes quickly from his and hurried back to the fire. Tamsyn sat upon the hearth, playing a rousing melody upon a flute. Lenore and Robert were dancing to the curious tune, while Kathryn, the Hume girls, and Mrs. Lawton laughed and applauded. Breathless at last, Lenore fell into a chair before the blaze. "Alas, if only it were England!"

"Are you so homesick, then?" Elizabeth asked her.

"Sometimes," Lenore admitted. "I should love just to see London this night! London, with her busy streets and carefree revelers and her churches, with the bells all pealing merrily. I should love to see Hampton Court; I would cherish a visit to Oxford. I would even love to walk the streets among the people. I *am* homesick, I suppose. I should not like to see the palisade—I should like to see Westminster Abbey and the shops—"

"Shops!" Robert groaned.

"Oh, come!" Lenore said, pouting. "I do not want to smoke meat and worry if we've enough candles and wood for the winter. Look at my hands! Alas, they are almost as bad as Jassy's. I have stooped to the making of candles and soap!"

They all laughed. Jassy was startled by her husband's touch when he picked up her small hand and smoothed his large fingers over it. The fire flickered, and it seemed that the room grew silent—even Tamsyn ceased to play—and Jamie studied her hand very carefully. "This is not a bad hand, as I see it, Lenore. It came to me rough and worn in the service of others, and now it stays rough and worn in the service of my dream. It is a fine hand. It holds great strength, yet it can touch with tenderness. I am quite fond of it, really. Tell me, Jassy, are you so homesick too? Do you still abhor the Carlyle Hundred?"

She could not snatch her hand away, nor could she understand the curious tone of voice with which he softly spoke, then so abruptly demanded. "I am here, milord, for you commanded it so. Remember?"

"Ah. You, too, would prefer London."

"You forget yourself, Lord Cameron. Where you go, I am thither commanded. And you choose to be here."

"Is it really so simple, then?"

"You have seen that it is so," Jassy replied demurely. She was trembling, and she didn't know why. She tugged lightly upon her hand and freed it at last. She looked about at their company and mumbled out some excuse about being exhausted. Then she fled them all, seeking the sanctuary of her room. Jamie would come soon enough, but he would not touch her. He would crawl into his side of the bed, keep his careful distance, and not disturb her.

Molly was not with her, and so she quickly disrobed alone and crawled into bed, shivering. She did not remove her pendant but held it between her fingers. *Cameron*. It was her name. Jassy Cameron. She had never stopped to realize it before, and now it suddenly meant very much. Holding the pendant, she closed her eyes and quickly drifted off to sleep.

It was not, however, a restful sleep. Of all strange times, her nightmares returned. And soon she started to scream again. To scream, and scream, and scream . . .

"Jassy!"

She awoke drenched in sweat, shaking convulsively. She was not alone. Jamie was back, and he held her tightly against himself. "Jassy, shush, it's over now. It's a dream, it's a nightmare. That's all. It is nothing real, nothing that can hurt you!"

She stared into his eyes. Against the soft light of the fire they were very blue and gentle. He touched her cheek and smoothed away the tears that she had shed in her sleep. "Jassy!" he repeated.

She had been as taut as steel, she realized. She went limp in his arms. It had been a dream. No specters haunted their bedroom, no corpses.

"I'm . . . sorry," she whispered. "I'm sorry that I disturbed you."

"And that I am here, not Robert Maxwell?" he said sharply.

She stared quickly into his eyes again, wondering if he was angry. He did not appear to be so, but the question was still intense, and she felt herself shivering again.

"I am sorry," she said softly, "that I disturbed you, milord, and nothing more."

"There is nothing that can hurt you here, Jassy. You are safe with me. You are safe." He smoothed back her hair and held her gently in his arms. "Are you all right?"

Her heart kept beating hard, but the pace was beginning to subside. The light of the fire had bathed the room in a soft glow, and she was leaving behind the shadowed world of her nightmarish terror. She nodded to him. He rose, shivering against the chill as he moved to the hearth to stoke the dying blaze with the poker. Then he returned to her, slipping beneath the covers and pulling her against him. She rested with her cheek upon his naked chest. Her hand also rested upon it, and her fingers were teased by the crisp mat of dark hair beneath them. He lay with his arm crooked beneath his head, stroking her hair, staring up at the canopy of their bed.

"Tell me about it. Tell me about the dream," he said.

She tensed, wondering if she could do so. He must have felt the new fear within her, for he reached for her chin and tilted her head so that she could meet his eyes. "No demons lie in wait for you here, Jassy. Tell me what torments you, and perhaps you will be freed from it."

She lowered her head against him again, rubbing her cheek against the sleek warmth of his chest. "It—it always starts with my mother," she whispered.

"And she is ill?"

"She is dying. I can see her: She is lying on the pallet in Master John's attic, and there is a sheet covering her, and I know what I will find, but I must go to her, anyway. I come closer and closer, and then I pull away the covers and she is there, but she is dead, and she has been dead for a very long time, for her eyes are nothing but dark, empty sockets, and it is as if the carrion and worms have preyed upon her. I stare at her and I stare at her and . . ."

"And, my love?"

"As I watch her, she becomes me, and I am in terror then that . . ."

"That what, Jassy?"

"I . . . do not want to die as she did," Jassy mumbled against his flesh.

He was silent for several long seconds. "She died the night that we first met."

"Yes."

"And you were trying to buy her some medication, or the services of some physician?"

"Yes," she barely whispered. The sound was a ragged breath of warmth that touched his flesh. Her fingers curled suddenly against him. "You must understand . . . Robert was very kind to me that day. She would not even lie in a coffin had he not insisted on paying the cost of it."

Jamie grunted. His voice took on a slight edge. "And that is it? The extent of the dream?"

She shuddered again, violently. "Sometimes . . . sometimes it is different."

"And tonight?"

"Tonight it was worse. I watched her, and even as I stared at her, she became me. I saw myself lying there, and I knew that I was dead. I was dead . . . as my mother had been."

"Was I there?"

She recalled the dream, Jamie staring down upon her, Hope sidling around him. She remembered holding the baby, the blue, pinched, stillborn baby.

"Yes, you were there."

"And what was I doing?"

"You were watching me. Very gravely, very sadly."

"Why?"

"Because . . . because the babe was laid upon me, and it was dead too."

"Jassy! Jassy!" He set his hands upon her and sat up, sweeping her into his arms and cradling her within them. His chin rested atop her head, and he held her close. He took her hand and stretched out her fingers, then laid her hand against the swell of her stomach. "Feel him! He kicks even now. He is strong and you are strong, and both of you will survive. I will not let anything happen to you."

She twisted against him, burying her face against his neck. He continued to hold her tight.

"Trust in me," he told her. He threaded his fingers through hers and laced them together over the bulge of their child. "Trust in me; I will be beside you, and I will never let you starve or want for anything."

Jassy had never known such a wondrous feeling of security.

Of being cherished . . .

She laid her head against him, savoring the sensation.

She yawned, exhausted again, certain that her dreams would no longer be haunted.

"Was there more to it?" he asked.

"What, milord?" she asked in sleepy contentment.

"The dream. Was there any more to it?"

"Oh . . . yes. Hope was beside you as you watched me."

He laughed suddenly, and with good humor. "You are a jealous little minx."

She started to stiffen against him. "Milord, I most certainly am not."

"You are."

"I am not . . ." She hesitated, for the baby was moving in great ripples against her stomach. "I . . . have grown so very large," she murmured.

He chuckled softly, nuzzling her head with his chin. "It will not be long now, madame. Not long at all. The end of February, the beginning of March."

"It will not be long," she agreed. She trembled, for she could not quite shake the fear. He held her closer. "I will be with you," he promised her. "I will be with you, and no harm will come to you."

She believed him. She gazed up at him with a tender, dazzling smile, and then she closed her eyes, and in a matter of minutes she was sleeping again, softly and easily this time.

Jamie laid her down, smoothed the hair from her brow, and studied her features, gentle with sleep, a smile still curved about her lips. She grew more beautiful daily, he thought, and he grew evermore beneath the shadow of her spell. He felt like a lovesick boy at times, watching her movements, watching her laughter, watching her when she frowned, concentrating intently upon some task or another.

Regrets . . . *He* had none.

He had determined to have her, and he had determined to marry her, and he had known that she had the passion and the spirit to rival his, to meet and challenge this brave new land. He had known that he had the power to make her his wife, and he even had had the sure confidence to believe that he could awaken the passion and sensuality that had lain behind the vehemence of her hatred and the volatility of her spirit. He had, in his arrogance known that he could claim her and awaken her, and command her here, to his side.

But he could not make her *love* him.

She was his wife. Soon they would have a child, and there was no reason that he should lose her.

No reason . . . except that he might well let her go. He could not love like this and keep silent. Nor could he lay his heart before her feet and lose his soul. She had wanted Robert. She dreamed of a man full of flattery and laughter. Someone gentle, easily led and maneuvered.

He clenched his jaw, hard and tight. He could not be a half-wit fool for her entertainment. If she could not love the man that he was, then he would have to let her go.

Misery clamped down upon him hard, and his muscles constricted, taut and painful. They would know soon enough, he thought. When the child came, there would be a time of reckoning. He would demand it.

And he would have it.

XVI

They were not to wait as long as any of them had anticipated for Jassy's baby to be born.

The doctor from Jamestown had promised to make it down to the hundred by the twenty-fifth of February, but it was only the fifteenth of that month when she felt the first startling pain.

She was out in the kitchen with Jonathan when she felt the constriction come around her, like a steel band tightening around her lower back. She had been bending over a pot of stew, and at first she felt as if she had merely stood over it too long. The last weeks had been wretched for her. She could find no such thing as a comfortable position, not to sit in, stand in, or sleep in. Rising was difficult, and walking had its annoyances, and she was ever in need of a chamber pot. She had grown very anxious and longed for the birth.

Straightening, Jassy held her hands upon her hips and stretched, and in a few moments the pain faded. Jonathan Hayes looked at her worriedly. "We can take stock of the spices later, milady."

She shook her head, smiling. "We don't know when the next ship is due, and I believe that we are running low on salt. Let's continue."

Jonathan went onward to assess the cloves, and Jassy

listened to him as he droned on, marking down the amounts of various herbs and spices in Jamie's ledger. Suddenly she could hear Jonathan speak no more, for the constriction came again, and no little twinge, but an agonizing knot about her. She jumped to her feet, gasping with it, squeezing her eyes tightly shut.

"Milady—"

"I am all right," she said, but the band constricted tighter and tighter. She fell back into the chair and looked at Jonathan. "I am *not* all right."

"I'll get help." Jonathan grabbed his cloak from the peg and went racing out into the yard. The pain began to ebb again, and Jassy worried that she might have given poor Jonathan a false alarm. She started to rise again, then felt a flood of water cascade from her, drenching her skirts and petticoats. She gripped hard to the table, for the cascade came with another pain, this one more fierce than ever before.

The door burst inward, and a cold gust of wind followed Tamsyn into the kitchen. He came hurriedly over to her.

"It is the baby," he said.

"It is too early!" Jassy protested.

Tamsyn smiled at her. "Jassy, girl, there's none can tell a babe eager to enter the world that it's too early. They will come when they choose to do so, and that's a fact. You need to get up to your bed, like a good lass."

"Then what?'

"Then, lass, you wait. Come, I'll help you." He set an arm about her shoulders. The door burst inward again, and Jamie was there. He stood, framed by the doorway, very tall and dark and forbidding. He looked at Tamsyn, and then his wife. He drew off his gloves as he came into the kitchen, tossing them upon the table. "Move aside, man!" he told Tamsyn, stooping low to sweep Jassy into his arms.

"No!" she cried, and she looked anxiously to Tamsyn. "Jamie, he studied at Oxford, please . . ." She hooked her arms around his neck, shivering. The birth water had made her very cold. "I am soaking you," she added in distress.

Jamie gave no heed to her sodden condition but stared hard at Tamsyn. He was not the same man he had once urged from the Crossroads Inn. He was clean-shaven, and he often smoked upon a clay pipe, but he seldom inbibed in anything stronger than ale, and he was frugal in that taste. Now, as he looked at the man, Jamie hesitated only briefly. He could not be sure of the man's credentials, but Jassy trusted in him, and perhaps that was the most important thing. "Come along, then," Jamie said.

Jassy whispered her thanks against his shirt.

He strode through the breezeway from the kitchen to the house, coming in by the dining room. The cold February wind struck them hard, and he felt her shiver anew. He saw Amy Lawton sweeping the hallway as he entered the main house, and he called to her quickly. "Go to the Tannen house. Fetch Molly. Where is Elizabeth?"

"I'm here!" Elizabeth called from the stairway.

"The babe comes," Jamie said briefly. He strode on up the stairs with Jassy in his arms. In their room he set her down and instantly set upon the hooks and eyes upon her gown. She looked up at him, shivering miserably. He tried to pull the gown over her head.

"You shouldn't be here," she whispered. "I am a disaster."

"Let's get this off." He pulled the gown over her head. She wore no corset or stays but only a shift and two loose petticoats. With the dress gone, she stood and backed away from him. "I can manage, Jamie, honestly."

"Get over here!" he commanded her gruffly. "You cannot manage."

"Jamie—"

Elizabeth had followed them into the room by then. She cleared her throat softly. "I'll find a new gown," she said.

Another pain seized upon Jassy hard, and she gritted her teeth as tears stung her eyes and she doubled over.

"Little fool!" Jamie chastised her. He caught hold of her, taking her hands in his own. She gripped hard in return. Harder and harder. "Easy!" he whispered to her. "Breathe deep, Jassy. Easy, love, easy . . ."

The band of agony eased, and she went limp against him. He took the opportunity to strip her of her petticoats and shift, and Elizabeth came quickly over to assist him, and to slide the clean, dry nightgown over her head. By then Tamsyn, too, was standing in the doorway. Jamie stared at him hard. "All right, then, man. What now?"

"Now she must lie down and wait, milord."

"That's all?"

"That is all that can be done," Tamsyn replied. Elizabeth drew back the sheets, and Jamie swept Jassy up and laid her out upon the bed.

Jassy caught his hand. "Jamie," she whispered. "It's too early."

"Not so very early," he told her encouragingly. He glanced at Tamsyn. He wished that he knew more about the birth process. He had learned so much in life. He could sail a ship, tramp his way through any wilderness, and survive off the land or the sea, but he didn't know how to ease a single furrow of pain from Jassy's brow, and he didn't have any idea if the babe was really too early, if it could survive at all.

"Two weeks," Tamsyn said, "if my old eyes don't deceive me. I'm a-thinking this lad might have found his roots on the very night of your wedding, milord, and therefore he has chosen to come just a mite too soon. Things should come well enough." He looked at Elizabeth. "Lady Elizabeth, if you would find Molly when she comes, have her tend to the water we need, and the cloths to wipe up his little lordship when he arrives, and for Jass—milady."

"What can I do?" Jamie said.

"Why, milord, perhaps you should go and smoke a pipe and have a whiskey. It will be a while."

Jamie shook his head. "I promised her that I would stay with her."

"Then stay with her, milord," Tamsyn said, and smiled

ruefully. "Cool her brow, hold her hand, and be at her side."

It was exactly what he did.

The man, Tamsyn, seemed awkward at first about touching Jassy in Jamie's presence. Then he seemed to shrug, realizing that Lord Cameron was in the birth room to stay, and that was that. Jamie knew that Tamsyn was aware of his doubt, and in the end Tamsyn squared his shoulders and spoke to Jamie as he worked over Jassy. Jassy winced and clung to her husband's hand. Jamie's flesh went white where she gripped against him, but he made no sound.

"We are in good stead," Tamsyn said cheerfully. "She has come far already, and the babe is in the proper position."

A sigh of relief escaped Jassy. Jamie looked at her pained features and knew that she was thinking of Joan Tannen aboard the *Sweet Eden,* and of the babe stillborn upon the vessel.

Her features screwed up into a curious mask. Jamie lay his hand upon her abdomen and felt the tremendous tightening in her womb. Her fingers shook, then dug into his hand again. "They come so fast!" she cried piteously.

And they did come fast. Elizabeth and Molly came back with the water and the cloths. Jamie wiped her face, and he spoke to her reassuringly each time that the pains subsided, but they came again and again, faster and faster.

She pleaded with him once to leave, but he met Molly's eyes over her form, and Molly shook her head. A second later Jassy's fingers crunched down upon his, and he held her, trying to take some of the pain away, trying to give to her some of his strength. At one point she seemed to sleep. Her grip eased from his. He stood, stared at Tamsyn, and paced the room, his hands locked behind his back. Elizabeth and Molly looked on.

Jamie threw his hands into the air. "Do something!"

"Do what, Lord Cameron?"

"Hurry this along. She cannot stand so much pain."

Molly, Tamsyn, and Elizabeth all gazed at one another.

Elizabeth stepped forward, reaching for Jamie's hand. "It is not so very long, Jamie. It has been just a matter of hours. Many more hours may go by before the babe comes; it is nature's way. You do not understand so much about babes coming into the world."

"And you do?" Jamie said.

Elizabeth flushed. "I was there when your sister bore your niece, My Lord Cameron, so, yes, I know something of it!"

Jamie lowered his head in acknowledgment. Elizabeth trembled slightly. She had never seen him even remotely humble before. She touched his arm. "I know that everything will be well, Jamie."

Jassy screamed suddenly from the bed, awakened by the ferocity of another pain. Jamie flew back to her side, his face dark, his hands shaking. "Easy, Jassy, easy."

"I cannot bear this—"

"You will bear it. Breathe."

"I cannot—"

"I command it, love. Breathe and hold my hand, and let loose of my son, madame."

"Let loose of your son!"

Her eyes opened in a flash of temper, and Jamie laughed. "Aye, lady, come now. You dally here!"

She lay back, telling him that he was a vile knave. When the next pain seized her, she swore like a dockhand and dug her nails into his hand, but she did not cry or weaken or scream. The pains were coming very, very fast.

Tamsyn realized that they would not be waiting hours and hours. The babe was coming before nightfall.

Lord Cameron's face was ashen as he watched over his wife. Tamsyn lightly touched his arm. "The babe comes soon."

Jamie started, sitting up. Molly awaited the child with swaddling, and Tamsyn talked to Jassy. "You never could wait for anything, lass. You never did learn patience, and you never could do things in half measures. You couldn't marry a merchant, but you had to have a fine lord, and that, lass, you did in a hurry too. Seems that this little lad will be one like his mother. Now push, Jassy, love. Give him a push."

"I cannot!" She fell back in exhaustion. Jamie caught her shoulders and pressed her forward. "Jassy, 'tis Tamsyn talking to you, and you must give him heed."

"Oh!" she cried out, and she tried to escape his hold and give up. He would not release her, and she was forced to bear down.

"I see a very dark head!" Molly cried enthusiastically.

"Again!" Tamsyn persisted.

"No!"

"Jassy, I will have my son now!"

"A daughter," Jassy said argumentatively.

"Push!" Jamie said gratingly.

And the baby came from her. It was the greatest relief that Jassy had ever known. Life spilled from her in a great, heavy gush, and the pain was numbed. . . .

And she heard the cry, the sharp, plaintive wail that came from her newborn infant. Sharp, plaintive, and very lusty.

"A son, at that!" Tamsyn laughed. "And very much alive and well."

"Oh!"

A son . . .

Just as Jamie had commanded.

The squalling infant passed from Tamsyn's hands to Molly, who quickly and tenderly swept him into swaddling and began to clean his little face. Jamie quickly and vehemently kissed Jassy fully upon the lips, running his knuckles over her cheeks. She was dazed, but still she thought that he looked upon her with great tenderness. But he was up then, and demanding his child from Molly. He stood in the candlelight and stared down upon the tiny new life, lifting away the covering and inspecting every bit of the child. He smiled, and he looked striking when he turned back to his wife with pleasure and exuberance.

"Perfect, my love. Ten fingers, ten toes, a stubborn chin, blue eyes, and very dark hair, I *believe*. It's quite sodden."

The new Cameron howled, and Jassy saw a tiny fist protrude from the coverings. A sharp sensation stung her breasts, and she felt them swell. "May I see him?" she whispered. She tried for the strength to sit up but was exhausted. Despite the cold of winter, sweat trickled through her hair and dampened her forehead.

"Jassy, one more time," Tamsyn said to her, and she looked at him in confusion. "One last time, love. The birth sac must come now. Push for me, lass."

It was not so hard that time. She was so anxious to see her son. She gritted her teeth and bore down, and again she felt the most wonderful sensation of relief. She fell back, closed her eyes, and breathed in exhaustion, but when she opened her eyes again, Jamie was hovering over her, and he very carefully placed the baby into her arms.

The love that swelled in her heart was instant and total. He seemed very tiny, but he was perfect. His mouth was open and his screaming was probably quite horrible, but it was delightful to her ears. His eyes *were* blue, a dark blue, like Jamie's, though she knew they might change and take on her lighter hue. His cap of hair was all Jamie's, though, very dark and rich and in startling plenty for a newborn. She loved his little gnome's face, wrinkled and pink and knotted up in the effort that drew forth his lusty howls. She, too, pushed the swaddling back. He *was* quite perfect. He was long and was very certainly a little boy, and though he wasn't chubby, he didn't seem to have suffered the loss of the extra weeks he should have spent in the womb.

She started to shake. Her nightmare vision was really at rest. Her son had been born alive, and he was beautiful.

"Oh, Jamie!" she whispered, and she was afraid she was going to burst into tears. "He is . . . fine."

"He is magnificent," Jamie corrected her. He gently touched his son's cheek with his finger, his hand seeming huge against the tiny face. Then he brushed her lip with his thumb, and she looked into his eyes. "He is magnificent," Jamie repeated.

Tears were welling in her eyes. Molly stepped forward very matter-of-factly. "Let him nurse, love. He won't get too much nourishment yet, but he needs to pull the milk in." Molly hesitated suddenly, looking from Jamie to Jassy. "That is, if you want it in. Ladies don't always nurse their own, do they, Lord Cameron?"

Jassy's breath caught. Did they not nurse their children out of choice? she wondered. She wanted nothing more than to have the baby as close to her as possible. She wanted to explore every angle of this new thing called motherhood, and she hoped desperately that Jamie would not deny her. Perhaps husbands chose wet nurses so that their wives would not be overly occupied with their newborns.

"We haven't a tremendous supply of wet nurses around," Jassy murmured.

"I'm sure that someone can be found—" Molly began.

"Jassy will nurse the babe," Jamie said firmly.

She gazed at him, grateful for his response. Beside her, he was every bit as fascinated with the infant, and he smiled at her and gently pulled upon the lace of her gown. Awkwardly, for her fingers trembled, Jassy set the baby to her nipple, and then laughed, her nervousness easing as he rooted about her breast, finding his hold upon her. He latched on hard at last, and a shaft of lightning seemed to streak through her. Love, as intense as the blaze of the sun, filled her with the strange new sensation. He began to suck hard upon her, sounding much like a little pig. Molly and Elizabeth laughed. "There's a hungry one for you," Molly said.

"Like his father," Jassy murmured, and then she realized what she had said, and looked up, reddening with embarrassment. But Jamie laughed then, too, and Tamsyn joined in, and it was one of the nicest moments of her life. She held the baby against her breast for a few minutes more, then Jamie took him from her again. He kissed her lips once more. "Molly says she's going to bathe you and set the bed right. Then you need to sleep. I'll come to you later."

Her eyes were already closing. She was dimly aware

that Molly asked for the baby back, that he might be bathed. Jamie turned the baby over to Molly and left the room. Jassy awoke somewhat when Molly moved her about to change the sheets and her gown, wiping her down with a wet cloth.

Then she slept, and slept hard, with no dreams or nightmares to disturb her.

Later that night she awoke, ravenous, and achingly aware of the howls and sniffles that aroused her from her slumber. She opened her eyes and found that Jamie was with her again, pulled up to the bed in the large captain's chair from his desk. The baby, now clean and swaddled anew in soft linen, lay upon his lap. He smiled when he saw her open eyes, then lay the baby at her side. The aching sensation seared her breasts, and she turned to her side and led the baby to nurse. He latched quickly and fiercely, and her eyes met Jamie's with delight. "I must do it right."

He chuckled. "Certainly so, madame. I never doubted you for a moment, and neither did he, so it seems."

She smiled, pleased and warmed. Jamie moved forward, stroking the babe's cheek, lightly brushing his fingertips over her breast. "He must be baptized first thing in the morning. What shall we call him?"

"First thing?" she repeated with a frown, and panic seized her. "Jamie, he is all right? There is no need to fear—"

"Jassy, he is in good health. Tamsyn assured me that it is so. It is only right to baptize him as soon as possible."

She nodded, lowering her head and wishing that she didn't betray her fears so quickly all of the time.

"Jassy, he needs a name."

"Don't—don't fathers usually insist upon naming their sons?"

"He is your son, too, madame. I had thought that after this morning you'd be quite loath to give me any of the credit."

She flushed, thinking that indeed it seemed far the

easier measure to be a sire than a dam. "James," she said out loud.

"For the king?"

"Nay, for his sire. He is the firstborn."

"Is that a promise for an army to come?"

"Nay, it is no promise!" Jassy said vehemently, and he laughed.

"If you wish it, he will be James. James Daniel Cameron, if that suits you, and we might, for the moment, call him Daniel to avoid confusion."

"James Daniel Cameron," Jassy murmured. "I like it." James Daniel opened his eyes wide to her. "James Daniel Cameron," she repeated. She bent down and kissed his impossibly soft and downy head. "I love you, James Daniel."

The baby's eyes closed. She stroked his soft skull with wonder, then she saw that Jamie was watching her. She stared at him and he smiled ruefully. "It is customary for a lord to present his lady with a gift upon such an occasion. I admit, were we home, I would have given you a rope of pearls, but alas, I have no such thing—"

"It does not—"

"I do have something else which I think is very fine." He produced a narrow string of rawhide, upon which was a striking and unusual amulet. The fingers of a man and a woman were etched primitively upon a pink shell. A sun burst above the two of them, casting rays about them both. A god seemed to peer down benevolently from the rays of the sun. With the baby asleep at her breast and his mouth half opened upon it, Jassy studied the amulet. She looked at Jamie and smiled slowly. "It is lovely."

"It was given to me once by a little girl."

"A little girl?"

He smiled. "The first time that I was here, I met Pocahontas. She had saved John Smith, but she was just an eleven-year-old child, and her fascination and generosity to the settlers was astounding. I was young myself, into my teens. She and Powan and I came together, first when the whites would have slain Powan, and second when the warring Powhatans might have gotten their hands upon me. I have always cherished it, and I hope that it will mean something to you, if it is only a symbol of the pearls that I will one day come to find."

He did not look in her eyes. He gently disengaged their sleeping son from her breast, then set him upon his shoulder.

"Jamie."

"Yes?"

"It is beautiful. I will cherish it, I swear it." She slipped it over her neck. He smiled at her.

"Molly has stayed. She will bring you something to eat in a minute. You must eat, and you must sleep, and—"

"I will be up soon, I promise."

"Milady, you will not. You will not rise for more than an hour or two for at least a week. Tamsyn has said so, and I will see that it is so." He smiled again, taking the sting from his words.

The door closed in his wake. Jassy pulled the covers close to her chin, and she smiled to herself.

She had never known that it was possible to be so radiantly happy.

In the days that followed, Jassy was absorbed with the baby. They never did call him James or Jamie; from the beginning he was Daniel.

He delighted Jassy, for he seemed stronger by the minute. He quickly lost his wizened appearance, and she liked to stare at him for hours, and compare every one of his little features to those of his father. He was remarkably like Jamie. Even being an infant, Daniel had certain ways of looking at her that pulled strongly upon her heart, for they were so similar to the very ways that Jamie could look at her. He could be silent and grave, and howl like the very north wind. She was certain that he had already learned to smile, although Molly assured her that it was a "wee bit of the air in his belly"—Daniel was too young to smile. Jassy didn't believe it for a second. He had come into the world determined, and now that he was within it, he was ingenious and precocious. She was certain of it. When she held him in her arms. she felt complete, as she had never been complete before. Something that she had done in life was right, and special, and entirely unique.

Her one unhappiness in those days was that it seemed that she saw less and less of Jamie.

He did not sleep with her the night that Daniel was born, nor the night after. Molly had determined to stay for a few days, and so Jamie had ordered that a cot be brought up for her comfort. A group of the laborers from the settlement had come with a gift for Jassy, and Jamie had brought them up to the room. She had greeted them from her bed, and she had been delighted with their gift, a cradle that had been lovingly carved from the best of the wood, and engraved upon the side with the Cameron crest. From the bottom of her heart she had thanked them, and John Tannen, who had led the group of them, was the one to speak to her, twirling his flat cap in his hands as he was so wont to do.

"Milady, if our gift pleases you, we are most humbly grateful. We were many of us a-fearing your arrival, for we thought that Lord Cameron's lady might be a harsh and cold mistress, demanding her distance from us all. But you came to us, lady, like a sweet angel of mercy, and we are, one and all, grateful. Molly and me are grateful, and I know that my Joan and our infant went to the Maker from a gentle touch. Lady, the best to you, and to the bonny boy!"

"Thank you, John," Jassy said. "Thank you all so much. We will keep the cradle forever, I promise you, and it will be cherished for the craftsmanship, and for the heart with which it was given."

She could not look at Jamie, who stood silently in the corner of the room. Emotions were churning too deeply within her. She had not wanted to come here, yet no place had ever been so much like home. She had married for gain, and if her driving desire had been a life without hunger, poverty, and want, she *had* accepted Jamie, knowing that he offered a life of much more, a life of luxury. There was little enough luxury to be found here, but that had long ago ceased to matter. It seemed so long ago now. All that mattered to her now was Daniel, and the welfare of her family and her dear friends and servants, and . . .

Her husband.

"Come down and warm yourselves with some ale, for it still blows cold beyond the doors," Jamie said, inviting the men. They left her with good cheer. Jamie's eyes remained upon her until he had left the room, but she could not tell what he was thinking.

Molly stayed for the week, and then she returned to her own newly acquired family. Jassy missed her, but she had Elizabeth with her, and Mrs. Lawton, and Charity and Patience.

She still didn't have Jamie.

The first night she hadn't questioned his disappearance. Then Molly had been there. But when Molly had gone home, he still avoided his own bed, sleeping across the hall in the room where Lenore and Robert had stayed. He did not wish to disturb her or the babe, he told her awkwardly one morning, slipping in to find more pairs of his hose. She needed her sleep.

Jassy, hurt, did not argue with him. She wondered if perhaps he did not want his own sleep disturbed, since the winter hung on and he was busy with survival.

But sometimes she heard him late at night, pacing the floor. At those times she hugged the baby to her, whether Daniel slept or not, and she bit deep into her lip, hoping that he had not ceased to care. She knew that they could not resume marital relations for some time, but they had not been together in that way for some time before Daniel had been born, and it had not mattered; it had been good to sleep beside him, to feel his heartbeat beneath her chin, to feel his arms around her. Tamsyn had told her that she must wait a month, a full month, and go carefully then. She did not know if Tamsyn had spoken to Jamie, too, or if Jamie simply had been aware of the ways of women and childbirth. Or if Jamie simply had ceased to care.

The nights when he paced disturbed her. The nights

when he did not pace disturbed her more. She didn't know where he was, or who he was with, or where his thoughts and yearnings might have wandered.

Hope was about too. When the snow melted, a group of the Indians came to the house, bearing gifts from Opechancanough. The great chief sent the baby a small amulet much like the one that the princess Pocahontas had given to Jamie, and that Jamie had given to her. She seldom took hers off, and though she was afraid that the baby might strangle on his, she tied it over his cradle. She wasn't sure why. She had sometimes lost faith in her own God, but she certainly felt nothing for the peculiar and demanding gods of the Algonquin peoples in the Powhatan Confederacy. Still, she felt that it was important the baby be protected by the amulet. The Christian God was just gaining a foothold here. The Indian gods had been around much longer.

To placate Father Steven, she also asked John Tannen to make her a crucifix to rest at the foot of the cradle. Father Steven objected to the amulet. Jamie was amused by it all. "Father, we acknowledge no craven images, so it seems to matter little what decoration we choose to use upon the lad's cradle. I'm sure that it will not sway him from growing up in the proper ways of the Church of England."

Father Steven threw up his arms and offered no further protest. Jassy cast her husband a grateful glance, but he didn't seem to notice. In his mind he was already away from her, anxious to attend to more important business.

Jassy was glad of his support in many things. If the question involved her in those days, he always deferred to her.

And still he stayed away. Jassy saw less and less of him.

When Daniel was two weeks old, the last of the fallen snow melted. Jonathan, who had been in the Jamestown settlement before he had come to work for Jamie in the hundred, told Jassy that maybe there would be no more snow that year.

February turned to March.

Tamsyn was no longer working in the stables. Jassy had been startled to discover that he had been set up in a small house of his own, and that the care of their medical supplies had been put in his hands. Little by little the people turned to him for help with their various woes and ailments.

" 'Tis your husband's doing," Tamsyn was quick to tell her. "When Daniel was born, he bid me follow him to the great room to the left of the hallway, and I near thought that he meant to say, 'Off with this man's head.' But he asked me about Oxford and my studies, and he was heartily angry, so it seemed, that I had let my life come to this over an indulgence in drink. I swore to him that I had no more difficulty, and he told me that it was a new world, a new life, and that he could not afford for me to waste my education and knowledge here. He gave me the house, and he sent the people to me. They came slowly at first. But I cured Mrs. Danver's stomach colic, and set Timothy Hale's broken arm, and they seem to have confidence in me now."

Jassy was glad for Tamsyn, and she offered her gratitude to Jamie that night. "I did nothing, madame," he told her impatiently, "but advise the man to use skills which we have grave need of here."

He dismissed her quickly and curtly, and she said no more.

March came blustering in with wind and rain, but by the fifteenth, on the day that Daniel became a month old, it seemed that spring was on its way. It was a beautiful day with a rich promise of warmth and a clear blue sky. The land had never seemed more verdant beyond the palisade. The farmers were preparing for their planting, everything seemed sweetly alive and awakened, and everyone seemed aware that it was almost spring, a season for warmth and laughter and gaiety.

Everyone but Jamie.

There were times when Jassy thought that he hated her, and there were times, too, when she thought that he had grown completely indifferent to her. He was very quick to anger, and he was almost constantly curt to her. He avoided her, staying out late at night, leaving the house by day.

And still sometimes she caught him watching her with a grave and brooding darkness to his features and his eyes, watching her as if he sought something. If she came to him, he would deny that he stared at her, and impatiently he would leave her.

Puzzled, hurt, and growing very frightened, Jassy watched him in turn. He loved Daniel, she was certain of it. He asked every evening that the child be brought to him, and Jassy would pensively hand her son over to Amy or Charity or Patience so that he could be brought to his father. Daniel did not return until he was squalling to be fed, and needed his mother.

On the fifteenth Jassy determined that she would have her husband back in her bed. She had not lost the least bit of her absorbing interest in her child, but she craved Jamie. She was young and in good health, and she missed him desperately, the way that he held her . . . the way that he loved her.

She dressed with special care, in a gown with a low-cut bodice and soft lace ruff that spilled over her breasts. She had spent the morning, once Daniel had been fed, washing and drying her hair, and it fell down her back like a cascade of sunshine. Anxiously pinching her cheeks, she sought out Jamie in the great room off the hall.

He and Sir William were involved in the business of charting out an area up the river they wished to map. Charts and quills were strewn over a large table in the center of the room.

The men looked up at her arrival. Sir William was quick to greet her with a smile of admiration and a quick bow. Jamie's eyes upon her were his only indication that he knew she had come.

'Good day, Sir William," she said. She looked at her husband. "I see that you are busy."

"Never so busy that it is not a pleasure for an interruption as beautiful as you, milady," Sir William said.

"What do you want?" Jamie asked curtly.

Even Sir William stared at him, shocked by his tone of voice. Then it seemed Sir William decided upon a hasty retreat, for he mumbled something about forgetting to see to the late guard. "I will return quickly, milord," he promised Jamie.

Then Jassy and Jamie were left alone in the space of the large room with a silence resting between them. Jamie stared at her hard, then issued a sound of impatience.

"What, madame, is so important that you must interrupt work and create a scene?"

"Create a scene?" Jassy repeated, her temper flaring.

"And disturb Sir William."

"Sir William did not seem at all disturbed."

"Ah, yes, you like compliments and admiration, and that he gives you willingly."

"Which you do not."

"I am not accustomed to fawning. Now, what do you want?"

"Neither are you accustomed to common courtesy, so it seems, my most noble lord! And what do I want from you? Nothing, nothing at all from you, but that which I have always craved—my freedom!" She spun around in a fury. She could barely see or hear she was so blinded with her anger and the surge of pain that his coldly spoken words had brought.

He caught her arm, pulling her back. She hated the power in his hold at that moment. She hated the viselike grip he held about her arm, and she hated the way that he towered over her and stared down at her with his eyes so dark and speculative. "Is that what you truly want, milady?"

"What?" she cried.

"Freedom?"

She hesitated, her lips gone dry, her tongue frozen. She ached to cry out, to pitch herself into his arms and let go with a flood of tears. She wanted to tell him the truth, that freedom from him would be misery. One word from him . . . a smile . . . a gentle touch . . . and she would do so.

She received nothing from him. Just his demanding, hard blue stare and the tense rigor in his muscles. Life had become so ironic, ah, yes, life, always the jest. She had despised him so. And now, when she had come to love him with all the heart and passion and aching need that lay within her, he had come to despise her.

"I have asked you a question, Jassy."

"I—" she began, but the door burst open, and Sir William came rushing back in.

"She's come, Jamie! The *Lady Destiny* ventures into the bay and will soon find her dockage in our deep harbor. She has come, ah, at last! Surely it *is* spring!"

Sir William hadn't seemed to notice the way that Jamie held Jassy, or the tangible tension that had riddled the air.

Jamie released her. "Let's hurry to greet the *Lady Destiny*, shall we?"

He walked out of the room, leaving Jassy to stare after him, feeling as if he had centered his sword well within her heart.

The pinnace came with supplies, with beautifully created clothing for Daniel, with guns and swords and ammunition, and with company too. Sirs Allen Wethington and Cedric Aherne arrived along with a cartographer, a metalsmith, and wives and children of the established settlers, and with new carpenters and laborers and craftsmen to make their homes within the hundred.

Jassy was pleased with their company.

Sirs Allen and Cedric were to stay in an empty house across the compound, but that was only to sleep. They dined in grand style that night at Lord Cameron's house, and Jassy was glad to be a hostess, she performed her duties with a fever.

If her husband no longer wanted her, she could prove that other men might.

Lenore and Robert came, and Elizabeth joined them shyly too. There was an abundance of fresh wild turkey for the meal, brought to them just that morning by a few of the Indians. There were meat pies and berries and corn bread, and the *Lady Destiny* had brought over a supply of coffee—becoming so very popular a drink in Italy now—and the fragile little cups for it so like the set Jamie had in the manor in England. When the meal was over, the men lit pipes, and still the party went on, for even Jamie was eager for news from England, and they were all soon laughing at Sir Allen's descriptions of the staid court of their dear King James and his Anne of Denmark.

Jassy realized quickly that Jamie had known Allen and Cedric in London; they had shared certain tutors at various times. They were all of an age, Allen reminding her much of Robert, for he was blond and blue-eyed and quick to smile. Cedric was a dashing redhead with a mustache and full beard, a bit of a portly girth, but great shoulders and heavy thighs to match. They were both charming to her, and she was delighted and on fire with the evening. Some sweet devil had entered into her, she knew. She wished, with all her heart, to provoke her husband's temper. She knew how to do it too. Not quickly, not with some overt action. But slowly. Too deep a smile for one man, too long a laughing touch upon another's arm. He never could have complained that his tavern wench of a wife did not have the manners of a lady, for she was soft-spoken and charming throughout the evening. She had gained their hearts upon a string, and she knew it.

"We'd heard that you'd run off and married, Jamie," Allen said. "And if you didn't find the loveliest demoiselle in all England. Where did he find you, my dear? Locked away in some north county tower? How is it that we missed you?"

Jassy held silent, her heart beating. She looked at Jamie, but he stood by the mantel, his elbow resting upon it, resplendent with dark good looks and subdued finery. His eyes fell upon her and he shrugged. "My wife and I met by sheer chance, gentlemen, upon the road, as it was. She was traveling to her family's home, conveniently close to my own. I was able to escort her, and as luck would have it, she came into my arms at precisely the right time."

Jassy's eyes fell. She was surprised that he hadn't denounced her in his present mood. "She is a tavern wench, gentlemen, and I met her in truth when she came to my room as a whore."

Perhaps appearances meant something to him, after all, she thought bitterly, and she lifted her chin. She rose swiftly to her feet and asked if she might get them something else to drink. She offered Robert Maxwell her most winning smile and refilled his glass with wine.

Charity came down the stairs then, excusing herself, and whispering to Jamie. He stared across the room at Jassy and smiled with a taut satisfaction.

"My dear, I believe that you need to excuse yourself for the evening." He looked to Sir Cedric. "My son is but a month old today, and still awakens in the eve, wanting his mother."

The men stood. Sir Allen came to her, taking her hand. "Surely, Jamie, you could have arranged for some assistance for your wife. That you could take her away from us . . ." His voice faded away with a tone of deep regret.

"But motherhood is quite a talent with my lady, gentlemen. She would have it no other way. *Good night*, my love."

Motherhood . . . it was her *only* talent, so it seemed, and Jamie was glad to order her from the party. She was eager to fight him, eager to assure the gentlemen that she would be right back. But then she heard Daniel, snuffling in Patience's arms up the stairway. Her breasts tingled and she was ashamed that she could forget her son—even in her vengeance against her husband.

She said good night and started up the stairway. Then she could not help but pause and call down to the company, sweetly assuring the men that she would see them on the morrow. Jamie's eyes touched hers briefly. She had angered him. She had taunted and teased and flirted very carefully, and surely her husband's friends would lie awake, wondering about her.

And perhaps her husband would come to her. . . .

He did come, and not twenty minutes later. She lay with Daniel. His tiny fist rested against her breast while he rooted at it. She had not changed but lay with her bodice apart, cradling her son to her.

She started at Jamie's appearance. He did not knock, he threw open the door to their room. She started and pulled away from the baby, holding her bodice together.

"You might have knocked." She gasped, stunned.

He stood tall in the doorway, implacable and unyielding. "You forget, madame, I am the *least* courteous man you know. And this is my bedroom, milady. I will never knock upon the door."

"You sleep across the hall, milord," she said, her heart thundering.

"I sleep across the hall. I will still enter here whenever I choose."

Daniel, interrupted from his meal, started to cry. Jamie's gaze fell upon his son, and he entered into the room, closing the door behind him. "Your son, madame," he said to her.

"If you have something to say to me, please do so, then I may return to my *talent* of motherhood. Tell me, milord, do you consider it my only talent?"

"You've many talents, Jasmine. Feed the babe. I am not leaving."

She bit her lip, quickly lowering her eyes. She flushed and burned, and heady, potent excitement filled her. She turned her back on him and brought Daniel back to her breast. He would stay. He was angry, but she had brought him back, and he would stay.

But he was silent, silent so long that she spoke herself. "What an interesting reply you gave your friends about the acquisition of your wife."

"What would you have had me say, my love? 'I married a tavern wench. You can see by the way that she whores and flirts about you'?"

"I did nothing of the kind!" Jassy snapped.

He was nearer to her. She had not heard him, but he hovered at her back. He leaned over and touched Daniel's cheek, his long, dark finger moving over the softness of the child. Jassy froze. His finger moved onward, stroking over the fullness of her breast. She did not care if they battled. Only that he came to her, that he lay beside her. She cared not if he took her violently, only that he did so.

He drew his hand away. "Take care, madame. I have decided that you may travel back on the *Lady Destiny*, if you so seriously crave your freedom. But while you are here, take care."

"What?" Jassy gasped.

"You may leave me. I am giving you permission to do so. Daniel stays, though. He is my son and my heir, and he will stay."

Daniel, the point of discussion, was forgotten. Jassy bolted up, her breasts spilling from her gown, her eyes a tempest. "I will never leave him! He is *my* son! I carried him and I bore him, and he needs me, he needs to nurse—"

"Don't fret, love. A woman can be hired to provide, I am certain. Good night."

"No!"

"We will discuss it, madame, in the morning."

"Jamie—"

"If you are so concerned about Daniel, Jassy, see to him now. He screams again that you should be so careless of his needs. Good night."

The door closed softly in his wake. Jassy bit hard into the back of her hand to silence the scream that threatened to erupt from her.

Daniel bellowed out loudly.

She swept him into her arms in stark panic. Jamie could not make her go away; she was his wife. He could not take Daniel away from her. He could not, he could not . . .

"Shush, shush, my little love!" she whispered to the baby. "I am here, I am with you, I love you, I love you so much. I will never leave you, I will never leave . . . him."

She lay down with the babe, and in moments his howls faded to the sound of his greedy suckling. Jassy's eyes were open in shock. Tears began to trickle down her cheeks, and then, in time, she turned her head into her pillow to muffle her sobs.

Then they dried. She would not leave. She would have her husband back. She was a fighter and a survivor.

Hadn't he always told her so?

She would fight him, and she would win. So help her.

XVII

They didn't speak in the morning. Jamie had to leave.

Lent had brought them to Palm Sunday, and with Easter coming early that year, the settlers began to plan for the holy day, and for the feasts they would all have within their homes.

The Cameron house was no different in that aspect, except that it was even busier than the others. Jamie had matters of government to attend to, and he had to spend two days in the Jamestown settlement. A legislative body was already at work in the colony, and Jamie, though he held his land directly from the king rather than the Company, was still a part of it. The laws in the Virginia colony were very much like those in England, and they were also maintained in much the same manner. Murder was a crime punishable by death, as was the stealing of an animal such as a horse or an ass or a cow, the type of beast that could mean a man's survival. There was very little crime in the hundred, despite the fact that some settlers had come to the New World to avoid fates in Newgate.

On the nineteenth, three days before Easter, Jamie returned. Jassy was perfectly cordial to him. She was warm to Robert and to their guests.

Jamie did watch her. He watched her, and the glow in

her eyes, and the striking beauty that it gave her. He watched her come alive for the other men, and despite his best intentions, his temper slowly simmered and seethed.

At dinner she laughed and flirted and played the perfect hostess. She was quick to suggest music, and she had certainly planned her entertainment, for she had musicians ready at her behest. He did not dance with her, nor did she carry the child any longer, and so he had no excuse to send her from the floor. He stared at her as she swirled in some man's arms, and he told himself bitterly that she was a hussy, had always been one, and that he had been a fool to marry her. Then he would remember that he had been the one to teach her what she knew about passion, and his throat would tighten and his stomach knot, and everything within him would burn. He had told her that he would set her free. He would do so.

Furious and anguished, he had but one avenue open to him. He left the house.

On Easter morning he rose early and looked into her room. Daniel slept sweetly in his cradle, but Jassy was nowhere to be seen. Anxious, Jamie ran out of the house and leapt upon his horse without hailing a groom. Bareback, he rode with a vengeance from the compound and out of the open gates of the palisade.

He found Jassy with Sir Cedric, far beyond the walls of the palisade. She was laughing delightedly and pretending a sweet innocence when it came to the use of firearms.

She was dressed in royal-blue velvet over a softer shade of linen. The gown was ruffed with white lace over black, and her breasts seemed to press quite dangerously against the bodice.

She was more beautiful that day than he had ever seen her, her eyes alive with laughter, the sound of that laughter like a melody of spring. Her cheeks were flushed, and she was as lithe and slender as a little wood nymph. She held the musket then, and flashed Sir Cedric her stunning smile as she looked to him for advice on the right position in which to hold the musket. A group of Indians came from the far western woods. Jamie raised a hand in acknowledgment, but other than that, he barely noticed them, for his eyes were on his wife. The Indians knew that the settlers were preparing for a Christian holy day. The Powhatans were probably bringing food and gifts, and they were certainly interested in the things that would take place. He should probably go greet them, but most of the Indians had good friends among the settlers and would be all right.

He was *not* all right himself.

Some invisible line in his temper stretched taut as wire, and then snapped.

He had done everything he could. He had made her his wife, and he had fallen in love with her. He had offered her freedom. . . .

And she seemed keen on taking him up on the offer. She was behaving as if she were free right now. No, she was behaving worse than that. She was a flirt, a tease. She was slowly and carefully cultivating and charming and possessing every man she met.

His head reeled with a jagged ache, as if it had exploded with a charge of black powder. Barely in control, he nudged his horse and came nearer the pair, watching as Sir Cedric helped Jassy align the musket upon the rest.

He paused at last behind the two of them. Jassy fired the musket and laughed with pleasure as her ball struck the target.

"Milady, you're a natural!" Sir Cedric congratulated her.

"Do you think so, really?" she asked, dimpling prettily, and flushing a lovely shade of rose. Her lips seemed like a shade of wine that day. Her hair was pulled back from her forehead with ribbon but spilled down her back and caught the glow of the coming sun. She was radiant and fascinating. Jamie's loins thundered along with his head, and he thought that it had been an endless time since he had touched her. It had been since he had realized how deeply and irrevocably he had fallen in love. Since he had worried about endangering their babe.

Daniel was over a month old now. And she was certainly behaving like a woman in the finest health.

"A perfect shot, my love. Alas, poor Cedric! She cons you, I'm afraid. Jassy *is* a natural, and has been for some time. Her accuracy is frightening. She aims her barbs, and they do strike, swift and sure."

Jassy spun around, looking at him. Cedric, at a loss, and yet aware of the terrible tension suddenly around him, laughed nervously. "Lady Cameron! You *have* had lessons before."

"Yes," she murmured sweetly. She kept a hostile and wary eye upon Jamie. "But none so gently given, Sir Cedric. You are a wonderful marksman, and a superb teacher."

"But the lesson is over," Jamie said, looking down at her from atop his mount.

"I rather thought that we had just begun," Jassy told him.

"You have thought wrong," he said softly. He dismounted from his horse and strode toward her. "I think we should go for a ride, madame."

"I do not care for a ride."

"And I do not care what *you* care for, milady. Come—now."

She stood stubbornly, hesitating for just a moment too long. Jamie stepped forward again and furiously swept her off her feet, striding back to his horse and tossing her rudely upon it. Her hair flew and tossed about her in a sudden disarray as she scrambled for her balance. Looking at her, Jamie knew what he wanted from her at that moment. He knew exactly what he wanted.

"Jamie Cameron, you—"

"Excuse us, Cedric, will you please?" Jamie said politely. He leapt up behind Jassy, nudging his heels hard into the horse's flanks. They took flight, southwestward, toward the deep forest.

Her hair slapped against his face with the force of the wind. He inhaled the clean, perfumed scent of her, the blond locks, and of her flesh. The wind seemed to rage, and the earth to churn beneath him, and all the while the violence and anger seemed to burn in his loins, to thunder in his head. Her body was rigid before his, and she gripped on to the horse's mane. His thighs locked against hers as they rode the animal bareback, coming closer and closer to the dense thicket of trees.

He at last slowed the horse, and when he entered into a trail that led to a copse of trees, he reined in. Visible through the pines and hemlocks was a brook, trickling softly and beautifully and white-tipped through the forest. Below them lay a bed of soft fallen pines, and all about them came the chirp and song and melody of birds.

Jamie did not notice much of nature. He dismounted, casting his leg over her, leaping to the ground. He turned around and stared at her while he reached for her. Her eyes were dusky, unreadable, in the green light of the forest, but he sensed that a spark of cold fury burned brightly within her.

"Come on, get down!" he snapped.

"You are the rudest individual I have ever met."

"Get down here."

"Make me."

"I damned well intend to!"

He wrenched her down from the horse and onto her feet before him. The vixen! She cast back her head and glared at him with a raw challenge. He held on to her shoulders, and he was tempted to shake her until she begged for forgiveness, until she fell to her knees before him.

She wasn't about to beg for anything, or so it seemed. Her hair was wild, and her breasts heaved excitingly with the flame of her exertion. "What do you think you're doing?" she spat out.

"Me?" He slipped a foot behind her ankle, causing her to cry out and fall to the earth, yet held in his arms, she came down gently upon the bed of pines. He came atop her, and then she swore, suddenly and furiously, struggling against him.

"You, *Lord* Cameron! You—"

"Me, milady, your husband. Alas, I am not the gentle teacher that Sir Cedric is! I haven't Robert Maxwell's flattering phrases, and God alone knows what else I lack. *Constraint*. I have offered you freedom aboard the *Lady Destiny*, but you can't even wait the time to board her to taunt other men before me."

"I have taunted no one!"

"You have swayed your hips and laughed and spoken and charmed and seduced. And, madame, you have done so well. God damn you, lady, for I meant to give you what you craved; you so despised this place that I meant to let you leave it, and—that scourge of your life—me, madame. But it seems that I have left you lacking, that I have perhaps been overly kind, for you only play the whore."

She tried to slap him. No, she tried to scratch his face. Then she tried to lift her knee and kick him, but he slammed his weight down hard upon her, and she cried out.

"Poor, innocent, demoiselle!"

"Savage jackal! Let me up. You fool. You—"

He ground his lips down upon hers. They punished and bruised. She fought him, and still the taste of her lips was wet and sweet and more potent than wine. He delved deeper and deeper into the dark recesses of her mouth. It had been too long since he had kissed her so. The memories reborn of the taste and feel and scent of her were so enticing that he shook with it. She twisted from him, trying to shove him aside. Her eyes were wild, and her hair was a halo about her, spilling over the pines. Her lips were damp and parted and bewitching. Her face was beautiful, beguiling, and filled with pride and hatred and the spirit of her fight.

"You fool! You will not do this on the ground in the dirt—"

"Nay, lady, you will not deny me, not today. Not this morning. Tomorrow you may do as you please. For today, madame, you have swished your tail one too many times in my direction, and I will have what I want. Nay, lady, what I *demand*!"

He forced his lips upon her again and caught her hands against the pines, palm to palm. He laced his fingers with her struggling ones and felt the pressure she wielded against him. He ignored it. He kissed her, drinking her in, tasting and seeking, and . . . gentle now. There was no more brutality to his kiss. She was open to him.

Her fingers curled against his.

He lifted some of his weight and removed his hand from hers. He pulled at the ribbons of her bodice, and then at her chemise, watching her eyes. She did not fight him but stared directly at him. He had no patience. The thunder rose painfully in his groin, driven by the weeks of waiting, and the nights of longing, and the anguished moments when he thought about her in the arms of another man.

He cast back his head and let out a loud groan. He buried his face against the spill of her breasts and thought of his son. He pressed his mouth to her flesh and felt her shudder. He would have pulled away, but she let out a soft, choking sigh, and when he released her hands, she held him there, against her. He tasted her as Daniel would taste her, and he filled himself with the feel and texture of her breasts, the thunder pounding ever more fiercely. He caught her skirts, pushed them up against her, and released the ties on his breeches. She still looked at him, her sapphire eyes glimmering in the green darkness. He touched her thighs and eased the stroke of his fingers against them. And still she looked at him with her luminous eyes and her beautiful face, defying him.

He nearly rammed into her but in time remembered that their child had not been born so long ago. He moved gently . . . but she spoke no protest, and he cast back his head, encased and shuddering, and groaned out the anguish in his heart and in his loins. She seemed to burst forth with a mercury, arching against him. He forgot everything else but the force of his desire, and he felt the thunder burst free from him, tear across the heavens and the earth, the blue sky and the verdant pines, and into her.

He cried out, and the sound of her voice rose with his own. The end came to him explosively, fiercely. He arched hard and held, and then fell upon the earth beside her, drained of his lust and his temper all in one, and suddenly, uncomfortably ashamed. He had raped his wife in the forest, upon the pines.

She was silent beside him, breathing hard, staring now at the sky. She made no attempt to adjust her clothing but lay so still that it frightened him.

"Jassy!"

She turned to look at him. There was a soft glaze of tears in her eyes. He swore, furious with himself. Pulling down her skirts, he rose, desperate to be away from her.

"Damn you!" he whispered, his voice shaking. He turned away from the striking and terrible innocence in her crystal-blue eyes, adjusting his breeches. He wanted to explain that she had pushed him to the limit, that no man could watch his wife with other men so long without going over some brink and landing his soul in a pool of dragons. He wanted to say so many things to her. He wanted to say that she had bested him in every way, that he loved her beyond measure. It would sound so very hollow now. . . .

He leapt to his feet. He did not help her up; he did not think that she was ready to rise.

"I'll leave you the horse," he said huskily. "When the *Lady Destiny* sails, I will give you my leave to take Daniel with you to England too."

"Jamie—" she began.

"I will not force you to stay, madame." He hesitated briefly. "Good day, milady. I am heartily sorry for my bad manners."

He left her, disappearing into the woods.

Jassy lay there, feeling the prick of the pines beneath her, for a long time. She listened to the ripple of the brook and felt the sun touch her cheeks through the trees. She brought her fingers to her face and discovered that her face was damp with her silent tears. How could she have failed so miserably?

She realized numbly that he had given her Daniel. He didn't even care if he kept their child anymore, he just wanted her to leave.

She closed her eyes, cast her elbow over them, and swallowed hard. He couldn't have ceased to want her so completely; he could not hate her so vehemently. She had wanted him so badly; she loved him. Loving was worse than the pain of hunger; it was worse than the fear of poverty. It was more painful than anything she had ever known.

She would *not* go. She had to talk to him. She had to make him stand still and listen to her. If she told him that she loved Virginia, that she loved the forest, primeval and so rich and dark, and the river and the Chesapeake Bay and the oysters that they pulled out of it. She loved the palisade, and the way of life, and she never had wanted to return to England. Even if he did not love her, he had to let her stay. She wouldn't go. She simply wouldn't do so.

Slowly, painfully, she came to her feet. She adjusted her clothing and tried to smooth down her hair and rid it of the forest floor. He had left her the horse, and he had gone off on foot—where, she did not know.

Wearily she looped her skirts together, took a handful of the horse's mane, and leapt onto the animal. At a very slow pace she started back toward the palisade. She was young and she was strong, and whatever came, she vowed silently to herself, she would survive. But she could not give up on her husband so easily. She could not.

When she broke slowly from the verdant foliage of the forest, she saw the palisade rising before her in the sunlight. No, it was not London, it was not Oxford, it was not even the Crossroads Inn. No grand Gothic or Renaissance buildings rose in mighty splendor against the coming of the morning. Yet what stood there was finer in its way, for what it was, was what men had built from a raw wilderness, and it was composed of blood and sweat and dreams of the future. The palisade was strong, and beyond it lay the church and her house and the potter's kilns and the blacksmith's shop and the homes of them all.

The gates of the palisade were open, welcoming visitors on the holy day. By the outer wall, one of the young farmers was cutting wood. A Pamunkee Indian was at his side, stacking the logs as the farmer cut them.

Then, suddenly, the Pamunkee snatched the ax from the young farmer and sank the sharp-bladed instrument right into the man's skull.

Jassy opened her mouth in horror, but her astonishment caused her to choke on her cry. Shocked, she reined in on the horse, disbelieving what she had seen with her own eyes.

The farmer clutched his head, fell to his knees, then fell flat, the ax still imbedded in his head. The Pamunkee calmly stepped over him to retrieve the ax, and looked toward the open palisade.

Jassy's limbs seemed to freeze, inch by inch. The cold and numbness overcame her, then struck pure icy terror into the very center of her heart.

"No!" At last her scream tore from her, and Jassy kicked the horse hard into a gallop, her mind racing. It was not just the horror of the murder she had witnessed. It had been the way in which it had taken place. The Pamunkee had stood with the farmer as his friend. They had been laughing, and then the Indian had grabbed the weapon and slain the man . . . then retrieved the weapon and looked toward the palisade.

How many of the Pamunkees were already inside the gates? They had been coming all morning—in friendship. Was it an isolated incident? Had the Indian gone mad?

Earth churned and flew as Jassy sped toward the gates. The Indian who had accomplished the murder was just nearing the palisade. He swung around, the ax in his hand dripping blood, and stared at her.

"Help! Sound the alarm!" she screamed. The blade looked lethal. She tried not to stare down at the dead body of the farmer. She urged the skittish horse around the body and kept her eyes upon the Indian. "Sound the alarm!" she screamed, hoping someone would hear her.

From somewhere deep within the compound came the sound of a scream. She and the Indian stared at each other warily. Jassy jammed her heels into the horse's flanks, and the animal reared, then bolted past the Pamunkee. She heard the sound of another scream, then she saw one of the soldiers come out of the guardhouse. He was wearing his helmet and his half-armor. He wore a look of wide-eyed shock as he stumbled out before Jassy, clutching his stomach. She realized that he held the shaft of a knife there. He had been skewered with his own weapon.

Jassy screamed herself. Another of the guards came out of the little house. "The alarm!" she shouted.

It was too late, for the two Indians had set upon the guard already. He battled them with a vengeance.

Still atop the nervous and rearing horse, Jassy looked toward the inner working steps of the palisade, those leading to the bell alarm and the cannon facing westward.

The cannon would do them little good. The enemy had come at them from within.

She had to reach the steps, and she had to sound the alarm.

Then she had to get home; she had to get back to her house. Daniel lay sleeping there. Elizabeth was there, and Amy Lawton and the girls. She had to get home, and she had to find a way to warn Lenore and Robert.

A man wearing a hastily donned shirt of chain mail came bursting wildly out of the guardhouse. Jassy saw that it was Robert Maxwell.

"Robert!"

He didn't hear her at first. He was looking sickly at the dead man with the knife protruding from his gut, below his half-armor. He stared at him, the knife he carried himself held in a white-knuckled grip, his features as pale as new snow.

"Robert!" she called again. He still didn't hear her. He

was in shock, she realized. "Robert!" Jassy urged the horse over to him. Still, he did not look up. She leapt down and shook him. "Robert! We have to sound the alarm. People have to know; they have to prepare. They have to fight back. We have to reach our houses. . . . Robert, the *alarm*!"

She slapped him, hard. He looked at her at last. "Oh, Jassy!" He was falling apart, she realized. He would be no help to her. She gave him a fierce shove. "Go, hurry! Warn them at my house, and hurry on to your own. I'm going to sound the alarm."

At last he moved. He looked back and saw the single guard still trying to fight off the two Indians. Jassy wondered if she should help him first, then she realized with a curious numbness that she might be killed, and if she were killed, she could never sound the alarm. She pushed away from the horse and went racing to the steps. She tore up them to the roof tower.

Just beyond the top step, at the tower door, stood one of the Indians. His chest was naked, and his well-muscled arms were laden with various tattoos. He wore only a breechclout, white goose feathers in his hair, and a necklace with a rawhide cord. He looked at Jassy and smiled slowly, awaiting her. She looked beyond him. Another of their armed men lay dead. He had been bashed on the head with a cannonball.

The murders were certainly not isolated incidents, Jassy thought furiously. The Indians had come to kill the white men. They were killing the settlers with their own weapons. They were killing them with anything at all that they could find at hand.

And the man at the tower meant to kill her.

Screams were rising now, near the gate. Soon everyone would know. Soon they would all realize the treachery . . . soon, as they lay dying.

"No!" Jassy screamed in a frenzy. She hurtled herself at the Indian with all her strength, and they toppled to the ground together.

Her attack upon the man had been a mistake. The warm, brown body that fell over hers was hard and powerful and relentless. She bit and she kicked and she struggled fiercely, but to little avail. The Indian was young and wire-sinewed, proud of his health and strength and entirely in his prime. She was strong, too, she knew. She clawed and scratched and caused him some injury, but she really had no chance, not from the very beginning.

He pressed his knee into her midriff, and all the air went out of her. Almond-dark eyes met hers with a glitter of amusement, and she knew that her fight was such a feeble one that he was enjoying the whole of it. He reached to his ankle, producing a knife from a rawhide sheath. He took hold of a strand of Jassy's hair and stared upon it for a moment, bemused. Jassy realized that she was about to be scalped.

She screamed, twisting and fighting in renewed fury.

Suddenly there was the soft and curious sound of a sickening thud. Blood spilled over Jassy's beautiful spring dress.

The amusement left the brave's eyes. He stared at her blankly, and she saw that a knife shaft protruded from the center of his bare chest. He grasped for it, his fingers convulsed, and then he went dead still and toppled over on her. She screamed, shoving him aside, and then she looked down the length of the ladder.

Jamie was there. His booted foot rested upon one of the steps, from where he had so swiftly and accurately sent the knife flying to kill the Indian. His eyes met hers, and despite the bloodshed, she trembled. He was solid like rock, as agile and stealthy as the Indians who knew their land so well. He was there for her, tall upon the steps, dark and fierce. He would never panic; he would always meet what came his way with dignity and undauntable courage. She had come to recognize and love the man that he was . . . perhaps *really* too late.

He moved and came racing up the steps toward her. He wrenched her to her feet. "What are you doing? What the *hell* are you doing! You should be back at the house, safe with Daniel!" His voice thundered; he was shaking with anger. He bent and retrieved his knife from the dead brave. He wiped the blade on his trousers and shoved the knife back into the sheath at his calf.

She was stunned, Jassy realized. As slow and as worthless as Robert. "The alarm! Someone has—"

He stepped by her and pulled hard on the bell cord. The sound began to peal, loud and strong. "Come on!" Jamie urged.

He dragged her down the steps into the compound. Three of the Indians were at the foot of the ladder. Like the Indian at the tower, these men were barely clad. They did not notice the cool breezes of the spring morning. One of them wore paint over his cheeks. They all stared at Jamie, tensing and bracing themselves for the fight.

It would be with knives. Twisting their blades in their hands, they stared at Jamie.

Jamie, warily keeping his eyes upon the Indians, shoved Jassy behind him.

"Get away! Hide! Find somewhere safe and stay there!"

"No—"

"Jamie!" came a booming male voice behind them. Sir William! It was Sir William Tybalt, alerted by the alarm! Jamie would no longer face their enemies alone.

"William!" Jamie said. He shoved Jassy quickly toward his friend. "Get her out of here."

"No! He must fight with you—" Jassy protested.

"William, take her. You are sworn to obey me, and I order you to take her out of here." He stared hard at Jassy. "When it starts, run from behind me. Get to the house. Get Daniel and Elizabeth and the others and make your way to the church. It's the only building of brick, and it is fortified. There are muskets in the back pews, and swords in the deacon's benches."

"I can't leave you."

"Come, my lady—" Sir William began. He had a firm grip upon her. He was Jamie's man, and would defend and obey him until the very end, that much she knew.

"I can't leave you!" she screamed again to Jamie.

"You have to leave me!"

"Jamie!"

She tried to hold on to his arm as they faced the Indians. Sir William pulled her away. Wetness streamed down her cheeks. She wanted to talk to Jamie. They were facing death, and there was no time to say anything, and she was choking on the tears that tasted of blood and metal in her mouth.

"Jamie—"

"Go!" he screamed to her. "For God's sake, Jassy! Do you think that I can concentrate on a fight with you behind me? Get out of here, get Daniel, *now*! William, for the love of Christ. . . !"

Sir William tugged hard upon her hand. Staring at Jamie, Jassy swallowed down hard on a sob, and blindly led by Sir William, she turned and ran at last. They stumbled along a fair distance, then, blinking furiously, Jassy pulled back and stopped.

"My lady!" Sir William urged her.

"Please, wait!"

"He knows what he is doing, Lady Cameron!"

Still, she had to see. The first Indian had already rushed Jamie. Jamie moved as quick as light, his knife blade reflecting the sun. The Indian came up taut against Jamie. He had been met with the knife in his loin. The two of them were face-to-face. The Indian breathed his last and fell. Now there were only two of the warring Pamunkees left. It was a far more even fight.

Jassy heard a scream behind her. She whirled around. Mary Montgomery, the blacksmith's stout wife, was laying a fire poker upon an Indian who had attempted to attack her with her own bread board.

Sir William rushed to help her, but Mary, on her own, did all right. She laid the poker flat upon the brave's head, and he fell without a sound. She looked at Jassy with satisfaction. "Another heathen gone to hell." She stared at the blood covering Jassy. "Lady Cameron, are you all right? Come in, Geoffrey and me will see to your protection. Sir William, you may well leave her with us."

"Thank you, good woman," Sir William said, but he

didn't need to go any farther, for Jassy was shaking her head.

"I cannot stay. Daniel . . . my son. I have to get my child." She was already moving. Men were rushing by her. They were grim-faced and determined, trying to reach the gates where Jamie had fought alone. There were bodies strewn all about. Some of them belonged to the white men. And women. And many of them belonged to the Pamunkees. She stepped gingerly over the open-eyed corpse of an older brave. "I have to find my son!"

"He'll be all right, milady. Bless us! Those treacherous devils! We'd all be dead if the alarm hadn't sounded!"

Jassy nodded, and kept stumbling along the muddy streets to her house. The sounds of the fighting continued. Sir William followed behind her.

Then suddenly an Indian jumped down from a thatched roof before them. Jassy screamed, and Sir William pushed her forward. "Go, milady, you are almost home. Run!"

The Indian fell upon him. Sir William drew his sword, and battle was engaged. "Run!" he shouted again to Jassy.

Daniel. Her innocent, vulnerable child lay at her house. Elizabeth and Amy and the other women waited there. Sir William would fare well enough without her. She nodded jerkily, and then she turned and ran once again. She could smell smoke. Some of the houses were on fire.

Bodies continued to line the way. Blindly choking, sobbing, she stepped over and around them.

She reached her own door at last and shoved it open. "Amy! Elizabeth!" No one answered her. She came tearing up the stairs and burst into her own room, where she had left Daniel in his cradle.

She stopped short in the doorway, her hand flying to her open mouth.

Daniel was still there, fast asleep. Elizabeth, ashen and terrified, was backed into a corner, held there at knifepoint by a young Indian. Another of the Pamunkees stood over the cradle, shaking his head. He looked at

Jassy, then he fingered the little amulet that Opechancanough had sent the baby as a gift. It looked as if he meant to touch the baby next.

"No!" Jassy screamed. She tore into the room and swept the baby up from beneath his eyes. She held him tightly against her. "No, no, no!" She narrowed her eyes and said the Indian chief's name. "Opechancanough! Opechancanough!"

The two Indians looked at one another, and then at her. Jassy flipped out her own amulet, the gift once given to Jamie by Pocahontas. Both Indians paused, then the first Indian indicated that she must put the baby back in his cradle. Daniel, awakened and sniffing his mother's scent, began to cry.

"No!" she screamed. She cradled her son closer to her. The Indian came to her. She stared into his eyes, but like Elizabeth, she found herself backed to the wall. "No! Opechancanough."

He came to her at last. He pressed the blade of his knife threateningly against Jassy's throat. She lifted her chin, tears stinging her eyes. Where was Jamie now? Was he alive or dead? Had Robert ever come to warn them here? Sir William! Surely he would come to her rescue at any moment.

There was a sudden sound of movement in the doorway, and Jassy quickly looked there with fervent prayers of rescue.

It was no rescue. It was Hope who stood there. Jassy wondered bitterly if she had known about the attack all along. Had she slain the whites who had taken her in?

Hope stepped warily into the room. She was dressed in European fashion, with a mass of petticoats holding out her skirts. She looked at Jassy with her curious green eyes, then spoke to the Indians in their own tongue. She was very quiet and very calm. The brave moved his knife away from Jassy's throat and spoke to Hope insistently.

"He says," Hope told her, "that the baby has Opechancanough's protection. He may stay. You are to come with him."

"What?" Jassy repeated. "But I am protected. . . ."

Hope looked at her with wide, greedy eyes. "But you are a woman. You are to come with them. You, and her"—she pointed to Elizabeth—"are his hostages, and you will get him out of the fort. You should leave your son." She hesitated. "They sacrifice their own sometimes. It would be wise to leave him. You must come."

Jassy shook her head. She glanced quickly at Elizabeth in the corner. Her sister seemed to be in shock, her blue eyes wide, open, and staring.

"I will not come," she said firmly.

Hope spoke to the Indian, and the Indian shook his head firmly, flashing a white, malicious smile. He spoke to her, and Hope looked to Jassy again. "If you do not come, he will slice out her heart and make you watch, and then he will kill you. He will do so immediately. It is your decision."

Elizabeth gasped and sank against the wall.

Jassy trembled, feeling the blood seep from her face. It took her several attempts to form words with her dry lips and speak. "Tell him that I will come."

"Both of you," Hope murmured. She offered Jassy a peculiar smile, and Jassy realized that it was one of concern. "I will come with you too. Do not be afraid. I will not let them kill you."

Jassy wasn't sure that anyone could stop this Indian from killing anyone. Still, ironically, she was very grateful to Hope. "Thank you," she whispered. She kept her eyes upon the lethal brave. "Hope, please take Daniel and put him in his cradle."

Hope shook her head. "I will carry him out. They might fire the house."

Hope took the baby from Jassy. He was screaming in raw fury then, his face mottled and red, his little fists waving. Her breasts burst forth in an aching reply, but she dared not touch him again. Tears threatened to spill from her in hysterical measure, but she braced her jaw and held stubbornly to a show of bravado. She edged against the wall, watching the brave, and sinking down by Elizabeth. "Come on, Elizabeth. We must go. We will be all right."

Elizabeth stared at her hopefully, her cheeks wet and stained with tears. "Jamie will come for us," she said.

"Jamie will come for us," Jassy agreed. He would come, if he did not already lay dead in the spring mud of the complex. "Come, Elizabeth. We will move slowly. Hope is coming too."

Hope lowered her head over Daniel's forehead. She turned around and started down the stairway.

The house seemed painfully silent as Jassy followed Hope, feeling the point of the Indian's blade at the small of her back. She held Elizabeth's arm, trying to give her sister strength. Elizabeth trembled, and silent tears fell down her cheeks, but she kept moving.

At the bottom of the stairway Jassy nearly lost control. A sharp cry escaped her as she saw that Amy Lawton lay upon the floor, the victim of an attack made with the dish of an English garden spade. Jassy fell to her knees beside the woman, rolling her over and seeking life.

Amy's eyes were open and seemed to mirror the final terror she had witnessed. There was no life left within her.

The brave behind Jassy growled out some warning and wrenched her back to her feet. They all heard a snuffling sound coming from the servants' wing. The second Indian started off that way, but Hope caught his arm, and pleaded with him violently, showing him the baby. At length the Indian nodded. Hope gazed at Jassy encouragingly, and hurried down the hallway. She appeared again a moment later, pulling along Charity Hume, who now held the screaming Daniel. "Tell her, Lady Cameron, that she will be all right. She must take the baby and go. They will burn the house."

Charity looked numb, and deeply in shock. She saw the Indians and started to shrink away. She was going to drop Daniel, Jassy thought.

"Charity!" she lashed out, and she knew that she had never spoken before with so much authority as Lady Cameron. "Charity! They are not going to hurt you. But if you harm Daniel in any way, so help me, I will! Take him quickly. Go to the church."

Charity stared at her for a moment, hardly believing her good luck that she might escape. She clutched the baby more tightly to her. "I will keep him, lady. I will keep him well. I will keep him—"

The first Indian was already setting fire to the tapestries and draperies about the hallway. The material caught the blaze quickly and hungrily.

"Charity, go!"

The young woman sped from the house. Tears burst from Jassy's eyes as they filled with smoke, and as her heart was torn raggedly apart by the pathetic wails of her son, slowly fading in the distance.

She had no more chance for tears or worry or emotion. The first Indian caught her by the hair and dragged her hurriedly from the house. He was taking no more time.

The streets outside were empty, except for a few strewn bodies. The Indian did not head for the gateway to the palisade but pulled her along toward the rear of the structure. She could hear Elizabeth choking and panting and sobbing behind her, and she knew that her sister was being dragged at the same frantic pace. Her scalp pained her mercilessly, the brave's hold upon it so strong. But at least, she reminded herself, it was still attached to her body.

They came to the rear wall. Jassy tried to stagger back. There were other Indians waiting there, about eight of them. When they saw Jassy and Elizabeth and their captors arriving, they began a rush up one of the rear stairways to the parapets and towers.

The Indian said something to her, jerking hard upon her hair. She was dragged up the stairs. Upon the parapet, she looked over the log wall. A hay cart lay beneath them. The Indian pushed her forward.

"No!" she cried in panic.

He lifted her up and tossed her over. Jassy screamed as she fell. She landed upon the hay, the breath knocked from her. She heard an echo of her scream.

Elizabeth landed beside her. Jassy tried to sit. She tried to help her sister. Some of the Indians were scaling the wall with ropes; three of them landed in the hay wagon too. Jassy desperately sought balance, but the vehicle suddenly jolted and started moving.

The wagon made it to the entrance of the forest, where the trails suddenly narrowed. The Indians had been prepared, Jassy realized. A group of horses waited in the clearing. She was lifted, struggling and fighting, from the wagon. She was thrown atop a horse, and a brave leapt up behind her. She tried to bite his hand. He slapped her across the cheek, a stinging blow.

Dimly she realized that she could no longer hear Elizabeth.

She did hear a soft whisper. It was Hope. "Don't fight him. This is Pocanough, and he will hurt you."

"Elizabeth," she murmured, dazed.

"Your sister has fainted. It is best for her."

Jassy swallowed and went silent. The Indian nudged the horse, and the animal leapt high and began a frantic race into the forest.

Jassy leaned back and felt the wind and the slick nakedness of the brave's chest, and she wished with all her heart that she, too, could pass out.

Jamie would come for her. Jamie would come . . .

If he did not lay dead in a pool of his own blood.

No, she could not believe it. He could not be dead. He could not. She would not be able to bear it if he was.

Tears spilled again from her eyes to her cheeks, but they went unnoticed, for the wind dried them even as they fell. She never would be able to lay down her pride and tell him that she loved him. She had been given everything in the world, and she had cast her heart to Robert Maxwell instead. And now she had lost even the opportunity to reach with all her heart for the things that once had been given to her so very freely. . . .

She closed her eyes against the wind, and in misery she endured the long and wretched ride.

It was all over but the burying, Jamie thought at last.

His white shirt was soaked in blood; his knife was caked with it. Indians lay about his feet in huge heaps, and his own men lay there too. How many had died? he wondered. Ten, twenty, maybe more?

He looked up at the spring sky, and he swore with a sudden vehemence. He had known! He had known not to trust Opechancanough! The wily chief had sent men slowly to befriend them, and then to murder and decimate those friends.

"My God! You have slain them all!"

It was Sir Cedric talking to him. Allen came rushing up at his side, cleaning the blade of his sword. He was glad that the knights had been with him during the bloodbath. They were brave fighters, and trained to the challenge. The Indians had attacked so stealthily that many would not have stood a chance against them.

Jamie looked down at the ground again. How many men had he killed himself? Ten, twenty? He did not know. Somewhere in the fierce struggle he had lost all sense of humanity. He had fought blindly, and with a blood lust of his own. They had attacked his home. They had attacked his palisade, and God help them, they had attacked his wife.

Suddenly he smelled smoke. He pulled Cedric close to him. "There are more of them. More of them, in the complex!"

"Come on!" Allen cried.

Men—the last of the trained and armed soldiers, the artisans and laborers forced into being warriors—followed behind as they all raced through the streets. The place was alive once again with survivors crawling about the streets, wailing over their dead, seeking out the wounded. The blacksmith's wife assured them that the Indians were gone from the compound. "There were but few who made it this deep, Lord Cameron."

That encouraged Jamie. He wanted to see Jassy. He wanted to take her into his arms and shudder and tell her that it was terrible, that he had seen so much death, that he had killed so much himself. He wanted to assure her first. He wanted to swear that he would take her home. He wanted to beg her forgiveness and ask humbly if they might have a chance to start all over again. He would bring her back to the manor in England, and even when he felt the urge to come back to this land, he would never expect it of her. Mostly he just wanted to hold her, and he wanted to hold his son.

"Lord Cameron!" a man cried. " 'Tis Sir William!"

"What?" Jamie cried. He hurried forward toward the man and knelt down upon one knee. His heart congealed. It *was* Sir William, slain. He had died fighting, for even as the blood had seeped from his great heart, he had brought down his opponent with him. A brave, with Sir William's blade through his gut, lay atop him.

Jamie quickly crossed himself. Prayer eluded him, but he knew that God would welcome such a brave spirit as Sir William. He clenched his teeth together tightly in pain for his good friend, then he came quickly to his feet, a new anguish searing through him.

"My wife. My God, he was escorting my wife!"

He tore down the street, and then he realized from where the smell of fire came. His whole street had been set to the torch.

His stomach lurched, and he stared at the flaming buldings. Behind him, someone called out orders to squelch the fire.

Jamie started to run again. He raced through the heat and the smoke for the church. As he reached it the doors opened, and Father Steven led his flock out to greet him.

"Lord Cameron, have we come through our test in the wilderness?"

"It is over," Jamie said curtly, staring into the crowd, into the smudged faces that met his. He saw Lenore and Robert. They were huddled together. There were many people there, many, many people. Jassy had saved them, he thought. She had remembered the alarm, and the people had surged into the church. The death toll would stand at twenty or thirty, he was certain, but most of the people had survived the attack, thanks to his wife's quick thinking—and courage.

"Where is she?" he said aloud. He gripped Father Steven's arms, and the man paled and did not answer him. He stepped forward into the church, reaching Lenore and Robert. "Where is she?" he repeated.

Then he heard the cry. Daniel's cry. He turned around, hope filling his breast, and he was instantly grateful to see his son.

But it was not Jassy holding the boy. It was the servant girl, Charity.

"Where is Jassy?" he demanded in a rage.

Charity shuddered. Jamie pulled the child from the girl's arms, holding him close. Daniel continued to cry, the sound echoing the howl in Jamie's heart. "Where in God's name is my wife!" he demanded.

It was Charity who answered him at last. She stumbled forward and sobbed out her story. They had come to the house, the Indians had, two men. They had come with gifts of pumpkin bread, and they had found Amy in the garden. Amy had brought them in, and one had taken the spade and killed her with it, and the other had taken the fire poker and slain Charity's sister, and then they had gone up the stairs. Charity had hidden, and she had stayed beneath her bed until the girl, Hope, had come and pulled her out. And then she had seen Lady Cameron, all covered in blood, her hair tumbling around her in awful disarray, but still very calm, her chin high and her shoulders straight.

"She had me take the babe, and she ordered me to bring him out, and she warned me that she'd have my hide were he hurt. Oh, milord! I ran, I was so scared. She made me. She said that they were going to burn the house. She knew it. She was holding up her sister, for Lady Elizabeth, she was so scared."

Lenore started crying softly. She fell into one of the pews. "They will slay them, they will kill them both! Oh, my God, Jamie, I have heard what they do with their captives—oh, dear God!"

Jamie stood very still, holding his screaming son. He cast back his head and let out a single cry of anguish, a sound more savage than any heard from the primitive tribes.

Then he clenched his teeth and drew his son to him

tightly. He held him that way for a long moment, then he gave the child into Lenore's arms. "Care for him with Charity."

"As I would my own," Lenore mumbled, cradling the baby. Daniel continued to cry. Jamie turned away, ripping open the pews and carefully arming himself.

Robert stepped forward. "Jamie, what are you doing?"

Jamie looked at him. "I am going after my wife."

"Wait. Wait until help has come from Jamestown, or from the Bermuda Hundred, or—"

"We do not know that there is any help to come," Jamie said.

Robert swallowed in fear. "I will come with you," he managed to gasp out at last. Jamie looked at his friend and slowly shook his head. "No, stay here. And you, too, Cedric, Allen. We haven't the power to fight the entire Powhatan Confederacy. If I am to get Jassy and Elizabeth back, it will be by stealth or negotiation. I am best off alone, and you are best off repairing our lives here, and mourning what we have lost."

He gathered what weapons he wanted, then turned away. people followed him from the church as he left it.

Thankfully the stables had not been burned. The house, and all the fine riches that Jassy had so cherished, were nothing but ashes. He stepped past the burning refuse and entered the stable and chose his own horse, Windwalker. He leapt upon the nervous stallion and started out of the complex.

"Jamie!"

As he urged his mount forward Sir Allen caught up with him, offering him a clean shirt and an unstained leather jerkin. He paused, taking them, and changed. When he was done, he smiled to his friend. "Thank you."

The people followed in turn. They offered him a water flask, and dried beef, and whatever else they could find that he might need. Sir Allen brought him a strong bow and a quiver of arrows.

At the gate to the palisade he turned and looked upon the smudged, bloodied, and anxious faces. They were all his friends, he thought. His people, his friends, and even before assessing their own losses, they were eager to minimize his. He looked over the tired and weary faces, and in them he saw strength. They would build again, they would build anew. They would bury their dead, but they would stay, and they would make the land theirs, make it good.

He lifted a hand to them all in acknowledgment, then turned Windwalker around and nudged the stallion into a gallop, westward, toward the forest, toward the Indian nations of the Powhatan Confederacy.

XVIII

They traveled all through the day and into the darkness, and when the rugged journey ended at last, Jassy was close to unconsciousness. She could not stand when the brave dismounted from his horse, and despite herself, she fell into his arms. She was lifted and carried along, until they came to the largest of their curious, long, arched-roof houses. There were many, many Indians there. They followed along behind her, laughing and making derisive noises. Thankfully she was oblivious of them. They spat toward the ground, but they did not touch her. The brave pushed them away, and she was brought into the house, and Elizabeth was carried in behind her. There was a sudden and curious silence. Someone spoke, and she was laid down. She heard a rustle of movement, and then an Indian was staring down at her. She tried very hard to focus upon him. He was nearly naked, dressed like the others in a breechclout, and wearing a strand of beads and shells about his neck. Dark hair fell to his shoulders and was parted neatly in the center of his head. His eyes were incredibly dark, and the very strength of his features was arresting. Startled, Jassy dampened her lips and tried to speak. "Powan!" she whispered.

"Cameron's woman," he said in acknowledgment. His

face wavered before her, then disappeared. He came back to her, shoving a water bowl into her hands. Gratefully she tried to drink, having little strength left. He lifted her head for her. The water was good. He let her sink back to the floor.

He rose then, walked to the entrance to his house, and spoke sternly to his people. Jassy was then dimly aware that he was arguing fiercely with the brave who had brought her in, the Indian Pocanough.

While the argument went on, Jassy heard a rustling, and then someone came close to her. She opened her eyes again. It was Hope.

"Pocanough says that you are *his* hostage. He took you. It is for him to decide if you should be tortured and killed, and if not, you should be his captive, his slave."

Jassy shivered uncontrollably. She was miserable and exhausted, and her breasts pained her mercilessly, swollen terribly because she had not nursed Daniel since early morning. Her head hurt and her thighs hurt, and her body seemed alive with agony, and still she didn't want to die.

And certainly not the way that the Pamunkees brought about death. Bashing their victim's skulls in upon their sacrificial rocks or altars. Or dismembering them and roasting their limbs one by one, disemboweling them while they lived . . .

"Oh, God!" she whispered. She tried to sit up. Hope helped her. Elizabeth was on a pallet, not far away. She inched over toward her sister. Elizabeth was still pale, her eyes closed. Jassy felt for her wrist and found that her heart was still beating. It was better this way. Elizabeth was being spared the awful agony of not knowing their plight.

"Powan comes back!" Hope whispered. "They will do nothing to you tonight. They will let you sleep."

Jassy came back to where they had lain her. She stretched out and closed her eyes. She sensed the presence of the Pamunkee chief as he came over to her, staring down at her. He said something to Hope, and Hope answered him softly in return. He made a sniffling sound and turned away from her. He sat before the open fire with the smoke hole above it in the center of his house. He snapped out some order—a command for Hope to come forward, for that was what she did. Something was cooking, and Jassy thought that he ordered Hope to prepare him a dish of food, for she did that too.

For the longest time Jassy lay awake, listening. She thought about escaping, but she knew that she hadn't the strength, and that she could bring Powan's wrath down upon her when he seemed to be her only chance of survival.

Finally Powan stretched out.

Soon she heard even breathing. He slept.

Looking back over the day, Jassy longed to rise, find his knife, and slit his throat. She trembled with the thought, aching to do so. But someone would come and slay her in turn. And they would slay Elizabeth, too, and maybe even Hope for good measure.

She didn't want to die. She wanted to live to return to her son, and to Jamie. If he lived.

If he lived.

She rolled over in a horrible agony. She had never wanted him so badly in her life. She wanted to pray, but she wasn't even able to do so.

Finally, restlessly, tears damp upon her cheeks, she slept.

The morning began with pure terror.

She awakened to the sound of raucous screaming. Opening her eyes, she saw a dozen Indian women staring down at her. They laughed at her, pulled at her hair, and spit at her dress. They were doing the same to Elizabeth. She heard her sister cry out in distress.

Her temper flared and exploded. Jassy leapt to her feet, snarling, and hurtled herself at the young woman who attempted to remove her hair from her head. She managed to bring the Indian maid down to the ground before Powan returned to the tent, and the women all fell silent. Powan came to her, dragging her off the maiden.

"Cameron's woman, you will behave," he told her.

"Tell *her* to behave!" Jassy snapped. Then she remembered that her life hung in the balance, and she locked her jaw. She still met his eyes. He smiled and shoved her back at the women.

"They will not hurt you. You wear the blood of our warriors, and that offends them. You will be bathed and cleansed, and that is all."

"That is all?" she whispered hopefully.

"For now," he said forebodingly. But she was to get no more from him. He left his house, and the women latched on to her arms. Elizabeth, too, was escorted from the house on the arms of the women.

They were taken past a village center. There was an interesting circle of poles and ashes there, and a large rock. The rock was red, bloodstained. Jassy paled, knowing what the rock was—the "altar" where men's heads were caved in. The sickening smell of fire and ash was still on the air.

She almost fell, buckling over with such strength that the women had to jerk her back to her feet. They had not been the only prisoners of the Pamunkee the previous night. Some captives had already met their fates upon the rock, and in the tortuous flames.

"Oh, God!" Elizabeth gasped.

"Come on, quickly, move, don't look!" Jassy urged her. She screwed up her own eyes until they entered into a trail of trees, and from there they came to a brook. Jassy shook herself free from the woman who held her, anxious to reach Elizabeth. She was too late. Elizabeth was violently sick, right into the bushes. Jassy held her up, smoothing back her hair, waiting for the spasm to die.

"It's all right, it's all right—" Jassy said.

"No, no, it's not. It is what they're going to do to us! I read John Smith's reports of the murder of John Calvin. They were in your house. I read them . . . I read about the Indians. They are going to torture and kill us just the same—"

"No, no, they're not. Powan won't let them."

"Powan will light the fires," Elizabeth said.

"Jamie will come," Jassy said.

She was wrenched away from Elizabeth. The women set upon them both, tearing and ripping at their clothing until they were both left shivering and naked and panting from the fight they had waged. They were shoved into the water then. The cold was shocking. Jassy rose, gasping for air. They were quickly joined by the women, who did not seem to feel the cold of the brook. Then they were set upon again, and scrubbed thoroughly with handfuls of sand and stones. Jassy hated every touch. Her breasts were in agony that morning, overflowing. No matter how she screamed and fought, they, too, were viciously scrubbed.

Finally, exhausted and panting, she and Elizabeth were left upon rocks to dry beneath the sun. Then they were given short, leather, apronlike dresses to wear, like the other women. They were not given shoes. Jassy thought that they were kept barefoot to hinder escape attempts, since most of the women did wear soft leather moccasins.

They were brought back to Powan's house then, and given bowls of meat in gravy. Jassy looked at the food suspiciously, but she was ravenous, and when she tasted the stew, it was delicious. Hope came back to them soon and told them that the meal had been rabbit, and that they needn't fear eating—the Pamunkees did not poison their captives; when they meant to kill them, they did so with a feast and lots of entertainment so that the deaths could be enjoyed.

"What is happening?" Jassy asked Hope.

"They are talking about you again in a council. Pocanough says that he wants you, and that he will have you. Powan says no, that he is the chief, that he will wait and see if your husband lived through the massacre and if he will come for you."

Elizabeth was poking at her stew. Jassy glanced at her quickly, then looked at Hope again. "Someone will come. They will come from the other hundreds—"

"Maybe. Eventually. But it was not only the Carlyle Hundred that was attacked. We came off very lightly, they are saying. The Indians managed to kill only twenty or thirty whites in a population of over two hundred. At Martin's Hundred, half were killed. It is the same at many of the others. Jamestown was spared, for the people were warned. Jamie saved many by being prepared; they say that *you* saved many by sounding the alarm."

"The entire Virginia colony was attacked?" Elizabeth whispered in horror.

Hope nodded gravely. "Opechancanough ordered it so."

"Why?" Jassy breathed.

"He wants his land back, I suppose," Hope said.

Jassy touched her hand suddenly. "Thank you, Hope. Thank you for coming with us. Why—why did you do it? You did not have to."

Hope shrugged. She lowered her head. "I lied to you. I was jealous. I wanted your husband, and I told you that I knew him to make you mad. He loves you. It was wrong."

Jassy inhaled softly. "I—I don't think that he loves me."

"Yes, yes, he does. He loves you very much." She smiled. "If he can come, he will. Powan expects him. He says that Jamie will come alone. Pocanough thinks that Jamie should be slain, but Powan says that Jamie is fair, and he will be fair too. If Pocanough wants to fight Jamie for you, that will be all right. Whichever man lives will have you, and if both are killed, you will belong to Powan. That is what I think that they are deciding."

Jassy shivered, then she looked at Elizabeth again. She couldn't tell what her sister had heard, and what she had comprehended. Elizabeth had never looked more fragile, or more beautiful. Her soft blond hair curled softly about her face and her flower-blue eyes. The leather apron exposed a great deal of her fair, silky skin, enhancing the fullness of her breasts and the long, shapely length of her legs. Jassy looked at Hope. Hope shook her head and left them quickly.

In the afternoon one of the women came back with a bag of grain and a mortar and pestle, trying to show them that they must work. Jassy shook her head, and Elizabeth stubbornly followed suit. The young woman looked at them angrily, then returned with one of the matrons with a long reed. The older woman began with Jassy, lashing out at her with hard, stinging blows. Jassy screamed and covered her face and fell to the ground so that the blows could be deflected by the leather upon her back.

Suddenly the blows stopped.

"Stop it! Stop it!" she heard Elizabeth shrieking.

Her sister—her sweet, shy sister—was on top of the Indian woman, wrenching the reed from her hands and wrestling her in a fury. Jassy staggered to her feet, hurrying to Elizabeth's aid. Just then, Powan came back into the house.

In a fury, he tugged up both her and Elizabeth by the hair. The older woman—with a bleeding lip, thanks to Elizabeth's tender touch—began to rant and rail and lash out at the white woman again. Powan thundered out in fury and pushed the two of them to the far rear of the house. He sent the woman away.

Jassy held still, watching the tall, muscled Indian pick up the reed. He came over to them and waved it in front of them. "Everyone works. You work too. Next time I will let them beat you until the blood flows from your flesh."

He dropped the reed and turned and left them. Hope returned with the wheat they were to grind. Looking at Elizabeth's smudged face, Jassy had to smile. "You *are* a fighter!" She laughed.

Elizabeth flushed. "She was beating you. I could not stand by and watch it."

Impulsively Jassy hugged her. Hope cleared her throat and told them that they must finish their work. "Everyone works to eat. It is the way that it is done," she said, looking at them anxiously.

Jassy and Elizabeth looked at each other and shrugged, and then set forth on their task. If it could remain so, if they could grind wheat by day and have Powan's protection by night, then they could survive until . . .

Until Jamie came, if he was alive to do so.

And if he could survive Pocanough.

If things could just stay the same . . .

But things were not to stay the same. That night, when Powan came back to his house, he dragged them both to their feet. He stared at Jassy and pulled on the amulet she wore around her neck so that it hung low over her breasts. His mere touch upon them caused her to wince, and he smiled, slowly and curiously. She gasped, stunned, when he ripped open her garment, baring her to the waist. Her breasts, so heavy and painful now, surged forth. She tried to cover herself, and he grabbed her hands, wrenching them around behind her back and holding her tautly to his chest with just one hand to imprison her. "You tempt me, Cameron's woman." She gritted her teeth against the humiliation and pain as he moved his fingers over the full globes of her breasts, pausing to flick the nipples and see them fill with milk. She wanted to lash out at him; she was afraid that she would fall, and she hadn't the strength to free herself from his powerful hold. "You tempt me, yes . . . but James Cameron is a man I will give a chance."

She opened her eyes wide upon his, aware that Powan was taunting her but that she would even be spared rape because of the man her husband was.

She heard a sudden hissing noise, and then fists slammed against Powan's back. Elizabeth! She was even daring to attack the Indian brave in Jassy's defense.

"Elizabeth!" she cried, but it was too late. Powan had already shoved her aside and clutched Elizabeth to him. He smiled, looking down at Elizabeth. He had her wrist and pulled her inexorably closer. "No!" Elizabeth murmured, shaking her head.

"Powan! Please—" Jassy began. She raced back to him, trying to swing the solid brave around. "Please don't. She is Jamie's sister-in-law! She is afraid of you, she will hate you—"

He started to laugh, and his eyes swept over her, lingering on her naked breasts and slim waist. "She is not his wife, and a captive need not love a captor."

"You can't!" Jassy cried, flinging herself against him.

She scratched, she raked, she sobbed, and she fought him very bitterly, but he was quickly on top of her, despite Elizabeth's harrying him from behind. Powan got Jassy down upon her stomach, and he laced her wrists together with a strip of rawhide, then dragged her to a corner where he tied the rawhide to a stake.

"Leave her alone!" Elizabeth cried, thundering upon his back. "Leave her alone!"

He tied Jassy securely.

"Leave her alone!" Elizabeth cried again. Jassy saw his jaw harden as Elizabeth's nails raked his bare flesh. He ignored the attack, and his dark eyes found Jassy's. "Don't make me forget who you are, Cameron's woman," he warned her.

"You can't—" she said, but he had already spun around and seized Elizabeth.

Jassy strained against her bonds in agony. She heard her sister scrambling away, gasping, sobbing, no longer seeking to attack but trying with all her heart to escape.

Bracing herself, she strained against the pole as she heard the frantic fight that ensued, a fight that was quickly ended.

She heard Elizabeth's piercing scream.

And she heard the sounds of Powan moving over her sister, breathing raggedly, ramming his body again and again. She heard the Indian's emission of a pleased grunt. She heard it all, burning inwardly and outwardly, wishing she could scream and scream and scream, just so that she would not have to hear what went on.

But she could hear. She heard Powan fall from Elizabeth, and then she heard her sister sobbing through the night. She could not go to her; she could not even talk to her. Elizabeth slept with the Indian brave. In the dim firelight Jassy could see that her sister was imprisoned by a strong brown arm. Elizabeth had gone silent, still and silent. Jassy wondered if she slept. She did not sleep again herself that night.

In the morning Powan slit the ties that bound Jassy to the pole before he left the house. Jassy stared at him with hard reproach, but he impassively ignored her. As soon as he had stepped from the doorway, she crawled over to Elizabeth. Elizabeth flinched from her touch and looked, dazed, into her eyes. "Oh, Jassy!" Tears welled within the deep blue pools. "Oh, Jassy, it was awful!"

Jassy held her and rocked her.

Then Elizabeth began to swear. She talked about how she hated the Indian and how she would one day cut his heart out and toss it into a fire while he still lived. Jassy finally encouraged Elizabeth to get up, and she worked on adjusting both of their outfits so that they might decently make it to the brook. People watched them as they walked, but no one tried to stop them. Jassy kept a sharp lookout, desperate now that they might find a way to escape. But although no one impeded their way, there were Indians everywhere, the men and the women, watching them. Escape would be difficult.

"He'll do it again!" Elizabeth stormed at the brook.

There was nothing that Jassy could say to reassure her. She could not fight and save her. Powan didn't give a damn about either of them, but in his curious way he did care about Jamie, and if she wanted just to spare Elizabeth, Powan still would not take her in her sister's stead.

"We'll escape," she promised. "We'll escape."

But they didn't escape that day, and by night, Powan seized Jassy and brought her, screaming and thrashing, to be tied to the pole again.

And he seized upon Elizabeth again. The only difference was that Elizabeth no longer cried when it was over.

They *had* to escape.

But two weeks later they had not.

They were coming to know the Pamunkee way of life. Powan was the chief of this tribe, and he spent much of his time in council meetings and debate. He was also a hunter and a warrior, and he expected his woman to serve him. A Pamunkee could take as many wives as he could provide for, so it was natural that he had laid claim to the women hostages, and that he held them for whatever trade it might take to return them.

After the initial torture by the other women, Jassy and Elizabeth were fairly much left alone. Hope continued to be their friend, and to keep them advised of what was happening.

In the morning they bathed and were set to work, either with grain or mending, or with plucking a wild turkey, or skinning or tanning. Neither of them took easily to the tasks, for although they were accustomed to days of work, preparing skins for clothing was hard and arduous. They were corrected many times by the Indian women when they stretched and scraped and cleaned and dried the skins. Jassy didn't mind the days. She came to like the mornings and bathing in the cool brook. She didn't mind the labor because it kept her mind busy.

She hated the nights. There was no way to avoid hearing Powan and her sister, and there was no way to avoid lying there and wondering if Daniel was all right, if he missed her, if he was being loved and cared for, if he was being fed and tended gently. And there was no way not to wonder about Jamie. If he was alive, he would come for her. He would have to. Whether he cared for her or not, he would have to come. It would be part of his code of honor. He would have to save her from the Indians . . . just so that he could send her home to England. Alone.

Somewhere in the third week of their captivity, things took on a subtle change, and Jassy was never quite sure just when it had happened. The noises she heard at night began to change. Powan had apparently determined to seduce rather than ravage. Jassy heard Elizabeth panting and gasping and emitting soft moans and whimpers, and then startling cries. Realizing what she heard now, Jassy closed her eyes in mortification and turned to the wall of saplings, gritting her teeth through the night. Once she had twisted to awaken and see in the firelight the two of them standing together, gleaming and golden, and Powan tenderly stroking her sister's nakedness. Ashamed, Jassy closed her eyes and rolled again, keeping her eyes tightly closed. She heard whispers that meant nothing, yet meant everything. She tried not to listen, but she could not help feeling an anguished longing deep inside and wishing that time could be erased, that she could be lying with her husband as Elizabeth lay with the Pamunkee.

Powan called Elizabeth his golden bird. He was coming to care for her very deeply, and Elizabeth was coming to blush when the Indian's name was spoken.

Jassy was growing desperate to escape.

On the twenty-fifth day of their captivity, she realized that by mid-morning there were few braves about. The women were busy and were accustomed to Elizabeth and her being busy too. If they came back from bathing, then calmly walked away into the forest, they might not be missed for several hours, enough time to give them a good head start.

Elizabeth argued with Jassy. "We don't know where we are!"

"The James River lies to the south of us. I need only find the river and follow it. I would have to find Jamestown. I can do it, Elizabeth, I can lead us home. I know it."

"We will run on foot. They will come after us on horses."

"We will hide. They will give up. And we might find white men in the forest, looking for us."

At last Elizabeth agreed.

The sounds in the darkness lasted longer than usual the night before they were to escape. Jassy thought that Elizabeth was telling her lover good-bye.

With the dawn, they went to the brook as usual. Hope brought them a turkey to pluck that morning, and Jassy whispered that they were going to escape. "Will you come?"

Hope thought about it for a minute. "No. If I am caught helping you, they will punish me as a traitor."

Jassy did not ask what they would do to Hope. She didn't want to know. She hugged the girl fiercely and promised her that they would meet again.

She waited another half hour or so, then tapped Elizabeth on the shoulder. They came out together and stretched, as if taking a brief break from their labors. No one paid them any heed. Jassy motioned toward the trail that had brought them to the village, and they calmly started walking along the dirt.

"I can't believe we're doing this," Elizabeth whispered. "We will probably perish. We will be consumed by insects. What if we are struck by a venomous snake?"

"Save your breath and walk," Jassy commanded her.

They had walked about an hour when they came upon the horses. Jassy grasped Elizabeth and pulled her into the bushes. One of the horses was a spotted mare. Jassy had seen it before. She had ridden upon it when Pocanough had abducted her to the village. "It is a hunting party!" she told Elizabeth.

"What will we do?"

"Just stay silent until they have passed us by."

Even as she whispered, the Indians returned to their horses, leaping upon them. Jassy saw Pocanough. He wore rawhide boots up to his ankles, his breechclout, a band with feathers across his forehead, and nothing more. He was with five other men. He already had several pheasants tied over his horse's haunches, brought down with his arrows.

The men all mounted. They laughed and joked, ready to ride on.

Suddenly Elizabeth gasped. Jassy heard the soft sound of a rattle. She looked around and saw that a snake, posing to strike, lay within range of the bushes where they hid. They must have disturbed the creature or its nest.

"Damn!" she cried in anguish, wrenching Elizabeth from their position and rolling with her far from the snake's possible strike zone . . . and right into the path of the Pamunkee warriors.

When Jassy looked up, Pocanough had stopped his mount right before her, the animal's hooves so close that he could crush her head any second.

He started to dismount. Jassy saw the malicious pleasure in his eyes. She leapt to her feet and ran.

She didn't care about snakes or brambles or the insects or anything else; she ran in panic into the trees and through them. She heard Pocanough thrashing behind her.

She ran until her heart hurt and her lungs burned and her legs were in agony. She ran until she felt that her insides were bursting, and that she would die if she took another step. Still she kept running.

But the Indian knew his way, and suddenly he was in front of her in a copse instead of behind her. Gasping, clutching her heart, and inhaling desperately, Jassy reeled back. Pocanough smiled, leapt upon a fallen tree, and sprang for her, knocking her to the ground with the impetus of his pounce.

She screamed and twisted beneath him. He tried to subdue her, catching her hands. She escaped his hold and rent a long scratch down his cheek. That angered him. He slapped her hard, and she caught her breath, dizzy from the blow. He lifted his hand to slap her again, and she thought that that was it; she could fight no more. Her strength was deserting her.

Then suddenly, out of the clear blue, a pair of bronze hands set themselves upon the warrior's shoulders, and Pocanough was wrenched cleanly and clearly away from her.

Jamie had been despairing, aware that he could never give up, but sinking lower into depression day by day.

Jamie had combed the peninsula. He had gone to Opechancanough, despite the massacre of the whites, and he had walked into the great chief's village with such arrogance that the chief had let him live. Opechancanough had told him that Powan had his wife and her sister but that he did not know where Powan was. Jamie would have to find him. It would be treacherous. Yes, he had ordered the whites attacked. All of the whites. He'd had a vision. They would keep coming and coming, and there could be no peace. The Indians would be absorbed into the earth, and the great Powhatan Confederacy would be no more. "The English must leave. My people know this. If they find you in the forest, James Cameron, they will probably kill you."

"You forget, Opechancanough, that I learned from the Powhatan how to move in the forest. I must have my wife. You know that. A man must do this thing."

Opechancanough agreed with him. He gave him supplies.

But the days passed, and he could not find the village where Powan was residing. He came upon tribes of Chickahominies, and though the Indians were not hostile to him, they could tell him nothing. Finally, the day before, he had ridden Windwalker into the domain of a curious old medicine man, and the medicine man had suggested that he try deep in the woods.

He had been riding since then. With the noon sun high overhead, Jamie had rested by a stream, tossing rocks into the water and torturing himself with his imagination. Opechancanough had ordered whites killed, men and women. The Powhatans did not mind taking female prisoners, but even then, it was possible that they would grow angry and kill the prisoners. And if they had not killed her . . .

He had learned that it was a warrior named Pocanough who had taken Jassy and Elizabeth. Powan was his chief, but Pocanough was a wily and temperamental young brave, and it was possible that he had demanded his way, that he had demanded the hostages he had taken.

His face contorted with pain, his body tensed rigidly, and he fought the piercing wave of agony that assailed him as he imagined her with the Indian brave. If she fought him, he would hurt her. If he lusted after her, he would take her brutally. If she kept fighting, he would beat her, until he broke her or killed her, one or the other.

Self-reproach paralyzed him, then he forced himself to breathe, knowing that it would stand him little good now. He had to find Jassy and Elizabeth.

And if nothing else, he had to kill Pocanough. He could

not bear what the man had done to his house and his home. He had slain his housekeeper, had taken his wife. Jamie went rigid again with the pain of it.

It was then that he heard the scream.

He did not know at first if his fears and dreams had collided and he had imagined the sound of the scream. Then it came again, closer, and he leapt to his feet, pulling out his knife. He looked around, and he heard the sound of foliage snapping and breaking. He stepped back, into the shadow of wild berry branches.

Then he saw the Pamunkee burst into the clearing. Grinning with an evil leer, the warrior waited in silence.

Then Jassy appeared.

Jassy . . .

Not as he remembered her.

Her eyes were incredibly blue against the soft tan glowing on her face. She was clad in buckskin, in an Indian maiden's dress, short and sleeveless, tied at the bodice with rawhide. Her hair was free and flew out behind her like a golden pendant as she ran. She was as wild and panicked as a pursued doe, beautiful and sure and lithe, and he ached from head to toe the moment he saw her, and he longed to call out her name.

The Pamunkee brave laughed and leapt from a fallen tree to accost her, bearing her down to the ground.

She screamed and screamed again, clawing him. And he struck her.

Jamie saw red. His temper split and flew, and he saw the red of the blood that had stained his home. He saw the hot red of the noonday sun, and of the fury that threatened to blind him. He sheathed his knife at his calf and leapt forward, placing his bare hands upon the brave and dragging him from his wife. The young buck was no coward, and no weakling. Jamie's anger was a powerful force, and he had been proven in many a battle. He slammed the Indian down to the ground and landed upon him. Again and again he drove his fist into the proud face. Then the Indian bucked in a frenzy beneath him, sending Jamie flying.

"Jamie!"

He heard the cry of alarm in her voice, and the concern in it was as sweet as nectar. He wanted to look at her. He wanted to sweep her into his arms, to touch her, to hold her. He could not. He needed to concentrate on the battle before him.

Jamie landed hard, but he quickly regained his footing, balancing upon the balls of his feet while the Indian charged him. He ducked, letting the Pamunkee use his own force to crash hard against a tree. Then Jamie came at him again with a rain of blows, to his lean, hard gut, to his face, to his gut again, to his chin, to his eye. The Pamunkee struck back. As Jamie reeled, the Indian pulled his knife. Jamie raised his own, and they faced each other, circling warily in the small clearing. The Indian smiled through a slit, half-closed eye. "Cameron," he said. "Cameron." Then he continued slowly in his native tongue, and Jamie understood every word. The white woman had defied Powan and escaped, and so now Pocanough could have her. He had found her again. And Jamie would be dead.

Pocanough lunged forward. Jamie met the drive and smashed down hard on the buck's shoulders. He fell forward on his knee, and Jamie brought his knife to the Indian's throat.

Suddenly a shot was fired.

"No!" A voice said firmly.

Jamie stiffened, holding still. He straightened and turned around but kept his knife flush with the Indian's throat.

Powan had come among them. He had ridden his big bay into the clearing, and he had ordered one of his men to fire off a musket round.

He had Jassy seated before him. With wide, blue, tempestuous eyes she stared down at Jamie in anguish.

"I have come for my wife, Powan, and the mother of my son."

"It must be done where men of the Pamunkee can see it," Powan said. He looked with distaste at Pocanough. "She belongs to neither of you now. She is mine. If you both die in battle, she will remain mine. If one of you slays the other in a fair fight before witnesses, she will then belong to the victor." He looked to his men. "Take them both. They will fight tomorrow."

Jamie dropped the knife. He could have killed Pocanough then, and he wanted to. But then they would have killed him. His only chance of getting Jassy back was to do it Powan's way. When the Indian escort came for him, he walked along willingly. He did not look at Jassy as he passed her by. He felt her eyes upon him and wondered at her thoughts.

That night the Pamunkees prepared for their entertainment. They danced erotically before the fire, and many of the women, with designs drawn upon their bodies with berry juice, danced naked and enticingly, reminding him of the time that he had traveled with Captain Smith in his youth. It had been so long ago now.

Then he had been a guest. Now he was part of the entertainment.

They had taken him to the brook to bathe, and then they had dressed him in a breechclout. He sat before the fire at Powan's side, across from Pocanough. They watched the dancing, and when the women had disappeared, the chief rose and told his people that in the morning there would be a fight, unto the death. If the white man survived, he was to take his woman and walk away unmolested. It was his, Powan's, word, and it would be obeyed.

Then he and Pocanough were taken and tied to posts. Two men, naked and heavily tattooed, began to dance around them, carrying claws of the brown bear. Suddenly the men raked the claws down the backs of the men who would fight. Jamie felt his flesh tear, and he ground down hard on his teeth, determined to make no sound. A Pamunkee would not cry out, and he, too, had to win this fight as a guest-member of the great Powhatan Confederacy. Inwardly he screamed, for the claws started at his shoulders and tore down to the small of his back. He felt the blood surge from the gashes.

When they untied him, he nearly fell, nearly blacked

out. He balanced himself against the pole, and he was glad to see that Pocanough was staggering too.

Jamie was led to one of the small houses near that of the chief's. He entered in and fell to his knees. He crawled to his pallet, and as he lay there the pain began to ease. They had left something to drink by the pallet in a gourd, and he rose and swallowed the mixture. He knew it was some drug against the pain, and to help him sleep.

Still, somewhere in the night, he awoke. He did not know what had awakened him at first. The fire in the center of the sapling house had burned down very low, and the light within was eerie. He felt something, some cool, sweet breeze. He looked up and started. He came up on an elbow and stared at the apparition before him.

It was Jassy.

Jassy, with her hair soft and nearly white-gold in the firelight. Jassy, with her eyes tender and wide and seductive upon him.

Jassy . . . erotically naked, her skin very bronzed over the length of her body, her breasts large and firm and provocatively swaying, the nipples very large and dark. He looked at her, and he saw that her buckskin had been tossed in the corner. He wondered if she was a drug-induced dream, or if his wife could really stand so before him, inviting his thirsting eyes.

"Jassy . . ."

She brought her finger to her lips. Then, miraculously, she came closer. She stepped over him, her legs apart. Then very, very slowly, she lowered herself over him. She sat upon his loins, and her hair trailed over his chest as she pressed her lips against his flesh, over and over again, moving against him sinuously. He felt the hot, sensual love of her tongue, and thought that he had lost his mind. Desire burst upon him in a flood, and he rose hard and swift and tried to sweep her beneath him. Her head rose. She stared at him with her hair trailing upon him.

"No," she said softly.

He hesitated.

Then she moved against him again.

All of her body moved and rubbed against him. She used her teeth upon his nipples and then licked them. She swept the softness of her hair over him and shimmied lower and lower against him. When she reached the fullness of his arousal, she took him into her mouth, until he did nearly lose his mind. He sank his fingers into her hair, and he pulled her against him. He brought them both to their knees, and he kissed her until she whimpered softly, then he drew his lips in drunken desire over her throat and shoulders, and he fondled her breasts and teased them with his lips and tongue and sucked them hard into his mouth. He worked upon her with a fascination, until her head fell back and she whimpered out whispers and cried of need and longing and desire . . . for him. Her milk spilled back onto her breasts, and he stood, dragging her to her feet. Then he did to her as she had done to him . . . kissing and caressing the length of her, forcing her to stand still while he ravaged her with the hunger of his lips and tongue. When she fell against him, he brought them together at long last.

And the night burst into splendor.

Nothing had ever been like this—the beauty of her seduction, the loveliness of her long, supple body in the firelight. If he dreamed, then he would gladly die in dreaming, for he had never known her touch to be so tender, so sensual, so impassioned.

And she had come to *him*. . . .

He moved upon her and within her, gentle and fierce, slow, and with impassioned fever. They soared to a summit together and plummeted softly back to earth in the shadow of each other's arms. and still the fire burned softly, and the darkness cloaked them, and it was real. They were together.

She rolled against him, sobbing softly. He tugged upon her hair, bringing her around to face him. "Why are you here?" he demanded. "Has . . . has Powan let you come?"

"Yes."

"Has Powan . . . touched you?"

"No. He has—he has taken Elizabeth." She shuddered and buried her face against him. "I am so frightened, Jamie. I'm so very, very frightened."

His heart hammered, and he tried to make her face him again. "Why? I swear, if I die, he will die with me."

A shattering sob escaped her. "Oh, God, Jamie! I do not want you to die for me! I have brought you nothing but misery and—"

He gripped her hair so fiercely that she cried out, but he had silenced her, and he spoke swiftly and vehemently. "You have brought me everything. You have given me Daniel—"

"Daniel!"

"Rest easy, he is loved and well. Jassy, if I die, I swear that Pocanough will die too. Appeal to Powan as the child's mother and he will let you go to Daniel. I know him well."

She sobbed against the sleek, bare dampness of his chest. "And he knows you, too, for you are here. Oh, Jamie . . ."

He lifted her above him and spoke, his passion naked in his taut features and in his voice. "Love me again, Jassy. Love me before the dawn threatens and you must go back."

She did. Again and again. Until the first pink light of dawn rose and she slipped back into her buckskin dress and tiptoed back into Powan's sapling house. Jamie did not sleep that night. He did not need to.

In the morning he was brought to bathe again. The Indians would all eat their breakfast, and then they would gather for the fight. Jamie did not see Jassy, not until he was led out before the crowd, barefoot, barechested, and unarmed.

She was seated on the ground before Powan and beside Elizabeth. The chief's hands rested on the two blond heads. Elizabeth tried to smile encouragingly. Jassy did not try. Her eyes were in torment.

Hope came up to him. She smiled, too, and Jamie knew that the half-breed girl believed in him with all her heart. He smiled in return. Hope gave him the short-bladed knife with which he was to fight. The blades were short, to make the battle longer—it would not be easy to give a mortal blow.

Then he faced Pocanough across the circle. A chanting rose on the air. Powan stood and spoke again. Then he dropped his arm, and the fight was on.

Pocanough did not wait a second. Snarling like a bear, he burst for Jamie, casting him off-balance. Both men came down to the ground, writhing and rolling and viciously attempting to stab each other. Pocanough's knife skimmed Jamie's back where the wounds from the night before lay open and vulnerable. Jamie nearly screamed. He kicked and bucked and sent Pocanough flying across the circle. He leapt to his feet and followed the brave. Falling upon him again.

Both had been smeared with bear grease, and it was impossible to get a hold upon the Indian. Jamie decided to break away, and regain his footing. He did so, and balancing carefully on the balls of his feet, he awaited the Indian's next move.

Pocanough leapt high and came down upon Jamie, smashing both of his feet against his chest. The air went out of him, and he fell, stunned and dazed, unable to move.

Then he heard her scream.

He looked up and saw that Pocanough was coming upon him now with the sure fire of triumph in his eyes, his knife raised and aimed directly for Jamie's heart.

In a split second Jamie rolled. The Indian smashed into the earth. Without a second thought Jamie swirled after him, implanting his blade with force between the cleft of the warrior's shoulder blades.

Pocanough raised his head back in a dying scream of rage and agony that ended in a peculiar gurgling sound. Then he fell face forward into the dirt.

Jamie staggered over to the chief. He fell to his knees. He looked Powan in the eyes. "I claim my wife and her sister," he said. Then he pitched forward, too, exhausted, wondering numbly if the very blackness of death itself was not seeping into him.

"Jamie!"

She called his name and fell down beside him, cradling his head into her lap. He opened his eyes and saw the tears in hers, and he smiled. Then he closed his eyes, and the darkness claimed him.

He slept until nightfall, and in his restless sleep he wondered again what had been real and what had been a dream.

When he opened his eyes again, she was there.

She was real.

He came up quickly on an elbow. He reached out to touch her. "Jassy . . ."

"You need rest. You need to sleep."

He shook his head, rising quickly. He was naked, he quickly realized, but his own European trousers were near his head. He quickly stumbled into them. "I don't want to sleep. I want to go home. I want to take you away from here."

"Jamie—"

"I want to go now." He caught her slender chin within his hands, wondering if the love and the tenderness and the passion could possibly be real too. "I am all right, Jassy, I swear it. I want to mount Windwalker and go home. Get Elizabeth."

Jassy left him and went into Powan's house, looking for her sister. She noticed that her palms were trembling and damp, now that it was over. The trial was over. . . .

Life was yet to be lived.

She found that Elizabeth was sitting before the chief's fire, studying the flames. Jassy hugged her. "We can go home now, Elizabeth. We can go."

Elizabeth studied her curiously, then shook her head ruefully, her blue eyes filling with tears. "I'm not going with you, Jassy."

"What?"

"I'm going to have Powan's baby. I don't think that they would care for my child back at the settlement."

"Don't be absurd. They will love your child! I will love your child and—"

Elizabeth laughed, touching her hand. "Yes, Jassy, you have so much wonderful passion and strength, and if you demanded it, no doubt, the people would all come to love my child. But . . ." She hesitated and spoke in a bare whisper. "I was always so afraid of men, and the world, and everything and anything at all. And now I am not afraid anymore. Jassy, don't laugh. Please don't laugh. I think that I love him. He will marry me, and he says that he will not need any other wives. Jassy, I am home. Please, please try to understand, and try to love me, anyway."

"Oh, Elizabeth, I will love you forever!" Jassy promised her. They cast themselves into each other's arms and hugged and cried. Jamie and Powan found them so together, and neither of the men had a word to say.

An hour later it was growing dark, but Jamie and Jassy were on the trail, mounted together upon Windwalker. Jassy had thought busily for the last hour of a way to start speaking. Jamie had cleared his throat a dozen times.

At last he found words. "Are you sure that you're all right?"

"I was never harmed," she promised him. She leaned back against him. She savored the warm strength of his chest, and she found incredible comfort in his arms, wrapped around her.

"Jassy . . ." He paused, and he sounded humble. She had not thought that he could ever sound so. "Jassy, if you wish it, I will take you home."

"But we are going home."

"I will take you to England. I will have to leave again, but I will never force *you* to stay here again. I had never imagined anything such as this massacre. . . ." His voice trailed away. They both knew then that hundreds of the English settlers had been slain throughout the Virginia colony. One of the greatest tragedies was that John Rolfe, the widower of the Princess Pocahontas, had been slain by his wife's own people. Thankfully their young son remained behind in England and had come to no harm. "I don't want you to have to be afraid again," he whispered to her. "I don't want you to be in danger again."

She twisted around, looking up at him. She touched his cheek, growing dark with the growth of beard. "I am not afraid," she said.

"I will see you safely home."

She hesitated, then pulled in on Windwalker's reins herself. She threw her leg over the horse's haunches, leapt to the ground, and stared up at him indignantly.

"Why did you come after me, my great Lord Cameron, just to get rid of me?"

"I said that—"

She smiled suddenly, thinking of her sister's words, and she interrupted him curtly. "You married me, Cameron, and you'll not get rid of me so easily. I *am* home!"

"What?" He raised a doubtful brow and stared down at her. To his amazement she cast a wicked blow against his thigh. "I am your *wife.* I have a right to stay, and I intend to." She hesitated and added more softly. "I am home, Jamie, *I am home.*"

He leapt down from the horse, taking her by the shoulders, the fires of hope leaping into his eyes. "We have no house!" he said harshly. "Except for the brick cornerstone foundations, we have nothing left. Nothing at all."

She bit her lip, aware that tears threatened to spill from her eyes. "If we have the foundation, haven't we really got everything that we need?"

His fingers clasped her arms so tightly that the grip was painful, but she did not cry out or protest. She studied the burning heat and tension in his eyes, and she began to tremble beneath his hold.

"You really would stay?"

"Yes."

"Why?"

"Why?" she repeated.

"Why?" he thundered, and there was no mercy in him. He was as hard and ruthless as she had ever seen him.

She wrenched away from him, the tears spilling from her eyes at last. Her nails dug into her palms, and she shouted back, "Because I—because I love you, you stupid, arrogant knave!"

"What?" he thundered again, coming toward her. She gasped, wondering if he meant to shake the insolence from her, but when she would have fled, he caught her about the waist and spun her around. She struggled against his hold, and they both landed hard upon the dirt. He straddled her and caught her wrists, then pulled them high above her head, laughing. "Tell me. Tell me again!"

"Stupid, arrogant—"

"No!"

"You told me—"

"The other. Tell me the other. Damn it, say!"

The tears were in her eyes again. She wanted to shout. She whispered, "I love you, Jamie."

"Again."

"I love you."

His lips fell upon hers. Sweet, hungry, exciting, evocative. He kissed her with a fascinating leisure for their curious position upon the forest trail. He kissed her as if nothing else in the world mattered, and maybe, beneath the green shadows of the forest, nothing else did. And when he ended the kiss, his smile so tender and gentle, she cried out and threw her arms around him again. He held her so for a long time without speaking, then he ran his thumb softly over her cheek and whispered to her at last. "Can you really love me?"

"I do," she vowed. "Oh, Jamie, please don't send me away."

"I never wanted to send you away. I only wanted to give you the freedom you wanted. Jassy!" He held her close, and his voice was filled with passion. "I did not marry you to survive this place, or to have a woman who could be dragged to a wilderness. I married you because of the spirit and fervor and passion in your soul, in your eyes. I married you to touch those things, and when I did touch them, I was not appeased but floundering ever further beneath your spell. Jassy, I fell in love with you so long ago—"

"I could not tell!" she interrupted in awe and reproach, and he laughed.

"Well, you were pining after Robert Maxwell. I am a proud man."

"I had not noticed!" Jassy laughed, but then she sobered and reached out, brushing the hair from his forehead. "Oh, Jamie, I was so wrong! It was you all along, wasn't it? You paid for my mother's coffin, not Robert."

He held silent, and she smiled. She would never tell him of Robert's lack of valor on the day of the massacre. It wasn't necessary. The truth was. "I fell out of love with Robert long, long ago, milord."

"How so?"

"He could not fill my heart or mind once you had set your claim upon me. Never, from the very beginning, milord, have I managed to forget you, as you promised me that I would not. And when you turned from me, I did not think that I would be able to bear it."

He groaned, burying his face against her throat. "I thought that you despised me still, and I could not love you and force you to remain any longer."

"Oh, Jamie! Could you not tell! When you touched me and I fell so swiftly to your command . . ."

"We are both proud and stubborn. It almost cost us so much. Oh, Jassy, I knew that I had your passion. I wanted your love."

"You have it all, all of me, Lord Cameron."

The trees rustled above them, a soft breeze moving over the land. He kissed her again, slowly and deeply, and the fires of spring came alight within them both, radiant and as beautiful as the burst of the sun, for their whispers were of love.

Jamie looked up and saw where they lay, in the dirt, in the road. He rose and swept her into his arms, carrying her into the brush, into the verdant leaves. He laid her down upon a field of green earth beneath the swaying branches of an oak, and he spread her hair against the earth. Then he laid himself against her, and he made love to her as he never had before, for her whispers of love filled his senses to bursting, and his passionate vows and promises urged her on to ever greater heights. And when it was over, they both lay in the wilderness, watching the canopy of the trees, naked and content in the green darkness of the forest.

He whispered again and again that he loved her. And she responded with awe, touching his cheek, adoring him.

At last he helped her dress, and they journeyed onward again. It was a long trip home but a good one for them both. During all of the journey they touched each other, talked of their pasts, and spoke of the future.

At last they came to the Carlyle Hundred, and when they were spotted, the people came milling out to greet them, waving excitedly. Jassy leaned back against her husband, trembling.

"Jamie, we are home."

"Home, love, is that burned-out shell."

She twisted to meet his cobalt stare, darkened with amusement and a curious tenderness. "The foundation is good. And upon that foundation we can build."

"We can build, my love. In this wilderness we shall build."

He smiled and laced his fingers with hers, and they both knew that the foundation was not within the bricks in the ground but within their own hearts.

Jamie urged Windwalker forward at a greater pace, and then the horse sped into an easy gallop. Home lay before them, and their infant son, and the sweet golden promise of tomorrow.